Acclaim fo

'Gorgeous! Exuberant writing,
Tracy

'Exquisitely detail
Heidi

'Absolutely wonderful . . . kept me spellbound'
Christina Courtenay

'An intriguing dual timeline tale that weaves together interesting characters and history'
Bella Osborne

'An epic love story, mixed with gorgeous settings, a great deal of mystery and intrigue'
Kim Nash

'Unforgettable and unique'
Clare Marchant

'A marvellous dual-time novel filled with mystery, fabulous detail and an enduring love story'
Maddie Please

'A wonderful, page-turning story full of intrigue and romance'
Victoria Connelly

'A beautifully written timeslip . . . Highly recommended. Five stars'
Erin Green

'A beautifully intriguing love story, that . . . stays with you long after the last page'
Rosie Hendry

'One of those wonderful, magical stories that appear rarely and stay in your heart forever'
Celia Anderson

'An enchanting storyline and engaging characters make this book a delight to read'
Lynne Shelby

'The perfect mix of mystery, magic, and romance'
Kate G. Smith

'I found the book enchanting'
Suzanne Snow

Jenni Keer is a history graduate who embarked on a career in contract flooring before settling in the middle of the Suffolk countryside with her antique furniture restorer husband. She has valiantly attempted to master the ancient art of housework but with four teenage boys in the house it remains a mystery. Instead, she spends her time at the keyboard writing women's fiction to combat the testosterone-fuelled atmosphere with her number one fan #Blindcat by her side. Much younger in her head than she is on paper, she adores any excuse for fancy-dress and is part of a disco formation dance team.

Visit her website: **jennikeer.co.uk** and find her on Facebook **/jennikeerwriter** and Twitter, Instagram and TikTok **@JenniKeer.**

By Jenni Keer

The Hopes and Dreams of Lucy Baker
The Unlikely Life of Maisie Meadows
The Secrets of Hawthorn Place
The Legacy of Halesham Hall

The Legacy of Halesham Hall

JENNI KEER

First published in 2022
by HEADLINE ACCENT
An imprint of HEADLINE PUBLISHING GROUP

Cataloguing in Publication Data is available from the British Library

ISBN 978 1 4722 9484 5

Typeset in 10.5/14pt Sabon Std by Jouve (UK), Milton Keynes

Printed and bound in Great Britain by Clays Ltd, Elcograf S.p.A.

Headline's policy is to use papers that are natural, renewable
and recyclable products and made from wood grown in well-managed
forests and other controlled sources. The logging and manufacturing
processes are expected to conform to the environmental regulations
of the country of origin.

HEADLINE PUBLISHING GROUP
An Hachette UK Company
Carmelite House
50 Victoria Embankment
London EC4Y 0DZ

www.headline.co.uk
www.hachette.co.uk

Clare and Heidi-Jo

This little beauty is for you – my fellow *Walkie Talkies*.
We never quite managed the walking (I blame the pandemic)
but luckily we seem to have no problem with the talking.
Thanks for always being there.

Chapter 1

1920

Suffolk

Phoebe stood in front of Halesham Hall and frowned. Not only was it a lot bigger than she'd expected, but it was also unlike any house she'd ever come across in her life. The jumble of spires and towers, with decorative crenellations along the rooftops, and high, narrow windows, gave it the feel of a medieval castle. It reminded her of a house she'd once seen in an illustrated book of fairy tales. The steep pitched roofs and multiple chimneys were all squashed together and elongated, giving the place a sense of otherworldliness. It was almost as though a small boy had made it from his brick box, determined to use every single brick, balancing them as high as he dared, and giving his imagination free rein.

It wasn't a house, it was a fantasy. And a slightly sinister one at that.

Despite the few brief details her parents had told her about the place, she'd failed to conjure up its sheer size or bewildering magnificence. The overall effect was enhanced by the brewing angry weather to the east, casting the Hall in moody and truculent light, with a thin strip of pale grey behind it, silhouetting its angles and spires. As she'd undertaken the two-mile walk from the centre of Halesham, the heavy, rain-laden clouds had appeared to her left and the gentle breeze had begun to whip itself up into a frenzy behind her. A storm was on its way – an ominous portent.

She swallowed hard. The Hall was in complete contrast to the tiny cottages she'd grown up in and made her feel even more insignificant than she usually did. Her life had hitherto been one of simple rural pleasures – unattended chickens wandering into the kitchen, and threadbare sheets cut into squares and hemmed for facecloths. If she wanted to go anywhere, she walked. The family meals came from the garden and were prepared and cooked by either her mother or herself. Before her now, however, was a world of servants and entitlement. The man she was here to see, the owner of Halesham Hall, had considerable wealth (if rather disturbing architectural taste) and a fearsome reputation. That knowledge alone made the knots in her stomach tighten and pull.

As she stood in front of the imposing gothic front door, with its pointed arch and height more than double its width, she noticed flakes of lilac paint on the neglected woodwork. Once upon a time, this door would have stood in purple splendour, perhaps to echo the multitude of lavender beds under the front windows. The blooms were long since over, but the borders well-tended, unlike the shabby exterior of the house.

The dull brass knocker was a slender hand reaching out from the engraved surround and the limp fingers curled around a solid ball. Phoebe reached for it, the cold and hard surface making her jolt. The way it hung in the air, so lifelike and so defeated, was unsettling. *She's trapped in there*, Phoebe thought, looking at the hand. *She's trapped inside and wants someone to let her out.*

After three sharp raps, she stood back and waited. There was a scurry of feet from the other side, a shout for 'Ada', and then disgruntled mutterings as the footsteps got closer. The door swung inwards to reveal a small, thin woman, with shrewd, emerald-green eyes and pinched-in cheeks. A pair of wire-rimmed spectacles was perched on the top of her head, threaded either side of her tight silver bun, and a bunch of keys hung from her skirts, indicating she was the housekeeper of this large household. She looked Phoebe up and down, perhaps deeming her more suitable for the back entrance, and narrowed her eyes.

'And what can I do for you, lassie?' The Scottish accent was thick and slightly intimidating.

'I'm here to see Mr Bellingham.' Phoebe managed to force the words from her rapidly constricting throat. It was too late now to abandon her plan – she had to see this through, whatever the outcome.

The older woman scrunched her wrinkled face into a frown, making each crease deeper. 'Is he expecting you?'

Phoebe glanced into the hallway – large black and white tiles, each one over a yard square, covering the floor. A marble bust of some ancient Egyptian pharaoh stood in the far-right corner, and there was a small collection of mounted cannonballs at his feet. It appeared the interior of the house was as peculiar as the exterior.

'Um, no, not exactly.' She paused. 'Not at all, in fact,' she corrected. If Mr Bellingham was given a hundred guesses as to who might be calling on him that overcast September day, she imagined her name wouldn't be among them. *Did he even know her name?*

'I'm afraid he doesn't usually see people without a prior appointment. May I ask what it's concerning?'

'It's a personal matter, but I'm certain he'll see me . . . Once he knows who I am.'

The housekeeper's interest was piqued. She leaned forward to study the young visitor more closely and Phoebe could almost hear the cogs grinding and clicking into place. There was a moment of realisation as she studied Phoebe's jet-black, wavy hair, tousled by the escalating breeze, her eyes so dark each iris was barely distinguishable from the pupil, and her delicate, almond-shaped face.

'May I say who's calling?' she asked, but it was obvious this woman already knew the answer.

'Phoebe Bellingham,' she supplied. 'His niece.'

There was, as it turned out, no time for the housekeeper to enquire whether Mr Bellingham would receive her. Within moments there was a pounding of feet descending the main staircase and a tall, darkly clothed figure with a neatly clipped moustache came striding across the wide, monochrome floor towards them.

'Sir, there's a wee lass—'

'Good God.' Mr Bellingham's strident voice cut across the housekeeper as he stopped dead in his tracks and stared at Phoebe. His initial flash of shock was quickly replaced with barely concealed distaste. He adjusted his face into a more neutral expression and narrowed his eyes. 'I heard he'd had a daughter. You really are the spit of your mother.'

'Mr Bellingham . . .' she began. 'Uncle.' The word felt unfamiliar and awkward. 'My father—'

'Sent a girl to do his dirty work. After all these years, I can't possibly think what he wants – unless it's money, and he won't get a penny from me.'

'No, it's not that.' She could feel the emotion battling to come out, and her voice started to crack. 'I've come to—'

'For pity's sake, spare me the amateur dramatics. If my brother wants to talk to me, he can do it himself. Sending a child, indeed. How utterly pathetic.'

Phoebe bristled at his remark. At twenty, she was hardly a child, even if legally she had another few months until she reached her majority. But she was small, slender and quiet, so was often mistaken for younger than her years.

'I'm afraid he can't do that.' Phoebe kept her calm and spoke in a gentle voice, in total contrast to Mr Bellingham's overbearing tones. She sucked in a deep breath. 'Both my parents were killed recently in a boating accident.'

The housekeeper gasped and her bony hands flew to her chest. Mr Bellingham's eyes flashed briefly wide, but he quickly repressed his shock. His eyes never left Phoebe's face and there was no further indication that she'd delivered news to him any more distressing than the weather forecast.

He approached the door and peered over her shoulder.

'How did you get here?' he asked, searching for signs of a cart or a motor car.

'I walked up from Halesham. I'm staying at the Bell.'

There was a low rumble as the threatening storm finally made its imminent presence known, and the light fell away sharply, as though blinds had been drawn closed in anticipation of the forthcoming spectacle.

'Then I suggest you start your return immediately as there is a storm on its way. Thank you for the information, but I'm afraid you're not welcome here.' He stepped in front of the startled housekeeper, pushed the heavy front door to an abrupt close, and abandoned Phoebe on the doorstep.

Chapter 2

1890

'This is a stupid game,' I said, hot, overtired and grumpy, throwing my little metal game piece across the room in disgust and kicking out at the table. Cook had spent all week cursing the flies and Murray had spent all week cursing the maids. Everyone's tempers were frayed and there was an unsettledness about the house that I felt keenly but couldn't understand.

My world revolved entirely around myself and I never gave the wishes or worries of others much thought. I wanted to spend more time with Mother but was not always allowed to do so. I wanted the best toys to play with and the sweetest foods from the kitchen – these I had in moderation. I desperately yearned for a companion of my own age to share my adventures, but Leonard was just over ten years older than me, and so my childhood was a lonely one.

I wanted my father simply to remember my name.

My brother had no desire to be cooped up in the nursery with me any more than I wanted him there. He longed to be outside, haring around the fields and meadows on his bicycle or climbing the old oak down by the river, but he'd been ordered to amuse me by Father as a summer storm had descended and put paid to any plans of outdoor adventures for either of us that day. Everyone hoped that the arrival of rain might end the week of suffocating temperatures and sticky nights, but I was most put out that it fell during the day, instead of stealthily and unobtrusively at night. As it was, it did little to clear the air.

'It's not my favourite pastime either – you know I'm not a game player – but it would please Father if he saw us,' Leonard said, picking up my horse from the rug and placing it firmly back on the seventh square. We were playing *Newmarket*, one of Bellingham Board Games's biggest sellers. My horse had fallen at the second hurdle, whilst his had raced ahead. 'These games pay for your governess, my schooling and this large house, Sidney. The least we can do is play them. Besides, I've missed you. School can be so tedious and there's nothing like being home for the holidays.'

Even at that young age, I knew I was being patronised. What was the point in having a brother if he was so much older? He was absent for the long school terms, having boarded since he was nine, and had little in common with me when he returned. My life was invariably disrupted the moment he descended on Halesham Hall – everyone bustling around after him and asking what he'd been up to, even what he might like for supper. He demanded a share of our mother's attention, talking to her about bookish things I didn't understand, and loitered in the kitchens, engaging in easy chatter with Cook, as though she were his friend, when in reality, she was mine. But most frustratingly of all, he reminded me that I was the second son, the spare, the baby. And I didn't like it.

It should have pleased me to have another male in the household, as we were sorely outnumbered. Mrs Murray, our housekeeper, was in charge of a staff of nine women, whereas Burton, the butler, oversaw only three men. And it was the female members of staff that I spent most of my time in the company of. When I wasn't attending lessons with my governess, I whiled away my idle hours trailing behind the chatty under housemaid, Daisy, or at the large refectory table in the kitchens, listening to Cook grumble about anything and everything, and sneaking cakes and gingerbread from the cooling racks when her back was turned. I didn't want to be stuck in the nursery playing, and losing, a silly horse-racing game with Leonard.

'Darlings.' Mother sauntered into the nursery with her hands outstretched. 'I've been looking for you both. May I sit and watch you play?'

She squeezed our hands affectionately, kissed our foreheads and then settled herself in the rocking chair, content to watch silently rather than participate. Generally a quiet woman, she didn't shout and complain like Cook, or jump up and down excitedly, like Daisy. She rarely left the Hall and only occasionally attended events with Father. When they held dinner-parties, which they did from time to time (my father's position dictating a certain amount of entertaining), she lurked in the background, and I wondered why he never pushed her to be bolder. But he adored his wife, I could see it in his eyes, and indulged her completely.

Daisy entered and placed a small sewing basket on Mother's knees. I was more interested in her needlework than my game, and watched her snip and pin, realising she was cutting up one of her old day dresses. Pale pink roses were scattered across the fabric, and it made me think of the rose beds that surrounded the knot garden, and how she would spend hours out there, pruning, gathering petals or dead-heading – depending on the season.

Sewing and gardening were Mother's two great passions. Father had thoughtfully turned the west tower into a space for her to indulge the former of these loves. I often found her up there alone, turning the handle of her sewing machine, when the only sound was the steady rhythm of the needle bobbing in and out of the fabric as she stared through the narrow windows at the gardens below.

'Why are you breaking up your lovely dress?' I asked, studying her face. She was physically present but somehow mentally absent, and often reminded me of the white porcelain figurine in the morning room – some classical figure draped in a flowing tunic, with a lost look about her face. She stood alone on the mantel shelf, staring across the room, beautiful but untouched, and never a part of what was going on before her.

'It's old and rather worn. I'm using it to make patches.'

The only Patch I knew was the gamekeeper's dog – an excitable terrier with a black patch of fur across one eye.

'For the dog?' I was confused. Animals didn't wear dresses, unless they were in picture books. Leonard snorted and I glared at him.

'No, my darling, my happy accident, my baby boy.' She gave me one of her elusive smiles then. They were rare but they were beautiful, and they lit up her whole face and everything around her. 'A square of fabric can repair a hole in something. But sometimes,' she said, giving me a strange look, 'they don't hide holes, they hide secrets.'

I didn't really understand. A secret was whispered. You cupped your hand and put it to the ear of someone else, telling them the thing that wasn't to be spoken aloud. You couldn't pin down whispered words and hide them under pieces of cut-up day dress.

'Remember that, won't you?' she said.

'Yes,' I said earnestly. 'Patches hide secrets.'

She smiled and patted my head, her slender fingers ruffling my dark curls, and then returned to her work. I liked it when she touched me. Father never did. Few people did, if I was honest.

Thrashing me soundly at the game, and far more gracious in victory than I would have been, Leonard took to the window seat and started flicking through a *Boy's Own Annual*, so I decided to set out my soldiers along the hearth. The rain continued to run down the panes, the clock ticked steadily on the mantel, and there was a companionship in our togetherness, even though we were all engaged in separate activities.

Rolling around on my back, looking at the magnificent ranks of my red-coated men from a variety of angles, I suddenly realised my mother was staring at me with tears in her eyes.

'Why are you crying?' I asked her.

She shook her head and I didn't think she was going to answer me at first.

'I'm crying for love – reminded that life can be a complicated blend of love lost, love found and love that endures – and you, my darling boys, will always be a love that endures.'

It sounded like one of the riddles that Father so often quoted. He enjoyed tongue twisters and word games, although they generally made me feel inadequate and stupid. I laughed and pretended to understand when Father supplied the answer to 'When is a door not a door?', but it was Cook who kindly explained later that 'a jar' could mean slightly open, as well as a glass pot brimming with tasty jam.

'You sentimental old bean,' Leonard said, hopping down from his seat and giving our mother a kiss.

There was a knock at the nursery door and Murray entered.

'The master is home,' she said, and Mother immediately jumped to her feet – always desperate to be with our father. We were the poor second choice when he wasn't around. The love that bound my parents together did so to the exclusion of all else, and I was jealous. I knew she wanted to be with us – just not as much as she wanted to be with him. She had been ours for a short afternoon and now we were being abandoned so she could be his once more.

As the door closed behind her, I looked across at my regimented men, arrayed in a neat rectangle – a solitary officer standing at the front, inspecting his troops. I swept my hand over their stupid black, shiny, painted heads and they tumbled like dead men on a battlefield.

'Come on, Squirt,' Leonard said, closing his book. 'Let's have another game of *Newmarket* and see if your little pony can make it off the starting line this time.'

I glared at him, noticing his smug smile as he anticipated another easy victory, and hated him then. I'd spent my short lifetime aware that simply through the order of our birth, Leonard would inherit everything about me that was familiar, even the house itself. He was destined to walk in my father's footsteps and become the owner of Halesham Hall and I would one day be forced to make a life elsewhere. He always had the upper hand, the leading role, whatever way I looked at our situations. Even my tin soldiers had originally been his until he'd tired of them. Was my life destined to be one of cast-offs and condescension? It was easy to understand how Mother got so overwhelmed by her emotions that they spilled out when she least expected them to. I picked up the board, carefully balancing the tiny wooden hurdles, metal playing pieces and ivory dice as I lifted it high into the air.

And then I smashed the whole lot against the nursery wall and burst into tears.

Shadows danced across my bedroom wall as the warm breeze shifted the curtains through the open gap in the window. The clouds of earlier had drifted across to the west but the rain had merely given temporary respite and the heat still hung over us – smothering and heavy. My quilt was too thick to sleep under, and my nightshirt clung to my body as I tossed and turned in restless frustration, more unsettled than usual because I had misplaced my bedtime rabbit toy. There was the sickly sweet smell of summer blooms in the night air, mingled with a less fragrant humid dampness.

One of the exterior doors to the Hall opened and closed, possibly the door from the kitchens, and the accompanying vibrations travelled up the walls. The sound wasn't loud, but in the still of the night, and with my sash window open, I heard it. I didn't have a clock in my room but knew it was late because the house was barely breathing. Gone was the heartbeat that pulsated steadily throughout the day: the bustle of Daisy up and down the stairs, the quick tapping footsteps of Mrs Murray prowling the corridors to scold idle staff, and the clanging of pans from Cook, especially when Father changed his dinner plans at the last minute. Instead there was only the whisper of hot shifting air playing with the curtains and the sounds of my own breathing.

I slid from under the sheet and wondered who could be entering, or possibly leaving, the house at this time? Was Daisy sneaking out to see the young man from Halesham that Cook said she was sweet on? Or were we being robbed? Some gypsy traveller making off with our silver? Perhaps the gardening hand Father had dismissed so angrily a few weeks ago was back for revenge? I crept to the window and peered out, but didn't have a clear view of the kitchen door as it was beneath me. I could hear shuffling, so I scampered next door to the nursery, which jutted further forward as part of the L shape of the house, to investigate.

The boxed Bellingham games had been returned to the ceiling-height cupboard after my temper that afternoon, but the floor was still strewn with my toys. Streams of moonlight gave the palest touch of colour to the objects about the room, and I carefully picked my way through them as I headed towards the window and clambered on to the brick box beneath it. My eyes, already accustomed to the gloom, fell upon a figure wrestling with a large bundle below. Was it one of the servants, doing something they ought not to be? It was certainly a woman, small and slight.

But in my desperation to see better, I tipped forward and fell with a crash towards the windowsill. The figure beneath, alerted by the noise, cast a desperate glance upwards, before scuttling across the courtyard and into the shadows of the trees that edged the gardens.

My heart began pounding so loudly I thought it might burst from my chest, and I gripped hard at the windowsill to calm my panicky breaths. I could not make sense of what I'd just seen.

Because the pale, frightened face that had looked up to the nursery had been that of my mother.

Chapter 3

Petrified that the crashing bricks would wake up other members of the household and I'd be discovered out of bed, I froze. There was the noise of a door being flung open from down the corridor, followed by the heavy footsteps of a man. I'd woken Father. I moved from the window and cowered by the wall. Tiny beads of perspiration formed on my brow, but not from the cloying temperatures. Conversely, my blood ran cold.

'Sylvia?' A door further down the hallway, possibly Mother's room, was pushed open, and Father's voice got louder. 'Sylvia?'

There was a moment of stillness, followed by a rising shout of 'No!'. More crashing and banging, then my father's pounding feet as he flung open every door along the way, until finally the nursery door was pushed inwards with such force it bounced off the wall and he stood in the doorway, a crumpled sheet of cream paper hanging loosely in his hand.

'Sidney.' He rarely used my name, so it sounded odd to me. I was always 'the boy' or 'the child', or occasionally 'Toad'. 'Where the hell is your mother?'

I couldn't stop my eyes darting to the window before constructing my futile lie – the deceptive skills of a child always lacking. 'I don't know, sir. I couldn't sleep and it was cooler in here.'

But my father was no fool. He saw the scattered bricks and strode over to the window, noticing that the curtains were pulled back, before returning to tower over me, his face contorted into an angry scowl. There were barely six inches between my nose and his as he took both my shoulders and pinned me to the wall.

'What do you know? What did she say to you?'

I was trembling and frightened, not sure how to answer. Instead, I focused on the blob of spittle forming at the corner of his lips, and the sensation of his large fingers digging into my flesh, pulling my nightshirt tight across my neck. That he should only ever be this close to me, that the only physical contact I had with my father was when he was angry, was a sad thing indeed.

'Tell me, boy. Tell me what you know.'

Mrs Murray appeared in the hall in a long white nightgown, her hair in a plait over her shoulder. She held an oil lamp aloft – an orange circle of light in the black.

'What on earth is all the commotion about, sir?'

'She's gone,' he shouted, turning his head but not releasing his grip. 'Damn well absconded like a criminal.' He waved the sheet of paper. 'This was left for me on her night stand. I wouldn't have found it until morning had I not been woken by the child, creeping around out of bed and knocking over the bricks.'

'Och, I can't believe the scheming wee minx was up to something so devious. I never for one minute imagined she'd dare do something like this,' Mrs Murray said, shaking her head.

I had hitherto been relatively indifferent to our housekeeper, a woman whose small, booted feet scuttled over the floorboards, usually hidden by the long, black dresses she wore. Her ability to appear without warning and catch the tardy maid or lazy hall boy shirking their work made her unpopular with the staff. Thin of face and diminutive of stature, she said very little but ran the house incredibly efficiently. Mother liked her well enough and for that reason alone, I'd never felt any ill will towards her. But now, the shock of her words hit me hard.

'This little toad knows something, I'm sure of it. Why else would he be at the window?' My father's grip remained strong and his face hovered uncomfortably close.

'I doubt it.' The housekeeper lowered her voice. 'Don't forget, she trusts me, sir, and if she was going to tell anyone, it would have been me. She wouldn't have confided any plans to the bairn.'

A nauseous feeling circled my stomach as I stared open-mouthed at the woman I had previously believed to be a friend of Mother's, and she had the grace to let her eyes fall from my glare. Even at six, I recognised a duplicity about her words, and wondered if she had been in league with my father the whole time; if any friendship shown to Mother had been a trick, like the games Father was so fond of; if all the time she had been reporting back to him and telling tales.

'Let the boy go,' she said. 'He clearly knows nothing.' She stepped forward and dared to briefly rest her hand on my father's arm. His grip loosened and I clawed at my throat to release the fabric that dug so painfully into my neck.

'Where is she, Murray? Where has she gone?' I'd never heard my father sound so desperate before. Although given to frequent outbursts of temper, he was fearsome and formidable. Yet for that one instant, he sounded afraid.

'She's fooled us all, sir. Appearing so sweet and innocent but secretly planning such a wicked thing. I blame myself. I saw no sign of this.' She shook her head. 'No sign at all.'

Father turned to me again, with a fire in his eyes that burned through to my core.

'What did you see at the window, boy? And don't you dare lie to me a second time, or there will be consequences.'

I swallowed hard. Father's consequences were meted out with the aid of his hickory cane – the tiger-eye knob gripped tightly in his hand, and the full force of swift repeated blows.

'Someone ran from the house. Perhaps it was a thief?' I offered lamely. 'Someone stealing our things?'

A low, guttural growl came from my father's throat and his nostrils flared wide. 'Get my coat, Murray, and see if you can raise one of the stable hands to saddle me a horse. I'm going after her. If what the boy says is true, she can't have got far.'

The pair of them left me alone in the nursery as I slid my body down to the floor and finally succumbed to the tears I'd been holding in since I'd been pushed into the wall. Father said they were a sign of weakness and should only ever be seen in women, but there was no one to witness my unhappiness, so I let them tumble down my cheeks.

I cried for many things that night – the loss of my innocence as I battled with the dishonesty of adults, the fear that my father would return to dish out punishment, the bewildering behaviour of my mother, and my guilt for admitting I'd seen a figure cross the courtyard. But in the drama of the night, I was forgotten about. A small boy, sobbing softly for things he didn't understand, alone in the dark of a nursery. When the tears finally ran dry and my lungs hurt from my strangulated gasps, I curled up on the hard wooden floor and fell asleep.

Sometime later I was woken by noises from below and stumbled out to the corridor, hopeful that Mother was returned and everything would go back to as it was before.

I crept towards the banisters of the main staircase, confident

I wouldn't be spotted in the shadows, and strained to hear the conversation.

'Did you find her, sir?' Mrs Murray's anxious voice drifted up the stairs, as the glow from her lamp advanced.

My father didn't answer the question directly. 'That damn garden hand I dismissed weeks ago was behind all this. I was right to be suspicious of her hours in the grounds. The landlord of the Bell said he's absconded, leaving debts and broken hearts far and wide.'

'Och, the wickedness of it all. I had no idea.'

'It's not your fault. She was more conniving than we gave her credit for. At least we know where she got the courage from. The timid creature could never have pulled something like this off on her own.'

'What will you do?'

'There is nothing further to be done. She'll not be coming back – I can assure you of that.'

His voice was measured and calm. Too calm, I thought, for the situation. I knew he loved Mother as much as I did. Whilst my world was in jagged shards about my feet, he appeared to have accepted she was gone, even though his anger still bubbled below the surface.

'I do, however, need a brandy, Murray. A large one.'

'Of course, sir. I'll see to it immediately.' And she scurried off towards the main body of the house, a circle of deep orange disappearing with her down the long hallway.

Father moved to the hall table so that he was now directly below me. The glow from the remaining lamp cast him in an eerie pool of light and, as he removed his hat, I could see where his hair was thinning on top. The damp smell of mud from the earlier rains drifted up the stairwell and I could almost taste his rage as his hands trembled.

He waited until the housekeeper was out of sight and then removed his gloves, laying them on the table beside him.

'. . . she'll not grace the Hall again. Ever . . .' he muttered under his breath, but all I could focus on, as I leaned closer to the light, was that both his large hands were covered in dark red smears of blood.

Chapter 4

The following morning, Leonard and I were summoned to Father's study – a room that we were hardly ever allowed to enter. It was his workspace, where all the genius that was his game design took place, and he refused to be distracted by tiresome children seeking his attention when he was busy. Although, in truth, there never seemed a convenient time or place for his offspring.

His business concerns were twofold. Shortly after inheriting the family printworks in his youth, he'd come up with the concept for a clever strategy game and utilised this business to produce the game commercially. Thus, the Bellingham Board Games company was born, and it was now so successful, he had business premises in London and shipped many of the games overseas. We were finally a family of note, power and influence, if not heritage.

It seemed strange to me that he made games for a living when he laughed so seldom and had no interest in his own children. Yet Mother had told me once that everyone in the country played his board games: from small children who indulged in the fun of *Quack, Quack, Oops*, to highly educated adults who might spend days conducting complicated games of *Empire*, or playing detective in *Find the Culprit*. Initially focused on board games, the company had expanded to include everything from themed packs of cards to unusual chess sets – all of which were personally devised or overseen by Father.

I stood before the paper-strewn desk and noticed the prototype board for his new Egyptology-inspired game, *Treasures of the Tomb* – a curling serpent, divided into segments, up which I assumed you climbed with each throw of the dice. Father had acquired a few related artefacts for the Hall over the years and the governess informed me that ancient Egypt had been a national obsession for most of the century. Napoleon had rediscovered it, Shelley had written about it, and jewellers, cigar manufacturers and even soap companies used their symbols and mythology to sell their wares. The game, she said, was certain to be a bestseller.

Still unsettled by the events of the previous evening, I focused on the board, as it was just below my eye-height, rather than meet the penetrating glare of my father. Leonard had a bedroom at the front of the house, rather than at the back like me, so had slept through the whole drama, but he had doubtless heard the inevitable whispers of servants.

'Your mother has left us,' Father said, as one might tell another they'd had eggs for breakfast. 'She will not be returning. It is a done thing and I am not prepared to answer any questions about her departure, nor do I wish to hear that you have been talking about the matter with either your peers or the household staff.'

His words were brutal to a young child, but I didn't doubt the truth of them for a moment. I'd seen her panicked face and wide eyes, and watched her run from the house as if the hounds of hell were on her tail – even though my six-year-old brain didn't understand why.

'You're not to try and determine her whereabouts and I

forbid her name to be mentioned in this house again. She has done an unspeakably selfish thing and betrayed the people who loved her most in this world. As far as I'm concerned, that woman is dead to us all.'

Leonard stared ahead at the heavy velvet curtains across the run of tall windows with wide, unblinking eyes, to subdue any reaction that might anger Father, but I couldn't prevent the trickle of tears down my hot, red cheeks. He stood and came to our side of the desk, towering over us and peering at my troubled face. My whole world had collapsed – my truest friend had deserted me – and I couldn't even ask why.

'Stop the pathetic snivelling – I don't hold with boys crying. She's abandoned you, just like she's abandoned everyone else, and I can guarantee she won't be shedding any tears over us. You think she loved you?' he asked, his face closer now and his brandy-soaked breath floating across my face. 'But she didn't love you enough to take you with her, did she?'

And these were the words that did the most damage. Whatever she had run away from, she had left me behind to face it without her.

'There is a lesson here, boys, and I want you to heed it and heed it well: women are not to be trusted.' Father almost spat the words out. 'And the sooner you realise this truth, the better.'

Every trace of my mother was removed from Halesham Hall within days of her departure. The wardrobe was emptied of her clothes, her dressing table was cleared, and anything she'd brought to the marriage, like the low, upholstered nursing chair, the pianoforte and, as I was later to learn, some quite valuable paintings and jewels, simply disappeared. I didn't dare ask what had happened to them, and could only assume they'd been sold, but this made no sense to me. If you loved someone, and I was certain Father loved Mother, how could you erase them from your life so readily?

I'd still not been able to find Mr Hoppity – the rabbit Mother had made me when I was a baby – and wondered if he'd been swept up in this purge. Daisy had a vague recollection of him being in the now-empty sewing room on the day of her departure, but our search proved fruitless, and I did not dare to ask Father, who had always scoffed at my attachment to such a childish toy. Mother had known how special he was, always tucking him into bed with me when I'd had a bad day. His loss, combined with hers, made everything so much worse.

One late summer evening, with the sickly smell of honeysuckle turning my stomach, I sat on the low wall that edged the herb garden. Everyone had been tiptoeing around Father, wary of the violent expulsion of hot ash and lava that was the eruption of his temper. He'd locked himself away in his study and entertained only an architect, the family solicitor and a handful of employees. There had been no comforting words for Leonard or me.

I was clutching a small bundle of letters to my chest, trying to find comfort in the one thing of hers that remained because Father didn't know of its existence, when Leonard approached. I hastily stuffed them into the pocket of my shorts and stared at my shoes – nearly reaching the ground but not quite – but he'd seen me conceal them.

'Hello, Squirt. Notes from Mother?' he asked, settling himself beside me. His long shadow made my world suddenly expand, and me shrink within it, reminding me of his size and age. He popped a piece of peanut brittle into his mouth and licked his sticky lips, as he offered me the paper bag, but I shook my head. 'Does she leave them under your pillows when you are upset or poorly?'

I nodded, wondering how he knew, but was wary of discussing this forbidden topic and cast my eyes around to see if anyone was nearby.

'Don't worry. We're quite alone,' he reassured me, reaching for my shoulder. 'And we need to talk about her, whatever Father says. It's one of the things I love . . . loved about her.' He corrected the tense, because it did feel like a bereavement in many ways. She was gone. No one anticipated her return. It was painful to acknowledge. 'Her little notes and letters when I was feeling low or anxious. Reminders that she loved me, even though we are a household where love is perhaps not demonstrated as openly as it should be.'

My stomach twisted. I thought that the notes had been something special between me and her. I didn't know she was writing to Leonard, too. And suddenly, it felt like a betrayal. A knife to the gut.

'She left us. She didn't really love us,' I said, Father's words echoing in my ears.

'Oh, Sidney, you're too little to understand.' Leonard squeezed my shoulder and let his hand drop.

'I *do* understand.' I jumped down from the wall and stuck out my chin. 'She ran away from nice things and nice people. Why did she do that when everyone here loved her so much?' And then I answered my own question. 'Because she didn't care about anyone else – not even me.'

My mind returned to the betrayal of Mrs Murray. Leonard knew nothing of this and I wasn't prepared to enlighten him. He sat there, thinking he was so grown up, pretending he understood this horrible situation, but he didn't know the truth of it. He hadn't overheard the things I had, he didn't realise that women told lies. Father was right – they weren't to be trusted – not one of them.

'It's all rather more complicated than that,' he said, in the same way that an adult might when they didn't have the patience or inclination to explain things to a minor. 'Mother was a good woman who was faced with difficult circumstances. Life is still black and white at your age, but enjoy your childhood whilst you can – there is a peace that comes with ignorance. My childhood is long gone, and I now have to face up to a future I do not want. I shall one day inherit the Hall and the responsibilities that come with it, and am expected to eventually head up the company. But I'm not convinced either will make me happy.'

I rolled my eyes and he noticed, leaning further towards me to stress his point.

'You don't understand what it's like to feel trapped, Sidney, and not see a way out. Even the woman I marry will be dictated by Father. And, unless I settle on the bachelor life, perhaps with a dog for company, I will see out my days in a loveless marriage, forced to remain at Halesham Hall, selling pointless games to pointless people.'

Although I didn't understand many of the Bellingham games, they intrigued me. The colourful boards were almost pieces of artwork in their own right, and the tiny game pieces were so detailed – like the beautiful lead horses in *Newmarket*. I was fascinated by the concept of rules, the rogue element of luck and how a bit of clear thinking could secure a victory. Numbers, generally, were beginning to appeal and my governess was delighted with my early grasp of multiplication tables. In fact, the only time my father had ever looked at me with any interest was when he'd discovered me learning dominoes with the head gardener in one of the potting sheds the previous spring.

I was fully aware, however, that Leonard had no interest in our family empire and only ever played the games out of a sense of duty. He preferred books and learning – words written by other people, telling you what to think. If you picked up a novel, you could read it a hundred times but there was only one way it would end. The very nature of the ink upon the pages meant the result was predetermined. Where was the fun in that? But a game – every time you played, the outcome could change, and the path to get there would be different. That was the real joy. I couldn't understand Leonard's indifference to our legacy.

He rubbed at his chin and I noticed a couple of pimples where he had recently shaved. Dark hairs would appear across his top lip and then, every so often, they would disappear. His voice was deep, like Father's, and he was nearly as tall. These changes would happen to me eventually, and I couldn't wait. Perhaps then people would take me seriously. I sat in his shadow, crossed my arms and scowled as he continued to lecture me.

'Promise me you will get out of here at the first opportunity, Sidney. Marry a sweet girl, move far away, start a family and choose a profession that makes a difference to the lives of others – medicine or teaching, perhaps. You don't want any part of this – believe me, you're better off being the second son. Your freedoms will be far greater than mine.'

'You're just saying that because you get everything.' Even at six, nearly seven, I understood that Leonard's birthright was part of the reason I found it so hard to love him. He beat me at everything, even life – an outcome determined before I was born. And now he was trying to convince me winning was a burden.

'I'm saying it because it's true. I get so . . . angry about it all, and sometimes my temper scares me. Mother leaving makes everything so much more unbearable. She was the only one who truly understood . . .'

I noticed his fists clench into tight balls until the knuckles turned white, and I thought about the times I'd heard him shout at housemaids, kick at tables and square up to the stable lads over petty grievances. These sudden bursts of temper came from nowhere, like Father's, but Mother assured me it was simply his age, and she took her eldest son's moods extremely calmly. Father, on the other hand, used the hickory cane to remind Leonard of his place. Yet her pathetic defence of Leonard's bad behaviour made me realise how weak and ineffectual she was as a parent. Weak, but, as we had subsequently learned, also duplicitous. My older brother was wrong about so many things, and his blind loyalty to Mother was one of them. I was now certain that she deserved no more of my tears.

I jumped off the wall, kicked at the dirt and walked away, determined to steal a box of matches from the kitchens and burn every single one of Mother's stupid letters.

Chapter 5

My father embarked on an extensive building programme at Halesham Hall that summer, and the first thing he commissioned was a tumbledown folly hidden in our private woods – its deep footings were dug with undue haste days after Mother disappeared. Despite installing a stunning stained-glass window of the sun, with glorious beams of yellow radiating from that central sphere, the remainder of the structure was shabby, with half-built walls and missing sections of roof. I couldn't understand why you would build something new and make it look so old and abandoned, but Leonard explained the whole point of such a building was that it had no point and, knowing our father as I did, it almost made sense.

The gardens remained largely unaltered, with the exception of an area given over to the planting of a yew maze. I initially had little interest in the rows of small, green bushes laid out by the garden staff, although I did take the time to record the layout when I was older and wiser to Father's devious games. I was far more interested, however, in the structural additions to the Hall itself. 'Enhancements', my father called them, but as the works progressed, they made little sense to me. Our home was already something of an oddity, with tall towers at the corners, elongated gothic windows, decorative crenellations and a lilac-coloured front door – all apparently done when he had married Mother. It was further proof of his love and devotion to a woman who'd so selfishly betrayed him and I understood his anger at her desertion all too well.

Now there were to be rooms tacked on to the existing building at peculiar angles, improvements to the kitchens (which didn't seem much like improvements to me), and a promised new wing on the east side, turning the Hall into a large, if cluttered, U shape. This second wing would incorporate a long dining room for entertaining, a bigger study for Father, and new bedrooms for the family – the thought of which was exciting, as he promised my new room would have secret cupboards and a special painting on the wall.

Leonard returned to school at the start of the term. Shortly afterwards, an army of builders moved in and the works commenced.

'All this mess,' tutted Daisy. 'Almost as soon as I've dusted, another layer settles. You could grab a cloth from my box and help, Master Sidney,' she said, hands on her hips, half-joking.

I was underneath a table in the drawing room, having taken to lurking in dark spaces to eavesdrop on staff, hoping their chatter would enlighten me as to the fate of my mother, but they appeared to know even less than I.

'Cook has put aside half a tray of biscuits for you,' she continued when I didn't respond. 'If you insist on remaining under the table, I shall eat them.'

I reluctantly crawled from my hiding place.

'I know it's hard but life goes on,' she said kindly, ruffling my hair, as her voice dropped to a whisper. 'Wherever she is, I'm certain she thinks of you and misses you every single day.'

We both knew to whom she was referring, without the need for a name, but I was not so certain, repeatedly questioning how she could have abandoned me. I had, however, bitterly come to regret burning Mother's letters, as my hopes of her returning diminished. They had been the last precious connection to the only person I truly loved – and now nothing remained.

'Go to the kitchens to collect your biscuits and then hurry to your lessons. The new tutor was looking for you earlier.'

'I don't like him,' I said. 'He's boring.' Father had dismissed my governess and replaced her with an insipid young man who was not many years older than Leonard.

'To my mind, you're lucky to have such a thing. I don't have no real learning and the most I can hope for is to meet a nice fella and start a family. The world will be your oyster, Master Sidney,' she said. 'One day, you will be a person of note and make us all proud.'

She patted my shoulder and, without thinking, I threw my arms about her – grateful to have someone who cared, someone who believed in me.

'What *do* you think you're doing?' My father's booming voice came from the doorway and Daisy stepped away from me, dropped her head and hurried from the room. 'This childish habit of following the staff about has to end immediately, boy. These people are not our equals. You do not talk to them, and absolutely do not touch them. If I find you mixing with them again, there will be repercussions.'

And so I stopped hanging around with the staff, which isolated me even more, and with scarce company of children my age, I was lonelier in the months immediately following Mother's disappearance than I had ever been.

Over the following two years, as the works progressed, I began to notice things that weren't quite right, and quickly realised that my father's hiring of men from outside the county was deliberate. It enabled him to keep his construction secrets away from staff and family, even though the builders could occasionally be heard scoffing at his bizarre requests. A window was installed in the new hallway, but when you pulled back the window-curtains, it overlooked nothing – the glass was barely inches from the bricks of another wall. He purchased mirrors with distorted glass and commissioned curious murals along the corridors. There was a curious second, smaller staircase at the far end of the east wing that led to a locked door. It was never opened, and never talked about, and so became known as *the staircase that led nowhere* by Leonard and me. The new dining room made me feel seasick for reasons I couldn't quite comprehend, and his decision to lower all the door frames to the maids' bedchambers in the west garret and replace the staircase to the kitchens with steps of unequal height was just plain mean. For the sins of my mother, it appeared all women would pay.

'It's amusing, is it not,' my father said, 'watching these stupid girls trot up and down the stairs, finding each step not as they expect?' He chuckled. 'Oh, how it slows them down. How they have to go carefully or risk tripping over. Why should I make it easy for them? Why should I care?'

I couldn't see the same humour in the situation as my father, but relished that I was being spoken to like an equal – that I was in on his joke, even if I didn't understand his glee. Because, since Mother's disappearance, he'd gradually begun to notice me. Perhaps now that she'd gone, and with Leonard away at boarding school, he had no one else to talk to – you could hardly converse with staff in such an informal way. So I didn't risk harsh words or brutal retribution by disagreeing or questioning him (his cuffs around the ear could sting for hours) and instead nodded eagerly. Suddenly I was important, ranking above staff, despite my age, and I found I rather enjoyed the attention.

He introduced me to the newly installed listening pipes that ran from the servants' hall up to his study. Staff would talk about the family, he said, in the most disrespectful terms, and were not to be trusted – but I was already wary of Mrs Murray. She tried to ingratiate herself with me by sympathetic looks and gentle words when Father was absent, but when it mattered, when he hit me or belittled me, she said nothing. I was not fooled, and my conviction regarding the deviousness of women was only reinforced when I overheard him talking to the family solicitor, Mr Dartington.

'It has to be dealt with, Clement,' I heard the solicitor say, as I sat crouched in the rose bed outside the open study window. (My tutor told me that my father's Christian name meant mild or merciful – how wildly inappropriate.) 'Her sudden disappearance, with no prospect of divorce or certain knowledge of her death, will prevent you from remarrying.'

'Ha – why would I ever wish to remarry?' His voice grew louder and he warmed to his theme. 'Women care for no one but themselves, and I was foolish to think I'd made a suitable marriage in the first place. They are deceitful and underhand – the sweeter they appear, the darker their souls. I now know with certainty they are fit for only two things – the bedroom and the kitchen.'

Although the true meaning of the bedroom reference was lost on me, I reasoned this was why the maids and the cook had not been replaced as my governess had – they were to be found in both those rooms.

'I'm sorry that you feel that way. I know how much you loved her, Clement.'

My father snorted. 'I never *loved* her. Tolerated her. Tried to look after her.'

'But you were always so attentive – forever showering her with gifts. I thought—'

'Huh,' he scoffed. 'I did my duty as a husband, but the truth was she bored me. I was furious when she abandoned us, but not surprised. Ungrateful bitch, after all I'd done for her. That she could leave the boys motherless makes me sick to my stomach, but I can assure you that I'm not heartbroken. I was never foolish enough to give her my heart.'

This revelation surprised me. I'd been so certain that he had loved her until she betrayed him – that she had, in fact, been the only thing he cared about – that I lodged his words in my young brain to fully analyse another time.

'Rest assured, no woman gets the better of me, Dartington. I may not have the marital bed, but I can satisfy those needs elsewhere. My focus henceforth will be the company, and I shall grow it until it is the most successful in the country. I've wasted too many years pandering to her and she was never once grateful for any of it. As a sex, I don't believe a single one of them can be trusted, and I'll be damned if I ever allow another woman close to me like that again.'

And as I wriggled about to get more comfortable under the window, I resolved to heed his warning.

Chapter 6

1920

As Phoebe reached the end of the winding, tree-lined driveway and stepped out on to the Halesham road, she heard the pounding of running feet from behind. A brief electric slash of jagged lightning cut through the dark blanket of sky above her, then barely a beat later it was followed by the low grumble of thunder. The storm was almost upon her, and the raindrops she'd felt walking away from the house were now heavy and fast, pelting the gravel beneath her feet. She pulled her coat tighter around her slim body as she turned to see who was approaching.

'Wait up, miss.'

The young man who skidded to a halt in front of her looked about her age but was much taller and broader. His clipped hair was short over his ears but a large wave of damp blond fringe fell across his forehead. He had a wide smile, tanned skin and a healthy outdoors look about him.

'Mrs Murray says you're to wait out the storm in the kitchen. She doesn't want you falling ill,' and he stuck out his hand like you might to a child in order to guide them somewhere. His eyes twinkled in the gloom. 'We need to be quick. I don't want to be out in this any more than you do.'

Still furious at Mr Bellingham's unfeeling reaction, but fully aware that the two-mile walk was not wise in the present severe weather conditions, she hesitated.

'My uncle ordered me to leave. He said I wasn't welcome.'

'Ah, but you don't know Mrs Murray.' The young man winked at her. 'Although technically the housekeeper, she's been at the Hall for decades and wields an awful lot of power. Bellingham's reactions are knee-jerk and he's famous for his foul temper. I've been given my notice twice but she always talks him round. C'mon.'

The storm arrived directly overhead at that moment with a simultaneous crack of thunder and flash of light, and water poured from the sky like a pump. There was no time to stand there shilly-shallying about the right and wrongs of the offer, so they scampered back to the Hall.

As they ran to the rear of the house, it became apparent that this extraordinary property was a horseshoe-shaped building built on a slight slope – the kitchens, where he was leading her, were half below ground level. Phoebe followed the young man down a run of stone steps and finally out of the driving rain, but she was so wet by that point, she was fairly certain that, had she made the decision to journey back to the Bell, she couldn't have got any wetter.

'Come in and dry yourself, lassie,' Mrs Murray said with an outstretched arm, as another crack of thunder shook the fabric of the house and rattled the high windowpanes. 'I don't know what he's playing at – sending you away. We haven't had a female Bellingham at the Hall for nigh on thirty years. He should be welcoming you with open arms.'

A sullen young woman sitting at the table was introduced as Ada, the head housemaid, and the young man who'd retrieved her was Douglas, the under gardener. There were clanging pots and the tuneless humming of a girl from the scullery, and a thin middle-aged man limped through the kitchen carrying an armful of pressed white cotton shirts.

Phoebe was offered a warming cup of cocoa and a towel to dry her sodden hair as she sat near the huge range to warm up, watching Mrs Murray making pastry.

'I'm sorry to hear about your parents,' the older lady said. 'I didn't know. Came as a shock. I remember your father as a bairn, screaming down the house, and can picture him now as a lad, laying out his tin soldiers in front of the fire, or running in from the woods, covered in mud. And your mother was a sweet wee thing, if a bit quiet – I didn't know her long.'

'Thank you,' Phoebe said. She knew her parents had married in Halesham and that the last time either of them had set foot in Suffolk was on their wedding day. There had been no contact between the brothers in the past twenty years.

'Without wishing to be indelicate, may I ask how they died?' the older lady said, crumbling butter and flour between brisk fingers.

'They drowned whilst on holiday in Scotland,' Phoebe explained, trying not to get emotional. It was still very raw, even more so for having been such a shock. One morning she'd received a cheery postcard saying what a splendid time they were having, and by that afternoon, she'd been informed of their deaths. 'Their pleasure cruise hit a submerged log and took water on board so quickly, not everyone was able to get out. My only comfort is that they were together. My parents loved each other very much and I don't think one would have managed without the other.'

'Aye,' Mrs Murray said, a misty look about her eyes. 'I remember.'

Before Phoebe had the opportunity to quiz the housekeeper

further, desperate to fill gaps in her knowledge of her parents' past, a bell rang on the far wall.

'The study,' Ada said, looking at the long row of question-mark-shaped wires, each with a small brass bell and labelled with a plaque of the relevant room.

Mrs Murray rolled her eyes. 'Never a moment's peace,' she said, wiping her floury hands on a cloth and disappearing up an unusually steep set of stairs into the main body of the Hall.

She returned after a few minutes and requested that Phoebe follow her.

'Mind the stairs,' Mrs Murray warned, 'they're different heights and will catch you out, especially if you hurry.'

'Could my uncle not get these altered?' Phoebe asked.

'Och, my girl, you don't know the half of it. This is the most peculiar house you'll ever come across. Wait until you happen upon the distorted mirrors – it's like living in a fairground sometimes.'

They entered the main body of the house and Phoebe followed Mrs Murray down a dark corridor, noticing strange illustrations painted directly on to the walls. There were a few traditional landscapes hung about, but a frieze of small figures, almost like a painted Bayeux tapestry, ran along both walls. Each figure was different to the last, from a juggler to a knight, a wizard to a king – all waving their arms about, engaged in various activities, and each one with a grotesque and bleak expression.

'The master's study,' the older woman whispered before leading her into the room where Mr Bellingham sat, hunched over his paper-strewn desk. He looked up as they entered.

'I've just been informed you're still here, despite me making it perfectly clear that you weren't welcome,' he said, rising from behind the clutter, pencil still in hand. All about him were sheets of paper covered in diagrams and drawings, open reference books and an assortment of dice, spinners and coloured game tokens. 'I explicitly requested that you leave and have been overruled.'

'Your housekeeper kindly allowed me to see out the worst of the storm at the Hall.'

'But I don't want you here. I've had nothing to do with my brother for over twenty years and certainly do not wish to have anything to do with his child. Am I not even master in my own home? That's all, Murray, you may leave us.'

The housekeeper nodded, closing the door as she retreated.

Alone with him in the eerie silence of the poorly lit room, cigarette smoke lingering in the air, Phoebe took the opportunity to press her case one more time. 'But I'm family.' This, she determined, was how she would get the man before her to trust her and let her remain at the Hall. She forced out her sweetest smile.

'Pah. Family. That hardly gives you any special status in the Bellingham household. My father was a bully – manipulative and calculating. My mother was a coward, running away and leaving her sons behind, not caring for a moment how that might affect *me*.' He frowned. 'And my brother . . . well, I strongly suspect you and I will have wildly different opinions of him. To you, he was doubtless an exemplary parent and all-round wonderful fellow?'

Phoebe shifted from foot to foot but held his eye. 'He was a kind and loving parent but, like us all, he had his faults.'

In truth, her father was a man of principle, but even her patient mother had become weary of the constant house moves that ensued each time those principles meant he fell foul of an unbending school board. He was stubborn and unforgiving of those who crossed him, particularly when he believed he had morality on his side, so the feud with his brother would never have been resolved during his own lifetime, even though she knew he had every right to feel aggrieved.

'Yes, he damn well did have faults,' Mr Bellingham said, choosing not to elaborate. 'And I was the victim of them . . .'

Phoebe couldn't believe the words that came from this man's mouth. How dare he imply that *he* was the victim, when it was her father who'd been banished from Halesham Hall – made homeless and penniless by his gloating and compassionless brother after he'd inherited the Bellingham estate? Although even this information was relatively new to her. She had always known she had an uncle somewhere in the world, and that her father had fallen out with him, but the family link to Bellingham Board Games and the reasons for the feud had never been discussed.

'. . . But then I believe our lives were blighted from the start. Perhaps he did not talk of our childhood? It was far from a loving environment.'

'Not much,' she admitted, forcing herself to sound neutral. In fact, this was the problem: she had scant information about either parent much before their marriage and move to Cambridgeshire. It was almost as if that was the point at which their lives truly began. 'I know that he was a lonely child, that Grandfather was a difficult man and that my grandmother mysteriously disappeared thirty years ago, leaving you both motherless. Yet I would have thought these things would have made you closer, not driven you apart.'

Mr Bellingham gave a laugh quite unlike any Phoebe had heard. She was used to giggles when the kittens in the barn tumbled around in the dust chasing pieces of string, or hearty guffawing when one of the locals made a cheeky comment after too many ciders, or simply the gentle contented chuckles of her parents as they shared some private joke. But this was dressed up as a laugh when in reality she knew it was scorn.

'Rather turned out that it was every man for himself.'

He walked towards the tall window and she felt slightly intimidated by his height and the self-assured way in which he held himself.

'However, I fear we are in danger of veering off track and I have no interest in opening up old wounds. As soon as the storm has passed, I want you to leave. And this time, I would ask that you don't return. There will be no fatted calf awaiting you at Halesham Hall. As I said before, you're not welcome.'

'But I've come all this way to make peace with you, Uncle. I have no family now. I have no one.'

'Sounds very much as if the problem is yours, not mine. Not something I need to be concerned with. Besides, family is a curse, not a blessing. Be with people because you like and admire them, not because they are related to you.'

'Your quarrel was not with me,' she persisted.

'But I *choose* to have nothing to do with you. That's my prerogative. Besides, you don't know me, and if you did, you might feel relieved I wish to remain estranged. In fact,' he said, 'the only reason I can think of that you sought me out now would be financial, and I will give no handouts.' He glanced back at the rain-spattered window and the lighter skies. 'The storm has wrung itself out and you have done your duty by passing on your news, so I am repeating my request that you leave.'

'Could I not call again? Would you not take just a little time to get to know me?'

This couldn't be it. She needed to remain at the Hall. He couldn't throw her out.

'I am weary of this nonsense.' His irritated tone was all too apparent. 'Why are women incapable of accepting an answer when it doesn't suit them?' He spun on his heels and walked over to the dark panelled door on the far side of the room. 'Leave now or I shall be forced to set Satan on you.'

'Satan? Please don't tell me you are going to summon up some malevolent spirit, or even the devil himself?' She almost laughed, but then she heard it – a whine from the other side of the door, and the increasingly frantic scrabble of claws against the woodwork.

'My dog. He knows his name.' There was a low grumble and the clawing became more desperate.

'You're seriously going to set a dog on me?' Phoebe was incredulous.

'If that's what it takes to get you to realise I'm in earnest, then yes.' He rested his hand on the carved wooden handle and paused. 'But when you have been savaged by the brute and are lying half-dead across my Persian rug, please don't say you weren't warned.'

There was a stand-off as the pair of them locked eyes. The man had every right to ask her to leave. It was his house, after all. But there was something amiss, aside from the injustice of his attitude and refusal to even give her a chance. She saw it in the flitting of his eyes and the way his hand hovered by the handle. Could it be the heir to the Bellingham fortune was testing her?

'I'll take my chances with the dog,' she said, sticking her chin resolutely in the air. 'I'm fond of animals. Even those forged from the pits of hell itself.'

He snorted as he turned the handle, swinging the door inwards, and commanded, '*Attack*, Satan. Get this girl from my house.'

Phoebe braced herself for some enormous wolf-like hound, with froth-covered jaws and sharp, elongated teeth, to bound into the room and take her down. Her hands scrunched into tiny fists, the nails biting into her flesh and her heart rate increasing, but she refused to move – to step back and show this man she was frightened. Besides, there was little that could hurt more than the pain of losing both parents. That was a wound she knew would never heal. Let him have his fun, if he must.

But to her utter astonishment, a dopey black and white cocker spaniel bounded into the room, long silky ears flapping as it ran towards her, tongue lolling from his mouth. The animal fell to her feet, tail thumping the floorboards in sheer doggy glee, and stuck all four paws into the air, waiting patiently for his belly to be rubbed.

Chapter 7

1892

The months immediately following my mother's departure were the loneliest of my life. Instead of dreading being sent to board, particularly after the tales that Leonard had shared about the ragging from the other boys and the harsh discipline of the masters, I began to look forward to a time when I would be surrounded by playmates. Even sleeping in the crowded dorms appealed, for my brother and I continued to have little in common, and I still resented him when he returned for the holidays. With each passing term, he became less of a boy and more of a man – and an increasingly angry one at that. Irritable and fractious, he had little patience with people and was often withdrawn and monosyllabic.

Burton had an annoying propensity to be everywhere, even on the wrong end of the listening pipes. I was summoned to Father's study once and thrashed for careless comments, forgetting the pipes would carry my words up the stairs. He'd been at the printworks that afternoon so couldn't have heard me, but I noticed the smug look in Burton's eyes. Apart from family, he was the only other person who knew of their existence. Murray had keys to most things, but not the locks in Father's study, and the pipes ran to a small cupboard at the back of that room with a listening funnel tucked inside.

I always felt Burton believed himself above the staff, as he lurked behind doors and scurried back and forth, spying on everyone and intercepting all post delivered to the house. It was taken straight to Father, regardless of the recipient, only to be later returned, clearly opened and read, and so I discouraged correspondence from my friends, isolating me further.

As a way to escape Burton's meddling and my father's judgement, I began to retreat to the folly more and more. I appreciated the romanticism of this lost little place, deep in the jumbled mix of evergreen and deciduous trees that made up Halesham Woods, and the fact that it was removed from both staff and family further added to its appeal.

Leonard talked of Mother's love for fairy tales and gothic romance, and I had vague, misty memories of her reading princesses and dragon stories to me. I knew that the towers at the Hall, the lilac-painted front door and the ornate four-poster canopy bed, swathed in lavender-coloured fabric and carved with dragon heads – had all been done for her. The west tower, where she had spent a large proportion of her time, was converted into a sewing room when my parents married, with every conceivable thing she might need for her needlework supplied. So, I had no doubt that the folly was built for her – the words *Sylvia – in silvis* above the window a direct reference to her name. Yet to dedicate this building to a woman Father would not even speak of, and professed to despise, confused me. Had he loved her? Even though he'd sworn blind to Dartington that he had not?

'You're to spend your evenings with me, boy,' he announced the November I turned nine. 'I wish you to have a thorough understanding of the Bellingham legacy. Enough with the tin soldiers and the picture books. It's time you were taught to play *Kings and Queens* and *Empire* – learn strategy and clear, unemotional reasoning.'

Previously, Leonard and I had been an inconvenience to Father, a distraction from his beautiful wife, but since her departure, he'd shown more interest in his sons, teaching us what he regarded as valuable life lessons, and shaping us into the men he wanted us to become. For example, he refused to let us abandon any ventures we undertook – perseverance was an attribute he considered vital. And on one occasion, he told me to jump from the boughs of a tree and into his arms, but stepped to the side at the last moment, letting me fall to the mud. 'Put your trust in no one – not even me,' he said, as he walked away, not offering to help me to my feet.

He bickered with Leonard often, however. At nineteen, my brother was all but a man, with his own opinions and beliefs that didn't always align with Father's – so it was for the best that he was away at university for much of the year. But Father got to me at the perfect time. I was a blank canvas, a lonely child desperate for someone, *anyone*, to pay me attention, even though his lessons were harsh and his games cruel, and I dreaded these evenings, because I didn't always understand the complicated rules or nuances of the activities we undertook. They started well enough, but he quickly became frustrated with me and frequently lost his temper. He made no allowances for my age, and I felt his disappointment keenly every time I made a mistake.

'You think me unkind, but I'm preparing you for life. It will be riddled with disappointments and people will show you no mercy outside these four walls – the sooner you realise that, boy, the better.'

I nodded. It was the safest course of action.

'We must also address your poor understanding of chess. It is known as "the game of kings", not only because the aim is to protect the monarch, but also in reference to its popularity as an idle pastime of the nobility. We may not have been born into elevated circles, but they are not better than us. Bellingham is now a name that commands respect and it has been my life's ambition to see it so. I refuse to be judged by a mediocre birth and scant heritage.'

Our family's humble origins irked Father and so he had ensured we attended the best schools and mixed with the right people. Even though Leonard was too young to be looking for a wife, I'd overheard a conversation about his duty in this regard. It was vital that the family line continued and that any future marriage advanced the Bellingham family name further.

'I have intellect and wealth, and have learned to win at life, despite my initially poor position on the board. Even my own marriage was a coup of sorts, her family believing I was not worthy. So, I shall teach you this game and you will learn something about life, for a good chess player has the edge he needs to succeed, and is always one step ahead of his peers.'

The entrance hall floor had been recently re-laid like a gigantic chessboard. When my chess lessons began in earnest, he stood one side of the tiles, me on the other, and I was instructed to cross the empty hallway in the manner of each piece. If I made a mistake, I was punished, and it proved a sharp learning curve, but an interesting one. *Being* the piece, I saw it all from another perspective which quickly improved my game and, he was correct, my ability to navigate life. Problem-solving, strategic thinking, pattern recognition, even sportsmanship and patience, were all skills developed by the proficient game player.

It was after one of our first evenings together, that my father announced my new room in the east wing was finally ready.

'Murray has supervised the transfer of your things and Daisy has made up the bed. Wash and change into your nightshirt, and then come to me in the library. You're not to go up to the new room without me, understand, for that will ruin the surprise.' His eyes twinkled and a small smile nudged at the corners of his mouth. I felt pleased that something had amused him. He so rarely smiled.

I nodded, a glorious excitement bubbling inside me. Father had promised a mural on my wall and I had seen the artist – a man from London – come and go over the course of several days. I'd spent so long obsessing about my highly anticipated new bedroom, and in quiet moments, when my tutor had finished with me and I had nothing better to do with my time, I'd sat on the bottom stair and listened to the workmen go about their tasks, sawing and banging, laughing and chatting. Mrs Murray bustled about and tutted at the dust, and Daisy periodically took up hot mugs of tea for the men, placing the tray down on the hall table to check her reflection – tucking a stray curl up into her mob cap and pinching at her pale cheeks before ascending, even though the looking glass reflected back a warped image of her face.

After preparing for bed, as I returned down the central staircase, I saw the back of my father disappear down the east wing corridor, and started to follow him. I was intercepted by Murray as I passed the drawing room.

'Your father is waiting in the library,' she said. 'What are you doing here, child?'

'But—' I began.

'To the library with you,' she ordered. Reluctantly, I turned about and trudged back on myself and down the west wing, almost to its furthest point, where our impressive library still remained.

I knocked nervously on the door, my bare feet cold on the floorboards and my breath condensing before me as autumn brought with it the colder nights and darker evenings. To my astonishment, it was my father's voice that commanded me to enter.

'Ah, you're ready,' he said, peering over his wire-rimmed spectacles as he selected a book from the high shelves before him. He placed it on a small tripod table. 'Then let us go.'

We walked almost the entire horseshoe of the house and climbed the new staircase in silence, me following behind until we reached the landing, when he finally allowed me to race ahead.

'This one is yours, I believe,' he said, and I looked at the panelled door, crisp and new. The shiny brass handle had a feather engraved along its length.

'Go on then, boy,' he prompted.

'Thank you, sir,' I said, remembering my manners, and launched into a grateful speech. 'It's kind of you to build me this room of my very own. I am a lucky boy.' I looked up to his expressionless face and beamed.

I pushed the handle down, wondering what pleasures waited within, curious about the mural and excited for a new bed and more space for my toys and books. But it went nowhere.

Above me, I heard Father snort.

'Come on, boy, you can't be beaten by a door.'

'It's locked,' I said, looking up at him for help.

'It's not locked.'

'But it won't move.' My voice was whiny and frustrated.

'How old are you?' he asked.

'Nearly nine, sir.' I wondered that he shouldn't know his own son's age, especially as my birthday was imminent, but said nothing.

'And yet you can't get into the lovely bedroom that I have spent two years building for you. Somewhat ungrateful, don't you think?'

'I don't understand.'

'No, you don't.' His voice was darker now, somehow more jagged and spiky. It was a voice you had to be wary around, in case you tripped on it and it tore at you. 'There is a beautiful room the other side of this door that little boys all over the world would give anything to have, but you expect to waltz up here and for it all to be yours without having to work for it? That's simply not how life operates, boy.'

'Perhaps I'll go back to my old room, just for tonight,' I whispered. I was cold, tired and confused. More games that I didn't want to play, not least of which was the careful selection of my words, in my efforts not to anger him.

'You will not,' he boomed. 'You'll stay here until you have figured out how to open this goddamn door. How can you expect to be part of the Bellingham empire, without an enquiring mind and a determination to overcome? Do you have no desire to wrestle with a simple puzzle or look beyond the obvious? I shall instruct that tutor of yours to focus more on your chess lessons and logic puzzles. Have I not told you repeatedly that if you want to win at life, boy, you must know how to play the game?'

And then, as suddenly as his spiky voice had appeared, it was replaced by the silkier, honey-coated drawl that I remembered him using with Mother. This switch between two personalities wasn't new, I realised, but it had never been employed on me before. And now that it had, I didn't like it.

'You do want to succeed, don't you?'

I nodded, terrified to do otherwise.

'Then don't think of me as harsh. It's for your own good. An uncomfortable lesson now will reap rewards in the future. I will not have you walked over or cheated, as I have been. You will get to know the tricks and lies that men, but most especially women, employ to further their own ends, and you will beat them at their own game. In time, you will learn to think on your feet and not be thrown when things are not as you anticipate.'

It's strange how memories drift back into your head and you interpret them differently with the passage of time. Standing in that draughty corridor, I recalled Father a couple of years previously, down on his haunches, hand on Mother's knee as she wept, telling her that it was for her own good, reassuring her that his aim was only ever to help. I'd believed him concerned for her, comforting and reassuring, but looking back at that moment, it began to appear more sinister. There was a nervous rolling in my stomach as I contemplated that he may have been the cause of the tears in the first place. Had he spent a lifetime playing games with her too? Was that why she'd fled?

He patted me on the head, his mouth smiling but his eyes most definitely not.

'I know you won't let me down. Not like my pathetic excuse of a wife. Open the door, Sidney, and get yourself to bed, because you are not to leave this corridor until you do.'

He abandoned me in the half-light, my toes frozen cold and my face hot with tears. I pushed furiously at the door, shouldering it repeatedly and taking my anger out on the stupid piece of wood standing between me and my father's respect, until my arm was sore and I had no more tears to cry.

Somewhere, lost in my terrifying dreams of doors and locks, corridors and shadows, there was a feeling of warmth. Something soft about my shivering body, gentle hands tucking material under me, lifting my numb feet to rest on a blanket. I felt a hand upon my head, my hair fleetingly caressed like my mother used to. And then I was alone again, tumbling back into my disconcerting dreams.

I stirred to hear my father's voice and opened my eyes to see Mrs Murray bent over me. Daylight was streaming in through the round window at the end of the corridor.

'The boy has clearly been crying like a girl. Utterly pathetic. I had hoped he was old enough to be beyond such weakness. And he's been here the whole night, you say?'

'Clearly,' she replied.

'Who gave him the blanket?'

'I have no idea. There was one folded on the window seat. I suspect he found it in the night.'

My father huffed and I heard his heavy steps begin to walk away. 'And the boy's clothes are all in the room?'

'Yes, sir, as you instructed. Everything of his is in the new bedroom.'

'Then he will be taking his lesson in his nightshirt, won't he?' There was a pause. 'Return the blanket to the cupboard and then leave him be, Murray. I don't have time for those who don't even try.'

I felt the warmth slide from me and opened my eyes, immediately catching Mrs Murray's gaze. Was there a flicker of compassion there? It had been so long since I'd seen it, I couldn't easily identify the emotion.

'Pull up, laddie,' she whispered, and swept the blanket into her hands, stretching it out wide and deftly folding it into a neat square, before trotting behind her ever-demanding master.

I shuffled to my bottom and stretched my aching limbs. My hipbone hurt where it had been pressed against the cold, hard floor, and I started to shiver again. Was I really to sit in the nursery and learn my multiplication tables in my nightshirt? The world felt heavy about my shoulders. I'd failed to open a simple door and my father was disappointed in me. Now I had to get up and present myself to the tutor, who would doubtless humiliate me even further.

Only Mrs Murray hadn't said 'Get up' – she'd said 'Pull up'.

I wondered . . .

As bizarre and unnatural as the action was, I tugged the brass handle upwards. The door to my new bedroom swung open, but my excitement had waned, for I was now scared of what I would find inside.

I stepped over the threshold, thinking about how Murray had covered me in the night and helped me to enter the room, and realised I'd badly misjudged the dour-faced housekeeper at Halesham Hall.

Chapter 8

1920

Phoebe's delighted smile as she petted the writhing bundle of silky fur beneath her feet contrasted starkly with Mr Bellingham's scowl. She'd called his bluff and could tell by his folded arms and tapping foot that he wasn't best pleased. Most people would see the funny side of the situation, but then she knew he was a man devoid of feelings, so she let him witness her amusement as Satan wriggled about, nuzzling against her caressing hands. So, he was playing games, she decided. Well, that made two of them.

'I don't mind admitting I was nervous there for a moment, but he's such a gorgeous dog, and *so* friendly.'

'He is the most stupid and useless animal I've ever had the misfortune to come across. Supposedly a gun dog but completely untrainable. I've been tempted to shoot him myself on several occasions, but he's not worth the bullet or the effort.'

Surely, he was joking? No one could be that unfeeling.

Aware his master was talking about him, but perhaps not that the conversation was so unfavourable, Satan rolled on to his stubby legs and waddled over to Mr Bellingham's feet, his tail wagging, gazing at him with unconcealed adoration. But

Mr Bellingham didn't interact with the animal or even look down at it.

The room was silent for a while, save Satan's heavy breathing and the clicking of his claws on the polished floorboards as he circled his master, unsure where to go or what to do. Phoebe stood up from her crouched position and wondered how long this unemotional man could prolong the silence. A full minute, as it turned out.

'Tell me how they died,' Mr Bellingham finally said, but Phoebe suspected his question came from a place of duty rather than interest.

It was painful, but she told him about her parents' holiday in Scotland and the pleasure cruise sinking.

'Mother loved the water and their holidays were always near the coast, a lake or a river. On this occasion, Father booked a day trip along the Clyde, but the weather was poor and the vessel hit a submerged log. Eleven people drowned. It made the newspapers but it was simply a terrible accident. No one was to blame.'

She'd done her weeping and said her goodbyes, and she would miss them both terribly, for the rest of her days, but there was no point in carrying anger and bitterness around with her. Doing so would colour her life and the lives of those about her, and her parents wouldn't have wanted that. Accidents happened – like Tommy, the nine-year-old son of the grocer who had been kicked by his father's carthorse and who died seven days later from his injuries. And following that terrible tragedy, Phoebe's mother had talked about coping with grief. Crying and being angry at the world were part of the healing process, and not to be ashamed of, but it was important to continue living, and to focus on positive memories. The grocer and his wife had five other children who needed their love and care and it was imperative that they remained strong for them. So Phoebe knew her mother would want her to live her life and be happy. And she was thankful that, unlike the grocer's boy, her parents' death had been swift. Drowning was supposed to be a peaceful end. She hoped so.

'And how did he earn his living?' Mr Bellingham asked.

'He was a teacher at our village school, and immensely popular with the children. His pupils were inconsolable when he joined up and left for France, and delighted when he returned, so you can imagine how hard his death hit them.'

He gave a small snort in response. 'And he distinguished himself, no doubt? Won medals for gallantry and had the undying respect of his men?'

'No medals,' Phoebe said. 'No gallantry.' Her father had been passionate about the cause, but had clashed with senior officers on occasion, so was content to return home when he'd fulfilled his obligation.

'He hated being away from Mother and vowed never to leave her side again.' The words began to swell in her throat, knowing he had kept this vow – even to the point of their deaths. A wave of grief swept over her. They still rolled in from time to time, but were less overwhelming than they'd been at the start. Mr Bellingham, witnessing her struggle, did nothing to alleviate her distress. Instead, he walked back to the tall window and stared across the gardens.

'Whilst I wish you no harm personally, the truth is he took something precious from me and I will never be able to forgive him for that. So, in return, I took something from him. The Bible does advise "an eye for an eye", after all.' He sighed. 'Although I must face the possibility that his victory was sweeter than mine.' He stabbed at a spider web, destroying the delicate and highly ornamental labours of that poor creature with one swipe of his finger, simply because he could not adequately articulate his emotions. 'We could never have reconciled, given the circumstances.'

It made her angry that he attempted to defend his actions. There was no justification for throwing out his brother and cutting him off so ruthlessly. Again, she fought to keep her expression impassive.

He turned to face her once more. 'He has been dead to me for twenty years, and in all that time I've not had the slightest curiosity about his life, and I doubt he had any interest in mine.'

His words didn't quite ring true to Phoebe – after all, he was the one leading this conversation. Whatever feelings (or lack of them) he professed to have regarding family, surely there was a part deep inside that had cared for his brother at some point in his life?

The door opened and Mrs Murray entered.

'How many will there be for dinner, sir?' she said, looking across hopefully at Phoebe.

'One. As always. The girl is about to leave and I remain furious that you went against my wishes and allowed her back into the house.'

'Och, sir, I couldn't see her out in that storm. It would be hard-hearted to make her walk back to town. The poor lass would have died of a chill. She was fairly shivering when Douglas fetched her in.'

'My God, why are women always so overdramatic? The rain has stopped, so she's free to return to Halesham. Perhaps you would be so kind as to ensure she actually leaves the premises on this occasion?'

'Can she not even stay for some food?' The housekeeper frowned and pinched her lips into a tight circle.

'It's fine, Mrs Murray,' Phoebe said. 'They'll provide me

with a hearty meal back at the Bell. You did more than enough by offering me shelter, for although I fully embrace being outside, I think even I would have struggled to walk the two miles in such ferocious weather.' Her face reflected the honesty of her words, but Mr Bellingham remained unmoved.

'It will be dark before the wee thing returns,' Mrs Murray persisted. 'Could Douglas not run her back in the motor car, at least?'

Phoebe smiled. 'Please don't concern yourself on my account. I'm not afraid of the dark and enjoy the stillness that descends upon the earth. There is something magical about the night, and if I'm lucky, I'll see a variety of wildlife scampering about in the dusk – a time the crepuscular creatures abound and the beauty of the world is revealed in a very different way.'

Mr Bellingham raised his eyebrows at her description. 'Crepuscular is a rather informed choice of word,' he said. 'What sort of education did you receive?'

'I was educated by my father.'

'You did not go to school?'

'I attended local village schools until I was fourteen and then he continued my education at home.'

He opened his mouth as if to make a further comment, but then creased his forehead in annoyance.

'Enough,' he said, perhaps sensing he was being inadvertently drawn into Phoebe's world, and wanting none of it. He addressed Mrs Murray. 'The girl is leaving and I have lost my appetite. Don't bother yourself making dinner for me. I shall pour a stiff brandy and retire early.'

'Honestly, sir, I'd have thought that your niece arriving like this, and what with the tragedy of her parents, you could see your way to letting her stay for a while. She's family.' The housekeeper made one last plea.

'I have no need of family.' He tossed his pencil on to the cluttered desk and returned to the centre of the room. 'Currently, the only things I have need of are a larger warehouse in London and a damn kitchen maid. Why you let her throw herself at that injured soldier returning from Africa, like some pathetic charity case . . .' Mrs Murray said nothing in her defence, even though Phoebe felt it rather unfair to blame the housekeeper for the romantic attachments of the staff. 'Women seem generally less willing to settle for a life in service than they used to. I blame the war – giving them foolish ideas of emancipation.'

Phoebe saw her chance and grabbed it with both delicate hands.

'I would gladly apply for the position.'

Until the tragic death of her parents, Phoebe had been assisting her father at the school and running the household with her mother, managing on a small personal allowance until she should either settle on a career or find a husband. Now without income, and not twenty-one until the following year, she would have to find some way of supporting herself.

The housekeeper looked at Phoebe and then at Mr Bellingham, who appeared to be considering the proposition.

'Och, what a ridiculous notion. She can't possibly stay here and work for you as a *servant*. What will folk say?'

'As if I give a damn what people think.'

'It's a very sensible solution,' Phoebe said. 'I'm used to kitchen work and I currently have nowhere to go. The cottage was tied to my father's job and everything my parents owned is currently stored in a disused barn until it can be sold or I find a place to live. I'll have to secure employment at some point.'

Mr Bellingham spun on his heels and turned to face her. 'Aha, so you *were* after handouts. Destitute and homeless, you tracked down a wealthy uncle to improve your situation.' He crossed his arms and a smug look passed across his face.

'Not at all,' she replied. 'I came here to build bridges, even though I don't understand how or why they were so irrevocably broken. Please consider me for the job, even just temporarily until you find someone else. I'm a hard worker and will be no trouble.'

Mr Bellingham toyed with the end of his moustache. 'Whilst I cannot deny I find a perverse delight in such a strange state of affairs, I don't understand why you would consider such a lowly position. You're clearly an intelligent girl and could easily find more suitable employment. Besides, Halesham Hall is a dark place. It eats at your very soul – you would not be happy here.'

'My world has collapsed,' said Phoebe, shrugging. 'The two people I loved most in the world have left me. I must find a way to carry on.'

'Ah, that sentiment, however,' Mr Bellingham said, not meeting her eye and studying the ornaments on the mantel shelf in undue detail, 'I do understand.'

Had she said enough? Would he let her remain at the Hall? It was absolutely vital to her plan that he should. Let him believe she wanted to connect with family and build bridges, but she had no intention of ever forming a close relationship with someone who had acted so ruthlessly towards his own brother. Because, very much out of her depth, and contrary to her gentle nature, Phoebe Bellingham was here for one thing only – revenge.

Chapter 9

Phoebe was bustled back down to the kitchens. Although Mr Bellingham had given tacit agreement to her taking the job, the housekeeper had every right to formally assess her suitability.

'He may be the master of this house, but even he'd not dare interfere in the running of it. The employment of female staff is under my remit and I'll brook no interference from him,' the stern-faced Mrs Murray explained. 'We are stretched to breaking point as it is, and if I don't think you're up to it, there will be no charity – family or not.'

Ada sat at the kitchen table repairing a white pillow slip, and had barely glanced at Phoebe when she returned. Douglas, on the other hand, broke into a wide smile as he washed his hands at the large butler sink. The overworked scullery maid, referred to as Betsy, could be heard scrubbing away at pots and pans in a room beyond, and the middle-aged man she'd seen previously walked through carrying a tray of silver cutlery. As soon as he was out of earshot, Mrs Murray told her his name was Sanderson and explained his limp was the result of an injury from his time serving in France.

'We're a much smaller household than before the war,' she continued. 'All the big houses have had to make economies, but I still have meals to prepare for seven. Mr Bellingham doesn't have horses any more, so we lost all the stable hands, and the gardening staff is reduced to two. Douglas's duties extend beyond the garden – he does the heavier work that Sanderson can't manage and occasional chauffeuring. The head gardener lives with his wife in a small cottage down the lane, but is getting on in years. Poor Sanderson is the only remaining manservant working in the house, juggling the roles of butler, footman and valet. It's a wonder that leg of his doesn't drop off entirely, the amount of time he spends on his feet,' she said, without the hint of a smile. 'I had hoped for the master to make a suitable marriage and perhaps have a wee bairn or two of his own by now, but he's less sociable since returning from the war and doesn't entertain on the scale he did ten years ago. He certainly knew how to throw a party back then – not that I approved of the bedroom antics of his guests, mind . . .'

Phoebe blushed, well aware her upbringing had been a sheltered one.

'Do you do all the cooking?' she asked, not wanting to comment on the debauched parties.

'Aye, along with the weekly accounts, overseeing the deliveries, and keeping an eye on my staff. But many of us in similar-sized households have been forced to take on a dual role, and the preparation of meals is now under my remit. When our previous cook left due to failing health, the need for a kitchen maid became even more of a necessity. I've tried to find a suitable girl . . .' The older woman sighed. 'But as your uncle so rightly pointed out, the factories, shops and offices pay better wages for shorter hours.'

'You'll find me willing and able. Mother and I did all the household chores between us. I'm used to making the bread for the day and I enjoy baking – particularly cakes. Last year I won

Best Fruit Cake at the village fete, and my father had a sweet tooth so I've had plenty of practice.'

'Aye, I remember his love of sugar. Forever stealing cakes and biscuits when Cook's back was turned. Hmm . . .' Mrs Murray took her spectacles from her head and peered at Phoebe. 'I'll give you a trial, mainly because I'd rather see you here at the Hall than wandering about the county with no place to lay your head. But that man needs some sense shaking into him, because it unsettles me, you being his niece and, I'm guessing, heir to all this, skivvying about below stairs.'

The housekeeper swept her hand across the room and Ada and Douglas stared at the new arrival open-mouthed – the thought Phoebe might one day be named as heir apparently not having entered their heads. To be fair, it wasn't an option Phoebe had seriously considered. It would be a big enough task to persuade Mr Bellingham to let her stay, as he'd made it perfectly clear she wasn't welcome. Her plan was more immediate – more damaging – but she lodged the possibility in the back of her mind.

'But I don't want the Hall,' she lied, and wished the housekeeper had kept this observation to herself. Although, from the few occasions her father had talked about his childhood home, she hadn't appreciated quite what an unnerving property it was – those spooky murals on the walls and the disconcerting way that doors, staircases and windows were dotted about, not quite where you might expect to find them. Never mind the sheer size of the place. Perhaps if she succeeded in her plan, it could be turned into a school. That would have pleased her father. The important thing was that she took it away from the current owner and made him pay for his wickedness. She had no wish to wait for God's divine retribution. The cruel and unexpected death of her parents had emboldened her to stand up to the bully on their behalf. It was somehow easier to find the strength to defend others than it was to defend oneself.

'But who else is he going to leave it all to?' Murray said. 'I can't see him marrying, not now. He's had his wild days and didn't find anyone suitable, and has the very definite air of a confirmed bachelor. You're the only Bellingham alive that I know of.'

'I'm only here to build a relationship with my uncle,' Phoebe said, forcing out a smile. 'In the meantime, I shall enjoy working with you all.' Despite Ada's coldness, the staff seemed friendly and she felt generally positive about this unexpected turn of events.

'Very well, then, you can start in the morning, but we must get you settled here tonight. I can't have you sleeping at a strange inn and eating alone. We've plenty of boiled ham to go round, and Ada can peel some more potatoes.' There was a grunt from across the room. 'Douglas, take the motor car down to the Bell, settle the bill, and fetch Miss Bellingham's things.'

He nodded and dipped his head, giving Phoebe a shy smile as he scraped the chair across the quarry tiles and swung a grey woollen flat cap on to his head.

'Two beautiful and eligible women at the house now. I'm feeling rather spoilt,' he said, grinning at Ada.

'Hope you're not looking at me. I wouldn't step out with you if you paid me.' She threw a sullen look in his direction.

'I was actually referring to Mrs M, who I happen to know possesses a pair of nicely turned ankles.'

Ada stuck her tongue out and Mrs Murray tutted. 'Be gone with you, laddie, before I give you a clip around the ear for your cheek,' and she made to swipe him with the rolling pin as he headed out the door. 'That boy treads a fine line. Trouble with a capital T.' She rolled her eyes and turned to Phoebe. 'So, how about you demonstrate some of those kitchen skills of yours and get some eggs on the boil to have with the ham?'

Preparing food Phoebe could do standing on her glossy black head, but navigating a kitchen surely designed to hinder rather than help was frustrating in the extreme. The sink, for example, had a brass tap that hung so low, it was impossible to put anything other than a small jug underneath it, so that filling up a saucepan involved several trips back and forth.

Mrs Murray picked up on her frustration. 'These kitchens were part of your grandfather's modernisations, after . . .' – she hesitated, choosing her words carefully, 'your grandmother left.'

'I can see what you meant when you said the house was peculiar. He didn't think some of his designs through very carefully,' Phoebe replied. 'The tap is totally impractical.'

'Och, he thought them through all right – he just wanted to make life difficult for us down here. Had a thing about women, did old Mr Bellingham, and not in a good way.'

Unsettled by this pronouncement, Phoebe swallowed hard as she set about the task required of her, keen to prove her credentials. She spied a large straw-lined basket of eggs in the corner of the room and looked for something to place half a dozen in.

'Where will I find a mixing bowl?' she asked.

Mrs Murray pointed to a cupboard at the bottom of a built-in dresser. Phoebe walked over and pulled the wooden knob. The door didn't budge.

'Welcome to the joys of Halesham Hall,' Ada said with more than a dusting of sarcasm as she barged past Phoebe with the sewing box. 'The knob is on the hinges side and serves no purpose. There is a hollow under the left top corner.'

'It really is all fun and games here, isn't it?' Phoebe

commented, rustling up yet another smile and trying to remain positive as she slid her fingers under the edge and wrestled open the cupboard.

'My girl,' Mrs Murray replied somewhat darkly from the other side of the table, where she was rolling out the dough for a jam roly-poly, 'this house is full of things that are not as they seem. Uneven stairs, deceptive doors, unsettling murals and a resident ogre. It's no wonder we have such a high turnover of staff. It's all about games with your uncle, and not all of them pleasant. I'm rather afraid he gets it from his father. The only difference is the old Mr Bellingham was malicious, but that wee laddie just does it because he's bored.'

It was amusing to Phoebe that Mrs Murray spoke about her employer as though he were still a boy, but then her father said the housekeeper had started working at Halesham Hall as a housemaid when his parents married, nearly fifty years ago. It was natural she would look upon the Bellingham boys in a maternal fashion, and it made him less scary to remember he'd been a small boy once. However, she couldn't agree with the older woman's assessment. To banish your only brother from his home and refuse to speak to him for twenty years for no reason that Phoebe could determine other than jealousy *was* malicious. Could Mrs Murray not see that?

'He trusts me to run the household, and he respects my opinion, when he's a mind to, but he can be the very devil when he's riled. Your father was lucky to meet your mother when he did. A chance of happiness came his way and he leapt upon it – escaping this house and its ghosts.'

'Ghosts?' Phoebe shivered.

'Och, I don't mean real ghosts. The only shadowy figure you'll see drifting about here at night is the master when he's had a few brandies, stomping about because he can't sleep. I mean the atmosphere. You can't shift it, somehow. Evil things happened here and I can't help but feel the remnants of those wicked deeds linger in the rooms – wailing in the walls and cold chills passing over you in the corridors. I hope you don't come to regret your decision to stay.' Mrs Murray looked up from where she was spreading jam across the dough to make sure she had Phoebe's full attention. 'Because the Hall has a habit of poisoning many who do.'

After a tea of mashed potatoes, hard boiled eggs and cold ham – basic fare but filling – Phoebe helped Betsy in the scullery, insisting it was the least she could do. Finally, as the large wooden clock on the wall struck ten, Mrs Murray led her up the servant stairs and along the back corridor towards the attics where the female staff slept. Some parts of Halesham Hall had three or even four storeys – all adding to the jumbled asymmetrical appearance. They were heading for the far corner of the west wing, part of the original house and about as far removed from the kitchens as they could possibly be, when they were intercepted by Mr Bellingham.

'I don't want the girl up in the garret,' he said, looking at Phoebe but addressing his housekeeper. She wondered if he'd forgotten her name or just couldn't bring himself to say it. 'I want her in the Blue Room.'

'That will complicate things, sir, if she's staff.'

'There are things she needs to understand if she's so desperate to be a Bellingham, and I intend to start by giving her the room her grandfather built for his youngest son. Although both the rooms he designed for his offspring were curious in their own way, this is the one I wish her to see.'

There was a look that passed between Mr Bellingham and his housekeeper. Phoebe spotted it, even though it was gone in a flash. Perhaps he wanted to make some point about her being a child by putting her in such a room.

'Ada has made up the bed and Douglas took up her trunk earlier. I shall show her there myself,' he said.

'But that room—'

'Thank you, Mrs Murray. I'll take it from here.' He gave his housekeeper a warning look and she shook her head, mumbling something inaudible and very Scottish under her breath. Phoebe followed Mr Bellingham out into the main part of the house; they crossed the hall and walked over to the east staircase.

'Is this part of my grandfather's renovations?' she asked, as they climbed the stairs.

'Indeed, the wing my dear father so thoughtfully built on to the Hall a quarter of a century ago.' His tone was far from enthusiastic about the addition. 'And here is the bedroom I talked of, presented to a young boy who'd dreamed of it for months, and was finally rewarded for his patience by his kind and loving father.'

He stopped in front of a panelled oak door and gestured for her to enter. Phoebe put her hand out to the handle. Along the length was the relief of a feather, its shape following a gentle curve, but when she tried to push it down, it wouldn't budge. Like so many things about the house, it was beautiful but bewildering.

Mr Bellingham stood by her side, observing but saying nothing. She released her hand and tried again.

'Is it locked?' she asked, her dark eyes wide.

'No.' He shrugged and turned to walk away, silhouetted in the glow of evening by the scant light from the curious round window at the end of the hallway.

This was a test, she realised. He was expecting her to ask for help, to whine, to complain, but she would do none of those things. She wouldn't give him the satisfaction.

This house is full of things that are not as they seem, Mrs Murray had said, and Phoebe thought back to the dresser cupboard. She tried pushing on the door, opening the other side, and finally she jiggled the handle and, contrary to all her instincts, lifted it up. There was a satisfying slide as the internal spindle pulled the bolt from the strike plate and the door sprang open. Perhaps the feather was somehow telling her to think of birds soaring up in the sky. Mr Bellingham heard the noise too – she noticed him hesitate with his next step – but he didn't turn.

'Oh, how enchanting,' she called out in her cheeriest voice. 'What an amusing little door handle. Goodnight.' And she stepped through the doorway into the dimly lit room, closed the door, and let herself fall heavily against it, dangerously close to tears and more determined than ever to see justice delivered for her father.

She would not be beaten by Mr Bellingham's unpleasantness. She simply would not.

Chapter 10

Phoebe woke up to a crack of bright yellow cutting through the gap in the curtains and the telltale chill of a departing summer in the air. When she'd entered the room the previous night, it had been dark and she'd been too weary to fumble about for lamps and matches. Instead, she'd tugged off her cotton dress and thrown herself across the large bed, its outline illuminated by the moonlight from the window now that the storm had moved on.

Her night had been restless for a multitude of reasons. It was a strange bed for a start, and the mattress was uncomfortable and hard. The room had a curious atmosphere. Every time she stirred, she had the weirdest sensation that she was being watched, and endless prickles danced across her skin. Added to this were the unrelenting memories of her parents which had permeated her dreams since the accident. Even a happy memory, such as being swung around by her father, or boiling up pickle jars with her mother, could make her so overwhelmingly sad.

It took her a few moments to work out where she was as she shuffled her body up the bed, resting against the headboard, and contemplated the dawning of a new day. Her new position at the Hall might not be one she'd planned, but at least the job gave her something to focus on, rather than allowing her to wallow in self-pity.

There was a tap at the door and Ada's sulky face appeared.

'You're to get up now,' she said. 'Mrs Murray said to let you sleep in the first day, what with all the travelling and that, but we need your help down in the kitchens. She's had me peeling potatoes all week and I ain't got time to be a kitchen hand on top of all my other duties. Especially now there's an extra bed to make up.' She stuck her chin in the air as she tripped across to the heavy velvet curtains and pulled them back fully to allow the gloriousness that was a mid-September day to stream across the room. Phoebe could see why it was called the Blue Room – the carpet was a deep indigo, the linen wallpaper was scattered with leaves of cobalt and teal, and the curtains were the colour of cornflowers.

'Of course,' she replied, drawing the quilt up to her neck as she adjusted herself against the pillows. She was in her undergarments, and felt embarrassed to have this girl look at her as though she was not only an interloper, but also a massive inconvenience.

'Although staff sleeping in the east wing ain't right, to my mind,' Ada said, under her breath. 'Forgot this yesterday,' and she dumped a cotton towel unceremoniously on the wooden rail by the washstand. As the housemaid left the room, Phoebe's eyes were drawn to a disturbing mural that dominated the opposite wall – one totally bare of wallpaper. It had been so dark that she hadn't noticed it the previous evening.

The painting had barely any colour, just hues of black and grey, with only minor shocks of brilliant white or blood red. In the centre was a woman, naked from the waist up – which Phoebe considered entirely inappropriate for the bedroom of a young boy. The woman's face was drawn, her eyes sunken and her lips slightly parted in an equally inappropriate manner, and snakes curled and hissed from her head in the place of hair – each with a vicious, flicking forked tongue. It was Medusa, she knew that much from her lessons, and around her stood stone statues of petrified men – all men, Phoebe noticed. The message was clear: women are dangerous – look what she's done to these poor souls.

Although there was nothing overtly horrific about the image, when daylight waned, it would have been a haunting sight for a young boy – especially her piercing eyes, following you about as you moved within the room. Could this be why she'd felt watched all night? She finally began to understand what Mr Bellingham had meant when he'd said that Halesham Hall was a dark place to be.

'Your uncle is in London today, and his soppy hound latches on to me when he's absent. You don't mind, do you?' Mrs Murray said, as she took Phoebe on a guided tour that first morning.

'Of course not,' Phoebe replied, bending to pat Satan's soft head. 'We had a scruffy little terrier called Nipper when I was younger. They're so dependent on you – taken from their mothers as puppies and desperate to be part of your pack. To fit in. To belong.' Where did she belong now? she wondered, feeling equally torn from her roots. 'If you show them a little kindness, they're always grateful. Dogs adapt quickly and have so much love and loyalty to give and, despite his unfortunate name, he's an absolute darling.'

In response to the conversation that was clearly about him, Satan sat adoringly at her feet and thumped his heavy tail on the floor.

'He's a wee scunner – that's what he is,' Mrs Murray replied. 'Forever running off with stolen trophies and getting into places he shouldn't.'

Not sure what a scunner was – something Scottish and mischievous, she decided – Phoebe smiled at the housekeeper.

The older lady, perhaps regretting her words, gave him a token ruffle of the head. 'But I feel sorry for the wee mite, much like I feel sorry for my girls,' she said. 'Even those who are only with us for a short while, and some only twelve or thirteen – placed in service and ripped from their families, rather like the dog. I try my best to guide and comfort where I can.' She pinched her lips into a tight circle as she thought about her words. 'Perhaps I'm getting soft in my old age. Never used to be like this. When I first became housekeeper, there was one wee lass who was petrified of me and called me the Scottish witch behind my back. But I've mellowed over the years. Not that I stand any nonsense, mind, but a kind word goes a long way when you've been slaving tirelessly all day for little pay and no word of thanks from your master, in a house that would give even the bravest of men the collywobbles. Honestly . . .' She huffed. 'At one point our turnover of maids was so high that I feared we'd run out of lassies in the county.'

Phoebe couldn't agree more. Perhaps Mr Bellingham's blunt manner had been acceptable when Victoria was first queen, but the tide was turning, and he would find there was no one willing to shine his boots, sweep his hearths or pluck his fowl if he wasn't careful.

They began their tour of the house in earnest and she was led along corridors and up winding staircases, pausing at the doors of various rooms to have their function explained, with an ever-eager Satan trotting behind. He repeatedly picked something up in his mouth that he shouldn't have, and on each occasion this was removed by a tutting housekeeper.

They walked through the entrance hall that she'd barely glimpsed that first afternoon. She could now clearly see the basalt bust of a pharaoh standing on a tall plinth – possibly Ramesses II – and a similar pharaoh of white marble by the door.

'The previous Mr Bellingham had a keen interest in Egyptology. *Treasures of the Tomb* has always been a big seller for the company,' the older lady said, noticing Phoebe pause by the first bust. 'He used to say those pyramids of theirs were the greatest puzzles created by man. I'm surprised he didn't commission one to be built on the estate, quite frankly. Mad as a hatter, that one, and I don't mind saying so now that he's in the ground.'

Phoebe didn't comment. It really wasn't her place.

The tour took nearly an hour and still she couldn't rationalise the layout of the sprawling Hall in her head. It was a confusing jumble of dead-ends, fake doorways and hidden corners.

'The dining room is such a lovely large space. Does Mr Bellingham entertain much?' They stood together in the doorway as Phoebe admired the long mahogany dining table that seemed to stretch into the distance like a Roman road.

'Ha,' Mrs Murray snorted. 'Walk down to the end and then look back at me,' she instructed.

As Phoebe advanced, she realised there was something off about the room. The walls weren't quite parallel, either vertically or horizontally, widening and leaning out as she progressed down its length. And the floor sloped – not by much, but it was unnerving. When she reached the far end, she turned to look back. The effect made her feel slightly nauseous.

'It's all wrong from down here.'

'Games, games, always games.' Mrs Murray sighed. 'That was your grandfather playing about with perspective and dimension. Impractical and horrid. People feel uncomfortable in this room, some not quite realising why, which I believe was rather old Mr Bellingham's intention. Sometimes I wonder whether he struck deals in here because the wine flowed freely, addling their already confused brains, and the poor souls agreed to anything just to leave.'

Phoebe thought back to the knocker on the front door. Did everyone at Halesham Hall, either resident or a guest, have that same desire to escape? she wondered.

'And in answer to the entertaining,' the housekeeper continued, 'hardly at all now. There was much more of it in the old days, when your grandfather first got married, but it dried up quickly, which was such a shame because his young bride loved giving dinner parties and meeting people. I remember her when they were courting – so pretty and gay – always laughing and lighting up any room she was in.' There was a dreamy look across the older woman's eyes. The Hall clearly held some happy memories for her, even though they had been disappointingly fleeting. 'They honeymooned in Venice and I had such high hopes for the union, but she didn't have that excited, flushed look of a young bride when she returned. Something wasn't right and I couldn't put my finger on it. He became increasingly protective and jealous of his wife – he tended to accept invitations alone and rarely entertained. It was a shame. I enjoyed seeing the place alive with guests.'

'But you say that the current Mr Bellingham hardly entertains at all?' Phoebe asked, seeking clarification, surprised this should be the case.

'There were some scandalous Saturday-to-Mondays before the war, but only occasional business dinners are held now. He may not be a lover of people, but even he realises you must engage with others periodically in order to get on in the world.'

And yet he couldn't bring himself to be pleasant to his niece. Well, that was fine, she decided, she had plenty of time to win him round. She would be sweetness and light until she found the information she sought, and then she would be his undoing.

The pair returned to the kitchens and her working day began in earnest.

Chapter 11

For the first time in weeks, Phoebe felt a wave of contentment wash over her as she threw herself into her new role. The Hall was unsettling, Mr Bellingham was a cold fish, and Ada kept giving her suspicious glances, but she was finally occupied. Cooking and baking had always been a joy, and even the more mundane tasks – gutting fish, preparing vegetables, plucking the poultry – gave her satisfaction. She'd been drifting since the death of her parents but finally had a purpose.

The sun was bright, even though it was losing heat with each passing day. It danced across her face as she knelt by the herb garden later that afternoon, selecting mint, sorrel and sweet marjoram for the beef stew Mrs Murray was preparing from her beloved and much-referenced Mrs Beeton. The housekeeper had no formal training as a cook and told Phoebe she'd clung to that book as if her life depended on it when her role within the household changed. 'Simple and wholesome' was her motto, and Mr Bellingham wasn't a fussy eater. Phoebe gathered he ate merely to survive, showing little interest in fancy fare or extravagant dining in recent years. Even though he was a tall man, he was as thin as a rake. Perhaps she could win him over through food, she mused, as Douglas walked past. He was carrying a bundle of fence posts across his broad shoulders, the muscles of his back tugging at the cotton shirt he wore, and his sun-kissed skin contrasting with the white of the fabric.

She didn't want to be caught watching him, so focused instead on selecting sprigs of mint as he disappeared behind the sheds. The scent floated in the air as she snapped each bright green leaf, reminding her of happier times with her mother, making mint vinegar or simply weeding herb borders together in companionable silence on sultry summer afternoons. There was an unpleasant lurch in her stomach, knowing that she would never see either of her parents again. She was alone in the world but was not a creature built for solitude, and she desperately missed her old life.

The last cottage they'd lived in had been picture-perfect and, rather unusually, they'd remained there for several years. Her father, restless since the start of the war, was frustrated that he was too old to enlist, even though as a teacher, he was exempt. However, much to the everlasting distress of her mother, he finally volunteered in 1917. Proof of age was not necessary, largely because the military was so desperate, so he resorted to taking five years from his age, determined to fight another noble cause. This denied him further opportunities to clash with his employers – only the superior officers in his regiment. When he returned after the conflict, he was less confrontational, calmer about things, somehow, and he accepted with weary resignation the restrictions imposed on him by the school board.

Phoebe and her mother had finally begun to put down roots at Stepping Stones. With its reed thatch roof bulging over the pink-washed rendered walls, like the top of a fresh-baked loaf as it spilled over the edges of the tin, it started to feel like home. There were always splashes of colour in the small garden – whatever the season. The oranges of the tree canopies and strong red berries of the hips and haws in autumn as you picked your way through shiny conker-covered pathways. The flame-coloured stems of the bare dogwood branches and bold greens of the neatly clipped conifers that edged the inevitable browns of winter. Deep purple crocuses and the bright yellow cowslips and primroses of spring. And then summer, when every colour conceivable was splashed around like the over-enthusiastic art-work of a child. But her favourite part of the garden was not the bobbing pastel hollyhocks or cheery red poppies, self-set where their land edged the fields, but the large rectangle of vegetable patch that covered most of the back garden. Narrow paths up and down the brown soil gave access to the crops for weeding and harvesting. And there was a long bed directly under the eaves to either side of the south-facing kitchen door, where her mother grew all the herbs needed for the kitchen and the medicine chest. Would the new schoolmaster tend the garden at Stepping Stones as lovingly as they had done? she wondered. Would he take the same joy and comfort in the flora and fauna of that small parcel of land?

Her eyes began to mist over with unchecked emotions and the world before her blurred, even though she knew that she would eventually come through this. Her future was still an unwritten book of wonderful possibilities . . .

'Well, well, if it isn't Dolly Daydream.'

The voice behind her made her jump and the small basket tumbled from her knees and spilled its contents over the grass. It was Douglas. He'd circled around behind her and caught her lost in memories. She blinked away the building tears.

'Shouldn't you be sweeping a floor or slicing up a mountain of onions? Instead of sitting out here in the midday sun and staring into the sky like a woman without a care?'

He gave her an open and wide smile, which she returned, pleased that he'd referred to her as a woman, whereas Mr

Bellingham had thus far insisted on calling her a girl. Douglas's joviality more than made up for his master's unpleasantness and Ada's scowling. She'd already fallen into an easy relationship with this affable young man, even though her insides were a spinning carousel of nerves and excitement.

'I'll have you know, I've just put a batch of fruit buns in the oven and scrubbed enough carrots to feed half of Halesham. And now you find me selecting herbs for Mrs Murray, which counts as work, so don't go telling tales and getting me dismissed.'

He dropped to his haunches beside her and she could smell traces of cut grass and engine oil drifting from his warm body. It was a strangely enchanting combination.

'I'm teasing. We're a pretty relaxed bunch when Mr Bellingham isn't around. He has a bit of a temper on him sometimes, but he's not that bad, once he's stopped spitting and hissing. It's all show. Have you noticed how Satan rarely leaves his side when he's at the Hall? And animals are pretty good judges of character. Here, let me help . . .'

He gathered up the scattered herbs and placed them back in her basket, Phoebe getting a further waft of him as he reached in front of her. His hands were rough with crescents of soil under the nails – workman's hands, she realised. Strong hands. Capable hands.

'So, what's your story?' he asked, as they began to pick the sorrel companionably. 'Old Murray said you're Mr Bellingham's niece, but I can't see the resemblance myself. Never even realised he had a niece, if I'm honest.'

'He's never been a part of my life, because my father and he fell out before I was born. The day I arrived at the Hall was the first time I'd set eyes on him in my life. But when my parents died, naturally I wanted to connect with the only family I had.' She paused, not sure if she should ask the question at the forefront of her mind. 'Do you know what their quarrel was about? I understand there was a puzzle involved.' She glanced at him, wondering what he might know.

Douglas shrugged and got to his feet. 'I was born the year after it happened and I've only been working here since the war. Old Mrs M is the one you should be asking, because she's been at the Hall for decades – although she has a curious loyalty to the current Mr Bellingham. They make an odd pair – both of them are prickly, but underneath all the spines, they have the soft underbellies of baby hedgehogs.' The thought of Mr Bellingham with a soft underbelly made her cough. 'Murray cares about her staff, as long as they work hard and abide by the rules. As for the master, I've seen him hit a wall in frustration and bellow at a maid for no apparent reason, reducing her to tears, but I've also spotted him with that soppy dog of his, when he thinks no one is watching. The trick is to pay attention to his actions, not listen to what comes out of his mouth. Clement Bellingham though . . . a real bastard, by all accounts. Word is he used to beat his wife.'

Phoebe shuddered at this new and unexpected piece of information. Had her father known about this? He'd never said anything, but then it was hardly a conversation he'd have with his daughter.

'I was told that my grandmother ran off thirty years ago, never to be heard of again,' she said, understanding this more now.

'Did she run off, though?' Douglas said. 'Or did she fall foul of her husband's temper one last time?'

Phoebe couldn't prevent her eyes from widening in surprise. 'You're seriously not suggesting—'

'I'm not suggesting anything, but my mother certainly has her own theories about what happened that night. She used to work here, you know, as one of the housemaids, so she might know something about the feud.'

'Phoebe?' came a shout from the direction of the kitchens. 'How long does it take to pick a handful of leaves?'

'I have to go.' She moved to her knees and Douglas reached out his tanned hand to help her to her feet. He gripped her tiny fingers, the strength of his arm whisking her from the ground as if she was made of nothing, and pulled her upright.

'Yes, Murray doesn't have time for shirkers. I'll be seeing you around.'

I do hope so, she thought to herself, because he was the first person she'd spent time with since her parents' death who'd enabled her to forget her sorrow, even if only temporarily.

Chapter 12

1899

The years following my mother's disappearance were tough and my childhood was not a happy one. Love and kindness were not words in my father's vocabulary, and my new bedroom was the biggest disappointment of my young life thus far. It was a space I continually felt unsettled in, which was deliberate on my father's part, as Medusa judged me every night and found me wanting. Mrs Murray might not be the enemy I had supposed, but she was not in a position to offer any substitution for the maternal love I lacked, and my brother's temper went unchecked if Father wasn't around. Although he eventually outgrew much of his adolescent hotheadedness, a subdued and bitter Leonard gradually emerged as he reluctantly undertook an active role within the company, resentful of a job he clearly had no great love for. Our roles were now reversed, as I was often away boarding and it was he who rattled around the Hall.

In the summer of 1899, aged fifteen, I returned to Halesham for the holidays with a temper of my own. Rather unusually, Father had not attended the school's annual speech day, always held three weeks before the end of term. Generally, he enjoyed swanning around his alma mater and reconnecting with old fellows. As an astute businessman, he was fully aware that there was a great deal of wealth represented by the parents of my peers, and he was never one to miss a business opportunity. But his health had been increasingly poor of late, and this was the first indication that the situation might be more serious than I'd assumed. So, he was not there to see me receive my prizes, nor to mingle at the garden party and enjoy the speech-day cricket match that was always played on this most auspicious of days.

However, even before his illness had taken hold, he had not once come to fetch me home on the final day of the school year, nor sent anyone on his behalf. Instead, I was always forced to drag myself and my trunk across the country on a train. It would have been easy enough to spare the coachman, or, if both coaches were in use, at least to send one of the stable boys to meet me and help with the trunk. But it was part of my father's plan to make a man of me. 'Be dependent on no one. Do not expect anything from anyone. The only person you can ever trust with absolute certainty is yourself.'

I liked school more than Leonard ever had, although academically he outshone me. I was always pushing the boundaries and rebelling, yet I performed well enough. Partly due to my sudden acceleration in height when I turned fourteen, I was popular amongst my peers, who revelled in my habit of challenging authority. I towered over many of the masters and could tell by their manner towards me that this did not sit well with them, particularly when they were raking me over the coals for some prank or for handing in sloppy prep. My lofty advantage was boosted by my father's tutoring over the preceding years that I was not to suffer fools gladly. I'd dared to say no to him once when I was seven and, without my mother to smooth things over with her soft words and gentle pleading, he'd hit me so hard I'd burst an eardrum. It was another life lesson: might, whether morally justifiable or not, was often accepted as being right.

On the last day of term, and after a journey that took half a day, I paid a man to drive me from Halesham station to our isolated and curious home. His horse pulled up outside and, free from the rules and regulations of others, I embraced my position in the household, shouting at the footman for his tardiness in retrieving my trunk and scowling at Murray as she greeted me at the door. I'd always found taking orders from others hard, and this was my chance to be fully in control. Besides, I was hot, I was tired and I was not best pleased that I'd been forced to arrive home on the back of a milk cart.

'It's wonderful to have you home again, sir,' the housekeeper said. 'Your brother is currently in Hampshire, staying with friends of your father for two weeks, and Mr Bellingham is in London on business, but should return the day after tomorrow.'

Not having seen Father since the Easter break, and only then very briefly, I was indifferent to his absence. If anything, it was preferable, because he was not there to make me feel inferior or scoff at my pronouncements, although I was surprised his health had permitted such a journey. Business, however, could mean several things: his increasingly frequent visits to an address in Harley Street which no one was supposed to know about, his decreasingly frequent liaisons with the long trail of ladies who had amused him since the departure of our mother, or genuine business matters concerning Bellingham Games – the last option being the most unlikely. For the past decade, a competent manager had overseen everything, freeing up Father to experiment with game ideas and indulge in the more pleasurable aspects of his position – the formal dinners and shooting parties. Our Suffolk paper mill and printers provided many of the game components, even though the boards were still coloured by hand, and the development of the games – Father's real skill – was largely undertaken at the Hall, but his banking was still conducted in the city.

'I shall eat at eight and have a fancy for beef,' I said, like a true Bellingham. I was emulating one of the older fellows from school, Sparshott. I'd fagged for him when I was younger and never forgot his superior tone and authoritative manner. Next year I was to be a prefect and could command boys from the lower school to fag for me. I would be allowed to stay out after lock-up and even administer canings. These things I looked forward to, as a sign of my maturity and progression through the school. I was determined that back home, with no father or older brother to take precedence over me, the staff would do *my* bidding.

'Cook has baked a salmon, followed by a haunch of venison for the entrée. It's your favourite and she thought it would be a nice treat for your return.'

'But I want beef, Murray. Can you not even fulfil that simple request?' I took my pocket watch from my jacket, inspecting the hands as though I had important things to be doing and no time to waste in idle chatter with staff.

'Very good, Master Sidney.' I couldn't fault her words but detected in her eyes a look that suggested I was getting above myself. 'Would you like something light to eat now? I'm sure Cook could rustle up some sandwiches and cold meats.'

'No, I rather think I shall take myself off for a walk, as the day is bright and the Hall is not.'

I'd been in a stuffy train carriage for too long and so, after changing into more suitable attire, I initially headed for the folly, where I often retreated to be alone with my thoughts. Despite Father still refusing to talk of Mother in our presence, I'd once come across him weeping on the stone bench of this architectural oddity, whispering her name over and over. I hadn't dared make my presence known and had returned to the Hall before I was spotted. His conversation with Dartington after her disappearance suggested her betrayal had destroyed any love he'd felt for her, but the building of the folly and subsequent pilgrimages there did not bear this out. Perhaps, I began to realise, his determination to cut her from his life was not because he hadn't loved her, but because she had not felt the same, and this humiliation had turned to anger. Bellingham men were not losers, they were victors.

This was a mantra he'd instilled in Leonard and me over the years, constantly reminding us of Grandfather's success in both business and society, against all the odds. The print works had been founded by Charles Bellingham – an entrepreneur and a hard-working man, who came into money after a tactical marriage. With access to trading routes via its proximity to the River Hale – a tributary that fed into the North Sea – the company did moderately well, printing local newspapers, religious tracts and books, and resulted in a healthy climb of both his fortune and his social standing during his lifetime. Clement Bellingham, his only son, expanded on this and was now looking to his own sons to continue the legacy.

But on that day, not wanting to think of Father or even Mother, I turned from the folly at the last minute and headed towards Halesham town and the stream that divided our land from the fields of the neighbouring farmer. This year, the main crop was wheat and it was a glorious honey-coloured sea of swelling grains, rippling in the distance. As I strolled out of the woods and along the sun-dappled path, I happened upon a young girl, similar in age to myself, kneeling on the grassy bank at the edge of the water with a small basket by her side.

I came to an abrupt halt and found myself noticing nothing else for those first few moments apart from her beauty. Her head was tilted towards the heavens, and her eyes were closed – long, dark lashes resting on her pale skin. Black hair fell loose down her back, which surprised me as I rarely saw the hair of young ladies so unconfined. One strand remained separate from the rest, curling and looping against her cheek as it fell across her chest. I became hypnotised by the gentle rise and fall of her breathing as she basked for those few moments in the warmth of the early afternoon sun.

With the stream behind her, and a collection of water reeds to her left, I was reminded of a painting I'd seen at the Royal Academy Exhibition at Burlington House in the Jubilee year. *Hylas and the Nymphs* by Waterhouse had made a lasting impression on me – a young man enticed into the water by seven dark-haired nymphs, tugging at his tunic, drawing him to his death. Before me now sat one of those bewitching nymphs and I felt similarly pulled.

Perhaps she sensed me, or I inadvertently made a sound, but her eyes flashed open and she jumped to her feet.

'You startled me,' she said, brushing down her skirts and taking a step back.

I was unable to reply immediately or to tear my gaze from her eyes – as rich as drinking chocolate but wide and wary. My mood, previously one of irritation and boredom, spun on its heels and danced away, as I felt a confusion of sensations flood to fill its place. My hands were clammy and my throat was dry and constricted. I swept my fingers through my hair and cleared my throat.

'My apologies.'

It struck me then how little I had to do with females generally in my life. School went out of its way to avoid any possible interaction between the sexes, convinced it would lead to illicit fornication and debauchery. Sports were encouraged, ostensibly to foster unselfishness and patriotism, but I suspected also to curb the excessive energy and frustrations of the hormone-ridden boys, cooped up together with neither girls nor war as an outlet for their pent-up and turbulent emotions. In truth, most of us were too frightened and in awe of the gentler sex to even converse with them – which was how I found myself at that moment.

Some of my housemates had sisters, younger and older, and knew something of how this curious species operated. I knew nothing. I had only the taciturn Mrs Murray and a handful of uneducated and dull housemaids who passed through the Hall with alarming frequency, and with whom I rarely interacted, unless it was to demand their help or reprimand them for their incompetence. I didn't even have a mother, who might give me clues as to what made this mysterious gender tick. The closest I'd come was spending the previous summer with Monty, who had a sister two years his junior. She proved the most annoying little thing and had taken a shine to me, trailing behind us wherever we went like a pathetic puppy dog, eager for attention. But a few carefully selected home truths soon put paid to her insufferable adoration. She was unattractive and slow-witted and I told her so. Yet, standing before this Waterhouse nymph, my tongue knotted itself like tangled wool. What did one say to a pretty girl?

'You're sitting by the stream.' I pointed towards the water and then immediately wanted to thrash myself for stating such an obvious fact. How disappointed my English master would be to hear me spout this banality, when usually I could express myself far more articulately.

'Yes,' she said.

'Are you hoping to paddle?' Again – maddeningly immature. Why could I not have thought of something more intelligent to say? A comment about the joys of the season or an observation relating to the scenery. We'd been studying Tennyson at school. I could at least have dredged up a few lines from 'The Brook':

> *I come from haunts of coot and hern,*
> *I make a sudden sally,*
> *And sparkle out among the fern,*
> *To bicker down a valley . . .*

Instead I had come out with a remark that made me sound like a village idiot. She gave a shy smile and a tinge of pink kissed her pale cheeks.

'I'm drawn to the water,' she said. 'The sound, like gabbled whispers, as it rushes over rocks and pebbles. How it's constantly on the move and never still, not even for one moment. Even in a stagnant pond, the creatures within stir and agitate beneath the surface. There is something mysterious and hypnotic about it.'

'Perhaps I should take more time to study nature,' I said, finally finding my feet in the conversation. 'I'm rather afraid I'm only out of doors for sports and end up in the water more often than taking the time to sit back and enjoy the view. There's nothing like launching yourself into the lake for a refreshing dip on a hot summer's day, and I row for the . . .' I'd been about to say school, but suddenly didn't want to admit to my age. Oh, the agonies of being on the cusp of manhood. I was bigger and stronger than both Father and Leonard, yet whenever I was in the company of either, they took pleasure in reminding me I was still an adolescent. Leonard had stopped ribbing me, however, now that I could pack a punch. 'I'm in a rowing eight,' I finally finished.

'Ah, too busy splashing about to enjoy the flora and fauna, I fear. But if you take the time to sit by the water, immerse yourself in nature and observe, you will find a plethora of charming sights – scampering otters, hovering dragonflies and, if you are really lucky, the occasional iridescent kingfisher darting between the banks to snatch a minnow from the water.' And then she quoted from the very poem I had toyed with moments earlier:

> *'With many a curve my bank's I fret*
> *By many a field and fallow,*
> *And many a fairy foreland set*
> *With willow-weed and mallow.*
>
> *I chatter, chatter, as I flow*
> *To join the brimming river,*
> *For men may come and men may go,*
> *But I go on forever . . .'*

'Tennyson,' we said together, and I grinned at her like a complete blockhead.

There was an awkward pause before she retrieved her basket and announced, 'Excuse me, but I must be on my way,' and dipped her head to signal her imminent departure.

Panic flapped haphazardly inside my chest. I didn't want this enchanting creature to scamper off over the fields and out of my life. I didn't even know her name. In truth, I didn't know what I wanted, only for her not to leave.

'You have to be somewhere?' I asked.

'Erm, yes.' She didn't elaborate, or even seem that certain of her answer, but I recognised that she felt uncomfortable, and for a moment I allowed myself to consider our situation from her point of view. We were in the middle of nowhere and I was a stranger – one who was considerably bigger and more powerful than her.

'Your name, at least?' I called, as she turned and made for the footpath that went to Halesham. With a name, I could make discreet enquiries. It was a small town and Murray would know if she was the right sort of girl or not – although anyone who quoted Tennyson surely must be. Besides, I was home for the whole summer. There was no need to rush these things.

She didn't answer immediately, or turn her head, but I saw her steps slow. 'Nancy,' she eventually said. Her steps quickened again as she climbed the shallow bank to the path, and with her glorious black hair swishing from side to side down her back, she disappeared into the distance.

Free from the monitoring of the school masters and the ever-judgemental eye of my father, I allowed myself to enjoy the moment. I was alone in the beautiful Suffolk countryside, with no one to answer to and nowhere to be, so took off my jacket and spread it on the ground to spare my trousers. I wanted to take a few minutes and experience the things Nancy had talked about. With my head leaning back on my clasped hands, I studied the drifting clouds and swooping house martins, I inhaled the sweet smell of the summer blooms, I listened to the gurgling of the water and rustling of animals scurrying about in the undergrowth. Finally, I let my eyes close and thought about the young girl who had so unexpectedly entered my life.

But as I lay there, my brain blurred images of the bare-breasted nymphs with the captivating Nancy. I didn't want to think of her in that way, yet adolescence is a time when your brain thinks of little else. I'd never seen a naked woman in the flesh – only in classical paintings, the illustrations of books and that damn mural on my bedroom wall. Some of the boys owned photographic postcards that showed breasts and more besides, and these were passed around the dorms after dark. And Monty claimed to have been with a girl the previous Christmas, but when pressed for details, they proved sketchy. It was more likely bravado in front of his peers, and something to make the younger boys regard him in awe – but I could never be certain, and had a begrudging respect for him either way.

Father had recently muttered about 'breaking me in' – again possibly forgetting my age – but I wasn't convinced this was what I wanted from the captivating Nancy. Confusing thoughts tumbled inside my youthful head. I was a bundle of contradictions at the best of times, but my opinion of the fairer sex, so long shaped by my father, was at odds with what I thought I'd glimpsed by the bank. I wanted something lasting with this mesmerising girl, not to simply use her for my own ends and then cast her aside. Yet how could I have these swirling feelings, circling around inside me and swelling like a tornado, when I'd barely made her acquaintance?

Still, I pondered what it might be like to brush away those stray strands of hair, to say something clever and make her smile, to lean forward and kiss those soft lips. She was not a girl to be grabbed from behind in the hay loft, but to be courted slowly and respected.

I imagined myself then, lying next to her on a rug by the brook, dappled sun filtered by the tall beech trees falling across her face as I quoted poetry to her. I dreamed of building a friendship around shared interests and simple pleasures. Of being able to boast to the boys in my house of a girl back home. Of the exquisite pain of waiting for each other. And, when we were both of age, of asking her to be mine for ever.

As these thoughts drifted through my head on that hot summer afternoon, I wondered at my reckless imagination after only ten minutes' acquaintance and concluded that the heat must have addled my brain.

Chapter 13

'I'm not sure I know any Nancys,' Mrs Murray informed me the following day. 'And I'm not sure you should be looking to, either. What do you want with lassies at your age? There is plenty of time for all that, Master Sidney.'

I gave her a penetrating look, one I had perfected over the years, having been on the receiving end of so many from my father. She dipped her head, reminded of her station. I had summoned her to the drawing room and lay sprawled across the leather Chesterfield, enjoying my temporary role as master of the house far too much.

We'd come to an understanding, she and I, since the departure of my mother. After the night she'd covered me in the corridor, I realised that, for all her brusqueness, she was a secret ally. Her position in the house constrained her actions, but I appreciated as I grew older that she was playing a game of sorts with my father and, unbeknownst to him, winning. She had to be outwardly harsh with the staff to win his trust, but often had their back. 'All lemon and no sugar,' Cook said of her, but followed it up with, 'but then I don't know how I'd manage in my kitchen without lemons.'

'Cook might know,' Murray suggested. 'She's often in town visiting her sister. Perhaps someone has finally taken on the manor house down by the rectory.' She glanced at her slim ladies' pocket watch. 'However, I must be getting on, sir, if you don't mind. Your father has written to confirm he will be back tomorrow, although I think he's forgotten you're here for the holidays as he made no mention of you.'

We both knew the atmosphere would change quickly upon his arrival, and not for the better. I was also painfully aware that any feeling of superiority I had would be quickly undermined. It was all very well for me to assume authority when I was the only family member present – even Mrs Murray had to defer to my wishes – but with Father's return, I would be reminded all too soon that I was legally still a minor.

'And as you're the only one for dinner, I thought I'd check if you had a particular preference?' she asked, raising an eyebrow in reference to my idle fancy and ill-mannered demands of the previous day.

'No.' I sighed. 'Whatever Cook has a mind to prepare.'

'Good, then perhaps a chicken and ham pie. The new kitchen girl is very good at pastry.'

'Not another one?' I said, but I knew staff never lasted long at Halesham.

'A young girl called Jane. Very quiet and unusually jumpy – appeared from nowhere, looking for work – but she knows what she's doing in the kitchen and is brighter than many we've had. She was lucky to get the job without references, but we were desperate, and it didn't take her long to realise why. Mr Bellingham has insulted her several times and she tripped up those hazardous stairs on her first morning. But two weeks in and she doesn't complain and works hard. Let's hope we can keep her for longer than the last one.'

I wasn't particularly interested in Murray's latest appointment. Whenever I returned there were new faces, scurrying about, their heads low and their thin, underfed bodies slinking into the shadows of my peripheral vision. My only interest was the sport I found in watching them negotiate the amusing curiosities of the house. One poor girl had fainted upon her first excursion into the formal dining room, so overcome was she by the confusing dimensions. It was always fun to watch them negotiate the uneven steps or wrestle with the backward doors.

'Chicken pie it is then.' I sat upright and slapped at my thighs. 'And now perhaps I shall head to the stables and say hello to the horses.'

In reality, I'd decided to meander through the kitchens and quiz Cook. She was Suffolk-born and bred, unlike our housekeeper, who'd come from the Highlands, and might know of the elusive Nancy or if any new families had moved into the neighbourhood.

But as I walked along the dark corridor below stairs and headed to the kitchens, I happened upon one of the aforementioned maids, carrying a tray between scullery and still room, and as we faced each other in the narrow space, I froze.

Because before me, in the grey cotton dress and white apron of the kitchen, her black hair barely visible under the lacy mob cap, was Nancy.

My earlier high spirits crashed to the floor as anger rose in my chest, like balance scales tipping in opposite directions.

The mysterious and beguiling girl I had been dreaming of for the past few hours was a lie. My water nymph was staff.

Chapter 14

Confronted by this unpalatable and unwelcome truth, I felt the vein in my neck pulse, as it did when my temper rose. An uncontrollable swell of pressure, building and building. Adolescence was proving a vexing path to navigate. Just when I believed I had a grip on my emotions, they lurched violently in another, and often unwelcome, direction.

'What the devil . . .' I began.

The colour drained from her already pale face and she dipped her head.

'Are *you* Jane?'

'I am so dreadfully sorry, sir,' she gabbled. 'I didn't know who you were and was nervous of giving my name to a stranger.' She shook her head. 'I plucked the name Nancy from the Dickens I'm reading.'

'You read Dickens?' I asked incredulously, and then remembered she'd quoted Tennyson at me the previous day. I felt bad for not doubting that a strange, beautiful girl standing by a brook might be educated, but here before me and working in our kitchens, I questioned it.

She bobbed her head. 'Yesterday was my afternoon off,' she explained. 'I wasn't doing anything I shouldn't have been. But, of course, I wouldn't have spoken with you like that if I'd known you were a Bellingham.'

'And I most certainly would not have engaged you in conversation had I known you were a servant.' I felt hot and angry all at once. Trying to muster some dignity from the situation, I stepped back into my temporary role as master of the house. 'On your way then,' I said dismissively. 'You do not have time to loiter around the corridors when there is work to be done.' I moved to the side for her to pass. Only when she was out of earshot and I recognised that my silly dreams of romance had withered, did I kick out violently at the wall and curse my foolishness.

I felt deceived by this girl, even though she had done nothing to deliberately mislead, apart from supply a false name. It was her afternoon off and she'd gone for a walk in the countryside. She had no more been aware of who I was, than I had been of her identity. But for a while, my overriding response was anger – predominantly anger with myself. I'd allowed myself to feel something for this girl, to yearn after her and to hope she would be obtainable, after such a laughably fleeting acquaintance. Once done, I could no more undo it than the clouds could recall the rain they'd dropped on the earth below.

I returned to the main body of the house, shouted at the footman to fetch my boots, and berated him for the speed at which they were delivered, before going into the grounds to clear my head. Like my father, and even Leonard when he'd been this age, I was unable to control these flares of temper, but had learned physical exertion allowed my building anger a form of release, and within half an hour of rowing furiously around the small lake on our estate, I felt measurably calmer.

*

'What are you doing, boy? Staring into space like an imbecile and doing nothing productive with your time. I don't pay for a top education for you to daydream.'

Father had happened upon me sitting on the bottom step of the curious staircase that led nowhere, my back against the wall and staring at nothing in particular, imagining the gentle whispers of my mother in my ear and the smell of her lavender perfume in the air. I jumped to my feet and felt the colour rise to my cheeks. How had I managed to displease him within moments of his return to the house?

'You're back,' was all I could manage.

'Of course I'm back. Do you imagine me a mirage? What the hell have I sired?' he muttered to himself. 'An unwilling heir and a woolgatherer of an understudy.'

His face was ashen and his posture stooped. In three short months he appeared to have aged by several decades. Leaning on his hickory cane – previously a symbol of his strength but now indicative of his weakness – he shuffled down the corridor towards his study, wheezing as he went. Whatever had occurred in London had soured his spirits and I would do well to steer clear from now on. Perhaps I should have taken Monty up on his offer of a couple of weeks down in Kent, I reflected.

Desperately bored, I was missing the interaction and stimulating conversation of my peers, and the prospect of a long, dull summer stretched before me. There was little to occupy my mind, and I was limited to the sports I could undertake alone – rowing, fishing and riding – although Leonard was more the horseman than me. I craved a companion, but there was no one with whom to play tennis, or even while away an hour or two with one of the Bellingham games.

It was strange that I so longed for home when I was away, yet upon my return, the high walls, long corridors and dark spaces held only unhappy memories and a constant feeling that I was trapped. Sometimes, I had the unnerving sensation that the ghost of my mother was in the rooms with me. Perhaps it was merely the flicker of something in one of the distorted mirrors my father had installed, catching my eye in the half-light. When I sat in the wing chair beside the fireplace in the drawing room, it was almost as if I was climbing on to her lap once more, her soft hands stroking my hair and her gentle lips kissing my cheek. At night, sleeping resolutely with my back to the mural and my face to the window, I heard whispers of her voice, her warm breath caressing my ear as she soothed and encouraged. But it was only my imagination playing tricks, for that part of the house was built after she'd left, and any notion of spirits meant she was dead, and I wouldn't allow myself to believe this was the case.

In my boredom, I took to walking, finding myself down by the brook time and time again, and disappointed on each occasion not to stumble across any enchanting nymphs. But as I returned to the Hall late one afternoon, I encountered Jane again in the gardens, picking blackberries from the hedgerow that ran along the back of the apple orchard. I'd tried to stay out of her way and, I am sure, she'd endeavoured to keep herself hidden from me. But looking at her again, as her dark eyes widened in surprise at this further accidental meeting, I couldn't help but recall that damned Waterhouse painting, because I was lured to her, yet again, like that dolt Hylas.

God but she was beautiful.

I took a steadying breath, noticing how my palms felt sweaty. Discreetly, I wiped them down my trousers, pulled my shoulders back and walked over to where she stood, a willow basket hooked over her arm, and began to pick the berries alongside her – silently and without allowing myself to look at her face.

I felt her body stiffen as I stood close, refusing to look in my direction.

'I'm sorry, sir. I realise you're angry at me,' she said. 'I should have said something but I didn't know you were Mr Bellingham's son. I thought you were in Hampshire and not due to return until next week.'

It took me a moment to realise that her words meant she thought I was Leonard, and I felt a flash of delight that I should be mistaken for my twenty-six-year-old brother. But I could not hide behind his identity any more than she could imagine herself to be Nancy.

'I'm Sidney. Leonard is my brother.'

She flicked her eyes in my direction as we both continued the task of selecting the firm, shiny berries, each one studded with tiny glistening black jewels, and placed them gently in the basket. Her tense shoulders dropped as she relaxed slightly.

I noticed this subtle action and it stung. She would know my age from the staff and it was obvious she no longer felt threatened, because I was not the man she had imagined me to be. And so I turned this hurt into anger.

'But I do not take kindly to lies from servants and have not decided yet whether I should mention this deceit to my father.'

I noticed the slight tremble of her delicate, purple-stained hands and turned to look into those hypnotising eyes.

'I need this job. Please don't get me dismissed.' Her bottom lip wobbled and I felt rotten. Something shifted in my chest and a wave of protectiveness flooded through me. She was like the baby bird that had fallen down the drawing room chimney in the spring, so fragile that when I'd scooped it from the grate, sooty and bemused, I'd been alarmed to find it weighed nothing. Its large black eyes had stared up at me, too big for the delicate head, and I'd felt a momentary flash of power. I could have crushed it so easily with my bare hands, simply squeezed my fingers around it and the thin, brittle bones would have splintered and snapped. But I hadn't wanted to hurt the tiny creature and had taken it to the gardens, placing it on a ledge beneath the window in the vain hope its mother might find it again and care for it. The same feelings engulfed me now as I looked at Jane. Her eyes were just as wide, her demeanour just as frightened.

'Of course not.'

It had been an idle threat, at any rate. It was important to me that she remained – even though my troubled mind hadn't worked out the logistics of this complex and confusing situation. All I knew was that I wanted to be near her, because I was already starting to recognise that I was a nicer person when she was around. My simple act of assisting her in the gathering of the fruit demonstrated that.

'Here, let me get those,' and I leaned across to pick the highest berries that she was straining to reach.

She stepped back and allowed me access.

'So, have you been here long?' I asked, even though I knew the answer, determined to put her at her ease and perhaps draw more information from her.

'Just three weeks.' Our hands brushed accidentally as we both deposited berries in the basket at the same time, and she pulled back sharply.

'Are you local? From Halesham, perhaps?'

'No.' She bowed her head and I realised my questions were making her uncomfortable. 'I'm, erm, new to the area.'

'Brothers? Sisters?' I asked, not really caring either way. I had this urge to keep talking to her, keep engaging with her, even though I couldn't think of anything witty or intelligent to say.

I noticed how the sun danced across her bare forearms and studied the soft dark hairs running up to her elbows. How her collarbone curved around her neck and dipped under the thin cotton print dress she was wearing beneath her apron. I could hear her breathing, see the rise and fall of her bosom under the starched white cotton, pulled tight across her chest, the material straining to contain the flesh beneath. Monty's gawky sister had been as thin as a pikestaff and these gentle curves were new to me. The air was thick with swirling currents of unsaid things and palpable attraction. I knew from her reserved body language and obvious nervousness, mirroring my own, that she felt it too.

'Thank you. I have sufficient for the pie now,' she said, avoiding my question. She smiled and bobbed a curtsey, which took me out of the daydream I'd been in for those brief moments where she was just a girl, and I was just a boy, and we were picking fruit in the warm sun of a glorious early August day. Her action was a reminder that our social situations were poles apart and it made me feel awkward. But as she stood before me, the gentle breeze romped through the hedge behind her and played with the grasses at our feet. It tugged at her skirts and rippled through the loose strands of hair escaping from her cap, backlit as she was by the sinking sun, and I was suddenly all too aware of her form. Her apron was tied tightly around her hourglass waist, and I realised how much taller I was than her as I looked down at her lips, slightly stained from the inevitable tasting of the ripe fruit she'd been sent to gather. Would those lips have the same earthy sweetness where the juice still lingered? I shook my head to free these disturbing thoughts. She was a kitchen maid and I was the son of a wealthy gentleman. What was I thinking?

Suddenly, it was all too much and a greater worry consumed

me. I spun sharply away from her. This stupid girl had no idea what she'd done to me. How my mind had followed her collarbone below the neckline of her simple dress and seen beneath the apron. How I'd imagined what it might be like to touch that pale skin and smell the glossy black hair underneath her cotton cap. And now the blood in my body had rushed to places I didn't command it to and made it impossible for me to face her any longer. Amusing in a schoolroom when it happened to another, but mortifying in the extreme for me in that moment.

I was aware of her hovering behind me, perhaps waiting to be formally dismissed.

'Go then, if you're going,' I snapped, twisting my body further away from her, wanting her to return to the Hall so that I could remove myself from the situation, and cursing the physiology of my youth.

Once I'd heard the patter of her small feet disappear into the distance, I ran to the nearest refuge – the folly tucked out of sight in the woods. My ears were hot and my pulse was racing. I needed to be alone.

I tucked myself behind one of the thick stone walls, grateful for the cooler temperature and the anonymity of the shadows. How had she done this to me by doing so little? I understood the science of it all well enough. I wanted her. My body wanted hers.

I focused intently on the patches of moss, leaning my head on the cold hard stone and struggling to control my breathing. The microscopic feathery leaves jutted in all directions, so delicate and fragile, and I was astonished at their perfection. I tried to think of anything other than her: the damp smell in the air undercut with the dustiness of the day, the way the light played with the rough surface of the walls, the sounds of a dog barking in the distance.

But it was futile and she returned to the forefront of my mind – Jane with her wide eyes, soft skin and gentle curves . . .

My head pressed harder against the slimy cold stone wall as I dealt with my frustrations in the only way I knew how, and my actions became faster and more urgent. My jagged breaths echoed around the small space, but it was only birds flitting between the treetops, scampering squirrels and timid deer who heard them, uninterested in the confused and angry juvenile struggling within. Finally my fist punched the wall, furious with her for making me feel this way, and even more furious with myself for not being able to control it.

Chapter 15

1920

Phoebe didn't mind hard work and, as September progressed, and the weather remained clement, she ploughed through the exhaustion of life below stairs. The plan was to keep her head low and hope Mr Bellingham's curiosity would eventually win out. In order to banish him, she would first have to befriend him, but for the moment, she was content to have the distraction of work and a place to lay her head. At the end of each weary day, she lugged her tired body upstairs and, turning her back on Medusa's unnerving glare, tumbled into bed.

The master, she was informed by Murray, worked largely from Halesham Hall – perfectly manageable with the advent of the telephone. One day a week he visited the print works in the town, and occasionally he travelled to London, but he spent most of his days confined to the study.

'He's not particularly sociable, as you may have gathered.' The housekeeper rolled her eyes. 'But he is somewhat of a creative genius.'

Perhaps a foul temper went with the territory, Phoebe thought. Flashes of genius and flashes of rage, vying with each other in a mind that was restless and highly combustible.

'He designs and develops most of the games himself,' the older woman continued. 'Shuts himself up in that study of his and works out the complicated rules and methods of play – occasionally shouting at that foolish dog for chewing up the board prototype or running off with his notes. He loves nothing more than wrestling with a good game or a difficult puzzle, even though he has few people to play them with.'

'Was it true that my grandfather set his sons a puzzle?' she asked, hoping she was trusted sufficiently now to be permitted to broach this topic.

'Och, you mean regarding the inheritance?' Murray stirred the stock she was making and put a spoon to her lips to taste it. Satisfied, she turned to Phoebe. 'Some nonsense that had the pair of them rushing about the house. I never fully understood what was going on, save that the master won. Such a cruel game to play with the wee lads.' She tutted.

'Do you know anything about it? What they were asked to do? If it was completed?'

Murray shook her head. 'You'll have to ask Mr Bellingham. Family business wasn't my business.'

Frustrated, Phoebe forced out a composed smile. Everything hinged on the puzzle and she was keen to instigate her plan. She might not be able to touch the company, but there was every possibility she could throw Mr Bellingham out of Halesham Hall and see him homeless, and that was enough for her.

Phoebe's duties rarely took her into the main body of the house and so she seldom encountered Mr Bellingham – designing games or otherwise. Her place was very much in the kitchens below, but, unlike the other staff, she had to use the main east staircase to access her bedroom. Two weeks into her new employment, as she headed downstairs for breakfast, Satan wandered past, his tail wagging in delight, with some stolen treasure between his jaws. It looked suspiciously like a game board and she was certain that Mr Bellingham would not be best pleased to find that his dog had absconded with it. She followed him to the end of the corridor and managed to gently persuade him to release the item. *Martian Invasion* was written across the top of the board and the scene was a planetary delight. With the happy-go-lucky mentality of the simple-minded, Satan immediately turned around and headed back whence he came, possibly to loot his master's study once more.

For the first time, she noticed another small staircase tucked at the far end of the east wing, with white panelled walls running up either side of the stairs. There were several staircases dotted about the hall, but this one hadn't been part of Mrs Murray's guided tour when she'd started earlier that month. She knew that the corridor on the floor above was blocked off at the far end where you might expect these stairs to come out, so Phoebe couldn't quite fathom what part of the house they accessed.

Her father had talked of a haunting staircase that led nowhere in a letter he had left for her in the event of his death – a letter so full of revelations and surprises that it was the very reason she'd travelled to Halesham. It implied the staircase was at the very heart of the heinous wrong committed against her father, and it was this wrong she was determined to redress.

Curious but wary, she decided to investigate, as there was no one around and it would only take a moment. A chill swept over her as she approached the stairs. She rubbed at her arms, before ascending a bewildering mix of quarter landings, brief runs of straight steps, and giddying spiral sections. There were no windows but light came from a circular glazed section of roof, thirty or forty feet above her. She finally reached the top, disorientated by the twists and turns, and stood on a small square of floor, with a door to her right. The white panels to her left were painted with a canal scene from Venice – possibly the Bridge of Sighs. The bridge was supposedly named after the sighs of prisoners glimpsing their last view of Venice as they returned to the prison, having invariably been sentenced to death. Although the scene itself was far more pleasant than most of the murals in the house, it was still inexplicably unsettling.

She noticed a brass sconce mounted off centre to the scene, with a stump of candle remaining in the socket. Most of the house was lit with lamps, but as this was clearly a place people rarely visited, she wasn't surprised to see this relic from the past. Her focus returned to the door, which had a pretty cut-glass doorknob. The flat edges reflected the light and on this bright morning the sun toyed with the beams, bouncing them backwards and forwards inside the knob, separating the colours within to throw a soft rainbow on the pale floorboards.

She twisted it, first right, then left. Just a tiny peek, she thought to herself, wondering what might lie behind, so isolated from the rest of the house. She pulled and pushed, and every combination thereof, remembering the curious door to her room, but it wouldn't open.

'It's locked,' a stern voice said from below, and she turned to see Mr Bellingham standing at the bottom of the last run of stairs, one of his unpleasant scowls across his face. An uncomfortable flash of heat passed through her, and her skin prickled at being so caught out.

'I'm sorry.' Colour rushed to her cheeks. 'I didn't mean to pry. I shouldn't be here. It's unforgivably nosy of me.'

She expected Mr Bellingham to be furious. She was, after

all, attempting to enter a room she had no business to be entering, but he was strangely calm and detached.

'Not at all. Find the key and you're welcome to open the door.' He leaned against the wall and made eye contact with her. 'We referred to it as "The Staircase That Led Nowhere" when we were younger, because it was permanently locked and there was little point in coming up here. One of my father's many games . . .'

Every time Clement Bellingham was talked about, the atmosphere shifted in an unpleasant direction, and Phoebe felt the slow slithering of disquiet crawl across her skin. Mrs Murray had clearly been deeply unsettled by the man, and dark clouds had passed behind her father's eyes on the fleeting occasions he'd spoken of his own father. What mad scheme had this man conjured up for his sons? Was the heir to the Bellingham estate about to enlighten her as to how he had come by his ill-gotten gains?

He met her eyes and held them. 'He sent us both on a treasure hunt, of sorts, to find the key just before he died, and said that all his most valued possessions were in the room at the top of these stairs, assuring us that whoever solved the puzzle would take over from him at Bellingham Games and own everything that lay within. Rather avant-garde, don't you think?' he said, raising his eyebrows, but still pinning her to the wall with his glare. 'Allowing both sons an equal opportunity to inherit? We assumed he was referring to the deeds of the Hall, valuable paintings from my mother's family, her jewels . . . and at the time we both thought it dreadfully unfair to pitch a young boy of nearly sixteen against a man of twenty-five. It was a crazy way to determine your successor, but my father was not a man you questioned. He was a man you obeyed. However, in the end, there was much more hanging on the outcome than even my father knew, and I solved it first – simply because I wanted it the most.'

She could tell the man in front of her felt smug and she wanted to shake him then, to grab him by his collar and scream at him. To demand an explanation for his subsequent behaviour. His victory was no excuse for such callousness. As the heir, he could have included his brother in the company, let him remain at the Hall, shared some of the family fortune. Instead, he had banished his rival and cut him off completely.

She took a breath and forced out a tiny smile. 'Was that what drove you apart then? You solved the puzzle, took the spoils, and you and your brother chose to part ways?'

He couldn't hold her gaze any longer and began studying the floor beneath his feet. 'It was rather more complicated than that,' he admitted. 'Although I'm not surprised my brother was scant on detail.'

'Then please enlighten me,' she said, unsure what he meant by that last comment. 'I would be interested to learn more about your estrangement.' Let him justify his actions if he could, she thought, and she folded her arms across her chest in anticipation of his lies.

'It all starts with two lines of a riddle that my father had framed. It is a clue to a destination and still hangs in the library. Would you like to see it?'

'Yes, please.'

He looked surprised, but also perhaps mildly amused, whereas she felt a flood of exhilaration at this unexpected turn of events. She'd assumed it would be more complicated than this, that she might have to beg him to tell her about the puzzle, or determine the start of it alone, but here he was leading her to it. And now she had her chance to redress the unforgivable wrongs he'd committed by stealing her father's birthright.

Because it was Sidney Bellingham, not Leonard, who'd inherited Halesham Hall. He'd overturned the order of things and become the heir, casting aside his older brother and relegating him to a life teaching in small village schools and wearing worn-out boots. For this he would pay.

The board was set and she'd moved her first piece. This was a game she was determined to win.

Chapter 16

1899

Adolescence is a tricky time, when passions run high and unchecked across all aspects of life, but particularly in matters of the heart. I was still finding myself, discovering my strengths, exploring my passions, and desperate to break away from unhealthy paternal influences. But most of all, I wanted to be loved, and so Jane, this simple country girl with a mysterious past, consumed me to a completely irrational degree. The only consolation was that I'd finally stumbled on an activity to keep me occupied for the holidays – the covert tracking and intensive study of our new kitchen maid.

Thoughts of her fully occupied my mind, and I had no respite, not even to sleep. I began to creep downstairs in the early hours and lurk in the shadows outside the kitchen, standing at such an angle that I could observe the staff through the narrow windows in their dim semi-basement. The scullery maid was first up, lighting the fires in the kitchen and under the copper. Jane followed a little while later, sipping slowly at her hot mug of tea, taking time to adjust to the hour. She was clearly not used to such demanding work – of this I was certain.

I loved watching her from my lofty vantage point as she

waited for the range to reach temperature and kneaded the dough. Her lips moved as she sang softly to herself, though I couldn't hear the tune. How wonderful to be so contented, especially with such a menial task. In these quieter moments, everything about her face spoke of joy and light. Her soft hands thumped and stretched as her body rocked gently backwards and forwards, and I was totally hypnotised.

Whilst the dough proved, she prepared breakfast for the staff and I was fascinated at how she scurried about the kitchen with never a moment of rest. Only when I saw the housemaid come in for the hot water did I return to the main entrance, letting myself in and stepping across the hall of monochrome tiles. I hurried to the east wing to settle myself in bed, awaiting a timid knock on my bedroom door, the sweeping back of my curtains, and the official start of my day.

Occasionally, mid-morning, Jane was sent into the gardens to collect any fruit or vegetables requested by Cook, and it was then that I took to open air activities where I might happen upon her, or at least be able to observe her from a distance. Sometimes, I found myself setting off for a walk on a route that began by leaving the Hall through the courtyard and invariably ended up at the folly – my quiet space and solace. I even took up reading – a most tedious activity, but one which, on fine days, gave me ample opportunity to seat myself on the edge of our formal lawns, where I could see her comings and goings from the rear of the house.

I reverted to my childhood habit of loitering in the kitchens – a place I'd been ordered to avoid since Mother's departure, but the lure of the beguiling kitchen maid was too great. This I could justify, because I was at an age when no amount of food could truly satisfy my appetite. Cook often commented that I would soon be as big as Goliath himself if I wasn't careful, but she always found a little something to suppress the inexplicable hunger that seemed to appear at such regular intervals.

'May I help you lift the fish kettle down?' I asked her, as I was substantially taller. It was proving more rewarding than I'd expected to be of assistance to the staff. I couldn't deny the warm feelings I experienced from their gratitude and kind words, even though I'd initially only undertaken these actions to prove my credentials to Jane.

'Thank you, sir, that will save me dragging the steps from the pantry.' (I was later to overhear her comment to Mrs Murray what a lovely young man I was finally turning out to be. Not enamoured of the 'finally', I found it was, however, gratifying to have my actions praised.)

I knew better than to address any conversation to Jane, or even to try and catch her eye. Instead, I surreptitiously observed her going about her duties and feigned a complete indifference to her presence. Burton didn't like me being down there one bit, but then I rather suspected he had something to hide, as even Daisy joked about his fondness for drink. A child below stairs was one thing, but a young man quite another – perhaps he even suspected me of spying for Father, as if the listening pipes weren't enough.

Late one afternoon, I happened across Jane as she carried two heavy pails of scalded bran and potato peelings down to the chickens, so I took the opportunity to make myself useful.

'Here, let me.' I took the pails from her and we walked towards the gate that led to the animal enclosures. Like many country houses, we were fairly self-sufficient, and we kept chickens, pigs and goats, even though we had our milk and beef delivered from town.

'Oh, thank you, sir. You're as strong as an ox. A fine young man.'

It was significant to me that she had used the word man, and I realised then that whatever my age might suggest, or others might think, she knew the truth of my maturity.

I placed the pails at my feet as I lifted up the heavy throw-over latch and swung the gate inwards, but I hadn't lifted it far enough and after some moments it toppled and crashed down again, catching the side of my hand as it fell. Blood, red and thick, oozed from the wound and a searing pain shot up my arm. I couldn't allow her to see any weakness and so whipped my hand behind my back and out of view. Her sharp eyes, however, had seen the same scarlet flash as me.

'Let me tend to that, sir. It's deep and needs washing.' She stepped forward and put out her hands expectantly.

I was about to argue, to present myself as not in need of help, but then I realised that this would prolong the encounter and have the added benefit of physical contact – something I'd forgotten how much I craved. Murray was fond of me, in her way, and she'd had my back ever since Mother left, but she was not a woman given to physical displays of affection, nor would it have been proper for her to give me that kind of attention. Yet I recalled Matron nursing me through measles at school two years before, and her kind words and gentle ministrations had almost made me wish for the illness to linger.

'You must let me clean it,' she insisted.

I nodded, re-latched the gate to prevent any birds escaping, and followed her back to the pump in front of the stable block. A couple of curious hens waddled towards the gate as we disappeared, giving frustrated clucks as they paced back and forth, unable to get to their meal.

Once in the yard, Jane operated the pump handle as I held my fingers under the ice-cold running water.

'Squeeze the wound,' she instructed, coming to my side and

lifting my hand to inspect it more closely. The heat of her tiny fingers around mine, especially now that the water had chilled them to the bone, was thrilling. As she tended to my injury, I was struck dumb, unable to utter a single word.

For the first time it occurred to me she might be a little older than me. She seemed more sure of herself in this situation and I was impressed by her calmness and presence of mind.

'Wait here while I fetch some strips of cotton. It's a clean wound and if you keep it free from dirt it will heal in no time.'

My heart beat violently in my chest as she returned within minutes and took my hand once again in hers, binding it with a thin strip of white cloth and neatly tucking the loose end under the folds.

I looked down at the top of her head and my eyes closed as I breathed in her scent – the tang from the carbolic soap and a hint of oranges and lemons, where she'd been preparing food that morning. She smelled heavenly, and I had a sudden fondness for those hard, red bars of Lifebuoy I'd hitherto only associated with frosty mornings and bowls of cold water in the draughty school dorms. In fact, my feelings overwhelmed me so completely that I knew at that moment I was in love with her and had never been more certain of anything in my life. I wanted to pull the cap from her head, drop my lips into her glorious hair, put my arms about her and hold her close. But it was not a thing I could do in the middle of the courtyard, and I was only too aware of how carefully I would have to play my hand. I couldn't afford to frighten her or put her position within the household at risk.

And then she raised my hand to her lips and kissed it.

'There,' she said, stroking the bound hand with her thumb, 'it will heal faster now.'

And through that simple action I knew that, however she had to behave in her situation as a servant, she felt the same.

Chapter 17

'Leonard has been delayed and will be away for longer than anticipated,' Father informed me the following morning as we sat together in the peculiar dining room he seemed so proud of, and one of the many architectural jokes he alone found amusing. I'd got used to its nauseating proportions, although my brother assured me it could make one feel rather queer if you were nursing any sort of headache or, even worse, the after-effects of too much strong drink.

Father looked grey, his face drawn, and his head hung forward, as though he didn't have the energy to raise it. I'd witnessed Burton helping him down the stairs that morning and wondered again at the true extent of his health issues. He shook his newspaper and then succumbed to a bout of coughing that was distressing to witness.

'He's sewn the Hampshire business up nicely but he's to be part of a shooting party at the Cross Ridge estate, on the Yorkshire moors, and has been invited to stay on for a while. The Glorious Twelfth and all that. He's not much of a shot but I'm not quite the ticket at the moment and a token Bellingham presence is better than none. I hope you'll take these duties more seriously than your brother when you are of an age to be part of that social set.'

'Of course, sir. I fully appreciate that deals can be struck over a dinner invitation and potentially important friendships forged over a game of billiards.'

'Excellent.' He nodded to himself. 'Excellent.'

It was the start of the red grouse season, and although it was not Leonard's thing, the owner of Cross Ridge had invaluable contacts in the United States, where we exported large quantities of our games (the Americans always hankering after our history and culture, having so little of their own). Plus, I understood that the gentleman in question rather conveniently had a daughter of marriageable age. Father was playing the long game, and part of that was for us both to make suitable marriages that would benefit the company, ergo our futures. I suspect he would have preferred to have attended the shoot with his eldest son – this wasn't the first time he'd complained that Leonard was somewhat lacklustre when it came to business and an abysmal shot when it came to hunting – but he was clearly not fit enough to do so. Leonard's bridge, however, was passable and we'd launched two new sets of playing cards – a nursery rhyme-themed pack aimed at children, and a rather charming set featuring an assortment of British wildlife. Father had commissioned a well-known local watercolour artist to provide the illustrations for the latter, and it focused largely on the birds and mammals shot by the rural elite. He was hopeful they would prove a hit in the country houses up and down the land, where the owners liked nothing more than to randomly execute the bewildered pheasant and exhausted fox for sport. To this end, Leonard had been sent with multiple packs of each and was expected to conduct some early research into this potential market on his trip.

'It grieves me to send Leonard to the slaughter, as the Cross Ridge girl has all the beauty and wit of a corpulent sow, but needs must. The trick is not to marry for love, believe me, but for financial or social advancement, and then to ensure she knows who is in charge. They need watching, women, because they are not to be trusted.'

It was a diatribe I'd heard ever since I could remember. Females needed a firm hand. They were conniving and would lead to your downfall if unchecked. Use them for your own ends but do not rely on them. However, I had started to question all this recently. Jane was not devious or complicated. She had no agenda and was not cruel – far from it. How could something so lovely and so pure ever be considered untrustworthy?

As if he could read my thoughts, he suddenly announced, 'Burton said you've been sniffing around the new girl in the kitchen, and this has been confirmed by things I've overheard through the listening pipes.'

I was furious with the butler. How dare he report back to my father. As for the pipes, I'd forgotten of their existence. I could only assume Daisy had been speculating about my visits below stairs. My rapidly flushing face gave away my guilt, and he continued without waiting for me to deny the accusation.

'I'm all for a bit of experimentation. I'm sure you've had your fair share of that at school, eh?' He gave me a knowing look over the top of his spectacles, and I didn't like the way his lip curled lazily upward as he said it. 'Smarts a bit, but you soon get used to it. You've doubtless got boys fagging for you by now, running around under your command, and what you choose to do with them is your business . . .' He broke off to catch his breath, wheezy now and thick in his throat.

'I start in the sixth next term, sir. I turn sixteen this autumn.' It was humiliating to admit, when even my own father assumed I was older than my years.

'Really?' He peered at me again, taking in my height, and

snorted to himself. 'Well, I understand you need to have a go on the real thing, as it were, but for the love of God, be wary when it's in your own backyard, eh? Be discreet. If Murray finds out, the girl will be dismissed and then I'll have that blasted Scottish harridan on my back, along with all my other woes.'

I knew my father had scant regard for women, and even less for staff, but I was still shocked. Jane, to him, was a commodity. He was all but giving me permission to use her.

'Extraordinarily beautiful, but then they're the ones to watch. Bewitching – and the clue is in the word.'

He took a slow and raspy breath, waving Burton away as he approached with a small after-dinner brandy on a silver tray.

'Anyway, on to more important matters. I've recently been forced to confront the future, and what that might mean for the house and the business.'

I wondered if he was about to elaborate on the health problems that we were all aware of but that he had never openly acknowledged. Burton was the soul of discretion in this regard, despite the increased frequency of Father's visits to London, but it was obvious the old man's lungs were failing.

'You've always been more interested in the company than your brother. You are also much more aligned to my way of thinking and I have high hopes for you, Sidney. I think you might have what it takes to succeed, whereas Leonard has a tendency towards sentimentality, which will only hinder him in life and in business. However, he is the oldest son and has every right to expect his dues . . .'

I wondered where this was going. We'd not properly discussed my future – indeed, I hadn't given it much thought myself.

'Ever since I fathered an heir, I have been conscious of my legacy, but I feel strongly that the next head of the Bellingham empire should have a game-playing brain. Competition and strategy, puzzles and problems, they're an important part of life, and you appear to have grasped this better than your brother. So when I was improving the house, I hit upon the idea of incorporating various puzzles as part of the refurbishments, with an eye to the future. The time has come to separate the wheat from the chaff, and to play the game. Solve the house and you'll find the key to opening the room at the top of the staircase in the east wing.'

At last. That damn door had haunted my childhood – always locked and never opened – accessed by a winding set of stairs which ran three storeys high to a single door off a tiny landing. There was always a disconcerting drop in temperature as you began the ascent, and faint traces of lavender lingered in the air. Sometimes, particularly when the weather was bad, I convinced myself I could hear a pitiful cry from within the walls, as if an animal was trapped behind them, or Mother was calling to me, but it was surely just my imagination.

Leonard and I had often speculated as to what lay beyond that door: a bedroom or a storage cupboard, perhaps? As a younger lad, and burning with curiosity, I had stolen Murray's set of keys and tried each one. I'd even dared to search through Father's desk drawers when he was away on one occasion, but to no avail. Why build a staircase that led to a perennially locked room? But then so much of what my father did defied common sense.

'Everything of value, my most precious belongings, are at the top of those stairs, and whoever solves the puzzle will inherit it all – the Hall, the company and all my wealth. My plans have been frustrated by Leonard's delay in returning home, but when he does, the game will begin, for I now know that we are running out of time. This is your chance to prove yourself worthy and snatch your brother's birthright from under his nose.'

I swallowed my shock at this unexpected announcement. He'd had puzzles built into the fabric of the house, and *they* would decide the future of his estate? Was he in jest? Father looked earnest enough and so my mind raced with the possibilities. For the first time there were avenues open to me that as the youngest son I'd dared not even dream of. *I could have everything.* Leonard would not inherit. And then I thought about my father's motives in all this. Even if he believed I was a more fitting successor, he was a callous man, pitting brother against brother, not caring what this might do to our relationship. We were not close – the age gap had seen to that – but I didn't particularly wish Leonard ill.

'You're silent,' he observed. 'I expected more questions, and perhaps an eagerness to begin.'

'What happens to the one who doesn't succeed?' I asked, and my father shrugged.

'He will have to make his own way in the world. I've given you both a good education and access to the necessary contacts. I have no time for losers. Dartington will handle everything and has overseen the legality of all eventualities. But do not fall foul of those softer emotions your brother so often displays, for if I have taught you anything, son, it surely must be that this is a world where the winner takes all.'

Chapter 18

I stood hypnotised as Jane walked across the yard, swinging an empty pail and heading towards the vegetable garden, doubtless instructed to collect potatoes or some such thing. Her hips swayed gently from side to side and her cheeks took on a rosy glow, bestowed by the warm outdoor air and her exertions. I wanted her so badly it physically hurt. The celebrated poets had warned me that with great love sometimes came great pain, and now I understood. I'd rationalised my anger at her unfortunate circumstances, and accepted her lowly situation was not her fault. And even though the gods may have conspired against me, I was a Bellingham – we always got what we wanted in the end.

I'd spent a restless night, mulling over the possibilities now open to me after Father's unexpected announcement. My life had taken two surprising turns in a matter of days. I'd fallen in love for the first and undoubtedly last time in my life, and although my age and her position made our situation difficult, these obstacles might easily be alleviated if I were to inherit Halesham Hall and the Bellingham fortune. Although I found many of my father's whims and schemes unfathomable, this one had the potential to change my life. For second sons, there was a weary inevitability of being the runner-up, but I'd suddenly been handed the opportunity to be the victor. And, as he had so often impressed upon me, to be a winner, one must act like a winner.

'Come here, girl,' I demanded, calling across the courtyard and adjusting my cuffs as she looked up to see where the voice had come from. I had a sudden desire to test both my potential power over her and her suitability as the object of my affections.

'I want you to do something for me,' I said, tilting my chin a little higher in the air and pulling my shoulders back.

'Sir?' She dipped her head but didn't meet my eyes. How glorious it was to have someone before me who was so biddable. It only made me look forward to the next term even more, when I would finally command respect and obedience from the younger boys. To take revenge for all the unpleasant things I'd been forced to do when I'd been at the mercy of the idle fancies of another. It was the circle of life, which I'd come to understand through my father's actions – you suffer and become stronger through it. Then you execute that power over those weaker than you, so that they might become stronger too.

'I left my straw boater in the centre of the maze. Would you fetch it for me?' I gestured towards the formal gardens as her anxious eyes followed my hand.

'But I've never been in there before, sir. How will I find my way?'

'Oh, come. A bright girl like you? It's not so very big and I'm sure you'd welcome the diversion on such a lovely day. Much more pleasant to be outside in the fresh air, wandering through an enchanting maze of yew, than be on your hands and knees scrubbing floors. I'll pop along and tell Cook I've temporarily detained you, but I really do have pressing matters to attend to and I don't want the hat forgotten.'

She looked conflicted but I knew she wouldn't dare disobey me.

'Hurry along now, there's a good girl, I don't have time to stand here debating the matter. There's a statue in the centre, and I left the hat at the foot of it. It shouldn't take you more than a quarter of an hour.' Remembering the lie that I was busy, I glanced at my pocket watch, as if I had places to be.

'Yes, sir.' She bobbed half a curtsey before depositing the pail at the edge of the path and turning towards the formal gardens.

Her acquiescence echoed in my head as she disappeared from view and my traitorous mind returned to unbidden carnal thoughts. I closed my eyes and perched on the edge of a low brick wall that bordered the courtyard, letting the sun kiss my face and allowing my mind to temporarily escape my surroundings. Scents of late sweet peas drifted in the air and the only sounds were those of whinnying horses, chattering birds, and in the distance a backdrop of Cook, clanking pans about in the kitchen and shouting at the scullery maid.

I conjured up a scene in my mind and allowed it to play out in my imagination: Jane before me, meek and obedient, as I towered over her and her wide, dark eyes looked up at mine. I ordered her to remove her grey cotton dress. 'Yes, sir.' Her words echoed in my head as I imagined the dress falling to the floor and me stepping forward to put my hands on her bare shoulders, milky white and as soft as butter. I ordered her to unpin her hair. 'Yes, sir,' and the ink black strands tumbled around her face. Lost in the daydream, my mind superimposed details from classical paintings, perhaps even the Waterhouse – small, firm breasts, wide rounded hips and that tantalising little triangle. I ordered her to come to me, to kiss me, to touch me . . .'Yes, sir . . . Yes, sir . . . Yes, sir . . .'

And as my body betrayed me again, a shout from the stables broke the spell. I opened my eyes and stood up, feeling a hot surge of uncontrollable anger, but not understanding why or how to dispel it. The courtyard was deserted. Embarrassed in case I should be seen in this state, I took myself off to the folly again.

The cool of the woods and the silence away from the bustle of the household calmed me immeasurably as I wrestled once again with the betrayal of my body. No one came near the folly – it was deliberately built off the beaten track and, precisely because it was so isolated, it continued to be my refuge. I felt closest to Mother here of all the places in and around the Hall, although I wasn't sure why. Perhaps because this was the only place where she was remembered – the Latin inscription across the stained glass the only tangible proof she'd ever existed.

I lay along the stone bench and curled my knees up towards my head. It was still the position I slept in, as I found it comforting, but no longer through fear, unlike when I'd been a child. The cold of the stone was welcome on that sticky day and, as I lay on my side, I studied the wide bands of deep yellow that fell across the leaf-strewn floor, elongated and creeping to the very edges of the space as the light found its way through the stained glass – focusing on anything other than Jane. A shiny black beetle scampered over the dead twigs, catching the coloured light as it went. I studied its haphazard journey until it disappeared into a gap in the wall and I let my eyes close.

I must have fallen asleep, because it was nearly an hour later that I stirred and fumbled for my pocket watch. I ambled back to the Hall, wondering how I might fill the remainder of the afternoon, when Murray approached me.

'Have you seen the wee kitchen girl?' she asked, looking anxious. 'She's been missing for the best part of an hour. Just disappeared without a word to anyone.'

My heartbeat accelerated. I'd completely forgotten about Jane, and hadn't told Cook that I'd borrowed her like I'd promised.

'No,' I lied, an uncomfortable feeling swirling inside me, undoubtedly my guilt. 'I'll scout the grounds if you like. I've nothing better to do.'

'Would you? Oh, thank you, sir. So kind.'

The housekeeper returned to the Hall, calling Jane's name in that sing-song Scottish accent of hers, and I raced back to the maze, the layout of which I'd memorised as a boy – sketching its twists and turns in my efforts to stay one step ahead of Father. He had, indeed, sent me into the maze when it had sufficiently matured, demanding I ascertain which statue he'd had erected in the centre. I'd long since realised it was a trick, the centre was enclosed, but my size was in my favour, as was the age of the yews. I was able to squeeze through the bushes and find Aphrodite, dejected and alone in her cage of green, and report back to Father – who hid his surprise that I'd succeeded extremely well.

As I approached the maze that August day, I heard a faint voice from within.

'Is there someone there?' She sounded weary, and I felt guilty that she had been lost in there all this time.

'Jane,' I called. 'I'm here. Keep talking to me and I'll find you.'

'Oh, bless you, Master Sidney. I'm so stupid to let myself get into this state.'

I took a left, then a right, then doubled back along a parallel path and made a final turn, to find her slumped on her knees, tears in her eyes.

'Oh, thank you.' She stood up and rushed towards me. 'It was terribly kind of you to come to my rescue like that.' To my surprise she put out her arms, perhaps overwhelmed by relief, and I pulled her to me and held her tight. Her spontaneous and overfamiliar behaviour was another indication that she wasn't a girl who had a background in service, and her sweetness and light underlined her character, reinforcing what I already knew – she was too good for this servile life and I would help her escape it.

'I called and called, but I don't think any of the garden staff are working this side of the Hall today.'

'Don't worry. I have you. You're safe.' I revelled in her warmth. 'Perhaps it was foolish of me to send you in. I overestimated your abilities and had no idea you'd be stumbling around for so long.' I couldn't admit to her that it was unsolvable. That I had sent her in for unkind reasons in response to my inability to navigate a whole gamut of powerful and unfamiliar emotions, and hadn't taken the time to analyse my actions.

She stepped back, suddenly remembering her station, and distanced herself from me once more. 'I must return to the kitchens. Cook will be furious.'

I nodded and began to retrace my steps as I thought about her gratitude at being rescued. It was such a splendid feeling, to have someone so thankful to see you in their moment of distress, that I began to wonder . . .

As she turned the last corner to exit the maze, a small cotton handkerchief fell to the ground. Not noticing the loss, she turned out of the maze and into the gardens, free at last. I stopped and bent to scoop it up, holding it briefly to my cheek, and then pocketed it.

Chapter 19

1920

Phoebe stood in the library beside Sidney Bellingham as he showed her the puzzle set by his father all those years ago. The puzzle she had come here to solve. He pointed at the two lines of copperplate script behind the glass of a small gilt frame.

Step inside and play my game.
The next move is checkmate.

'You have to admire the old man really,' he said, toying with his moustache. 'Breaking with convention and putting the inheritance on the table like that. Who says the oldest son is the most fit to rule? Would your father really have had my dedication and love for the company? I doubt it. He was never much of a game player.'

'What game?' she asked. 'I don't understand.'

'This is the first of several clues. Solve it and it will lead to another, then another, and so on. It takes you on a merry little treasure hunt, until you find the key to the door at the top of the staircase.'

It wasn't much to go on, Phoebe reflected, and she really didn't like that first line. The player was being manipulated by the game master and she felt like Gretel, standing at the open door of a gingerbread house, being invited inside by an old woman with a child-sized pot bubbling away over the fire. But she wouldn't allow herself to be deterred.

'May I try and solve it?' she asked, wide eyes looking up at him.

'I don't see why not, but don't expect to get very far. You don't know enough about the house, or how your grandfather's mind worked, for that matter. But you may amuse yourself with it for a while, if you so choose.'

This was a challenge if ever she'd heard one. She focused. He actually wanted her to attempt to solve it, if only to see her fail.

He stroked his moustache as he contemplated her request further.

'You have my permission to access any part of the house or grounds in pursuit of the clues, and I'll inform Murray you are not to be challenged should your investigations take you into places you might not otherwise be permitted.'

Something else to stick in Ada's craw, she thought.

She turned back to read the words once more. 'It's clearly referring to the game of chess and I'm sure this house is bursting with chess sets. I'll have to give it some thought but *I will* solve it,' she said, with more conviction that she felt.

He looked at her determined face and raised an eyebrow. 'Then prove you are worthy of my time, and that the Bellingham blood truly runs through your veins,' he challenged, and Phoebe swallowed hard, because she knew something Sidney Bellingham did not . . .

She was not family and she had no right to be at Halesham

Hall or to attempt this puzzle. Leonard Bellingham was not her father, but he had tried his best to fulfil that role, and she had loved him with her whole heart. Sidney had treated this honourable and kind man abominably and for that, she would make him pay.

Two months before arriving at Halesham Hall, Phoebe had sat in a draughty office on the top floor of a crumbling townhouse in Cambridge as the solicitor picked up a small cream envelope and passed it across the large expanse of oak that was the partners' desk. It was a week after her parents' death and there had naturally been matters to settle. The will had been straightforward – she would inherit what little her parents had put aside upon her majority – so she couldn't understand what further information this letter might contain.

'I'm not privy to the reasons for the addition of this correspondence, nor its contents, but it was lodged with us not long after Leonard Bellingham enlisted in 1917.' The solicitor had shaken his head slowly from side to side. 'Very busy years for us, for the saddest of reasons. So many young men were suddenly only too aware of their mortality and the implications their premature passing would have on loved ones. My guess is it contains particulars he was anxious for you to know should he not survive the war, but as we had no further instructions relating to it when the conflict ended, I am honouring my client's initial wishes to pass it to you in the event of his death.'

She recognised the elongated uprights and distinctive slant of her father's handwriting, and for a moment she could do nothing except hold it tightly to her chest. He had gone from her life so unexpectedly and so finally, and yet here he was, reaching out to her from beyond the grave.

'I'll adjourn next door and give you some time alone to open it.'

Phoebe nodded her head gratefully as she leaned forward to accept the proffered paper knife, sliding it under the seal. She took a deep breath, knowing that reading his words would be difficult.

20th June 1917

Dearest Phoebe

I write you this letter sincerely hoping that it will not be needed, and that I will be around to watch you grow and blossom, to wonder at the beautiful woman you will doubtless become. But with my departure for foreign shores imminent, and the harsh reality of a war that has seen so much death and destruction already, I fear my return is not a given. This letter is merely a precaution. There is something you must know and I want you to hear it from me.

The first thing you need to understand is how much I love your mother. Everything rests on that. She was a beam of light appearing between the parting clouds – a sudden love that I hadn't been looking for and it took me by surprise, falling at my feet and causing me to halt my stumbling. From the very first moment I held her in my arms and looked into her dark, hypnotic eyes, I knew I had found safe harbour. You have those same mesmerising eyes and will one day have an equally devastating effect on some poor chap who will not be able to fight his feelings any more than I could. I just hope he deserves you.

I rashly declared my feelings to your mother not long after we met, sitting at her feet in a tiny garret bedroom as she recovered from an accident on the stepping stones of the brook near my family home. And yes, this is why we named the last house as we did, for I think we both knew, even from that first meeting, that it was love. I could hardly believe she felt the same, but your mother was reluctant to declare her feelings, because she carried with her a troubling secret and warned me I would not want her after I knew the truth.

You were that secret.

But as I looked into her eyes, I knew that it didn't make a jot of difference. I loved her, every part of her, even the child that she was growing inside. Your mother offered a pure and uncomplicated love. I needed nothing more than that, even, or perhaps especially, after my brother's unforgivable behaviour . . .

You have often questioned why I so rarely talk of my past. The truth is my younger brother snatched the Bellingham inheritance from me when he solved part of a ridiculous puzzle our father set nearly twenty years ago to decide his heir. Sidney turned my father against me and was rewarded for his treachery with ownership of the company. After Father's death, he could have offered me friendship, but instead cast me out with nothing. And yet I get a certain amount of satisfaction from knowing that the puzzle remains unsolved in its entirety, and the Hall and the family wealth remain there for the taking. This information was told to me by my dying father – perhaps his final attempt to dissuade me from what he saw as an unsuitable marriage to your mother. Locating the missing deeds was key, he stressed. Not interested in more cruel games, I refused to participate further, but the staircase that led nowhere haunts me still.

Over the years I have occasionally reflected on my choices, but I know that what I have with you both is worth more than a fancy building and coins in the bank. Let Sidney wallow in his empty rooms, eating the finest foods and drinking from our father's cellar of vintage wines, for I have long since made peace with the situation.

I only tell you all this because you are entitled to know the history of the family name you carry, even if that name is not of your blood . . . And yet, though biology may tell me differently, you were my daughter from the moment I saw your red angry face, screaming down the cottage to announce your arrival. I have wept by your bedside when you were ill, and my heart has soared at your triumphs. I witnessed you taking your first steps and delighted in hearing your first words. And my love for you grew stronger still as we wrestled with the sadness of not being blessed with any further children.

As for your real father, you may naturally quiz your mother about that. I never once asked and she never once said. It was not information that would change anything and so it did not matter to me, even though I often suspected she was a victim of someone who had abused a position of trust. She was disowned by her family when her condition was discovered, but the loss is theirs, so do not blame her for the actions of a bad man.

Should I fall on some battlefield far from home, I will meet my maker and stand by my decisions. The lies we told came from a good place. We didn't want you frowned upon or called names. The sins of the father should not be visited upon the child.

Throughout your life, love will come and love will go, but know that my love for you will always endure, whether or not I survive this conflict. You are worthy of the very best life has to offer, Phoebe. Do not let anyone make you believe otherwise.

Your affectionate and ever-loving father

Leonard x

The slow ticking of a large grandfather clock standing in the far corner of the office had been the only sound for the following few moments. Each tick reiterated the facts. Leonard was not her biological father. Her mother had been rejected by her family. Leonard had been robbed of his birthright by his younger brother. Everything she thought she knew had changed in a heartbeat.

The solicitor had returned after a decent interval and saw her out into a warm summer's day. As she stumbled down cobbled streets, past gothic limestone buildings, and along the banks of the River Cam, she tried to make sense of everything she'd learned that afternoon. The biggest pill to swallow was that her beloved parents had kept the truth from her. She so dearly wished they had spoken to her about this. Leonard's nurturing made him more of a father than biology ever could, and she would always think of him as such, but his death had robbed her of the opportunity to let him know that his big secret would not have altered her love for him. So instead, she chose to focus on a wrong that she could right – Sidney's harsh treatment of his older brother. Leonard keeping the truth from her had pure motives. The younger Bellingham all but exiling his brother was an act of spite.

A growing anger had bubbled inside Phoebe, not an emotion she generally wrestled with, and it ate away at her over the following weeks. Sidney and Clement Bellingham were surely to blame for everything – from Leonard losing his birthright in a ridiculous game, to her parents being cast aside, and perhaps even ultimately their deaths. They'd never been well off and had often struggled financially, and yet they could have had a very different life, one where her mother needn't have worn dated dresses or spent a year saving ha'pennies in a jar for a precious few days away with her husband. As these feelings fermented, a timid Phoebe became emboldened and determined to redress the balance. For once in her life, she would take action, and she would do it for her parents, even though they were not around to benefit.

With her chin set high and her heart thumping wildly, she had set off for Halesham Hall to undo Sidney Bellingham. And the knowledge that she was not blood and did not deserve the spoils made the task seem all the sweeter.

Chapter 20

Phoebe could already detect a change in Sidney's attitude towards her, she reflected the following day as the puzzle fluttered around her head. He clearly knew nothing of her true parentage and honestly believed himself to be her uncle, because, had he been privy to the truth, she wouldn't have lasted five minutes at the Hall. However, from being unforgivably rude and throwing her out that first afternoon, he was now decidedly curious about his estranged niece, and was toying with the notion that she was worthy of his interest. Sharing the puzzle with her was proof of this. She had hooked her fish. Now it only remained to reel him in.

She was slow to acknowledge that her own attitude had similarly changed. When she thought of him now, it was more as Sidney, rather than the formal Mr Bellingham title she'd previously assigned him. He didn't deserve that kind of respect, although this levelling of their status, even if only in her own mind, was more disconcerting than she cared to admit.

'Halesham Hall *is* the puzzle,' he'd told her in the library. 'Perhaps the grandest of all that my father designed. He was a genius, in many ways, but a dangerous one.'

Phoebe enjoyed games as a rule, and there was nothing like the satisfaction of guessing a correct answer or coming first. It was where she differed from many of her childhood friends – young girls who shied away from exercising their minds outside the domestic challenges of neat stitches and perfectly risen soufflés, and the sum of whose ambitions amounted to securing a husband who could support them and producing healthy offspring in return.

It wasn't marriage she objected to. After all, she had witnessed one of the most supportive and loving marriages between her parents. But for all her mother's talk of suffrage, intellectual thought and lively discussion between *both* sexes, it was only talk at the end of the day. Her mother had constantly deferred to her husband, which had frustrated Phoebe no end as he wasn't always in the right.

Perhaps coming to the Hall had been a reckless move on her part. It was increasingly obvious that she was out of her depth. This wasn't her world. She was a simple country girl with little life experience, and she was playing with fire. But, on the other hand, she had nothing to lose – her life was already empty. Her good, honest and kind parents hadn't deserved their frugal and difficult lives. This struck her as all the more poignant because the wealth surrounding her was the wealth that her father had been denied.

Unsure quite what to do, she nestled the Bellingham riddle at the back of her mind. In the meantime, she would throw herself into her role as kitchen maid, and looked forward to being busy, knowing baking was one of her dearest pleasures.

That afternoon, however, her optimism was put to the test when Mrs Murray twisted an ankle on the uneven servant stairs and Phoebe's duties multiplied.

'You'd think I'd be used to them after all these years, but I was running late with the master's afternoon tea and I'm not as young as I used to be,' the housekeeper said as Phoebe lowered the older woman's foot into a tin pail of cool water and gently manipulated the swollen area. 'You're going to be rushed off your feet, I'm afraid, although Betsy can pitch in, and Ada knows her way around a mincer.'

It was the limping Sanderson who now responded to every ring of the bell, whilst Mrs Murray tried to manage things as best she could from the large lathe-back Windsor near the range. They muddled along reasonably well, helped by the fact that Phoebe was a competent cook. But everyone was astonished when Sidney visited the kitchens to see for himself how his housekeeper was faring, having been informed of her accident.

He appeared in the doorway, and there was a moment where he looked over to Phoebe, up to her elbows in meringue mixture, and froze. His hand reached for the architrave before he steadied himself and walked over to his housekeeper.

'Nothing broken, I trust?' he asked, towering over the smaller lady as she polished the silver cutlery in her lap – one of the few jobs she could do from her chair. There was genuine concern in his expression, Phoebe noted with surprise, as she looked at them from across the room, beating egg whites to stiff peaks in preparation for her delicate lemon-flavoured kisses. She'd missed baking for the afternoon teas that the vicar had been wont to attend, and she'd had quite the reputation for her dainties, from her almond madeleines to her cherry strips.

'No, sir. I'll be right as rain tomorrow. I just need to rest the ankle for a bit.'

Clearly uneasy below stairs, Sidney nodded, wrung his hands and looked about him. Phoebe felt his eyes bore into her and she tried to avoid his stare as she sieved the fine sugar into the egg whites. There was a rack of cinnamon biscuits cooling at the far end of the table and his gaze drifted to them and then back to her.

'Ah, I see now why I have been spoiled with such sweet treats of late. Murray is more of a wedge of apple pie or chunk of sturdy fruit cake sort of cook.' He sauntered over to them and picked one up. Without thinking, Phoebe rapped the back of his hand with the wooden spoon, much as she used to do when her father tried to steal her cakes the moment they came from the oven.

'What the devil . . .' He dropped the biscuit in shock and Phoebe felt colour and heat flood her cheeks.

'I'm so sorry. I wasn't thinking. My father used to . . .' She trailed off, realising that such talk wouldn't be welcome.

'I know you aren't familiar with the rules and formalities of such a large household, but I am master of Halesham Hall and should I choose to eat the whole rack of biscuits right this instant, I shall do so.'

Phoebe bobbed her head and squeezed her lips tightly together to prevent herself from saying anything inappropriate as she began to drop spoonfuls of her meringue mixture on to the parchment-covered baking tin.

Sidney's eyes narrowed again – in fact, in their short acquaintance they had narrowed so frequently, she could only suppose he had extraordinarily heavy eyelids. He placed his hands behind his back, however, left the biscuits untouched and walked over to the windows, looking up at the drifting clouds.

'Douglas did a splendid job of trimming the maze last month. I would like to show it to Phoebe,' he said to no one in particular, and then he turned to face her. 'Finish whatever it is you're doing and then meet me outside, if you will.'

'We're preparing dainties for the afternoon tea you organised,' Mrs Murray pointed out.

'Damn and blast, yes, the ladies of the church committee coming to remind me of my charitable duties in the community and poor attendance at church. They'll be after more money, no doubt, for the restoration of the bell tower. Still, as it is their husbands and sons who make up the majority of my workforce at the printworks, it is as well to keep them onside.' He rubbed at his chin as he contemplated the afternoon ahead. 'However, you *will* manage without the girl for a while.' It was an unequivocal statement. There was to be no further discussion as he spun on his heels and left the room.

'Och,' the housekeeper said as he departed. 'He really has no consideration for our workload, and me stuck in this chair until my ankle heals. Perhaps I shouldn't grumble. He often puts his hand in his pocket for local causes. Just a shame that he doesn't have the necessary charm to reap the benefits of his largesse.' She rolled her eyes. 'Pop those in the oven – I'll keep an eye on them – and then do as he bids. He's not a man who likes to be kept waiting, especially when he's set his mind on something.'

'Your grandfather designed it,' Sidney said without emotion as she gazed up at the high hedges before her. They were confronted by the spiky green leaves of a dense wall, with a narrow entrance half way along.

'It's a maze of yew – one of the faster-growing varieties. It was planted when I was a boy and didn't take long to mature to a height that made it impossible to peek over the hedge tops to cheat and find your way out. There's a statue in the centre and if you can tell me what the statue is of, I will give you five pounds.'

She stared at him in disbelief. Not that the money wouldn't be welcome, but she was astonished that he could fritter such a sum away on an idle notion.

'That's ridiculous. You pay me twenty pounds a year to work for you. How can you justify such an extravagance?'

He shrugged. 'Everyone has a price and I'm curious to see if you can solve the maze.'

'I can't be bought, Uncle,' she replied. 'I have work to do. Mrs Murray is waiting and it is more important for me to carry out my duties when people are relying on me than to play in your maze.' It was a totally unreasonable request – surely he must see that.

Sidney's tone deepened. 'You have work to do if I say you have. I'm your employer and I say you are to solve the maze.'

His expression darkened and Phoebe recognised he was a man who quickly became irritable when he didn't get his own way. She remembered her father once mentioning how his younger brother had been spoiled and cosseted by their mother. After she'd disappeared, he said, it had become vital for Sidney to win at things, to be the best, the strongest, and to assert ownership, which only became worse the older he got. Perhaps the loss of a parent so young had engendered in him a need both to control and to be independent of others.

She shrugged. Although there was a part of her desperate not to pander to him, she was in his employ and therefore under his authority. Ultimately, she needed him onside, so what harm could it do?

'All right,' she said. 'But I won't accept the money.'

He settled himself on a low bench that overlooked the entrance and crossed one lean leg over the other. 'Suit yourself. You have half an hour,' he said. 'Shout if you need help, but that will be counted as failure.'

'*Half an hour?* Mrs Murray will go spare. There's so much to do. Never mind all the baking for this afternoon, she needs me to crown half a dozen pigeons for the suet pudding she's making.'

'Leave old Murray to me. Off you trot then.' He waved a

hand in the direction of the gap and then placed both hands behind his neck as he tilted his body back in a leisurely manner. Phoebe couldn't help but notice a wry smile cross his lips.

So, she was to be his sport for the day. This man was to test her at every turn – as though she had to earn a place at this house, as though he wanted her to fail, to cry, to surrender. Well, it wasn't going to happen. If she'd learned anything from life, it was that bullies revelled in your reactions.

From the exterior of the maze, she knew it was about a hundred yards square but the walls within would be narrow and high. This was a tricky sort of challenge. Everything was guesswork, because she had no overview and gathered fragments of information as she progressed. It would be trial and error until she happened upon the solution. She turned left as she entered – both options had equal chance of success or failure – and she started to draw a map in her head of where she had been for when she, inevitably, had to retrace her steps.

Knowing that the smug man lounging back on the bench in the afternoon sun was enjoying every moment, she tried to focus. He clearly had a twisted sense of humour – one that delighted in the misfortune or confusion of others – and she would not let him witness her failure. Determined to get to the middle of the maze even if it took her all night, she pulled back her shoulders and set her face forward. He could explain to Mrs Murray why the pigeons were still hanging in the larder and the fruit tarts not made.

As she walked along the first path, she passed a gap in the yew to her right. Should she take it? Or continue straight? Common sense told her that turning right would take her closer to the centre, but mazes were duplicitous things – often the route to victory was the most tortuous. A small metal plant label at the base of the hedge marking the gap caught her eye. She bent down to examine it, expecting it to tell her that the hedge was *Taxus baccata*, but there was simply an elaborate letter N within the frame, which meant nothing to her. Standing upright as she debated which path to take, she heard the pounding of running feet from behind and a hand violently grabbed at her shoulder.

'Stop,' Sidney commanded, spinning her to face him. 'I've changed my mind. Come out now before you get ensnared in this warped version of hell. In fact, I command you to escape Halesham Hall whilst you can. The whole place is a web of misery and tricks. There are secrets buried here that should never be unearthed. You're too innocent to be sucked into all this, and I should never have agreed to you working in the kitchens.'

He stared intently at her startled face. Although she couldn't swear to it, there appeared to be a silent torment swirling within the golden syrup of his irises, and it scared her.

She frowned. 'But . . .' She gestured towards the heart of the maze.

'It can't be done. It's impossible,' he said. 'The centre is enclosed, although there is a statue of Aphrodite in the middle – the goddess of love. I believe your grandfather was trying to make some point about love being unattainable, because there was no way to reach her.' He started to pace back and forth along the narrow path, wringing his hands and periodically glancing up to her. 'He enjoyed watching people waste their time trying to solve it, because their frustrations somehow matched his own romantic disappointments. I thought I would equally enjoy your fruitless efforts and that it would be a victory to hear you call for help and admit defeat, but I don't want any part of it. I want you to return to Cambridgeshire.'

That explained the generous reward then – he knew she wouldn't be able to claim it.

'No, I . . . I don't want to. There is no one there for me.'

'Equally, there is no one here for you at Halesham Hall. I don't know what you're trying to achieve, but it's foolishness to hang around waiting for me to undergo some great epiphany and welcome you into the bosom of the family. It's never going to happen, so you are to pack your trunk and be gone by the morning, and I forbid you to make any further contact with me.'

He stopped pacing and reached for her shoulder again. Much like when he'd visited the kitchens to check on Mrs Murray, she saw genuine concern and compassion etched across his troubled face. The thought that such a heartless man could feel such emotions hadn't occurred to her before.

'Do this one thing for me, Phoebe. Can't you see I'm trying to save you, you foolish girl? I cannot let Halesham Hall destroy you too.'

And for the second time there was the faintest whisper of doubt in her mind. Perhaps her father failing to inherit Halesham Hall had not been such a bad thing after all. He'd escaped, while poor little Sidney had been left behind to be consumed by it and all its unpleasantness.

Chapter 21

'Mr Bellingham has asked me to leave,' Phoebe said, stepping back into the kitchen and wearing a frown. 'He wishes me to be gone by the morning.'

Mrs Murray's relieved smile that her kitchen maid had returned so quickly dropped as she made her announcement.

'Goodness, child, what did you do to upset him so? You weren't gone many minutes.'

'I have no idea.' The truth was she really didn't understand Sidney's unpredictable and inconsistent behaviour, but she explained to the housekeeper what had happened in the maze.

Mrs Murray put down the last of the fish knives she was buffing. 'That laddie,' she said, shaking her head. 'And I always think of him as a wee lad, despite his nearly two score years on this earth, when he behaves like this. Although I can't deny that this house has not been a happy place for a long time, if ever, I earnestly believe it has the potential to be. Sending away a drop of sunshine like yourself isn't going to help matters. Och, if I was bigger and he wasn't my employer, I'd be tempted to box his ears.'

'Is that why you stayed?' Phoebe asked, intrigued by the forthright words. 'Because you wanted to see the Hall have its happy ending?' She washed her hands in the sink and took up her duties again, determined to do her job until the last. The guests would be arriving in a couple of hours and she was keen to impress. He'd asked her to be gone by the morning, so she would work until then.

'I couldn't leave the boys, especially wee Sidney. I knew I'd never have bairns of my own and I'd been working here since before they were born, so they were like my children in a way. Even though he wasn't the easiest of laddies growing up, I can still remember him at six years old, his heart torn out by his mother leaving. I've done my best and I've watched out for him all these years, even though I'm not the sentimental sort.'

Phoebe took a moment to remember that Leonard had been significantly older, and thus he'd had the benefit of growing up with his mother around. Sidney had been so young when Sylvia had disappeared, and had not. It went some way to explaining his behaviour, she acknowledged.

The cinnamon biscuits were cool now, so she began to stack them in a tin.

'It wasn't so much the lack of a mother, as the presence of a nasty father. That poor wee laddie turned seven the autumn after his mother left and old Mr Bellingham announced that for his birthday Sidney would have "a gift greater than God". He told his son, "The poor have it, the rich need it, but if you eat it, you'll die." I watched the child tear at the brown paper with wide eyes and an eager anticipation, only to find an empty box as that cruel man laughed to himself. "What a shame you did not take the time to solve the riddle and spare yourself the disappointment," he said to a distraught Sidney. "You cannot expect things to fall on to your lap. Life simply doesn't work that way."'

Phoebe's heart flipped. The answer to the riddle was, of course, nothing. What an unkind trick to play on a child. The more she learned about the history of Halesham Hall, the more she realised how special her upbringing had been. Her heart ached for the Bellingham boys. There was so much physical contact in her childhood – the arms of a loving parent, affectionate ruffles of the hair, tender goodnight kisses. Indeed, only last year, she had sat on her father's knee as they both balanced on the wide swing which hung from the sycamore in the schoolyard, watching a sunset together. She had thought this was normal, because she knew no different. But her life had been sheltered and she could see this now. And those people whom she might conceivably envy, those with money and social standing, were sometimes the worst affected of all. Babies were taken from their mothers to be cared for by a nanny, overseen by a governess, and then sent off to boarding school as soon as possible – at least, the boys were. For all Sidney's wealth, she would not wish for his childhood in a hundred lifetimes.

One of the housekeeper's bony fingers went to the corner of her eye and Phoebe saw her wipe away a tear.

'The master needs someone's arms about him, someone to tell him everything is going to be just fine, and that he can stop kicking out at the world. I'd dearly love to see him find a wife, but I'm running out of years. I'll be sixty-nine next month and the physical demands of this job are starting to take their toll. What will happen when I go? Who will care for him then?'

Phoebe shrugged. She would not allow herself to get sucked into this and for her resolve to slip. Yes, his childhood had been traumatic, but it did not excuse his behaviour. If she could get her hands on the Hall, she could use it for good – not leave it to decay whilst one entitled and difficult man swanned around, believing himself to be better than everyone else.

'It's not right that he should spend the remainder of his life alone. Your poor uncle has had his heart broken twice,' Murray continued. 'No one deserves that. First as a small child when his mother abandoned him, and again when he was older and fell in love. And that twisted father of his used both these experiences to foster a disrespect and mistrust of women. All Sidney ever wanted was to love and be loved, and I believe he still wants that to this day.'

Neither did Phoebe care about Sidney Bellingham's disappointments in love. He hadn't cared a jot about his brother when he'd thrown him out.

Mrs Murray dug deep for a smile and patted her lap in determination. 'But your arrival has changed everything. He has family now and someone to care about other than himself for the first time in years, so I refuse to allow him this silly tantrum.'

Phoebe was thankful she had someone on her side, if only because should she be thrown out of the Hall, she wouldn't be able to execute her plan.

'If I've managed to persuade him that young scallywag Douglas should keep his job before now, I'm certain I can do the same for you. Keep an eye on that onion sauce and slice some bread for the sandwiches – nice and thin, mind, those church ladies are fussy.' She rolled her eyes. 'And take those kisses out of the oven by half past. I need to see a man about a dog.'

The housekeeper set her face in a most resolved manner before hauling herself from the chair. Phoebe rushed over to her, concerned that she was not in a fit state to mount the stairs, but she was brushed away, and Mrs Murray crossed the kitchen with quite a determined hobble.

Whatever power Mrs Murray had over Sidney, she exercised it well. Half an hour later and Phoebe was not to leave after all, although the older lady warned everyone to give Mr Bellingham a wide berth that afternoon, expecting inevitable repercussions from the master being undermined by his housekeeper.

The staff gathered in the servants' dining room later that evening, waiting for Ada to return from taking the supper tray up to Mr Bellingham before commencing their meal. His afternoon charity tea had been a success but his foul temper had returned the moment his guests had left. Too out of sorts to eat a proper meal, he had requested merely 'a plate of those fancy meringues and the cinnamon biscuits' – which Phoebe counted as a silent victory. Ada duly returned, slipped into her chair, and apologised.

'The grumpy devil is in a rum mood,' she commented, scowling at both her plate of food and the new kitchen maid.

'It's not appropriate to talk about the master like that,' Mrs Murray reprimanded from her position at the head of the long refectory table. She'd told Phoebe that when the old Mr Bellingham had been alive, the butler, Mr Burton, had occupied the opposite chair, but it was now empty. Sanderson was not deemed quite senior enough to merit the seat.

A moment of silence swept the table as everyone's eyes turned to the stern Scotswoman.

'For what we are about to receive, may the Lord make us truly thankful.'

They all bowed heads, muttered 'Amen', and then lively chatter broke out as cutlery clinked against crockery. There was a bustle of condiments being passed around, and the large bowl of steaming mashed potatoes made its merry journey from person to person. Delicious wafts of pigeon pudding and onion sauce swirled around the room.

'Do you have tomorrow afternoon off?' Douglas asked Phoebe as she handed him the hot dish of shredded cabbage.

She nodded.

'Would you like to walk into Halesham with me? Nothing funny,' he added, hastily. 'I need to stop at the ironmonger's for some nails and a coil of wire, then I'll pop in on my mother. She always does a nice little tea of cakes and scones for me. I thought you might enjoy it as you don't have family near – well, apart from old sour-chops, and he's such a cold fish he treats you like a servant, not a niece.'

'Some respect for the master, please,' Murray said again. 'What is the world coming to? Staff were barely allowed to talk at mealtimes in my day.' She tutted as she scooped up a forkful of the rich suet pudding.

'That would be lovely.' Phoebe's heart gave a little skip at the thought of a pleasant walk in the countryside and perhaps sitting in a cosy parlour, having tea and scones, something she'd done with her parents. She swallowed down the rising lump in her throat as happy memories engulfed her.

'You can take over a dozen of our eggs as a thank you for the jar of bramble jelly she sent back last time, Douglas,' Mrs Murray said, joining in their conversation. 'With all those mouths to feed, I'm sure she'll be grateful.' And then she turned to Phoebe. 'Daisy worked here years ago, before she married. Hard worker but terrible blether and rather emotional, forever either weeping or giggling, but her heart was in the right place.'

'An afternoon to look forward to, then,' said Douglas, a shy grin spreading across his sun-tanned face and his eyes dipping to his plate as soon as Phoebe's connected with his. Something warm and unfamiliar bubbled in her chest and she focused intently on a small knot of wood in the table before her as she wrestled with what the peculiar sensation might be.

Chapter 22

The day was bright and clear as Douglas stood in the courtyard, nonchalantly leaning against the wall of the house and chewing on a blade of grass. He had a canvas bag across his body which Phoebe assumed contained the eggs. His woollen flat cap was slightly askew, which she thought was endearing. Had she more courage, or known the young man better, she would have adjusted it for him.

'Sorry to keep you waiting. I had to pop upstairs for my hat,' she announced, pushing a pin through both hat and hair to keep it in place. 'Let's go.'

The pair exchanged a smile and Phoebe's heart fluttered. This man was everything Sidney was not – fair-haired and open-faced, young and carefree. He wore a broad smile when you spoke to him, and had a studied look of concentration when he was working. She'd seen him planting spring bulbs in the front gardens – carefully measuring the distance between each one and focusing intently on his task. There was no edge to him – he appeared to drift along in the world like a paper boat bobbing down a stream, letting the ripples and currents toss him about as he continued to sail onward on his predetermined course.

'Shame,' he said. 'It hides your eyes and you have lovely eyes.' Phoebe felt her cheeks flood with heat. 'Never seen a pair so dark. Like the twinkling black glass beads on my grandmother's favourite necklace. Meant more to her than anything, because my grandfather bought it for her just before he died.' He paused, his mind obviously wandering. 'I imagine real jet would shine even brighter but you don't earn that sort of money tilling the soil, and you also don't make old bones. Worked for others all his life, all weathers, for little pay and even less respect. But then the world is full of haves and have nots – all dictated by the accident of your birth. My poor grandfather never even made fifty.'

'I'm sorry,' she said, but he merely shrugged and rolled up his shirtsleeves, revealing his strong forearms – solid muscle from his heavy labouring – and slipped off his cap to fan his face. Her cheeks grew hotter but it wasn't the sultry September afternoon that sent the blood coursing through her veins.

They walked across the kitchen garden and along the edge of the orchard – Bramleys, russets and Pippins now ready for harvesting. A few windfalls were scattered at the feet of these fruit-laden trees, and excitable wasps buzzed around, drawn to the fermenting, sugary juices.

'Look at all those glorious apples,' she said, briefly leaning on the post and rail fence that edged the orchard and shielding her eyes from the strong early afternoon sun. 'They do so remind me of my mother. She used to take a paring knife and whizz around the skins, peeling them in one long, unbroken curl. Pippins were her favourite – the streaks of yellow and red bleeding into each other.' A moment of nostalgia swept over her.

Douglas hopped over the low fence in a sudden and swift movement and walked to the nearest tree, gently twisting a ripe apple to release it from its reluctant parent. A hop and a skip later and he was kneeling at her feet, holding it aloft.

'For madam. I very much hope it is to her liking.'

She smiled and lifted the ripe fruit to her nose, inhaled the sweet, slightly floral scent, and then took a bite of the crunchy flesh as he returned to his feet.

'We've already begun to harvest them. I've been clearing out the apple shed and lining the drawers with straw. If we're lucky, the fruit will last through until next spring, but old Murray usually makes a batch of apple jam and also adds it to various chutneys. I found an ancient cider press in the back barn and have a mind to try it out, given that we've got such a bumper crop.'

'Are you happy at Halesham Hall?' she asked, because at that moment, his joy and enthusiasm about the imminent harvest was plain to see. 'I gather my uncle can be a difficult man to work for.'

'For the moment, and the attractions are growing by the day . . .' He gave her a shy smile. 'But I'm not sticking around for ever. Working for other people is a mug's game. I have plans,' he said, as they began walking down the winding dirt path towards the woods. 'Problem is you need money in order to make money, and I don't have two brass farthings to rub together. But I'm no fool – when I see an opportunity, I grab it. I might even sell off some of that cider on the quiet. Bellingham wouldn't know.' He grinned. 'Ultimately, though, import and export is where I'm headed – oranges, lemons, almonds, dates and figs. There's a real market for these and I'd love to be in on it. As much as I enjoy being out in the sun, the life of any labourer is a short one. Those fancy-suited men behind their huge desks with their three-storey town houses, club memberships and tailored clothes – now that's the life.'

Living in the town wasn't for her, but she understood there were advantages and disadvantages to both the rural and the urban lifestyles. Her heart, however, would always be in the countryside.

'Is that a building in amongst the trees?' she asked, spotting a stone wall and possibly a window as a beam of light glanced off something smooth and shiny, catching her eye. They were still on the Bellingham estate, as Douglas had explained that their land included the large private woods. The stream marked the boundary with the neighbouring farm and Phoebe wondered if this was the brook mentioned in her father's letter.

'Mmm . . . of sorts. I'll show you,' he said reluctantly. 'Come with me.'

'Oh, how beautiful,' she said, as they approached a curious tumbledown building, the clearing where it stood bathed in a small circle of light. 'Such a shame it's been left to ruin. What was it originally? A medieval chapel?' She frowned. 'It's somewhat off the beaten track.'

'It's a folly, built about thirty years ago, Mum said, but made to look centuries old. An example of people with more money than sense, if you ask me. Why pay builders to build something and then get them to do half a job? Looks quite ghostly at night but pretty enough in the day, I guess, particularly when the light catches the coloured window – although I must admit to always feeling rather uneasy when I'm here.'

'Oh, but it's positively darling.' Phoebe skipped towards it, her curiosity aroused, and looked up at the impressive arched window at the south end. 'You're right about the beautiful stained glass.' Each golden ray came from the central sun and was picked out in bright yellow. She poked her head around the broken wall to look inside. 'And a stone bench. One might come here to escape and contemplate. Such a delightful place.'

'Really? I always think that bench resembles one of those tombs you find in churches, with the carved effigy of a knight lying on top. There's something about this place I don't like. I was asked to cut back the trees here last autumn and I had the feeling I was being watched the whole time.' He shuddered. 'Mum said the folly went up shortly after Sylvia Bellingham disappeared. The name Sylvia means of the woods or the forest, so Ma says. Look,' and he pointed to the Latin inscription, *Sylvia – in silvis*. 'She always felt like it was some kind of memorial to Mrs Bellingham. Let's face it, the woman hasn't been seen for thirty years. She surely must be dead by now.' He grimaced. 'Don't you feel it?'

'Feel what?'

'Never mind.' He shrugged. 'Come on, let's get going or we'll lose the best part of the day, hidden in the gloomy woods.'

They crossed the bridge over the stream. Phoebe's heart jolted as she noticed the stepping stones below and realised this was where her parents' romance had begun. As was so often the case with these unexpected memories, she felt both happy and sad, but she tried not to let Douglas witness her conflicted emotions.

They eventually approached the clustered houses of Halesham and her companion explained that it was a small market town, the main employers of the two hundred inhabitants being either Bellingham's printing press or the large fertiliser company with its factory by the River Hale. His father had worked for the latter all his life and lived in a row of workers' terraced cottages on Blacksmith's Lane – one of the narrow roads off the main square.

It was, he told her as they stood in the centre of town, admiring the town hall clock, a thriving parish that could be traced back to the Domesday Book, and it had the usual blacksmith, tailor, cobbler, butcher and grocery stores. Most poignant of all was a stone war memorial with the names of thirty-one men commemorated, which had only recently been erected. He paused to point out his nineteen-year-old cousin, shot dead in a forest in Belgium, and she saw a cloud pass over his bright eyes.

'Were you a part of it?' she asked, not sure if asking was the right thing to do.

'Very briefly, towards the end,' he said. 'And it's why I can't lead the life of my father. At someone else's beck and call, with no hope of rising above my allotted station in life. But times are changing, Phoebe, and I promised myself when it ended I'd do something with my life in memory of the men who gave their lives – the men who did what they were told, without questioning their orders, and then paid the ultimate price.'

He reached out to stroke his cousin's name – his thumb caressing the letters – and took the longest breath in she'd ever heard. Phoebe knew better than to pursue the conversation. These men had witnessed terrible sights, done unspeakable things, and she understood they needed to forget and move on – or, at least, try to. Even her father had been unable to talk about his time at the front, much to her mother's distress. They shared everything and always had, but he couldn't bring himself to share that.

Whilst Douglas popped to the ironmonger's, Phoebe remained in the square, soaking up the rays of the late summer sun and enjoying the bustle of traders and shoppers. A woman was selling books from a small wooden barrow, so she looked out a penny from her purse and bought a slightly battered green cloth copy of *The Wind in the Willow*s, tucking it under her arm. She missed her books, all packed away in boxes whilst she decided what to do with her life, and had remained fond of children's stories – their innocence and simplicity appealed to her far more than the racy novelettes some of her friends read.

Money was tight, but a penny spent on a book was money well spent. Unless she could succeed in taking the Hall from Sidney Bellingham, she would never be well off, and even then, she wasn't sure if she would keep it. Stealing it away from the man who had betrayed her father was enough. She wouldn't come into much when she reached her majority and was perfectly content to be frugal until the end of her days. Her parents had lived a modest but contented life and their extraordinary wealth couldn't be counted in pounds, shillings and pence. Instead it had been measured out in kisses, kind words and the making of happy memories.

'Right, let's go and see the old girl,' Douglas said, reappearing with a couple of brown paper packages. 'Hope your ears are up to this. You might not get a word in edgeways. She's a talker, is Mum.'

Douglas led her to a small, mid-terraced house. Assorted grubby children sat on the pavement edge, their scuffed shoes kicking about in the gutter – others ran after balls, laughing and shouting. A somewhat battered black baby carriage was parked outside a shabby front door, doubtless having gone through multiple children, if not multiple families. The silently sleeping occupant remained untroubled by the noisy street.

They were greeted at the door by a plump but flustered woman who Douglas introduced as his mother.

'Come in, come in,' she bustled. 'Excuse the house, but it's too small for all the bodies and there never seems to be enough room to give everything a proper place.'

'I have a *lot* of sisters,' Douglas explained, leading Phoebe down a dark corridor to a tiny kitchen at the back of the house.

'I thought we'd stopped at six,' his mother chipped in. 'Dougie was our first and our Harry so wanted another boy, but after five girls in a row, even I knew it was time to quit. Why the good Lord saw fit to bless me with so many little madams I don't know, but at least each one was healthy, so I decided not to push my luck, and then we got a surprise two years ago. The only part that wasn't a surprise was that it was yet another girl.' She rolled her eyes and motioned for Phoebe to take a seat, hastily removing a pile of laundry from the chair. 'Call me Daisy. We'll have to have our tea party here in the kitchen, I'm afraid. Harry's mother lives in the front parlour. Bed-bound and foul-tempered, as if I didn't have enough to do.'

For a moment the older woman looked as though she might cry, and Phoebe remembered Mrs Murray mentioning Daisy's mercurial emotions. But she rallied and plastered a cheery smile across her rosy cheeks. Douglas got his smile from his mother, she realised – broad and engaging.

'Ah, here she comes, little minx,' and a tiny blonde-headed child crawled in through the open back door, clutching a wooden rattle. 'Please God she's the last.' Daisy sighed. 'I love 'em and everything but they're so draining. Right then, tea?'

She put a copper kettle on the stove and began to clear the circular kitchen table, stacking plates and cups near the sink and chattering away as she bustled about. Realising the milk in the glazed white pitcher had turned, she sent Douglas next door to beg a jugful.

'So what's life like up at the big house?' she asked Phoebe, over her shoulder. 'There was something off about the old Mr Bellingham. He was a bit handsy, I've been told. *After* the wife left, mind, never before, so I was glad to be out of there. Our Dougie says his son's got you working in the kitchens. He's not the rotten apple his father was, but he was rather a confused and neglected child. Desperately unhappy, poor bugger. His mother leaving was the start of a downward spiral for that boy.'

It was perplexing to Phoebe that so many people felt

sympathy for Mr Bellingham, jarring against her casting of him as the villain in her mind. Even her father had occasionally talked of his little brother as a casualty in the family breakup, and Mrs Murray, too, implied he'd been an innocent victim swept up by his father's bitterness. Perhaps he'd had a rotten start in life, she acknowledged, but her father hadn't turned out that way and he'd grown up in the same twisted household.

'I've come to Halesham to mend bridges,' she said, 'but it's hard when I don't know what happened between him and my father that was so terrible that they chose not to speak to each other for twenty years. This was personal, I'm sure of it, and nothing to do with the bizarre legacy of my peculiar grandfather. After all, my uncle could easily have let his brother remain on the estate, but instead chose to heartlessly throw him and my mother out.'

Daisy leaned towards Phoebe, her eyes wide with surprise. 'You poor girl,' she said, clutching her hand. 'Has no one told you? Sidney Bellingham was *desperately* in love with your mother, and *never* forgave your father for stealing her away.'

Chapter 23

1899

'Oh dear,' I said to Jane, as we hurried back across the lawns from the maze. 'Father will be terribly cross with me for asking you to do a job that took you so long. I foolishly assumed you would be in and out quite quickly – the maze really is terribly straightforward. And Mrs Murray will be fuming that you disappeared for a whole hour. I'm sure I don't want the wrath of my father and you don't want to be dismissed.'

'Would she really sack me for this?' Those wide eyes stared at me again, but I persevered with my scheme to get myself out of trouble and for her to see me as the hero of the hour, rather than the villain.

'You don't know her like I do. A harsh woman with a cold heart. She tolerates no excuses. The truth is there was a . . . um, dog in distress. I happened upon it as I was returning to tell Cook you'd be delayed, and in my haste to help the injured animal, I forgot to inform her that you were undertaking a task for me. However, on reflection, I think I shall be in trouble for diverting you. We shall just have to come up with a plan.'

'Shall we?'

'Yes, and I have just the thing. We'll tell them that it was you who found the injured animal and were tending to it, to save both our skins.'

In point of fact, it would be me in hot water should my foolish whim to send the poor girl into the maze be discovered. Murray gave the impression of ruling with a rod of unbending iron, but I knew that there was a kind side to her. Yes, she would berate the shirkers and scold the clumsy, but she would also send an exhausted girl to bed early and cover for anyone who was poorly. She was in charge of the housemaids, but she'd been one of them many years ago, and never forgot it.

'I feel uncomfortable saying things that are untrue.' She paused for a moment, something dark sweeping across her eyes. 'One should always tell the truth, even when one is not believed and is punished regardless. God knows when we lie and it is a sin.'

Was she thinking back to some truth she had defended? Was she in Halesham now because she had not been believed? It was frustrating that she wouldn't share her past with me. I wanted to know everything about her, to help her, to protect her, and she wouldn't let me in.

'Nonsense, we aren't harming anyone. In fact, we are sparing me from the wrath of my father – and possibly the rod – and you from dismissal. And all because you were not able to find your way to retrieve my boater, and I came to the aid of a dog in distress. We are hardly committing the most heinous of crimes. Father can be cruel and unforgiving, and he simply won't listen to reason when he's made his mind up over something.'

'I had a strict father too,' she said, her eyes repeatedly flicking up to mine and back to the ground, clearly unsure whether she should be sharing this confidence. 'Very religious and very righteous. I was once caned for daring to disagree with him. I like to think he loved me, but he loved God more – a fire and brimstone believer. Everything was to please God and anything perceived as a sin was severely punished.'

'And he's dead now?' I surmised, delighted that she was finally opening up to me.

She paused. 'Let's not talk of him any more. I just wanted you to know I understood, having spent a lifetime trying to please him.'

'It's tough, isn't it?' I said, realising this was something that pulled us together. She would understand those parts of me I struggled with, that I knew were far from perfect, and appreciate how we are all shaped by our parenting – for good or ill. 'Do you have any other family?'

'I have no one,' she said, and I wanted to reach for her and tell her she had me. She would always have me. But it was too early to lay my cards on the table. Instead, I tried to find out more about her background, a topic she had always avoided before, by a more circuitous route.

'How do you come to know Tennyson?' I asked. 'You have a surprising education for a kitchen maid.'

She avoided my eyes and instead picked at the edge of her apron with her slim fingers. 'The village schoolmaster was a poetry lover. He saw my interest and encouraged it, although I don't know why. My father saw little point in educating girls beyond their domestic duties.'

'Do you play chess?' I asked, going off at a tangent and wondering if I could engage her in some activity as a ruse to spend more time with her. Such a cerebral game would surely demonstrate whether she was truly worthy of my affections.

'No.'

'Then I shall teach you.'

'I'm not sure it would be appropriate . . .'

'Oh, come along now, we can meet on your afternoon off. You say you have no family, then let me be your family – a surrogate brother, if you will, because I'm just as lonely as you.' There was some truth in my words, but I was manipulating her emotions for my own ends. I ploughed on, noticing her begin to waver. 'The head gardener told me the weather will be fine for a couple more days, and alluded to deep red sunsets, open pine cones and other such country nonsense I didn't understand. We can meet by the brook. I'll bring a blanket. Please?' I begged. 'It's so dreadfully dull here with no Leonard and this long and empty summer stretching before me. I don't see why we shouldn't be friends. We don't have to tell anyone.'

'Maybe.' I could tell that she was torn between the offer of friendship and the moral ambiguity of our situation.

As we crossed into the courtyard, Mrs Murray appeared. 'And where have you been, my girl? Cook's language is getting coarser by the moment.'

'It's not her fault. She was helping an injured dog, alleviating its suffering and returning it to its master. Come now, Murray, don't tell me you wouldn't have done the same?' Anything to avoid admonishing looks from the housekeeper if she realised I'd sent Jane into the maze when there was work to be done. She'd be disappointed in me. Truth be told, I was disappointed in myself for playing such a mean trick.

'Hmm . . .' The housekeeper pursed her thin lips and gave me a look that suggested she thought my story was dubious. 'Well, young lady, if you can appear with those potatoes you were sent out for in double quick time, I'll say no more about it, but consider this a warning.'

And as the poor girl scurried back to her abandoned empty pail, she threw a last grateful look back at me and I knew she considered herself in my debt. I would capitalise on that.

Chapter 24

How was it I'd failed to notice until my sixteenth year that there was so much beauty in everything around me? Nature was truly wonderful and I'd been rushing through my life without taking the time to appreciate any of it – the deep purple petals of the morning glory unfurling at daybreak as they searched for the sun, tiny glass droplets of water sitting on the large leaves of the hostas after a summer shower, a black caterpillar making its steady journey up a tree trunk, each hair quivering as it rippled upwards in search of food. Everything smelled so fresh and clean now that a storm had broken the prolonged spell of hot weather – the head gardener's forecast had been wrong. Even about the Hall, my attention was drawn to the smallest of details that I'd walked past a hundred times before – from the crenellations and hideous gargoyles that adorned the rooftop of the west tower (my mother's sewing room many moons ago), to the intricate patterns on the rugs Father had imported from Turkey.

'These dominoes are remarkable,' I commented to Murray one morning as she passed me sitting on the bottom step of the main staircase.

As part of Father's remodelling, the banisters had been replaced by pale sycamore hexagonal balusters and handrails, with tiny decorative dominoes burned into the wood at the base of each spindle. Pyrography had become terribly fashionable and this was yet another example of his passion for games being reflected in the fabric of the Hall. I'd also not noticed until recently the card suits painted around the doorframe to the games room, the snakes and ladders carved into the uprights of the bookshelves in the library, or the amazing details on the figures that danced down the east wing corridor. My world had opened up to the wonders around me and I knew it was because I'd found love at last. I wanted to see the world through Jane's eyes, to embrace every detail and wondrous thing of beauty around me.

'And they've been equally remarkable for the seven years they've been in that exact spot, but it's good to see you in a cheery mood, Master Sidney.'

I grinned. 'Would you ask Cook to make me a picnic lunch?' I asked, getting to my feet. 'A sizeable one. I have a hearty appetite today.'

She looked me up and down. 'Hardly surprising. You've shot up like a beanstalk this past year. You must be as tall as the head groom and half his age. I'm sure Cook will be happy to oblige.'

And so that afternoon I found myself sitting on a blanket, down by the brook, with a wicker picnic basket bursting with treats (my efforts to make myself more helpful to staff in recent days was reaping unexpected rewards), and in the company of a shy, somewhat nervous kitchen maid.

'Relax, no one comes down here. We're still on Father's land, and we aren't doing anything untoward,' I tried to reassure her as she cast her eyes about and finally looked back at me. 'We are as brother and sister, enjoying a picnic on a summer afternoon.'

Her shoulders dropped a little. 'Yes, of course.'

I'd hoped she might make some remark alluding to the fact that we were far from that, but I'd learned enough from my cynical father to know that courtship was a game, and women often underplayed their hand. Society expected certain things of them, and they presented themselves as unworldly and cautious as part of their virginal charm. Yet she had not only kissed my hand, but also agreed to this meeting – unchaperoned. We were both dancing around our mutual attraction and, whilst I planned my next steps, I was more than content to act as a disinterested party.

It occurred to me that when Leonard returned, he could give me some advice. Not that he was in any way an expert in these matters, in recent years being too much like our reserved mother, and less the angry adolescent that I remembered when she'd disappeared. But now that he was of marriageable age, and Father had sent him off to court a possible engagement, I assumed he knew how these things were done. Although we'd never been close, surely that was part of his duty as an older brother – to school me in the ways of the world.

'Why are there both stepping stones and a bridge at this spot?' she asked, pointing to the smooth, flat stones that formed a pathway across the babbling brook.

I shrugged. 'The stones are ancient, but a bridge is more practical, I guess. You could hardly take livestock into town over the stones. The bridge was built in my grandfather's time. I have a vague memory of tossing a paper boat from it with my mother and chasing it downstream.'

'I never use the bridge,' she announced. 'It is far more romantic to find yourself standing in the middle of the brook, with the running water gushing and swirling at your feet. I simply adore the water. Perhaps I was a mermaid in a former life.'

As I arranged the pieces on the board, Jane crossed the stepping stones to pick a small posy of wildflowers from the far bank. She returned to place them in the basket and then settled opposite me for her lesson.

It was satisfying to me that my suspicions regarding her

intelligence should be correct, as she proved a fast learner. She was well educated – far better than someone of her position had any right to be – and I was hopeful that the mysterious details about her former life would come out eventually. I had to be patient.

Once we had covered how all the pieces moved, we managed a rudimentary game. I even elicited a shy smile at one point and my already elevated spirits soared higher than the treetops that towered above us.

'You must look through the family games and see what you might like to play next,' I said. 'We can sneak up the main stairs on our return, as I should very much like to show you my legacy. Daisy and the under housemaid are also off on a Wednesday. We won't be seen.'

'That would be lovely. I used to enjoy playing games with . . .' She stopped herself, instantly regretting her unguarded words.

'With whom?'

'It doesn't matter,' and she shook her head. What had she been about to tell me? I knew she was hiding things. A beautiful orphan girl showing up out of nowhere, who could read and write, with a lively brain and sunny disposition but a protective reserve that forbade me to get too close. And she was working as a kitchen maid for low pay and long days of physical labour. It was all wrong. Sometimes, it was as if she didn't understand how to behave in her position, like when she'd kissed my injured hand, or embraced me in the maze. It added to my conviction that she was running from something or someone, and that her background had not been in service.

'What is your story, Jane?' I asked, leaning back against the gnarly trunk of an aged oak, as she tidied away the board and set out the picnic. 'You don't talk of home and old Murray implies you turned up at Halesham Hall like the autumn leaves blown in by the wind.'

'There is no story. I lost my parents and needed work, so I came to Halesham seeking employment and someone in the town said the Hall was often looking for maids . . .'

'Yes,' I agreed. 'We get through staff rather quickly. My father has an unfortunate sense of humour and a quick temper. Our trick cupboards, uneven stairs and the disturbing murals would test the patience of even the most forbearing of women.' I didn't mention the unsolvable maze.

'He strikes me as a sad man,' she said, but avoided my gaze, realising she was speaking out of turn.

'Why do you say that?' I leaned forward to take a piece of cold chicken pie. I didn't think of Father as sad – angry and vindictive, perhaps.

'I see it behind his eyes. People aren't usually unkind without a reason. I think he carries great pain around with him.' She paused, her face crumpling into a delicate frown. 'Forgive me if it is inappropriate to ask, but did your mother pass away? No one speaks of her.'

'She left when I was six,' I volunteered, giving her the official version, although her total lack of contact over the years and the blood I'd seen on my father's hands that night often preyed on my mind.

Jane put her hand on my arm as I bit at my bottom lip, self-inflicting a physical pain to suppress the emotional one.

'Oh, Master Sidney, I'm so sorry.' Genuine concern saturated her face. 'No mother? And no sisters? Did you still have a nanny at that age?'

I shook my head. 'I had a governess, but Father replaced her with a tutor after Mother left. A tolerable man, if somewhat dull. My father has little time for women, believing them to be the root cause of all his woes.'

'Yes.' She looked down to her pale hands resting across her

lap. 'History often casts us as the villain. Consider poor Cleopatra, written into the annals of time as an evil seductress and responsible for the downfall of Egypt. Perhaps she was just doing her best to protect her country with the only methods open to her in a male-dominated world. Our voices are not heard. We do not get the chance to defend unjust accusations.'

Her cheeks flushed pink after delivering the longest speech I'd heard her make since our first meeting by the brook, when she'd been oblivious of who I was. Impassioned by her theme, she'd leaned towards me, but now fell back on to her heels and chose to look across the brook – studying the swirling waters as though they had the answers to whatever troubling thing was obviously on her mind.

I was impressed by both the arguments in her speech, and her courage to speak to me in such a bold manner. She might present herself as a meek little thing, but under the surface there was a bubble of passions, opinions and surprising historical knowledge – all bursting to escape. This kitchen girl had totally bewitched me and, as I stared at her pale face, my father's schooling came to mind. 'If you want victory, you must formulate a plan to achieve it. Never leave things to chance – for chance bestows equal favour on the undeserving.' And so I began to plan my next move.

If she wasn't completely in love with me already, she soon would be.

The scheme I eventually hit upon was linked to her gratitude the day I'd covered for her in the maze. With a small degree of preparation, everything was ready, although I had to wait a full week in order to be able to execute it.

Stealing a jar of lard from the kitchen, I'd been down to the brook before luncheon to smear each of the stepping stones. I suspected Jane would head out there on her afternoon off, especially as the weather was so pleasant, and the thin soles of her boots would offer no grip against the greasy surface. My plan was simple – she would slip and I would come to her rescue.

Once the stones were prepared, I concealed myself behind some trees, far enough away to make the whole thing look like a coincidence, but near enough so that I would be the first to arrive and earn her eternal gratitude.

I heard her approach before I saw her. She was humming to herself, as she often did – usually some rousing hymn I vaguely recognised. I watched her pass by and waited for her to turn left and head to the brook. It was important to establish that she'd taken the footpath, on the off-chance she had other plans, when I would need to ensure the stones were wiped clean to avoid anyone else from injuring themselves.

I crept further back, deeper into the woods, and listened out for a cry or a splash. After a moment, a piercing scream cut through the still air and I raced to rescue my damsel from her distress, knowing that any thoughts she might harbour of me being simply a boy would be quickly dispelled as I swept her up in my arms and carried her back to the Hall. Monty said all the mawkish romance books that his sister read had dashing heroes who saved the heroines from peril. My strength, my kindness and my timely appearance would all be in my favour.

But everything I had envisaged, all my carefully laid plans, were suddenly in jeopardy as I heard the pounding of horse's hooves and the concerned voice of a man. I'd been beaten to it. All my hopes began to dissolve, like the morning mist, with each thud of my booted foot on the soil. Someone else would lift her from the water. Someone else would hold her fragile body in their arms and look into her grateful eyes. And it was only as I stepped out from the trees that I realised that the someone would be Leonard.

Chapter 25

'Is everyone all right? I heard cries.'

I played the part of bewildered passer-by as my brother bent over Jane's wet body, having dragged her to safety. A small empty basket lay on the bank and a horse stood patiently nearby, his reins hanging loose, nibbling the lush grass below.

'Sidney! Thank God.' Leonard looked across at me as he lifted her up into his arms. 'Grab the reins, there's a good chap – don't want Star wandering off. This poor girl has slipped into the stream and damaged her ankle – perhaps even broken it.'

I felt a guilty twist in my stomach as I saw tears trickle down Jane's face at her obvious pain. I'd been rash and rather naive with my plan, because I'd never once considered that she might break a bone. It was much like when I'd been reprimanded by the headmaster for my thoughtlessness in selecting one of the smaller boys to move the heavy goal posts and the lad had broken a toe by dropping it on his foot. But this was all wrong. It was supposed to be me who cradled her limp body close to mine. I should be the one caring for her, comforting her, not Leonard.

'What the devil are you doing back?' I asked my brother, frozen to the spot as everything unravelled before me. 'Murray said you were returning tomorrow.'

'I'm a day early, but we can discuss that later. There are clearly more pressing matters,' he said pointedly, and then I saw him glance over my shoulder. 'Reins!' he shouted. 'Honestly, Sidney. You are useless in a crisis. Do as I instructed and fetch the damn horse, or it will wander off and then where will we be?'

It felt humiliating to be reprimanded in front of Jane, but I turned to grab the reins. Leonard was correct – the horse needed to be secured – and whilst I wanted to point out that the animal was his responsibility, I knew that he had dismounted in haste to help her, as anyone would have done.

'Can you help me get her on to Star?' he asked. 'I'll take her back to the Hall. Old Murray will know what to do.'

'It's just a sprained ankle and a bruised elbow,' Jane murmured, now beginning to shiver despite the summer temperatures and nurse her stomach, as though the shock of it all might make her sick.

'Let me do it?' I offered. 'I'm bigger and stronger than you.' Drawing attention to my size was a small victory in the situation, but one I fervently grabbed with both hands.

'Nonsense, I'm a far better rider.'

'Then let me carry her back. It isn't far. Being on horseback will jar the injury.'

'Sidney . . .' Leonard's tone irked me. 'Just do as you are asked, there's a good lad.'

I took the small compensation of holding a bedraggled Jane briefly as Leonard mounted the horse, inhaling the scent of her as I bent my head imperceptibly towards her hair, and holding her tighter than was strictly necessary. The warmth of her damp body travelled through me as I pressed every part of me as close to her as I dared.

'Pass her up, then,' Leonard said.

Between us we manhandled her on to the horse as she winced

in pain, and then I watched them ride off towards the Hall. I stood alone by the brook, the only sounds that of the chattering water and curious birds, feeling more furious with Leonard than I'd ever been in my entire life.

'I'm not best pleased that dinner has been delayed.' Father tapped at the table with his fingers and glanced at the ormolu clock that stood at the far end of the room. His increasing health issues hadn't done anything to soften his temper. 'When I ask for a meal to be served at eight, I expect it to happen. I feel like docking their pay. Women are so prone to idleness if not monitored.'

I was surprised that he'd wanted to join us for dinner, as he'd been eating most of his meals in his room recently. It had been quite the undertaking to get him down the stairs, and Burton had enlisted the help of the footmen.

'The kitchen maid had an unfortunate accident this afternoon,' Leonard said. 'And it's thrown everyone into chaos. I came across her when I was out riding and brought her home. Nasty sprain.'

One of the aforementioned footmen arrived with a tray of soup and placed a bowl in front of each of us, Burton mumbling apologies for the lateness of our meal.

'Damn foolish girl. And what the hell were you doing on the estate?' Father said, flicking out his linen napkin with shaky hands. 'Murray said you were back early and then no one knew where you'd gone. There are important matters to discuss regarding the company and I've been anxious to get things sorted before it is too late. I am running out of time. You should have informed me that you were home.'

Leonard and I glanced at each other across the wide table, and then both dipped our heads to focus on the bowls of steaming beef broth before us. Burton remained statue-like in the corner of the room, doubtless knowing more about my father's health issues than either of us. This was the second reference Father had made to what I could only assume was his impending demise. How interesting, I pondered, that I felt nothing on either occasion when I was presented with the knowledge that he would not be with us for much longer. Absolutely nothing.

'Your brother is aware of some details regarding my plans, but I need to speak with you both about what the future holds for the Hall and the company . . .'

He proceeded to address Leonard, who carefully rested his soup spoon on the edge of his bowl as our father told him about his bizarre legacy, stipulating that each clue, once solved, must be left as it was before, to give us both an equal chance of finding the key. Father always played to win, but he never cheated, a principle he had instilled in both of us.

'This is utterly ridiculous, sir,' Leonard said. He'd become increasingly agitated as the grand plan had been explained. 'You're pitting brother against brother, and attempting to overturn the established laws of the land. I'm the eldest. I should inherit. Indeed, I've spent the last few years working for you, fully expecting this to be the case.'

'But you have no real interest in the company, no passion for the games. You have shown no inclination to be involved in their design and development, nor have I seen any evidence that you even enjoy such pastimes. Granted, you perform your duties well enough, but I remain far from convinced you have the necessary enthusiasm, drive or ambition.'

I allowed myself a small smirk. By implication, Father was bestowing those qualities on me. Leonard noticed my expression and so my gaze dropped to my lap.

'If you wish to prove me wrong, Leonard, then I suggest you find the key . . .'

Father's words were followed by an unpleasant mucus-laden cough, his face turning almost puce. For one dreadful moment, I imagined he was about to pass away, right then and there, before our eyes. Leonard and I exchanged the briefest glance of alarm, but said nothing. We both knew better than to offer him assistance.

'And what happens if neither of us solve your ludicrous puzzle? What then?' Leonard said, after Father's coughing had subsided.

'As I told your brother, Dartington has covered all eventualities and made sure my wishes are backed up by the appropriate legalities. You can both remain in the house until such time as the puzzle is solved and then it is of course up to the new owner to decide who may stay under his roof. You will each be granted an income from the company – enough to live on and live well – and that will continue throughout your lives, should the puzzle not be solved. We are Bellinghams, a name that now commands great respect, and I do not wish our standing in society to be compromised. But all the papers that relate to company ownership, house deeds and access to my fortune are together in one place and only the person who locates them can step into my shoes.'

'Utterly ridiculous.' Leonard slammed his napkin down on the table and rose from his seat. 'You are seriously considering playing a stupid game to decide the future of your legacy? That you might even consider allowing a child to be head of the family when you have a twenty-five-year-old son waiting in the wings. My whole life has been in preparation for this – despite my preferences otherwise – and now you tell me we are to conduct some childish treasure hunt to determine the most serious of matters. I have suddenly lost my appetite.' And he rose from his chair and stormed out of the room.

'I'd be pleased to inherit the company, sir. I feel I have an aptitude for the business. I am academically capable, and have developed a shrewd business acumen, and through your tutoring, I have come to appreciate the beauty of games,' I said, toadying up to my father after my brother's outrage. 'Not only the aesthetic of the finished design, but the elegance of playing the game itself.'

If I had hoped my little speech might curry favour, or give me some advantage, I was mistaken. The same cold eyes met mine.

'Then beat your brother to the key and prove it,' he said, and leaned over his bowl to scoop a spoonful of soup to his mouth with his shaky hand.

Chapter 26

The following day, perhaps wisely allowing Leonard a brief cooling off period, my father presented us with the first two lines of his puzzle – framed and hanging on the library wall.

Step inside and play my game.
The next move is checkmate.

It took me moments to realise that 'step inside' referred to Halesham Hall itself, where you were immediately presented with a chessboard at your feet, but I did not allow my face to give anything away. To race there now would give my brother equal advantage, and I could tell by his disgruntled mutterings that the clue meant nothing to him. So I did what my father had always taught me – I played my hand slowly and carefully.

Perhaps my father had given me a head start, thinking I was at a disadvantage because of my years, or, more likely, had spotted my potential and had skewed the game slightly in my favour. He'd not spent hours with Leonard in the hallway, as he had with me, allowing me to think of that monochrome floor as the chessboard it represented. On the other hand, it was most unlike him to offer anyone concessions, and he tended to beat me ruthlessly at all our games, even when I was a young boy. To win by anything other than your own merits was a hollow victory, he'd drummed into me.

So it was later, when I was certain that Leonard was absent from the house, that I took myself to the entrance and investigated the words of the puzzle further. It was now blindingly obvious that the two busts of the pharaohs represented the kings in a game of chess, and it therefore followed that the white jardinière was the castle and the mounted cannonballs were pawns. These items had not been in the hallway when I'd been made to cross the board as a boy, but had been added in recent months, possibly because Father realised his time was up and the puzzle would soon be needed.

I stood back and assessed the layout. If the castle moved to the furthest rank, the black king was trapped behind his pawns. It was checkmate. There was nothing else for it other than to actually make the move, so I slid the jardinière towards the back. It was phenomenally heavy, but it glided across the polished floor relatively easily. The base was a soft material, offering no resistance – and clearly designed to be moved. Not sure what might happen, I certainly didn't expect the weight of the white castle to make the tile drop a good two inches. It was on springs and opened up a gap under the floor, which revealed a small wooden panel with the words *I, Andrea, am reformed to help you gather letters* written across it.

I had the next clue, but the answer didn't immediately present itself, so I returned the jardinière, making certain to leave everything as it was before and not to give Leonard any indication I'd been there.

All this time, Jane had been uppermost in my mind – not only was I concerned for her welfare after my thoughtless trick at the brook, but also, in solving the puzzle, I would have something to offer her. Should I inherit, I would be a man with prospects. Naturally, she would have doubts about our future, but if I were named heir, these obstacles would be surmountable. It was more imperative than ever that I beat Leonard in this game.

Murray had earlier reassured me that the damage to Jane's ankle was only a sprain. She'd prescribed a day of rest and elevation of the foot, but it was to be kept from Father, who had dismissed staff previously for having the insolence to be unwell. I still felt guilty for causing her injuries and so decided to pay her a visit, even though it was forbidden for men to enter the female servants' bedrooms.

I climbed the servants' back stairs that ran up to the attic rooms of the west wing and to the maids' quarters. (As was usual in larger houses, and with the sole aim of preventing any untoward intermingling of the sexes, the male servants slept in a small block near the stables, with the exception of Burton, who had a bedroom near the butler's pantry to safeguard the valuables.)

I was eager to share my news and beg her to be patient. Plus, Leonard's face as he lifted her on to his horse had been niggling me, and I was desperate to remind her that I was there for her, even though it hadn't been me who had carried her back to the Hall. Such rotten luck that he'd been on the scene and thwarted my plans. As I walked along the dimly lit corridor, I noticed how much colder it seemed in this part of the house, and how much creepier. If I thought my mural was disturbing, then it had nothing on the paintings along the walls leading to the staff bedrooms – twisted images of what might conceivably be an interpretation of Dante's journey through the nine circles of hell. I'd had no idea, as I'd lain awake with my back to the unsettling Medusa, that the girls in my father's employ were faced with such gruesome images. I could only assume they were designed to prevent maids from wandering the corridors late at night, when they should be tucked up in their beds. And, typical of my father, these images were painted directly on to the walls – rather than hanging pictures, which could be removed or covered. It all brought to mind the medieval doom paintings, designed to guide the God-fearing congregation away from their sinful lives. Perhaps he was hoping to scare his staff into doing the same.

As I reached Jane's room (Daisy, easily engaged in careless chit-chat, had told me it was the third room along), I bent down to peer under the unfeasibly low door lintel and was furious to find Leonard sitting on a small wooden kitchen chair at the foot of her bed. The door was left open, as propriety demanded, but his presence in this part of the house was not permitted. I failed to acknowledge that my behaviour was equally inappropriate.

Jane's face lit up when she saw me, and she shuffled herself into a more upright position. Her complexion was pale and it was obvious she was not well. Had she caught a chill from entering the icy stream? Again, I chastised myself for the rashness of my plan.

Leonard stood up abruptly, the legs of the chair scraping across the floorboards and catching the corner of the worn rag rug. It was a shabby and cramped space, the ceiling curving in as it tucked itself behind the eaves. An ancient chest of drawers, with patches of broken veneer and two missing knobs, was along the back wall, and a small table stood by her bed. I'd never thought about the staff outside of their serving us in our privileged lives. This sparse and unwelcoming room was where Jane came when her working day was over, and it was not a place that offered any cheer or comfort.

'What are you doing up here?' Leonard asked, looking decidedly guilty as I bent myself nearly double to enter the room.

'What are *you* doing up here?' I replied, my eyes boring into his as I straightened up, feeling like Gulliver in Lilliput.

'What are the pair of you doing up here?' came Mrs Murray's stern voice from behind. As usual, her silence and stealth enabled her to appear like a spirit – unsummoned and unwelcome. 'I do not allow menfolk in the maids' quarters, even if they are masters of the house. Kindly both leave the servants' garret *at once*,' and she gave us a stare that brooked no dissent.

'You shouldn't be fraternising with Jane. She's a kitchen maid,' I mumbled to Leonard as we walked back along the corridor.

'But an unusually beautiful and educated one.'

'Back off, Leonard. She's my friend. I won't have you appearing from nowhere and clomping your way into my life and my friendships.'

Leonard stopped and put both his palms up to face me, as if to calm me down.

'Steady there, little fella,' he said, somewhat ironically, as he tilted his head slightly to look up at me. 'No one is stopping you talking to the girl. I know you've been friendly with staff since you were a boy, and you jog along with old Murray better than most. Seek refuge with the servants, I don't blame you in this godforsaken house, and it's really no concern of mine, as long as you keep it from Father. I completely understand you get bored here over the holidays, with no one of your age to mix with. As for Jane, having stumbled across her in her moment of need, I was merely concerned about her recovery – as I would be with any member of the household who had suffered an injury.'

Unsatisfied with his defence, I followed him down the winding staircase. You don't leap hastily to your feet if you have nothing to hide, and I suspected that my brother was another Hylas, bewitched by my nymph. But he couldn't have her. I'd seen her first. She was mine. And I would do everything I could to keep it that way.

I began to tackle Father's puzzle in earnest and a couple of days later I realised the second clue was leading me to the maze.

It was the word 'reformed' that I kept coming back to, as I puzzled over its meaning. Was there an Andrea who had undergone some kind of reformation? There were very few famous Andreas – Andrew the Apostle was the first to spring to mind, and becoming a disciple of Christ was perhaps a reformation of sorts. Yet it was Paul who wrote letters in the Bible, not Andrew. Researching in Father's library, I also came across the renaissance architect, Andrea Palladio, and a fifteenth-century artist, Andrea Mantegna, but neither of them made sense with reference to the rest of the clue.

Only when I realised that *I, Andrea* was an anagram of Ariadne, did my Greek mythology come back to me – she was the woman who led Theseus safely from the Labyrinth after he'd slayed the Minotaur. Suddenly I had a connection with Halesham Hall – my father's dratted maze. I'd worked out how to get to the centre years ago – or rather, as close as I could, so gathering letters was as simple as locating the small plant labels as I followed the path out, with each letter spelling out two simple words: *Ascending bones.*

I had the next clue.

Chapter 27

I'd never been one for treasures as a boy. There was no small box of childhood mementoes under my bed – perhaps because my childhood held few happy memories that I wished to be reminded of. But within days of Jane arriving in my life, I'd begun to gather a small box of keepsakes, closely guarded and often looked through, which I secreted at the back of my wardrobe. It contained the abandoned handkerchief I'd pocketed in the maze, a clumsy attempt to press some of the flowers she'd gathered from the brook the day I had taught her how to play chess, a few strands of lost hair carefully wound around a square of cardboard, and an offcut of fabric from when she'd altered one of her dresses. I took out the handkerchief and brought it to my face, holding it there, inhaling softly, desperate to find some lingering trace of her scent. Occasionally, I slept with it under my pillows, returning it to the box as soon as I awoke, to avoid it being discovered by the housemaid.

I didn't believe in magic, often struggled with the existence of God or indeed anything of a metaphysical nature, and yet I was convinced that owning these articles would ultimately bind Jane to me. It was as if, by touching them, small particles of her would drift in my direction, and where they led, the whole of her would follow – like the first few grains of sand falling through the hourglass that heralded the way for the rest. I was so desperate for her to be mine that had I stumbled across a love incantation instructing me to drink the blood of a rat and chant mystical words, I would have hastened to the outbuildings and checked the traps.

Extraordinarily early one morning, I heard footsteps along the hallway outside my room. I rose from my bed and opened the door a crack, to see the back of my brother disappearing down the staircase. It was an ungodly hour to be up, unless you were staff, and so, brimming with curiosity, I followed him. He crossed the hall and out into the barely awake dawn of a cool late summer morning. The birds were at their most talkative, and the sun floated steadily up into the eastern sky, like a blazing hot air balloon.

He walked to the rear of the Hall and stood in the shadows, just as I had done on many an occasion, positioning himself at the correct angle to peer down into the kitchens as staff scurried about, preparing for the coming day. But it was the raven-haired kitchen maid, humming to herself as she kneaded the dough for the breakfast rolls, that had his full attention.

And I knew then, regardless of what he'd said to me in the garret, that Leonard had fallen for Jane, too.

Rage bubbled in me like a furiously boiling pot on the stove as I returned to my room and paced back and forth, my fists clenched and my teeth grinding. I cursed myself for trying to rush things with the stepping stones and inadvertently allowing them to meet. I might as well have placed her in his arms myself and said, 'Here, hold her, feel her, inhale her – isn't she glorious?' Yet I knew my feelings were reciprocated by Jane – the signs had been indisputable. She'd chosen to spend time with me, laughed at my jokes, studied my face, thrown her arms about me and kissed my hand. In the end, I decided the best thing I could do was confront her about the situation when she returned to her duties. Lay my cards on the table, tell her it was now a distinct possibility that I would inherit the Hall, and get her to admit that she returned my feelings. The time for her games had ended – I needed her to openly acknowledge the truth, and promise she would wait for me.

'I rather think Leonard has taken a shine to you,' I said to Jane, hoping for a shocked exclamation that she most certainly did not feel the same.

It had been several days before I could catch her alone. Due to her weak ankle, the scullery maid was feeding the chickens and collecting vegetables, and so Jane was not venturing outside. It was only by loitering below stairs that I saw her alone in the still room, grinding coffee beans one morning, and knowing that Murray was otherwise engaged, I seized my opportunity.

'I don't know what you're talking about, Master Sidney,' she said, but her flushed cheeks told a different story and not one I was expecting. Was she flattered by his attentions? Or was Father right about the machinations of the fairer sex? Had she hopes of being mistress of Halesham Hall and had transferred her affections accordingly? My stomach rolled at the thought.

It's hard to size up your competition when it's your brother. He was, unlike myself, legally allowed to take a wife. But I didn't think that was his game. Leonard didn't love her like I did. How could he? He barely knew her. She would be a plaything, a distraction, until he tired of her and settled down with someone like the Cross Ridge girl. And I didn't want her spoilt like that.

'You know that Leonard might not inherit? That our father is a huge advocate of ability and passion over birthright and entitlement?' My first thought was to make her realise how unsuitable my brother was.

She stopped turning the handle and looked at me.

'He has set us a challenge and whoever finds the key to the door at the top of the back staircase in the east wing gets the company, the Hall and the Bellingham wealth. He recognises I am a more suitable heir and is giving me the opportunity to prove it.' Her eyebrows rose at my bold statement, and yet still I blundered on. 'Leonard hates working for Father and I fear had he been born to reduced circumstances, he would have amounted to very little. No drive. No ambition. And certainly not a lover of puzzles. So I rather suspect it will be me who inherits the Hall, me who runs the company, me with the wealth.'

'I'm sure whoever inherits will do a good job,' she said diplomatically, emptying the wooden drawer and tipping the smoky, bitter-smelling coffee into a small pot. 'Leonard strikes me as a kind man, and you are a very bright boy, who will go far, I'm sure.' Still she fiddled with her machine as she reminded me of the remaining obstacle. My age. Before Leonard had returned, I'd been 'a fine young man – as strong as an ox'. Now he was here and she could draw comparisons, I was once again a child.

'I'm not a boy. Look at me. I said *look at me,* Jane.' I made her raise her eyes to meet mine as her hands dropped to her sides. 'You must see beyond my years and understand I have the body and mind of a man. Surely, being of a similar age, you understand how frustrating it is to be judged for that alone, rather than for your merits?'

'I'm nearly twenty, sir,' she said, as my plans took a further hit and my stomach ruckled up.

How could this be? Her slight frame and short stature had

led me to believe she was about sixteen, perhaps a little older. I knew Daisy had started working at the Hall at an exceptionally young age, only twelve, and so many of the young girls in service were indeed just that – girls.

'You look younger,' was all I could muster.

Why was everything against us? Our wildly different social positions, Leonard intruding on my schemes, and now issues with our respective ages?

'I appreciate that you're wary, that fate has played a cruel trick with our births, but the years between us are nothing. I know you feel it too. I'm just asking you to wait.'

'Wait for what?' Her face crumpled into a frown.

'For me. Until the law enables us to be together.'

'I'm not sure I'm following you, sir,' she said, her eyes scrunching in further confusion.

'Our love,' I said simply, because it was ultimately such a simple thing – love. It was absolute and all defining, and the complications were surmountable.

Her mouth parted slightly in surprise and I noticed her body tense. 'I am so sorry, but I think you have misunderstood. I am very fond of you, sir, but I don't love you. Not like that.'

'You do,' I replied, standing on firm ground and wondering why she would deny the truth. Perhaps more coquettish tricks on her part. 'You've kissed my hand, put your arms about me, chosen to spend time with me unchaperoned, and we have talked – really talked about things that matter.' I clenched my fists and took a measured breath to calm myself. Why was she toying with me in this way?

'Yes, like I would spend time with a friend. Like I have tended to the bruises and scrapes of the Sunday School children. Like I would care for a younger relative. It was, as you said, as if we were brother and sister. I was scared in the maze.

I didn't stop to think because I was so relieved to see somebody, imagining myself lost in there for ever.'

'I don't understand. All the time we spent together. It meant nothing.' My heart was thumping now and my hands felt clammy. Uncomfortable feelings swirled in my stomach. Had I got this all wrong?

Jane's face crumpled as if she was in pain, or perhaps to demonstrate that she could feel mine, and then she began to shake her head slowly from side to side. 'It meant a great deal, Master Sidney. I came to Halesham Hall knowing nobody, and you befriended me. Perhaps I didn't think through the implications of our friendship. You've misunderstood my actions, but it was you who insisted we were like brother and sister and, once having had a brother about your age, I transferred those affections to you.'

Concern and compassion lined her beautiful face, but I was having none of it. She put a cautious hand out to mine, but I snatched it away before she could touch me. I backed away, too angry even to comment on the news that her family was larger than she'd let me believe.

'You led me on,' I shouted. 'You made me fall in love with you.' I was trying not to succumb to tears but they were pricking at my eyes and there was a fury rising in my chest. The truth of everything was now laid before me. Each touch, each kiss, was a lie. She was as devious and cold-hearted as Father claimed her sex to be. 'I love you,' I reiterated, but it was a faint echo of my earlier bold statement.

There were footsteps in the corridor as Burton rushed past to answer a bell, and we both slunk into the shadows and lowered our voices.

'Oh, Sidney, you don't. Not really. You think it's love, but it's not. I've felt this way too, in the past, and it is a powerful and all-consuming emotion, but sometimes we fool ourselves, and only when real love comes along – unselfish and undemanding – do we look back and realise that it was a pale shadow of the real thing.'

'Don't speak to me as if I'm a child,' I said, calmer now and better in control of my emotions.

'No, Master Sidney, never that,' she said, so earnestly, I almost believed her.

'You don't know what's in my head. You can't tell me how I feel. I *do* love you, Jane, and will never feel this way about anyone again.'

'But I don't love you, Sidney.' It was said kindly, but nothing could take away the sting of those words. There was no balm to soothe the searing pain of her admission. 'I'm enormously fond of you and I'm sorry if you've misunderstood that affection.'

I saw it then, the truth of my father's words. She had her eye on Leonard – she was attracted by his position, his prospects and his wealth. It had been about the inheritance all along. Women were intrinsically the same. It wasn't my age per se, only that I was the second son. Had I been a year younger than him, she still wouldn't have looked twice at me. She wanted to become mistress of Halesham Hall and reap the benefits of such a position.

'No,' I said, feeling anger bubble inside. 'You're just confused.'

I lurched forward and tried to place my lips on hers – the thing I'd fantasised about doing since our first meeting. My attempt was clumsy and ill-conceived, but once she had connected with me in this way, once our bodies were close, she would know. She would understand. And she would stop lying to herself and to me.

I brought both hands up to cup her face and found her mouth

with mine, not quite certain of what I was doing, and trusting everything would come naturally, but instead of responding, her body went limp. My mouth pushed repeatedly against hers, looking for that connection, that reciprocating kiss, but nothing. I pulled back to see tears streaming down her face. And then, with a sudden pang of regret, I dropped my hands and stood still.

'He doesn't love you,' I said, confident now in my assumption. 'He's using you. But then perhaps you are using him too.' And I spun on my heels and walked out of the room.

Each step I took away from Jane, my anger grew, so that by the time I'd returned upstairs to the main body of the house, my body was practically convulsing. My world had collapsed and Leonard, waltzing back to the Hall unannounced, was to blame. I sought him out to exact my revenge, finally locating him in the library, at the end of the west wing. His back was to me as he ran his hands idly along the spines of various volumes. I studied him for a moment as I clenched and unclenched my fists, the building anger making my chest swell and my head lift.

And then, without a thought for the consequences, I ran at him, growling like a rabid dog.

'You absolute bastard,' I shouted, as I rugby-tackled him to the floor and swung at his face. Although smaller than me, he was nimble and he moved his head at the last minute so my fist met with the hard wooden floorboards. The shooting pain up my arm only increased my fury.

'What the hell is this about?' he shouted. 'Whatever it is, you can't solve it this way. Talk to me. Sidney – STOP!'

I came at him again, pulling back my arm but this time catching him square in the stomach as his head reared up in pain. He could bop his head around all he liked, but his torso was an immovable target as I straddled him and my weight prevented him from rolling over.

Visibly winded, his head fell back to the floor as he coughed. He managed to wriggle one arm free and grab my wrist.

'Sidney,' he shouted. 'For God's sake. I get it – you're stronger than me. Punch me all you like, but what we really need to do is talk. If you insist on giving me a good thrashing, at least let me know my crime.'

I sat back on my feet and dropped my hands. Leonard put his elbows to the floor and tried to pull himself from under me. I reluctantly rolled to the side and let him sit up.

He brought his knees to his chest and coughed some more, before putting his hand on my shoulder. I shrugged it away.

'Is this about Jane?' he asked. 'I know you like her.' He frowned. 'Do you have romantic feelings for her?' It was as if the thought had only just occurred to him, so I tried not to let him know I was rattled, as Father had always taught me.

'Don't be ridiculous. The bloody kitchen maid,' I spat out. 'I don't know what she told you, but she's delusional. I was having some fun at her expense. Stupid girl. Can't you see she's been daydreaming about ensnaring one of us and angling to become mistress of this place – playing us off against each other? As if I would have any serious affections for staff,' I scoffed. 'I hope you haven't been sucked in by her just because she has a pleasing face. You shouldn't be chasing around after an ignorant girl.'

'She is far from ignorant, Sidney, and you know that.' Always reasonable and in that moment, frustratingly calm.

His face was serious and I cast my eyes down.

'Perhaps not. But you've stomped all over my friendship with her and I'm furious that you are leading her on.' I needed to justify my punches somehow, without admitting the truth of my affection. Attacking him had been ill-thought-out. 'Besides, she's hiding something. She's turned up here out of nowhere and refuses to talk about her past. Don't trust her, Leonard. Don't be fooled by a pair of pretty eyes and her pathetic act of helplessness.'

'She's a kind person and an honest sort. You know these things. We've been so long without tenderness that we don't always recognise it. Perhaps you don't remember Mother like I do, but there is something about Jane that reminds me of her.'

I hated him for pointing out all the things I knew in my heart but refused to acknowledge in my despair. I kicked at the bottom of the fitted bookcase with my foot and curled my top lip.

'Do *you* have genuine feelings for her?' I asked. 'Because Father will never allow it. And it won't do you any good in the long term. You surely must be playing with her. Using her as a distraction until you're married off to some business contact of Father's.'

'I'm not that sort of man, Sidney, and you know it.'

'So what, then? You're in love with her? You're going to marry her?' I laughed a bitter laugh, amused at such a ridiculous notion.

'Yes,' he said, as my world imploded. 'If she'll have me.'

Chapter 28

1920

So many things suddenly made alarming sense to Phoebe, even though Daisy's unexpected information created nearly as many questions as it answered.

Her mother had fallen in love with Leonard Bellingham, oldest son and heir to the Bellingham Board Games fortune, and after a whirlwind romance, they'd married – partly because she was on the way. Her father's letter had explained this much, but he'd not mentioned that Sidney was caught up in this romance. Could it possibly explain the lifetime of animosity between the brothers? He'd got the girl and his little brother hadn't?

'Is that why my uncle hated my father so much?' she asked, beginning to understand.

Daisy shrugged. 'I just witnessed a moody and unpleasant Sidney transformed in the space of days into a helpful and polite young lad when he met your mother. She turned up at the Hall that summer and he doted on her, followed her around like a sheep, and believed himself to be in love.' She passed over a plate of scones and tried to ignore the whining child by her feet.

'Believed?' Phoebe questioned.

'He was only about fifteen or sixteen at the time, and Jane

was older, closer to my age, perhaps twenty. It would never have worked.'

Of course. Phoebe kept forgetting the huge difference in the brothers' ages. Over ten years, her father said, so that in many ways they'd both felt like only children during their childhoods.

'It was one of them schoolboy infatuations, and then when your father returned to the Hall after some trip up north, there was an accident out in the woods and Leonard was like a dashing Lancelot to her distressed Guinevere. He was even riding a horse when he stumbled across her, can you believe? And when someone has swept you so dramatically up in their arms and taken you to safety, you're all but obliged to fall in love with them. Wish my Harry had swept me into his arms, but the only lifting he does is a pint of mild at the Bell.'

Despite the older woman's smile, Phoebe recognised Daisy was living an unfulfilled life. She'd been in service until her marriage, and the following two decades had been dedicated to childbirth, the rearing of her offspring and meeting the various needs of her husband. Meanwhile Harry, by all accounts, had spent his life at the factory, shovelling fossilised animal waste, in a job that had few prospects and poor wages – when he wasn't sipping pints. It was easy to see why Douglas wanted to break free of this life, and she understood and admired his drive.

'They really loved each other, you know,' Daisy continued, hoicking the little girl up on to her knee and valiantly continuing the conversation, despite being poked in the face by a chubby and inquisitive hand. 'Happened in a flash and they barely took their eyes off each other. But then she was a real looker, your mother. Men were mesmerised wherever that girl went. She was incredibly beautiful.'

'Yes,' Phoebe agreed, a lump forming in her throat. Beautiful inside and out.

'As are you. In fact, you gave me quite a turn when I first saw you. You're the spit of her, with very little of your father about you. And I can't help but wonder if that's partly why Mr Bellingham is being so mean. It's like she's back in his life again, opening up old wounds.'

It hadn't occurred to Phoebe that her strong resemblance to her mother might be against her, but then she hadn't known about Sidney's unrequited adolescent infatuation. Was that why he'd registered such shock when he'd set eyes on her that first day? It had been brief, but she'd spotted it – a panicky flit of alarm and surprise had dashed across his face. Something similar had happened when he'd come across her working in the kitchens. She was a cruel reminder of the disappointments of his past.

'I felt sorry for him,' Daisy continued. 'But I was with my Harry by then and, having fallen in love myself so many times, I thought he'd get over it. I always did. Gossip from the Hall was Sidney lived quite a wild life after that, certainly up until the war, but then so many young men who made it through the conflict came back altered by the things they'd seen, and he was no exception.'

'But surely losing a girl to his brother couldn't have resulted in so much hate that they didn't speak for twenty years? Most people suffer romantic disappointments at some point in their lives and move on. There's more to all this, I feel certain of it.'

Having badgered her mother for such a long time to be up on her lap, the little girl was now restless to get down, and Daisy lifted her down to the floor and had a whole minute of blissful peace until her daughter began pulling at her boot laces.

'I was married that autumn because little Dougie was on the way,' she said, conspiratorially. 'So I don't know much more, except there was an awful fight when I thought they were going to kill each other, and then your mother all but eloped with

Leonard Bellingham. Mrs Murray was not best pleased to lose two maids within the month.'

Phoebe's mouth dropped open and she stared at Daisy. Surely the woman was confused? 'My mother was the daughter of a clergyman and grew up in a rectory. Her family died and she was left alone in the world.'

She stuck to the lie that her mother had told all these years, rather than exposing the pregnancy and admitting her mother had been cast out, but she felt uncomfortable that her parents had kept another truth from her. Details of her mother's life before her marriage had always been scant, and there had certainly been no mention of her employment at Halesham Hall as a low-paid, overworked domestic servant. What else had her parents kept from her?

Daisy registered the look on her visitor's face and paled. 'Did you not know? I'm so sorry, I just assumed . . .' The former housemaid put her hands to her lips, as if contemplating whether to continue.

Phoebe leaned forward. 'Please tell me what you know,' she begged. 'You can't hurt them now.'

'Your mother turned up out of the blue, July I think it was, desperate for work and more jumpy than a skittish foal. Murray took her on in the kitchens as we was desperate. Your father returned in the August and your grandfather went spare when he found out his oldest son was sweet on her and forbade him to marry below his station. Burton told us the master wrote him out of the will for bringing such shame on the family.'

'My grandfather disowned him?' Phoebe was confused. She'd believed all the blame had been Sidney's. Yet Daisy was saying his own father had cut him off. However, the dates of the former housemaid's tale proved her mother had been carrying her before she'd come to Halesham, making it unlikely that she would ever uncover the identity of her real father.

The fact that her parents had lied to her, or at the very least, concealed elements of the truth, sat uneasily. She'd forgiven them from hiding her paternity, but further deceits were tumbling out and made her wonder who she could trust. She'd come to Halesham Hall so certain that she was on the side of good, honest people, seeking retribution for the wrongs of the past, but perhaps there was more to this matter than she'd first considered? Despite herself, she was already experiencing pangs of sympathy for Sidney after his terrible childhood, and was beginning to understand that there were reasons for his volatile behaviour.

Daisy noticed Phoebe's pale face. 'Blimey, girl, I think you're gonna need something stiffer than tea.' And she walked to the sink, pulling back a pretty floral curtain and reaching for a bottle of gin, concealed behind a bucket of cloths and brushes.

Phoebe shook her head.

'I think I might, if it's all the same.' There was a popping sound, and then Daisy slugged back a mouthful before replacing the cork and then the bottle.

'All right, girls?' said Douglas, returning from the yard and popping his head around the doorframe to the small kitchen. 'Here's the milk you asked for, and she said not to be a stranger.' He planted a kiss on the top of his mother's head.

'Get them plates off the dresser for me, love,' she said, and Douglas took down three tea plates and set them on the table.

He pulled out one of the pine kitchen chairs and his hand accidentally brushed the back of Phoebe's neck as he took his seat. Or was it an accident? Her own hand went up to the soft patch that he'd touched and then she discreetly slid it back on to her lap as he lumped down next to her. He gave her the broadest grin, before shyly looking down at the table, his cheeks flushing an endearing pink. Daisy, perhaps aware the conversation was delicate, changed the subject and Phoebe determined to enjoy her afternoon and deal with this new information later, when she was alone and could think more clearly. She focused on her scones, not quite up to the standard of her mother's, or indeed her own, and sat back to spend an hour listening to Daisy put the world to rights as the exhausted woman wrestled with her increasingly overwrought infant.

'She likes you,' Douglas said, as they undertook the two-mile return journey.

In many ways, Phoebe had felt more at home in the cramped kitchen of Douglas's mother than she did at the Hall. There was a sense of family and belonging in that tiny house, however crowded it was and hard up they were. Daisy might be frustrated with her husband and her life, but Phoebe knew she loved her children and did her best.

'Wears her heart on her sleeve, my mum. Every emotion is written across her face like the headlines on a newspaper sandwich board. If she hadn't taken to you, believe me, you'd have barely got a grunt goodbye.'

She smiled. 'I liked her too.'

'Was she able to tell you any more about the Bellingham feud?' he asked. 'You were a bit on the quiet side.'

'Parts of it.' Her mind was still reeling from the knowledge that her mother had not only been loved by both Bellingham brothers, but had also been forced to leave her comfortable previous life to work at Halesham Hall. Her father's letter had talked of her being disowned by her family, but surely they hadn't been so cruel as to cast her out with nothing? Was that why she'd had to take the position of lowly kitchen maid? For her mother to perpetuate the lie that her own parents had died, there must have been no hope of a reconciliation. Her rector father clearly hadn't practised the Christian forgiveness he undoubtedly preached.

They entered the woods and Phoebe realised that dusk was fast approaching, as the light was sinking rapidly below the horizon. The sleepy sun cast the last of her deep orange beams between the black silhouettes of the thick trunks to their right. Her steps slowed as she picked her way through the treacherous undergrowth, hindered by the strips of dark shadow and her own tired legs. A trailing bramble, creeping its suckering shoots across the open path in search of light, snagged her skirts and tugged her backwards. Realising her predicament, Douglas knelt to unhook the offending prickles.

'Thank you,' she said, as the handsome young man knelt at her feet for the second time that day.

There had been a few lads starting to pay her particular attention back in Cambridgeshire, but her mother was insistent her daughter shouldn't be in a hurry to tie herself down – that the right one would come along and she would know. And Phoebe was fine with that, because the right one hadn't come along, and she'd been content to smile at the potential suitors, certain that her heart was safe for the moment. However, looking down at Douglas now, with his open face and sparkling eyes, she was beginning to understand what her mother had meant.

'Not at all. I'm sorry we left so late, but Mum can talk for England. We're losing the light now and I don't want you tripping and spraining an ankle. Mrs M wouldn't be best pleased to have her kitchen maid hobbling around and unable to carry out her duties properly, especially as she's barely mobile herself.'

Phoebe's tiny-heeled button-up boots weren't as sturdy as his brown leather hobnailed work boots, but then women's clothing was generally less practical, she reflected. Skirts were truly designed to hinder, rather than help. In the heat of a summer's day, the layers of material were almost unbearable, and in the cold and wet, they soaked up the snow and mud, so the heavy fabric clung around your ankles and weighed you down.

Douglas put out his hand to help her navigate a fallen tree. Despite spending the whole afternoon together, there had been sparse physical contact between the two, the brushing of her neck aside, so when his warm, strong hands encircled hers to hoist her over the trunk, she felt prickles of excitement travel up her arms. As the things she thought she knew about her life were starting to unravel, the realisation that here was someone who could anchor her down was enticing. In the dimming light, her eyes locked on his. She could make out their greyish blue from under the brim of his cap. Her heart beat a little faster and she boldly held his gaze a little longer.

Safely over the obstacle, their hands fell apart, but now that the connection had been made, it was as if neither could bear to separate entirely from the other. They walked much closer together, her arm bumping into his on several occasions as it swung gently by his side. The conversation dried up because Phoebe simply couldn't think of anything to say and, as they walked, her thumb traced those areas of skin that had come into contact with his.

She swallowed hard. Her mother would have been horrified that she should be out in the woods with a young man at this time of day, unchaperoned, but times were changing. The war had empowered women and, although in many ways life had reverted back to the old order of things when the men returned, there was a sense, certainly amongst the educated ladies she knew, that a precedent had been set. Even Lloyd George had recognised the invaluable contribution of the fairer sex when the menfolk had been called to foreign fields to fight for their country, and had rewarded a select few with the vote. Twenty years ago, being alone with a man like this might be considered scandalous, but women of her generation were bolder, and the world was a little less judgemental. Besides, her virtue was safe with Douglas.

'How long are you going to play your uncle's silly game and work in his kitchens? It's not right. You should be a guest at that house, not a paid drudge.' He broke the silence.

'It suits me for the time being,' was all she could muster.

Douglas paused his steps and rubbed at his chin. 'Yes, I suppose it's currently your only option. At least you're in his household, and after a while he will come to realise what we all know – you are a kind person, caught up in a quarrel not of your making. You deserve to be eating with him in the dining room, wearing fine dresses and real jet necklaces. I'm sure he'll eventually accept that you are family.'

Phoebe didn't respond. She didn't want those things – she wanted only to bring the Bellingham empire down for what Sidney had done to her father. At least, that had been her plan when she first arrived. Things were muddier now . . .

The pair emerged from the shadows and out into the open fields that led up to the Hall. They paused at the stile, which Phoebe was more than capable of negotiating herself, but Douglas put out his hand for hers and she grasped it with all the desperation of a drowning woman and stepped down on to the dusty path.

They set their faces to the Hall, now bathed in the last of the golden light, and strode towards home. This time, however, neither of them let go.

Chapter 29

Entering the courtyard, Phoebe and Douglas were greeted by Mrs Murray climbing the steps from the kitchen. Their hands immediately dropped apart, like guilty lovers.

'Ah, there you are, Phoebe. Mr Bellingham is asking for you. He'd like you to join him in the drawing room for the evening.'

'But it's only half past six and I don't have to be back on duty until nine. It's my afternoon off.'

'Aye, well, he never was one for putting the needs, or indeed the liberties, of others above his own.'

Despite being initially indignant at Sidney's request, Phoebe realised this was a small victory. The only way she could get to the truth of the past was to make him believe her motives were pure, that all she wanted was simple friendship and to connect with family. In reality, she had a puzzle to solve and an inheritance to claim, and needed all the help she could get.

Douglas gave her an encouraging smile. For those last few hundred yards, with his large hand wrapped around hers, she'd pondered what might happen when they reached the Hall. Would he suggest they sat quietly together somewhere, away from prying eyes? Might he even kiss her? Now these fancies were moot. Sidney was demanding her company. They were both in his employ and as he paid the piper, he called the tune.

'Go,' Douglas encouraged, his eyes crinkling as he gave her a soft smile. 'You need to build these bridges. It's important.'

She followed Mrs Murray inside and unpinned her hat, carefully poking her coral pin back into the straw so as not to lose it, and hung it on a coat hook. As she walked up the stairs, she heard music coming from the drawing room, so followed the sound and entered.

In the corner of the room stood a cherrywood Edison phonograph – she'd noticed it before and been curious. Her parents had not been able to afford such luxuries, but she'd seen them in magazines, and the vicar had a small Edison Standard. This machine was larger, encased in a slim cabinet with an attractive fretwork pattern cut into the front and a handle protruding from the right side to wind it up. A shiny black disc was spinning on the turntable and lively music echoed around her – a chirpy, clear melody on the piano with the competing sounds of brass and wind, providing a series of squeaks and scales, which somehow worked, even though it had no right to.

'I like this music. What is it?' she asked Sidney. He didn't stand for her, she noticed.

'Jazz.' He was reclining in a deep-red velvet armchair, swirling a brandy around his glass, cupping it in his palm as the stem rested between two fingers, but never once taking a sip. Even though she was across the room, she could smell the heady spiciness of the drink. 'It's all the rage in the city.' He studied her face. 'I find it hard to believe you've never heard jazz music before. You really have led quite the sheltered life, haven't you?'

'Not particularly.' Phoebe felt defensive. 'Just because my world was small doesn't mean it was sheltered. But then perhaps it is usual for girls of my age to be married.'

'Exactly how old are you?' He frowned.

'Twenty-one next year.'

He rubbed at his whiskers. 'Ah, that makes sense, although I'd assumed you were younger. You do rather present as unworldly and vulnerable, but then your parents were never going to hang around before procreating.'

'I'm not unworldly.'

'Have you even been to London?' he asked.

She shook her head.

'Have you never ventured to your local assembly rooms and danced the Castle Walk to ragtime? A young gentleman leading you around the room?'

'No.' She stared at her feet.

'Then you most certainly have not been to a night club and attempted the Argentine tango with a total stranger – now there's a dance to scandalise and an opportunity to hold a woman closer than one ought in public.'

For a moment her thoughts flitted to Sidney holding some exotic woman close to his body and her cheeks flushed. She shook the unsettling image from her mind.

'And yet, you don't strike me as the sort of man to dance,' she rallied, feeling emboldened by the knowledge that he had no right to speak to her in this way. 'It is a sociable activity, engaged in by those who enjoy the company of others.'

Sidney finally got to his feet and gestured for her to sit. 'Oh, I did all manner of things before the war that you wouldn't believe,' he replied, with a wicked but humourless grin, slumping back into his chair and finally taking a gulp of his brandy. Perhaps swallowing the drink made the memories more palatable. 'Things that would make your pretty face blush, and of which you most definitely would not approve. Carnal knowledge of another that should not exist outside marriage – now *that's* what I call a sociable activity.'

She studied him briefly as he spoke. He had a maverick look

about the eyes, despite his formal attire, and in anyone more pleasant, it would have made him quite dashing, because they were his defining feature. They locked on to hers, undoubtedly with severe disapproval, and almost physically pinned her down. A hazel-syrupy brown that matched his dark colouring. It was easy to understand how he'd ensnared so many women in his youth. He was, she reluctantly admitted to herself, strangely attractive.

She stared back at her boots, feeling shocked and uncomfortable. Everything he said seemed designed to embarrass or hurt. She wasn't so naive that she didn't realise these things went on – her own mother being an example. But subjects such as these shouldn't be discussed openly, and certainly not by a man who believed the woman before him to be his niece.

'I hope I can assume that you have always behaved properly with young men of your acquaintance.' His eyes narrowed.

'Of course. How dare you suggest otherwise.' She was angry now and had left her manners out in the courtyard when he'd summoned her to him on her afternoon off. These were not appropriate questions, regardless of their true relationship, and to even suggest she might not have done so was insulting.

He leaned forward and focused intently on her face. 'And yet I understand you waltzed off to Halesham with Douglas this afternoon. The pair of you alone together in the dark woods where anything could have happened.'

Ah, now she understood where he was coming from and why she'd been summoned. He'd heard about her outing and was determined to blacken even that innocent relationship.

'Don't be ridiculous. I have no friends or acquaintances in the area and it was a kind gesture to introduce me to his *family*,' she said pointedly. 'It was all perfectly respectable. I had afternoon tea with his mother.'

'Ah, yes, young Daisy. Only not so young now, I suspect. An intriguing woman who was rather given to drama, as I recall. But we digress.' He sat up straight for the first time and his expression darkened. 'You do realise Douglas is sniffing around you like a tomcat? He has something of a reputation with the ladies and, despite my lack of affection towards you, I feel as your only living relative a sense of duty to point this out.'

'Douglas is my friend. There was absolutely no impropriety in his behaviour towards me whatsoever.' He was being unkind again and she was certain his accusation had no grounding. It was an attack on something she held dear, an attempt to make her question her beliefs and decisions. Besides, it had taken Douglas all afternoon to pluck up the courage just to hold her hand.

'Oh, you naive and gullible fool. He is an attractive young man with healthy appetites and even I can recognise that you are a pretty enough little thing. Quite a coup for a working-class lad, to secure the hand of a Bellingham. Perhaps he is hoping to marry into money, although I'm not sure how that will sit with his socialist values . . . but then everyone has a price.'

Phoebe swallowed hard, said nothing and instead distracted herself by looking about the room. There was no point protesting Douglas's innocence when Sidney's mind was so clearly made up, though it was somewhat premature of him to be thinking that one outing might lead to marriage. Silence descended as the phonograph stopped playing.

'So, how are you getting on with my father's puzzle?' Perhaps he felt he had made his point as he moved the conversation on.

'I've not had a lot of time to focus on it, to be honest.' She couldn't help but feel she was missing something obvious. If the clue suggested the next move was checkmate, there had to be a game set up somewhere, or even something more abstract, like a painting of a game in progress, but she'd not come across either.

Sidney smiled, placing the flats of his hands together as if in prayer and letting the tips of his fingers rest on his lips. Something was clearly amusing him.

'Do you play chess?' he asked. 'Because I fear you won't solve it if you don't.'

'Yes, do you?'

He couldn't prevent one of his eyebrows bopping up in surprise. Whether it was because she played chess, or because she'd had the audacity to question whether he did, she wasn't sure.

'Naturally. I'm a gentleman with a thorough education, and my family fortune and working days revolve around board games. You've had a slightly more . . . provincial upbringing. I imagine your leisure time was spent picking turnips and herding sheep.'

It was on the tip of her tongue to say that she could only assume his leisure time revolved around ringing bells for staff to help prepare him for some mind-numbing activity embraced by the elite, such as the hunting down and tearing apart of an innocent fox, where the right sort of clothing was paramount, drink flowed freely and no one actually cared whether the fox lived or died, as long as business deals were struck and loveless marriages arranged. Instead, she bit back her comments and tried to look demure.

'I'm certain my standard of play will not match yours, but I would happily give you a game, should you wish?' Damn the man for reeling her in, but perhaps he would let out something related to the puzzle, and she hoped his vanity and male ego might be enough for him to accept. He would, after all, be certain to win, and in her experience people who knew their victory was a given were far more likely to undertake a challenge.

His brow wrinkled as he contemplated her offer.

'Excellent idea. Fetch the set from the corner cabinet,' he ordered as he dragged the large circular tilt-top table that stood to the right of his chair in front of him.

She returned with the set and a wooden chessboard, and between them they began to lay the thirty-two pieces out. They were rather unusual and slightly sinister – each one had a face, except for the pawns, which resembled tombstones.

'Ivory and rosewood. My father had it commissioned,' he said as he set down the last queen.

Phoebe walked over to collect a chair and he reached into his breast pocket to take out a cigar.

'Do you mind?' he asked.

She shrugged. 'It's your house.'

'Hmm . . .' he pondered. 'Technically not, but let's not concern ourselves with irrelevant details.'

It was interesting to her that he openly acknowledged this. She knew the truth, but wasn't expecting him to admit it.

She sat down as Sidney spun the board so that she was white.

'You shall make the first move and I shall be black – perhaps a reflection of the colour of our souls?' he joked, and lit the cigar, inhaling deeply and pausing before slowly exhaling the smoke into the space between them. Phoebe was fascinated as the vapour curled around his head before the long swirls petered out into nothingness. 'Besides, I feel you should have the advantage, since in all other areas of your life you are at a distinct disadvantage to me.'

And yet, Phoebe thought, her heart suddenly and unexpectedly heavy for the damaged man in front of her, I had a childhood surrounded by loving parents.

The game began in earnest and the conversation largely dried up. There were long pauses as he contemplated his moves, and Phoebe found her mind wandering.

'Do I bore you?' Sidney asked when the game was well underway, noticing her dreamy expression. 'You appear to be off with the faeries. Perhaps preferable to being stuck here with me?'

'Not at all. But there is nothing wrong with indulging yourself with quiet moments of reflection, or indeed ridiculous fantasy.'

Her reply was met with a snort. 'If you are dreaming about that garden hand, I've told you, forget it. I won't allow any such nonsense.'

'No, just the faeries, Uncle.'

He raised his eyebrow again as if to say touché.

Finally, he made his move, and it was a clever one, so she leaned forward and tried to focus. She wasn't a proficient player, not possessing the sort of brain that lent itself to the necessary deviousness or ability to plan several moves ahead, but she knew how the pieces moved and had often played an enjoyable enough game with her parents, and occasionally the retired postmaster from their village.

'My mother taught me to play,' she volunteered, testing the water by mentioning the woman Daisy claimed had been the reason for the Bellingham brothers' feud, and still reeling from this revelation.

'Did she, indeed?' He looked thoughtful for a moment. 'Leonard never was into games, even when he was working for Father. Your mother, however, was quick-witted and enjoyed learning new things.'

'You knew my mother, then?' she ventured, wondering whether he'd admit to his affections for his former maid and confirm Daisy's story.

Sidney took a thoughtful puff of his cigar and exhaled with equal deliberation. 'She scrubbed our kitchen floors in the summer of 1899 and my brother took a fancy to her, but our father did not approve and forbade the relationship. And so they ran off to marry. I can't say she made any lasting impression on me. Staff rarely do.'

What lies, she thought, but said nothing. He'd just admitted he knew her well enough to know she played chess. But his words backed up the assertion that her mother had been a lowly domestic servant. Yet again, she questioned why her parents had never talked of any of this to her. She would have understood.

She slid a pawn forward, simply because she couldn't think of a more impressive move, fully aware that she played a defensive game – the postmaster had told her so.

Sidney studied her face for a while and then moved his knight. She saw at once that it threatened both her bishop and her queen, so she moved her queen to safety and sacrificed the bishop.

'I think you're going to win,' she conceded, shrugging her shoulders.

'Of course I am, because you don't want it enough. You aren't hungry for victory. And you play an alarmingly unsophisticated game.' He sat back in the chair and picked up his brandy, swirling it around again and bringing it to his nose to inhale the aroma. 'I can read you like a picture book, and a particularly elementary one at that. Your game is transparent and amateur. I see every thought cross your face, every hesitation, each surprised look. I know what move you'll make even before you know it yourself.'

He gave a wry smile and picked up his queen with a flourish, placing her directly in front of Phoebe's king, who was trapped behind a row of his own men and had no escape route. She realised she could not take his queen without moving into check.

'Checkmate,' he said.

She peered at the offending monarch, smiled, and then reached her hand across the board.

'Well played, Uncle.'

'And now you congratulate me without a hint of sarcasm?' He shook his head. 'Generally, I find those who are content to lose rarely have the drive to win.'

'Whereas I find that those who lose graciously learn from their mistakes and are better people for it. I, for example, shall be wary of a knight fork in future and ensure my king is not boxed in. My game has improved and I thoroughly enjoyed the experience – for that I thank you.'

He raised an eyebrow and then gulped back the remaining liquor in his glass. 'What else do you play?'

'Despite the delicate family politics, I am fond of several of Bellingham's more popular games. I particularly enjoy *A Grand Day Out* – racing around the map of England in a motor car, visiting landmarks and collecting points. There was a sleuthing game of yours that the vicar's wife owned, and Mother and I often played *Treasures of the Tomb*. And cards, of course.'

'Poker?' he asked, but she shook her head. 'Yes, it is rather new to this country. Draw poker is quite popular in America and I'm trying my damnedest to get it picked up over here, but the British are terribly snobbish about it. The skill involved really separates the men from the boys. I shall teach you.'

Not 'Would you like to learn?', Phoebe noticed.

'I'm also currently developing a wider range of wooden picture puzzles for adults. They are strangely addictive and I think there may be a potential market amongst the lonely spinsters of this world, stuck at home, poor of mobility and with little to occupy their minds. You can give me a female insight and help me select the designs.' Yet again, it wasn't a request, but an order.

Phoebe sighed inwardly and glanced at the mantel clock. 'You really must excuse me now.' She began to place all the chess pieces back in their wooden box. 'I have an early start.' And she collected up the last pawn and swung the tiny brass hook on the front of the box into its eye. She walked over to the cupboard and when her back was to the room, he spoke, yet again, in that authoritative tone that brooked no discussion.

'You are to spend your evenings with me from now on, unless I am otherwise engaged, and begin to reduce your duties in the kitchen. Murray will advertise for a replacement.'

Although this was a small victory and a sign Sidney was warming to her as she'd hoped, it was the third demand he'd made of her in quick succession. She was beginning to dislike his superior tone and assumption that everyone was merely on the earth to satisfy his whims. How satisfying it would be should she solve the puzzle and claim the house. Perhaps, she thought fleetingly, she could offer him the position as butler and watch him scurry up and down the uneven stairs to answer her bell. But then her true nature won out.

'I appreciate I am in your employ, Uncle, and you are entitled to make such a request, but you do have a rather unfortunate manner. The occasional please and thank you wouldn't go amiss, particularly in your dealings with staff. After all, everyone likes to feel appreciated.'

She gave him one of her genuine smiles, worried she'd said too much. Perhaps she'd overstepped the mark, but she was neither used to employing staff, nor being employed in such a capacity. However, he frowned and made no response, as if he was seriously considering her words.

Although it was satisfying that he was starting to think of her more like family, she realised that she enjoyed her job and was reluctant to relinquish it. The work was hard but the people below stairs were fun to be around, and being treated as family rather than staff would give her fewer opportunities to come into contact with Douglas.

'Whilst it is lovely to be invited to spend time with you, the truth is, I'm happy working here. Being busy takes my mind off the loss of my parents and I have always enjoyed baking. Your staff are friendly and make me feel like family.' He could take that last remark whichever way he chose.

'But I *need* company in the evenings.'

Astounded by his selfishness and sense of entitlement, she stared at him in utter disbelief. It was like listening to a spoilt child.

'Besides,' he continued, 'you are, unfortunately, a Bellingham and I do not wish for the tittle-tattle regarding your position within the household to reach my associates. It was a fun diversion for a while, but it no longer amuses me. You'll stay at the house as a guest whilst I decide what to do with you,' he paused, '. . . if you would be so kind. Which will have the added advantage of removing you from Douglas's machinations. Making a play for a kitchen maid is one thing, but even he must know that a garden hand aspiring to court the niece of his employer is quite another.' He paused again. 'It's always the damn garden hands . . .'

His last remark implied Douglas was not the first gardener to cause him trouble, but she made no further comment. Instead, she walked over to Sidney a final time and collected the board to return it to the cupboard. Slipping it under the box of pieces, she focused on the grid of eight alternating black and white squares and the pretty border of scrolls and leaves, rather than Sidney's unkind and determined efforts to interfere with what she was certain was her burgeoning romance with Douglas.

And then her heart thudded with excitement, for she was certain she'd just solved the first part of Clement Bellingham's puzzle.

Chapter 30

'The entrance hall is a chessboard,' Phoebe announced, closing the cupboard door and spinning round to face Sidney.

'And . . . ?' he prompted, placing his glass down and leaning forward with interest, which only confirmed her suspicions. Her mind raced.

'And there are two pharaohs – one black, one white – standing in the hall. They must be the kings,' she said. 'The Valley of the Kings is probably the most famous archaeological site of the last hundred years, so that means . . .' There were a couple of other items in the hall, but she couldn't remember them clearly and so, mid-sentence, she dashed out into the corridor, towards the front of the house. Sidney followed behind.

'This is the white castle.' She stood in the middle of the chessboard floor and pointed to the jardinière, with its crenellated top. 'And these are black pawns.' She pointed to the mounted cannonballs. How had she not seen it before?

After a quick assessment, she heaved the jardinière into a checkmate position, without any offer of help from Sidney, who observed from the bottom of the staircase, and was rewarded with the next clue.

'*I, Andrea, am reformed to help you gather letters*,' she muttered under her breath. Although she had no idea how many clues there were in this mad chase to the end, solving the first one was a massive boost to her confidence. The clue itself needed further reflection, but she was one step closer to her goal.

She turned to Sidney and smiled. For a moment he glanced over to her with something resembling pride, almost returning the smile with his dark eyes, and reminding her of looks from her parents when she'd won a prize at school or come first with a cake at the village fete. But as quickly as it lit up his shadowed face, it disappeared.

'Then the game is afoot,' he said, and he spun on his heels and strode down the corridor without so much as a goodnight.

After lengthy discussions the following day, Phoebe and Sidney reached a compromise regarding her future employment. Mrs Murray would advertise *again* for a maid and Phoebe would continue with her role in the meantime, especially as Sidney had a large dinner party for a handful of important business contacts organised for early October. When, or rather if, a suitable girl could be found, Phoebe would become a guest at the Hall, but would still be permitted to help in the kitchens, as long as she was discreet. She enjoyed it – besides, she would be terribly bored rattling around with nothing to do. He finally accepted she had a point.

'And it's your wee niece who's been making all those fancy cakes and bakes you've been so impressed by,' Mrs Murray chipped in. 'I've noticed that you've been rather partial to them of late, so don't you be cutting off your nose to spite your whiskered face.'

Sidney looked thoughtful. 'Yes, she proved her worth with the afternoon tea. Baking was never your strong point, Murray.

So . . . she's trying to win me over through my stomach?' He turned to Phoebe. 'I hope you haven't been adding anything untoward in these sweet treats of yours? Slowly poisoning your wicked uncle with cyanide in the almond fingers?'

Ah, so he knew his behaviour was reprehensible, then.

'Only a sprinkling of magic from my friends, the fairies,' she teased. 'Something to make you more pleasant.' Mrs Murray nearly choked on her own tongue.

The eyes narrowed for the umpteenth time, but on this occasion they were accompanied by the flicker of a smile. He really couldn't fight it, she thought with satisfaction. Despite himself, more joy was creeping into his life and she was the cause. There was a small heave of guilt as she reminded herself that her friendship towards him was fake and dripping with ulterior motives.

'You are forbidden to mention your current position in the household to any of my guests,' he said, returning to their initial topic of conversation – the imminent entertaining.

'I'm hardly likely to find myself talking to any of them, and I highly doubt they will wander down to the kitchens.' Although she would relish the challenge of preparing more ornate dishes with Mrs Murray, she wanted nothing to do with the stuffy businessmen, and planned to keep herself tucked away for the duration of the party. But Sidney had other ideas.

'Perhaps I have not made myself clear – you will be attending the dinner. Several gentlemen will be bringing their wives and so a female Bellingham would be a bonus. Sadly, I can't keep you hidden in the scullery for ever. I may be an utter bastard . . .' – Mrs Murray blanched visibly at his unsavoury language, '. . . but I don't need to advertise it. You will attend and I shall introduce my niece to my friends and acquaintances.'

Suddenly she felt *utterly* provincial. The occasional

Sunday lunch with school governors and benefactors, and her parents inviting the vicar over for tea, was the sum of her formal entertaining experience. The thought of preparing fancy dishes excited her. The thought of conversing with fancy people did not.

A fortnight of frenetic and focused activity went by. Invitations were sent out in Mrs Murray's best copperplate hand, the requisite food was ordered, delivered and stored. Phoebe was rushed off her feet with extra jobs from the housekeeper as she became increasingly involved in the preparations, and Douglas was only ever at the Hall at the end of the working day. The demands of the season kept him extremely busy on the estate and they only saw each other at mealtimes. She had her suspicions that Mrs Murray was deliberately sending her on errands as soon as he appeared, and it was now Betsy's job to collect the vegetables.

That was the problem with domestic service – you were never permitted to be alone with members of the opposite sex, and barely had time to nod a hello, never mind hold a conversation. You might snatch a few words across the pews of a Sunday, but even that was frowned upon. All deliberately orchestrated, of course, and it added to her romantic frustrations. In her idle moments, her thoughts returned to Douglas's strong hand clasped around hers on their walk back from Halesham, and several times Mrs Murray caught her staring into space as she imagined what a future with this open-faced young man might hold.

When the day of the dinner finally arrived, Phoebe worked non-stop, preparing sauces, filleting fish and setting delicate arrangements of exotic fruits in aspic. Mrs Murray was impressed. Knowing the housekeeper had never been given the opportunity to train as a cook, Phoebe took the time to show her how the presentation of the dishes could make a considerable difference and give them a professional edge.

'Ooo, aren't we la-di-da?' Ada said as she passed through the kitchen, lugging her heavy housemaid's box brimming with dusters, brushes and polishes. She'd been sent into the dining room to prepare it for the evening's entertaining, and eyed the tray of fancies ready for the oven and the intricate sugar flowers Phoebe was making.

The maid had been even more unfriendly since learning of Phoebe's imminent elevated status to family member, *and* that she would be helping in the kitchen at dinner that evening to cover for the absence of the young Miss Bellingham. Mrs Murray had been forced to hire a young woman from the town as an extra pair of hands for the day, as she still hadn't found a suitable replacement for Phoebe and the household remained woefully understaffed.

'Would you like me to show you how to make these flowers? They're ever so easy.' Phoebe was making tiny daisies of gum paste to place on top of the lemon fancies and she could see Ada's glances from across the room.

The housemaid paused and her curiosity won out. 'Maybe.' So Phoebe beckoned her over and stepped to the side. 'Quickly, though. I've got to start laying the dining table now the room has been thoroughly cleaned.'

Ada was a fast learner. At one point she almost smiled when she was complimented on her delicate petals. But Phoebe's mind was restless and unfocused, and she was relieved when Ada returned to her duties. She hadn't seen Douglas all day, but every task she undertook was linked in some tenuous way to him in her mind. The floor she was scrubbing, his feet had walked across. The potatoes she peeled, he had planted and nurtured during the preceding months. The cup she washed, his lips had touched.

At lunchtime, she hid her disappointment when Betsy was asked to take a small parcel of cheese sandwiches and an apple over to him. Both he and the head gardener had been out since dawn, tidying the driveway in preparation for the arrival of the guests, dead-heading and weeding, clipping and sweeping. Her gaze returned periodically to the wall clock above the window as she counted the hours until he joined them all. The staff were eating early so everyone could focus on the entertaining and, although Phoebe wouldn't be eating until later with the guests, she planned to stay until the last possible moment, helping with the preparations.

In the dining room, the Georgian mahogany table had been unwound and the two footmen hired for the evening had carried extra leaves from the storage room to enable the table to comfortably seat fourteen. Phoebe was sent to deliver the recently polished cutlery to Ada. The housemaid explained, as she carefully positioned numerous hand-etched glasses on the highly polished surface just so, that tablecloths were no longer the thing, much to everyone's relief, as candle wax, red wine and greasy gravy were the very worst stains to remove. Between them, it took fully half an hour to set out the complicated arrangement of cutlery. They were joined by the housekeeper, doing her best to decorate the bases of six large candelabra with the bright orange crocosmia and Chinese lanterns selected from the garden.

At five o'clock, by which time they were satisfied that they were largely on top of things, the servants' tea was served. Douglas bounded into the kitchen with his usual cheery hello and an armful of further greenery that he'd been asked to collect. He looked exhausted but still had that endearing twinkle about his eyes. Phoebe jumped up from the table and offered to take the sprigs of ivy and eucalyptus, following him into the passageway and discreetly inhaling the bewilderingly intoxicating sweat of a man who had done an honest day's work. She was rewarded by one of his cheeky winks, but both seemingly remained wary of any open displays of affection. Their shy holding of hands had been a prelude to something that neither had defined yet. He hadn't asked her to be his sweetheart or made any further overtures. There had been no conversation about that afternoon, other than the fictional ones she'd repeatedly played in her head the last few nights – awake and restless in the early hours, tracing her own hand over the curves of her body in the airless room, quilt flung to her feet, and trying to imagine how it might feel if the hand was his.

How had she gone so quickly from a relative indifference to men, to this desperate longing and all-consuming obsession for Douglas? Was she desperately trying to fill the void in her heart left by the death of her parents? Or was it simply that she'd finally met the right man? He *was* the one, of this she was certain. Her body told her so every time she saw him, thought of him, or even simply breathed.

'I hear you're to be an honoured guest at the dinner tonight,' he said. 'You're finally getting somewhere with that irascible uncle of yours. I'm so proud of you.'

She blushed under his gaze.

'My mother has been asking after you,' he continued, resting the greenery on a small pine table in the dark passage. 'She wondered if you'd like to go for tea again sometime?'

'I'd love to,' she gushed. 'I had such a wonderful afternoon.'

'So did I. And the best bit was the walk home.' He lifted her hand and squeezed it as a reminder of the simple holding of hands that had thrilled her so. How could something so commonplace suddenly be so incredibly intimate? She'd held the hands of schoolchildren often enough when helping her father, leading them in from their play, or marching to the church with them for worship. Why did her body react as if he'd run his lips across her neck, or traced his rough fingers down her body?

He leaned forward and studied her lips. She felt a lump rise in her throat as she tried to swallow. Bending towards him, she rose up on her toes. He was about to kiss her, of that she was certain, and she'd never wanted anything more in her whole life.

Ada bustled into the passageway and barked at Phoebe to stop dallying, shattering the moment.

'Take that foliage through to the entrance hall,' she snapped and then turned to Douglas. 'We need to have words . . .'

And as Phoebe scuttled down the corridor, she wondered what exactly those words might be.

Chapter 31

Sidney had requested that Phoebe join him in the drawing room half an hour before the guests arrived, so she finished up in the kitchens and went upstairs to change. A simple dress of pale blue silk that her mother had made for her to wear to a church fete the previous year was laid out on the bed – the only thing vaguely suitable in her wardrobe. The material clung to her body as she slid it over her head and, although the cut was dated and it lacked adornment, the colour suited her. Anything too dark made her pale skin look positively anaemic.

She studied her reflection, spinning and bobbing before her in the long cheval mirror. (Mrs Murray had kindly lent Phoebe hers, as the mirror in the blue room was next to useless with its twisted glass.) It was interesting how a piece of clothing could transform you both inside and out. Phoebe felt like a woman for the first time since arriving at Halesham Hall as the silk swirled around her ankles and fluttered at her collarbone, and she longed for Douglas to see her like this. Modern cotton print dresses and aprons didn't lend themselves to sensuality or femininity, or have the figure-enhancing nipped-in waists of the pre-war styles. Women increasingly resembled sticks, straight up and straight down, with a generous bust now viewed as unfashionable. Was it possible her boyish figure might now be to her advantage?

She fastened her mother's slender string of pearls around her neck, sprayed a mist of lavender across her exposed skin, and took a fortifying breath before heading downstairs.

Disappointingly, Douglas was nowhere to be seen as she popped her head into the bustling kitchen, nearly twisting her ankle on those damn uneven stairs on the way down. How bad would it look if she attended the evening hobbling about?

'An absolute picture,' Mrs Murray said through a cloud of steam as Ada crashed and banged about in the background. Betsy poked her head through from the scullery and sighed a wistful and admiring sigh.

'Aww, you look like a leading lady,' she said. 'A real Lillian Gish.'

'He ain't here, if that's what you were hoping for, and we ain't got time to watch you parading around,' Ada muttered as she rushed past Phoebe, her jibe obviously referring to Douglas's absence.

Phoebe smiled graciously, tipped her chin up and mounted the stairs, determined not to react to Ada. She completely understood the housemaid's resentment and conceded that appearing in the kitchens had been thoughtless on her part.

She lingered briefly in the doorway to the drawing room before entering and was amused to witness Sidney bending over and ruffling Satan's ears. The dog looked up at his master adoringly and she watched the stern-faced man's lips break into a small smile before he bobbed his head to plant a kiss on the black wet nose of his companion. She coughed as she entered and he spun round, pausing for a moment to look at her, and for the first time in their acquaintance, appeared genuinely lost for words.

'You look so like your mother,' he finally managed. 'She was very beautiful, if somewhat lacking your rather alarming propensity to speak your mind. For a moment, I thought it was her. Ah, the ghosts of the past pick cruel moments to reveal themselves.' He sighed and gestured for her to take a seat. 'It struck me tonight that the one thing Halesham Hall has sorely missed these past thirty years is a female Bellingham to head up the household.'

Yes, she'd noticed the distinct lack of a feminine touch about the place. Mrs Murray did her best, occasionally arranging a tall vase of flowers in the front entrance hall, or ordering new furnishings through necessity, but she wasn't a feminine woman. She always wore black and favoured very little ornament. The enamel thistle brooch that had been her mother's, and a plain silver ladies' pocket watch to help her keep an eye on tardy servants, were her only accessories.

Sidney frowned as she walked past to sit down, and leaned towards her.

'Lavender?' he asked, as he sniffed at the air between them. She nodded, unable to tell from his expression whether this was a good thing or not.

He offered her a drink, but she declined, and then he wound up the phonograph again. Music filled the air as he paced in front of the fireplace for a few moments, clearly at a loss for conversation, and then finally cleared his throat.

'I shall take the arm of Colonel Deben's wife and lead everyone into dinner. You will take her husband's arm and enter last. Try to limit your conversation to banalities so as not to embarrass either me or yourself, and at the end of the meal, I will give you the nod to rise and bring the ladies back into the drawing room, so we may talk politics and smoke.'

It was all terribly behind the times and rather a slur on the female intellect, she thought, as if they were not to have political opinions. Yet he accused her of being dated. Back at

Stepping Stones, everyone had remained at the table after formal meals, and lively discussion was encouraged for all – not just the men. But then she knew her parents were different. Her mother was passionate about equal education for girls and had been an active member of the suffrage movement before the war. Her father, perhaps somewhat frustrated by the domestic situations of those he taught, had shown considerable interest in the relatively new Labour Party. Phoebe suspected Sidney would reach for a stiff brandy if she announced her father had voted for Lloyd George in 1918. She could see now that the parting of the ways had been inevitable for brothers Leonard and Sidney – with or without the added complication of affairs of the heart.

'I'll do my best, but it is not the company I am used to keeping. I've lived a far simpler life.' She knew that amongst the guests that evening there were local politicians, industry moguls and financiers. Not the sort of people to pop by the local schoolmaster's cottage for tea and cake – however fancy the schoolmaster's daughter's baking may be.

'Tell me about your home,' he said, raising an eyebrow. 'I should like to picture Leonard in his life. I've often wondered what exactly it was that he gave up Halesham Hall for.'

'But he didn't give it up, did he?' She tipped her head to one side. 'He lost his inheritance in a game and you threw him out.'

Sidney swirled the contents of the small glass he'd picked up from a side table. 'That's what he told you, is it?' He didn't wait for her to respond. 'That his evil younger brother cast him aside? I can't argue with a dead man, nor would I want to, for out of respect, I do not wish to undermine your father in your eyes, but the decision to separate himself from this family and move away was very much his.'

Again, there was that feeling that her parents hadn't told her the complete truth. Even though Sidney would inevitably be biased in his retelling of past events, and his manner was always abrupt, she believed him to be honest. After all, he had nothing to prove to her – no reason to lie. She backtracked and answered his earlier question.

'We lived in a modest thatched cottage provided by the school,' she said. 'It was by a stream, which Mother always said was the nicest part of the whole house, and she renamed the cottage Stepping Stones. She loved the water . . .'

'Yes . . . I remember.' Again he forgot his pretence not to have known her mother well. Phoebe didn't comment.

'We grew much of our own food, as you do here, only we didn't have staff, just a woman who came in daily to help with the laundry and housework.'

'Your father had no manservant? *He dressed himself?*' Sidney was unable to hide his shock. 'What a come-down for him, to go from the life of a gentleman, where every need was answered by the pull of a bell, to living in a tiny cottage like a farm hand.'

He was taking obvious glee in over-simplifying what she said, but that was his issue, not hers, and her face continued to shine with joy as she talked of her parents.

'I remember how much he enjoyed physical tasks, like digging over the garden or polishing his boots until they shone like fresh conkers, and he was always proud of mending things. Mother used to laugh and say, "Oh, Lenny, a blind man could have done a better job," but he insisted practicality was more important than beauty. Have you never buffed a pair of your own shoes and inhaled the glorious, waxy smell of boot polish?' she enquired.

'No, why on earth would I?'

'To feel the satisfaction of a job well done, and to look down and know that the gleaming pair of boots upon your feet was achieved by your own hand,' she replied.

Sanderson entered and dipped his head towards his master. 'The first guests have arrived,' he announced, and Phoebe sucked in a slow breath as her heartbeat thudded in her chest.

There was a marked difference between buffing glasses, painstakingly arranging cutlery and folding napkins into complicated roses, and arriving at the unparalleled spectacle of a fully laid table, illuminated by the shimmering golden light of half a dozen flickering candelabras, being seated by a footman, and finding yourself surrounded by impeccably mannered guests in all their finery. Phoebe was certain that she appreciated the display far more than anyone else present because she knew the hours, if not days, of preparation involved in organising such an occasion. She noticed a couple of the ladies cast their discerning eyes over the flower arrangements, possibly to reassure themselves that anything adorning their own dinner tables was far superior, and then the carousel of courses began. They started with mock turtle soup, accompanied by a fine sherry, and Phoebe felt a touch of empathy for the pale-faced girl sitting diagonally across from her, who also looked out of her depth as she stood in for her recently deceased mother. It was going to be a long night.

The soup course was followed by fish, then the entrée of mutton cutlets and sweetbreads, and then the remove, Mrs Murray's speciality – roast suckling pig with her spicy pease pudding. This proliferation of courses was somewhat old-fashioned, but Halesham Hall seemed behind the times in many regards. The quantity and the richness of the food had almost defeated Phoebe by the time the pork arrived on the table. She battled on, however, determined not to let Sidney down.

Phoebe had managed thus far to largely smile and nod, ask polite but neutral questions, and give simple answers when quizzed about herself, but she felt unnecessarily scrutinised. She noticed the critical gazes of some of the ladies pass over her dated dress, the admiring glances of the men (who didn't pay much attention to what she wore, as she was pretty enough to distract them from her wardrobe), and even Sidney seemed to be studying her to an unusual degree.

'Excellent claret, Bellingham,' a stout man said from across the table, raising his glass in the direction of the host when they reached the game course – pheasant in this instance.

'I'm lucky to have inherited a fairly decent cellar from my father. This is a ninety-three Château Margaux, but the war has played havoc with French wine – both the import and the production.'

'Absolutely. The destruction of the vineyards in the Champagne regions was a particular tragedy,' someone further down said. 'Damn shame. I do so love a bottle of Bolly – and, against the odds, the fourteen turned out to be a splendid vintage.'

Phoebe remained silent. She knew little about wines. Her mother had made a pleasant elderflower, and occasionally a blackberry, but village schoolmasters did not lay down extensive wine cellars, or lament the unavailability of continental luxuries.

Recalling her earlier conversation in the drawing room, she thought about what her father had lost by leaving Halesham Hall, regardless of whether he'd been thrown out or had chosen to walk away. It had been his birthright to host occasions such as this and command the wine cellar.

Sidney was toying absent-mindedly with his food as he tried to look interested in the endless chatter of the pinch-faced woman to his right, and she remembered why the trappings of wealth had never bothered Leonard Bellingham. Despite his riches, Sidney was miserable. True happiness was not a good French wine, but being on the receiving end of unrelenting and selfless love. Sidney had never found that and she pitied him, for all his fine clarets, and again questioned her plan. What was the point of revenge when she knew in her heart that her father wouldn't have been happy at the Hall? Did she really hate Sidney that much? She studied him; handsome and commanding respect from all around the table. An unexpected shiver rippled up her spine and she felt cross at herself for subconsciously acknowledging his attractiveness.

The plates were once again swiftly and efficiently removed, and the next course was served by the almost invisible footmen.

'I say, this brûlée is superb. Did old Murray throw this together? She's certainly upped her game,' the gentleman across from her said.

'No, I—' Phoebe began, before Sidney cut in.

'Hasn't she just?' he said, and Phoebe withered under his stare, realising her error. She swallowed hard.

'So, you're old Lenny's daughter,' said Colonel Deben, leaning towards her and raising a monocle to his left eye, reminding Phoebe of the now sadly deceased Chamberlain. 'I heard he'd had his head turned by a pretty girl and was tricked into marrying below his station, but I can see she passed her beauty down to you. Quite a scandal though – a scullery maid or some such.' Even though he was addressing her directly, this bumptious man clearly had no respect for her feelings. 'Bellingham said the pair of them drowned. Rotten luck. Still, the wages of sin and all that . . .'

Phoebe gripped the handle of her spoon so tightly her knuckles went white, staring at the man, unable to believe such cruel words had come from his mouth.

'And what part of my father marrying my mother was sinful?' she asked, trying to keep a smile on her face, furious he should consider that her father had been tricked into the union. His letter had made it quite clear that the decision had been his – not that this ghastly man knew the truth of the situation.

'Now, now, my dear. Don't look so cross. We all know there is only one reason to marry in haste, particularly when the marriage is beneath you.'

The accuracy of his words stung, but there was a love behind it that this man would never understand. There was no doubting that her parents would have married regardless.

'I'm certain they were neither the first nor the last to engage in such activities out of wedlock, but I can assure you theirs was a love match. If they married in haste then it was only because they couldn't contain their love.' She allowed her spoon to clatter into her bowl, not even caring should it dent the fine French-polished surface. 'How many of you around the table can own to taking responsibility for the women you have been with outside of the marriage bed? The hypocrisy of the elite makes me sick to my stomach.'

Her words tumbled out, perhaps helped on their way by the excellent claret. She offered a challenging stare to each of the men present, and a disturbing silence followed as her words hit the air with more volume than she'd intended.

'Oh, come, gentlemen,' she pressed, determined to defend her parents and try to open the male guests' eyes to the flaws in their reasoning. 'If the wages of sin truly are death, then how many of you here tonight are imminently expecting a knock on the door from the grim reaper himself? Shall we lay an extra place for him, so that he might join us for the dessert before collecting his dues?'

There was a titter from the pale-faced girl, and a building

chorus of coughs and mumbles from the more baritone and bass timbres in the room.

'Excuse the amusing outspoken exuberance of my niece.' Sidney spoke up from his end of the table. 'I fear she is not used to the drink. Perhaps it would be a convenient moment for the ladies to retire? Burton, fetch the brandy.'

And as she swept past Sidney, leading a trail of shocked women to the drawing room, she noticed that, in his anger, he could not even bring himself to look at her.

Chapter 32

It was nearly midnight and the guests had left. Phoebe changed out of her silk gown and back into the simple print dress and apron she wore in the kitchens. Within minutes of the last motor car pulling off the drive, she'd joined Ada and Betsy, who were busy dealing with the acres of dirty pots and pans. It wasn't strictly Ada's job, but everyone was pitching in. Phoebe hadn't appreciated before quite how like a family the servants of these larger houses were. The way they'd all pulled together for the dinner party, and the pride each and every one of them had in the finished result, was a joy to witness.

'What are *you* doing down here? Has Cinderella finished at the ball?' asked Ada, hands on hips, and she paused her frantic scrubbing of the copper skillet, the smell of vinegar hanging in the air.

'I'm here to help. I didn't ask to be included in the ridiculous dinner. I'd much rather have been down here with you.'

Being a part of the entertaining that evening had only proved what she knew in her heart to be true. She didn't want to be a part of this world. What was she doing trying to solve the puzzle? Her father wasn't alive to benefit and she certainly had no desire to swan around this ghastly house, barking orders at servants and filling her days with pointless pastimes.

'You can't marry him, you know, if that's your game. The Bible says so.' Ada turned back to the butler sink and picked up the next dirty pan.

'Whatever do you mean?' asked Phoebe, confused.

'Mr Bellingham. He's your uncle.'

In her irritation, she nearly told Ada that Sidney Bellingham was not blood and she could damn well marry him if she chose. How the housemaid's sour face would have paled. But out of respect for her mother, she didn't react.

'To be honest, the dinner party was a thoroughly unpleasant experience. It was full of stuffy men with outdated opinions, and I'm afraid I rather embarrassed myself. Uncle Sidney was most unhappy with me. The food was lovely though. And everyone commented on how beautiful the table looked. You did wonders.' She couldn't help smiling at Ada, who almost smiled in return. 'I feel awful that you've all been slaving away down here, while I've been sitting at an elegant dining table, having my meal served to me by footmen – of all things.' She giggled. 'I've never been served by a footman before. Here. Pass me that cloth and I'll dry those pans.'

But Ada and the young girl were standing on a duckboard to keep their feet off the scullery floor, which was awash with water, and there wasn't much room for a third.

'If you really want to be helpful, put some milk on for cocoa. We're parched,' Ada said, her posture slightly less aggressive now.

Phoebe returned to the kitchen as Mrs Murray appeared. The housekeeper was carrying a tray of bone-china dinnerware through to the butler's pantry, where all items of value had to be counted out and back in again at every formal function, and all breakages accounted for. Sanderson had sharpened his pencils that afternoon in anticipation.

'You looked every inch the hostess in that beautiful blue silk. I don't mind telling you, there was a moment there when I felt a lump rise in my throat – thinking back to those early days when the newly wed Mrs Bellingham hosted some of her first dinner parties. I hope you did your uncle proud,' the older woman said.

'Far from it, I'm afraid,' and she relayed how her tongue had run away with her when she'd felt her parents had been attacked. 'I'm fully expecting to be banished from the Hall in the morning. Again.'

Mrs Murray put the tray down on the refectory table with a little too much force and the delicate coffee cups rattled alarmingly.

'Why is it that those who think themselves above us in life also think themselves above the judgement of the Lord? The only reason anyone was cross in that room was because they knew you had a point. "He that is without sin among you, let him cast the first stone at her." Your father was a good man. Any haste over their marriage was purely to do with his desire to escape Halesham Hall, I can assure you of that.'

She scooped up the tray, but as she headed for the butler's pantry, she left the young Miss Bellingham with a disturbing piece of information.

'This house has a dark past and I'll tell you this for nothing, lassie – the whole sorry situation got so violent at the end between Leonard and Sidney, one of them had to leave, that's for sure, or I swear they'd have killed each other.'

Daisy had told her much the same thing, but Phoebe was still horrified that the brothers had hated each other so much that they'd had murderous intentions, regardless of whether the feud was over the inheritance or her mother. Her mind reeling, she unhooked a small copper pan from the pot rack and measured out milk from a large white jug, before setting it on the range, and standing in the dimly lit kitchen alone with her thoughts.

There was the sound of footsteps, followed by a series of bumps, and then a loud curse. Phoebe poked her head around the corner to see Sidney on his backside at the bottom of the stairs.

'Bloody steps,' he groaned, and Phoebe couldn't help but smile at the grumpy and somewhat crumpled heap of man at her feet. There was the steady clip of claws and heavy panting, as Satan followed down the steps and then sat, looking adoringly up at his master.

She put out her hand to offer assistance and, to her surprise, he grasped it, heaving himself upwards. His hands were softer than Douglas's and there was a strange sensation of warmth flooding up her arm as they made contact.

'Yes,' Phoebe reiterated, 'stupid, impractical, unkind steps,' and she gave him a hard stare as their hands dropped apart. She was fairly certain he was in the kitchens either to tear her off a strip or two, or to demand she leave the Hall. Probably both. In that order. She'd disgraced herself already so had nothing left to lose by speaking her mind.

'What are you doing down here, Phoebe?' he asked, a frown creasing his perennially morose expression as he followed her back into the kitchen. So, he hadn't come down for her, after all.

'More to the point, what brings you to the kitchens, sir?' asked Mrs Murray, reappearing from the shadows with the now empty tray and bustling back into the room. 'Have the staff overlooked something or do you require a nightcap? Some cocoa to take upstairs, perhaps?'

'Not at all. These are my kitchens and I will visit them if I choose. I actually came down to congratulate you all on a *largely* splendid evening.' He looked at his niece as he emphasised the almost-perfect nature of the event.

Two surprised heads poked out from the scullery and Mrs Murray raised an unconvinced eyebrow, but Phoebe realised he was taking her previous comments on board. Manners cost nothing.

'Thank you, sir. I'm sure we all appreciate you taking the time to visit us and impart those kind words.' The housekeeper's face remained wary, as though she was expecting her master to follow this up with a sting. 'Back to work, girls,' she said to Ada and Betsy, perhaps worried the unexpected praise might go to their heads and prevent them from finishing the pans.

'Give everyone an extra couple of shillings for tonight. They've earned it.'

'Very good, sir.' Mrs Murray nodded. 'If you'll excuse me, I have things to see to,' and she continued on her way.

'Well, young lady.' He turned to Phoebe. 'What an outrageous display of ill manners.'

Her eyes fell to the floor. 'And you're here to dismiss me for being so rude to your guest,' she surmised. 'I apologise for embarrassing you, but do not apologise for defending my parents. Father did not marry below his station. She was the well-educated daughter of a rector,' Phoebe said, 'and they loved each other. I knew nothing about her employment here as a kitchen maid until recently.'

Sidney stared beyond her, his eyes not focusing on anything in particular, but instead giving her the impression that he was looking inward. 'The truth of her background does not come as a surprise. I had long since suspected she was not born into the servant class. She told me her family were dead. That she was alone in the world. Her reduced circumstances forcing her to find employment.'

Phoebe stuck her chin into the air and faced him with fortitude, much as she had done when he'd threatened to set Satan on her, but, as ever, his expression was totally unreadable. 'Regardless of the truth of her past, it was not the Colonel's place to belittle them or cast aspersions about the reasons for their marriage. Dismiss me if you must, but I will always defend those I love.'

'How wonderful it must be to have someone stand by you, fight your corner – even after you have passed on.' He looked fleetingly mournful. 'But the fact remains, I was extremely embarrassed by your behaviour tonight. Do you not think there are occasions when I have suffered unjust slurs against my own character and been forced to stomach them for the sake of propriety? Besides, when you have as much money and influence as most of my guests this evening, you can say what you damn well please, as those who disagree run the risk of losing your patronage.'

'I'm sorry if I have affected your business interests in any way. That was never my intention.' Perhaps she'd been rash to leap to her parents' defence. Did it really matter what some pompous old man thought of them? She knew the truth. Leonard had been more than honourable to take on another man's child without a second thought and never once judged her mother for her situation.

'I continue to make allowances for you, Phoebe, because this is not your world and these are not your people, but you have to meet me halfway. Your provincial behaviour and dated clothes, your strange compulsion to voice the things you believe, and your blind faith that being good and honest will be enough to combat the evil in this world, sadly mean that you will struggle to fit in here.'

'Equally, I make allowances for you . . .' she looked him straight in the eye, determined to say what was on her mind now, whatever the outcome, 'because you had a childhood devoid of love. The world is a horrible place where unjust things happen, and it has made you detached and cold. Being loved, and giving love in return, makes it bearable. If remaining here means I have to compromise the things I hold dear, then perhaps it is better that I leave. Isn't that what you came down to do anyway? Dismiss me?'

Sidney rubbed his chin and let out a long, slow breath. 'I am not as eager as I once was to see you gone from the Hall. Perhaps I was also hasty to behave towards Leonard as I did all those years ago. My quick temper has been my downfall on many an occasion, and so I will take a more considered approach this time. You were terribly ill mannered, Phoebe, but then so was the Colonel. Besides, he was more relaxed about the incident after his third brandy. Told me you had pluck.'

Phoebe wasn't sure whether to be relieved that her behaviour had been excused, or furious that her outburst was clearly being patronised. To be called plucky was a way of belittling her further, as if women having opinions was not only unusual, but also incredibly brave.

'Perhaps you might refrain from such silly tantrums in the future, but I don't wish to dwell on tonight. I was wrong to hire you as staff but I would very much like you to remain at the Hall. Forgive me. You are the only family I have left in the world.' It was a heartfelt apology.

He wasn't the man she'd thought he was when she marched up the long driveway all those weeks ago, determined to expel him. Her view of Sidney had been coloured by her father's prejudices and the Bellingham stubbornness they had both inherited. There were so many secrets and untruths echoing around the empty corridors that she could no longer bear to be part of the lies. If she was to stay, there was something that the man standing before her had to know.

'Family is important,' she agreed, 'but even those who don't share your blood can share your heart and help fill those gaps left by the loss or absence of others.' She was thinking of Leonard at that moment, knowing that she could not have loved him more, even if he'd been her real father.

They paused their conversation as Sanderson limped into the room, silently replaced something in the dresser and returned to his pantry. When he was no longer in sight, Phoebe lowered her voice and leaned towards Sidney. 'Could we step outside for a moment? I must tell you something in confidence.' What she had to say was not for the ears of staff.

He frowned. 'Of course. I feel a headache coming on, and some air might do me good.' He opened the kitchen door for her, following directly behind as she climbed the steps. Satan, who had been lying across the knotted rug in front of the range, jumped up and trailed behind them both, tail wagging.

There was something about being outside in the dark, the moonlight kissing the edges of everything around them and the breeze gently caressing her skin, heightening all her senses and making her acutely aware of every nuance in her environment. She stopped and turned as Sidney halted in front of her, becoming equally and uncomfortably aware of him, his scent, his height, his concerned eyes burrowing into hers.

Phoebe took a deep breath. It was time for the truth of her paternity to come out.

'After my father died, I found out that he wasn't my father.' She was phrasing this badly, but it was so complicated and it was such difficult news to deliver. 'My mother was already carrying me when she arrived at the Hall and Leonard took us both on, bringing me up and loving me as his own from the start. I'm not family. And you aren't my uncle,' she said.

Sidney stared at her, his mouth dropping slightly open, and he reached for the top on the iron railing by the steps. For the following moments, he didn't move or respond. Whatever he'd expected her to say, it obviously wasn't that. In order to fill the silence, she continued.

'I was born in the February after they met and even you must know the dates are wrong. I have no right to be here, or to try to solve the puzzle. I came because I wanted revenge for the past – for the things that happened to Leonard – but I see now that life isn't as simple as good and bad. It is shades of everything in between.'

Phoebe studied his eyes more closely. There was real emotion behind them – hurt, confusion and bewilderment – and he looked vulnerable for the first and only time since she'd known him. Something inside her fluttered, and she had the strongest compulsion to reach out and stroke his cheek, although she managed to resist.

'You lied to me,' he said.

'By omission, yes. And you lied to me. You were in love with my mother, and that was the real reason you fell out with Leonard.'

A beat.

'Ah, he told you.'

'No, my parents never mentioned it. Daisy—'

'Of course,' he interrupted, rubbing his hand across his chin. 'Yes, I believed myself in love with your mother and Leonard took her from me. It hurt me badly at the time but the truth is that she was never really mine in the first place. Ah, the adolescent heart is a wild and untameable beast that will not listen to reason or logic.'

He looked lost in thought and for several moments the courtyard was eerily silent as he massaged his temples with his fingers. Finally, he spoke.

'So now we both have the truth laid before us and must decide what to do with it. But I'm afraid there are echoes of the past and implications for the future that I am too weary and full of drink to deal with at this moment. It has been one hell of a day. Please excuse me.'

He shook his head, before spinning on his heels and climbing down the steps into the bowels of the house, as Satan padded down faithfully behind him.

Chapter 33

1899

My father's rapidly deteriorating health meant the clock was against me and this urgency spurred me on. It was imperative to solve the puzzle whilst my father was still alive to witness my victory. I'd spent a lifetime trying to prove I was good enough for him and this was my final chance to do exactly that.

However, I couldn't imagine where bones, referred to in the clue, might go upwards. My first thought was graves, and how a person's soul might ascend to heaven, briefly considering our small parish church, but it was not part of Halesham Hall and we had no chapel on the grounds. It was noticing our head gardener, a wiry man in his fifties whose wild greying beard was practically a garden in itself, wheeling his wooden barrow past the drawing room window, that I recalled with fondness our games of dominoes . . . or 'bones' as he always referred to them. I knew that early dominoes had been made from animal bones, and Father had embraced this aspect of their evolution when Bellingham Games produced a somewhat disturbing set of dominoes with a skull on the back of each tile and tiny inlaid bones of ivory representing the pips. The popularity of the adventure novel *Treasure Island* and the ongoing fascination with the legend of Blackbeard convinced Father these would sell well. He was correct as usual – always on top of popular trends and fashions – as boys across the nation loved nothing more than the thrill of a swashbuckling tale.

I deduced, therefore, that *ascending bones* must refer to the domino-decorated staircase in the east wing, and after much head-scratching and a few frustrated kicks, I worked out that the hexagonal balustrades were on spindles and could be rotated so that, starting from the bottom step, I was able to match up the dominoes as I ascended. With a satisfying click, the last one turned and the oak handrail lifted a few inches to reveal another clue burnt into the wood.

A Chappe's revolutionary idea for the fleet leads you to study.

Chappe, I quickly decided, was surely a name, and it was as simple as flicking through some dusty encyclopaedias from the library to connect the Frenchman Claude Chappe with the invention of semaphore during the French revolution. The frieze along the east corridor suddenly made sense. The waving figures were signalling with their arms, even though they weren't holding flags, and so the juggler with both arms at right angles to his body, as his balls flew in the air above him, was an R, and the athletic-looking acrobat about to perform a cartwheel or some such was a T. By referring to the chart I'd found in the same encyclopaedia, I was able to spell out the next clue, and realised 'leads you to study' was a direction, not encouraging book-learning, as I'd first assumed.

Turn the tables on Winchester's three destinations.

No immediate solution presented itself and I spent the whole of the next day wrestling with what it might mean, my increasing frustration matching my increasing bad temper.

I could only assume Winchester referred to the former capital of our great and glorious land, famous for its cathedral and college, and investigated the train lines that ran into and out of this Hampshire city, but failed to see any connection to the Hall. I thought then of the American rifle and hastened to secure the key to the gun room from Burton. I'm not sure he fully understood my request, but he was persuaded to part with the key. His sobriety issues had become more pronounced in recent weeks. Perhaps it was only to be expected when the man oversaw the wine cellar and had a tendency to consume those leftover inches in the bottles cleared from the dinner table.

I was disappointed again, however. Aside from the numerous shotguns, the only rifles were Lee-Enfields. Besides, what could the destination part mean in this context?

Finally, in my desperation, I asked Murray if she knew of anyone with the name Winchester, perhaps someone who had an association with my father or a former employee, but again, nothing. And as this latest clue had somewhat hindered my pursuit of victory, I could only hope Leonard was much further behind with the puzzle.

It was gut-wrenchingly painful for me to accept that something was going on between Leonard and Jane, and that it was mutual. I couldn't believe, however, that he really meant to marry her. My constant monitoring of my brother's movements became obsessive. Not only was I desperate to see what they were up to, but also I needed to know where he was with solving the house.

I'd refused to speak to him since his declaration, but I had watched them interacting from afar, standing in the shadows when they met and listening at doors as they talked. Leonard contrived excuses to loiter in the kitchens and walk through the walled gardens when she was collecting vegetables – much as I had done only a few days earlier.

I realised that Father had been right all along – women were not to be trusted. How foolish I'd been not to heed his lesson. I'd been deceived, tricked and manipulated by Jane, who clearly had her eye on the bigger prize. But I was a good game player and thought perhaps I could outwit them both – if only I could get my head around the damn Winchester reference.

On the following Wednesday, I spied Leonard crossing the courtyard from my chosen vantage point, the nursery, shortly before I knew Jane was to finish her duties. Facing the rear of the house, it had always afforded an excellent view of people's comings and goings over the years – including on the night my mother had fled from the Hall.

It was Jane's afternoon off, and if Leonard had left for the woods, I was certain she would shortly follow, so I raced down to the kitchens, hoping to catch her leaving.

'You do realise that I was playing with you?' I said, stepping out in front of her barely ten minutes later as she appeared in the corridor. 'When I told you I loved you the other day. It was a joke. I was testing you.'

I was desperate to undo the damage of my hasty actions from before, but she glanced about nervously, perhaps worried I might try to thrust my unwanted attentions on her again. How I bitterly regretted trying to kiss her in the still room.

'Of course,' she said, summoning up a smile. 'You're a good . . . person, Sidney. You've been a real friend to me since I arrived, and I need friends. I would hate anything to spoil that.'

'Excellent. Then as it's your afternoon off, perhaps we could go for a walk, *as friends*, or play a game of *Round the World* together? It was one of the games I showed you in the nursery last week that you were particularly interested in – remember?'

I was keen to show off, like the pricket deer that I was, the genius of my father and the heritage that was our family company, as if it would make me a more attractive proposition by association.

'I'm so sorry,' she said, not meeting my eye. 'I have other plans today.'

'Oh?'

'Erm, yes, I'm meeting an old friend in Halesham.'

Lies, I thought, and my nails dug into my tightly clenched fists, but I kept my face neutral. She had no contact with anyone from her previous life and had never received so much as a letter since working at the Hall – I knew because I'd been watching her for weeks, forever curious about her mysterious past.

'Just for afternoon tea and cake at the tearoom off Market Street.'

Lies, lies, lies. They came from her tongue so readily and plausibly. I nodded, my face revealing none of my true suspicions, so disappointed that the object of my affections had the capacity to deceive. She was not meeting a friend – she was meeting Leonard. He'd been restless all morning, after announcing to Father at breakfast that he was unwell and couldn't go to the print works as planned. But he was no more ill than Jane had suddenly reconnected with someone from her previous life.

I accepted her excuse with calm grace but underneath I was fuming. How could she lie to me and yet insist we were still friends? She excused herself and I retreated back upstairs, ringing the bell and asking Burton to fetch my walking boots and a green checked Norfolk jacket that might help to better conceal me in the countryside. I left the Hall and took myself beyond the garden in the direction Leonard had been heading, tucking myself behind a tree that overlooked the footpath through the woods and into Halesham.

Sure enough, not many minutes later, Jane came tripping along the path, having now changed out of her working clothes. She was almost skipping, her head turned to the sun, and was humming a merry hymn to herself. Once she was a safe distance ahead, but not so far that I would lose her, I followed through the trees, taking a parallel route.

I hoped she might turn right at the brook and make her way to town, and that I was mistaken about where she was heading. But she turned left, weaving through the trees directly ahead of me. A turtle dove purred in the canopies above and she turned to look in my direction. My heart thudded as I took cover behind an old hornbeam, its wide, grey, twisted trunk weary with years and leaning slightly to one side. For a moment, I was fearful she'd spotted me, but she continued her journey, and I let out a silent breath, only for my stomach to contract when I spotted my brother.

Leonard leaned casually on the wall of the folly. My folly. The place that had been a refuge and retreat for me over the years. He'd shown no interest in the place before, declaring it senseless and unnerving when Father had first built it. But now, there he was, a huge grin spreading across his face as she approached, stepping into the small patch of sunshine that pooled on the woodland floor.

My heart shrivelled like the abandoned berries on the leafless winter trees as I watched her pick up her pace for the last few yards and run into my brother's arms. He pulled her close and swooped his face under the brim of her hat to kiss her. This time she did not freeze, did not drop her arms away and refuse to reciprocate. Instead, her lips were only too eager to connect with his.

Everything was betrayal with these two. How had I believed them both to be allies in my troubled life when nothing could be further from the truth? I wanted to shout out, to kick at something, to punch Leonard so hard he would never get up. Before me was a scene I had no desire to witness, and yet I couldn't tear my eyes away.

It made for uncomfortable viewing as my brother pulled back and lifted his hands to her head, carefully removing her hatpin and lifting the straw boater. Still, they had not spoken, their eyes locked as they communicated without words. They were so utterly absorbed in each other and oblivious to the world around them that a flaming meteor could have sailed through the skies and crashed into the earth and I don't believe either of them would have noticed.

The hat was dropped gently to the ground at his feet and then he raised his hands once more and pulled at the tortoise-shell comb that held her glorious black hair, so that it fell loose about her shoulders. She shook her head and I noticed how her hair caught the light, like a waterfall of black ink. Leonard toyed with the ends, wrapping a loose strand about his fingers, and still not taking his eyes from hers.

Suddenly, and with the lock of hair still in his grasp, he jerked her forward with a roughness that took her breath away. She gasped as their bodies collided but followed it with a silky laugh, before they kissed again, with a passion that I'd never witnessed and only dreamed about. He bent towards her, Jane arching as his body forced hers backwards, and then he slid his right hand around her waist and his left hand under her knees as he lifted her up and carried her into the folly and out of sight.

I stood there for some moments, staring at Jane's hat, cast

aside and forgotten in their passion, and felt some sympathy for that abandoned object. I knew what was happening in the dim shadows, up against the mock-gothic stone walls. Walls that had seen so many intimate moments of my life over the years – the tears and abject loneliness of the child, the restless irritability and uncontrollable anger surges of the boarder home for the holidays, and more recently the sexual frustrations of the young man.

Punishing myself further, I walked towards the stained-glass window and crouched beneath it, hearing soft moans and heavy breaths. I repeatedly smashed the back of my head against the wall, scrunching my eyes up tightly to prevent the tears from escaping. Everything in my world was falling apart – crashing to the ground with a thunderous boom. It would have been more bearable had she resisted, if my brother had forced himself upon her, but she'd now lost all respect from me. How could she behave like a common whore? Throw herself at my brother so willingly? He might profess to love her, but he must know Father would have none of it, and then where would she be? Jane was the mistress of her own destiny the moment she had allowed him to lie with her, and would have to reap what she had sown.

I slid down the bumpy wall and let myself sit in the damp, mulchy soil. I can't be certain how long I was beneath that window, as each sound and each silence killed me in equal measure. Finally, Leonard spoke.

'I've had so many years surrounded by bitterness and suspicion that I'd forgotten that there were people full of kindness. I can't imagine my life without you.'

I picked at a hangnail, pulling it back so violently that I drew blood. Naturally, he would roll out meaningless flattery – he was basking in the afterglow of his conquest. I watched the scarlet droplet swell between my nail and the torn skin, and then trickle down my thumb and fall to the rich humus of the woodland floor. I scuffed the mud with my boot and let my blood become part of the decay.

'Our union brings you no advantages, only complications. I'm nothing.' Her voice was a whisper.

'You're *everything*, Jane. It is I who offer nothing. Sidney will solve this puzzle before me, I'm certain. I'm playing catch-up with every clue. He will inherit and I will be left with very little.'

I cannot deny the satisfaction I felt when Leonard acknowledged this, as I'd spent my entire life playing second fiddle to him. Oh, how the worm had turned.

'We don't need it, Leonard. We have each other.'

There was the sound of shuffling and soft murmurs as they revelled in their contentedness. To further punish myself, I imagined the kisses, his lips in her hair and her arm across his chest. But the unbelievable speed of their attachment only proved that both parties were duplicitous. She wanted the Hall and was playing a very clever game by denying exactly that. He merely wished to use her body, and would continue to profess his love until she'd served her purpose.

I started to heave myself up, deciding I'd heard enough, when Jane's words made me freeze.

'I've been wondering what Winchester could refer to. I think there might have been a game of your father's that had a Winchester in it. I'm not certain – perhaps it was a Watson or Williamson – but there was some detective game he devised that I'm sure the village schoolmaster purchased. He was a big fan of Conan Doyle. Sidney and I were looking through the games in the nursery recently and it reminded me.'

Two things struck me as I hovered half to my feet, half leaning against the folly wall: firstly, I hadn't realised that Leonard had caught me up with the puzzles, and secondly, Jane was right. She had solved the next clue.

Chapter 34

1920

The following morning, restless and anxious, Phoebe was given a couple of hours off by Mrs Murray. There was a surplus of food from the dinner party, which would feed the staff for the next two days, so not much cooking was required. Perhaps sensing her kitchen maid was troubled, or possibly worried she was feeling the after-effects of too much wine, the housekeeper suggested that she went for a walk in the grounds to clear her head.

Instead, Phoebe wandered into the study hoping to stumble across Sidney to further apologise for her deception. He was absent, but she was amused to find a large collection of *Boy's Own* annuals spread over the desk. Picking up a couple, she noticed the colourful illustrations on the front covers: boys tobogganing down a hill, cowboys astride rearing horses, a collection of childhood paraphernalia, such as fishing rods, guns and cricket bats. There were no children in the household, so she could only assume they were connected with his work.

'I've been looking for you.' Sidney's voice made her jump.

'If it makes any difference, I only found out the truth after my parents died . . .' she began, immediately on the defence and before he had a chance to condemn her for withholding such a shocking revelation. He'd slept on everything now and she wondered what his judgement would be.

'Are you worried I'm about to banish you as I banished Leonard?' He walked over to the desk, running his hand across the loose papers and the badly stacked books.

'No, I—'

'Last night, I remembered a curious thing your mother said to me when we first met. She told me her name was Nancy – identifying herself with a character from the Dickens she was reading.' He rubbed at his temples with his hand, as if he were still wrestling with the consequences of Phoebe's news. 'I should have worked it out. Poor Jane. I have no doubt she was badly used and I also have no doubt, looking back, that she was honest with my brother from the start.'

Although it was quite incredible that her mother had managed to conceal the pregnancy during her short time at the Hall, Phoebe remembered her once saying how lucky she'd been when she was expecting – not having suffered much from sickness in the early days. Of course, at the time, Phoebe hadn't known the circumstances surrounding her conception.

'The decisions my mother made were to protect me. I was told she was thrown out by her family. She must have been very frightened and I doubt she thought much beyond surviving each day.'

'I understand that. But your lies – they are not so easy to justify.' He sighed. 'I must have been painted as quite the blackguard by my brother for you to keep this from me for so long. If, however, Leonard accepted you as his daughter then I will honour that commitment, as legally you are a Bellingham. The truth can be kept between the two of us and no one need ever know. To everyone else we remain uncle and niece.'

'But why would you agree to that when you don't even like me?'

Instead of contradicting her last statement, he took a more circuitous route to justify his decision. 'It's taken me twenty years, but I'm starting to realise how important Leonard was to me and I wish things could have turned out differently. I can't go back and undo the wrongs committed in the past, but I can make things right from now on. Perhaps I need to be less hot-headed in my judgements. See, Phoebe, what a good night's sleep and a period of reflection can do for a man?' He almost smiled.

She really hadn't been expecting such calm resignation from him. He was wrestling with his more compassionate side and was prepared to forgive her, when he had every right to lose his temper, throw her out, and request that she leave. Her motives had been far from pure.

'But I came to the Hall to—'

'I've been wondering,' he said, not letting her speak, 'if you were the reason old Lenny kept away from me all these years. He never once tried to contact me and he was a more forgiving sort than me. I would have capitalised on this information if I had come by it twenty years ago. He was protecting you and your mother, and keeping her secret. Whereas I have no such excuse – I could have reached out to him. I made unfair judgements about you when you turned up at the Hall, believing you to be the child of my traitorous brother . . .'

'Yes, a child,' she said forlornly.

'But that's my point. You are far from that, Phoebe.' He locked eyes with her and she noticed his Adam's apple bob slowly up and down his throat as he swallowed. 'Never that.' Something inside her flipped over, leaving a tight feeling across her chest. 'Perhaps we could be friends and start again? Call me Sidney, if it makes you more comfortable, even if only when we are alone. Let us be two adults on an equal footing. I like you as a person, whether relation or not, and am a better man when you are around. I've been forced to take a good, hard look at myself since you've been at the Hall. You have been a refreshing breeze in the dank, closed caves of my life. Besides, you were quite correct – I lied too, even if only by omission. Neither of us are angels.'

She contemplated his words and found that the idea was not altogether unpalatable. She had nowhere else to go and was desperate to remain near Douglas. If their relationship should develop, as she was sure it would, Sidney would have no legal powers to prevent it. He'd not been named as guardian, and besides, she would be free to make her own decisions in February. In the meantime, if she could foster his respect, he might even come to realise that Douglas was a good match for her, and see his way to support the union.

'And don't forget, we have plans. I'm to teach you poker and you are to help give me a female perspective with the wooden picture puzzles,' he reminded her.

'Yes.' She held up one of the *Boy's Own* annuals. 'You seem to have the male perspective nicely covered. Or was this a little light reading for your own enjoyment?' She couldn't resist teasing him.

'I do not read them for fun. It's work. The boys that read these volumes are the boys that play my games. It is vital I understand their psyche, that as a company we latch on to the prevailing hobbies and interests of the young. I research all my games thoroughly – it's why I maintain such an extensive library.'

'Pity your father designed the house so that it was about as far away from his study as it could possibly be.'

'Ah, not as far as you might think,' he said, giving her a

curious look . . . but she knew that it was a fair walk from the far end of the west wing to his study in the east wing, especially if you were carrying heavy books.

'So, you spend your days reading *Boy's Own* annuals and pretend it is research? I shan't tell if you don't.' She returned the book to the table.

Sidney gave her a genuine smile – not a mocking curl of the lip but the sort that made his eyes crinkle at the edges and his cheeks lift. He gestured for her to take a seat, and then slipped into the chair on the other side of the desk.

'Think what you will, young lady, but there is a reason we are the leading board games manufacturer in this country. The genius that was *Empire* started it all. My father had the idea as a lad and it is from this that the family fortune now stems. Have you ever played it?'

She shook her head.

Animated by the subject, Sidney leaned towards her to make sure he had her full attention. 'The idea is to build a navy, invade territories and develop your acquired lands. The board is a map of a fictional world, overlaid with hexagons. There are bonus cards to help you, like the discovery of gold or oil on the land, and those that hinder – a savage uprising or bad weather where you lose ships or harvests fail. I shall teach you, and perhaps we can look at some of our other best sellers also. Which of the Bellingham Games did you enjoy the most?'

'When I was little, the horse racing game, *Newmarket*, and *Treasures of the Tomb* was always fun. There was some highly engaging detective game the vicar's wife taught me when I was older, but I can't recall its name.'

'Ah, *Find the Culprit*. Good, good.' He nodded to himself. 'Father had so many marvellous ideas, some more commercially successful than others, but it is I who have taken the company to the next level, analysing his past efforts in much greater depth to discover what might make a game popular before it is launched.'

'In what way?' she asked, genuinely interested in this aspect of game development.

'Making learning part of play particularly appeals to the middle-class parents, for example, whereas the more wealthy care not what their child does in the nursery as long as Nanny keeps them out of the way when they have company. Our educational games, like *Kings and Queens*, sell well because in order to win you must lay down the kings and queens of England from your hand in the correct chronological order. Similarly, *Virtue or Vice* – a game of morals and manners – is welcomed by all in their efforts to produce polite and virtuous offspring. And yet totally frivolous games such as *Thank You, Mrs Moggins*, with absolutely no educational benefit, are popular simply because they are fun.'

'So you do understand the concept then?' she asked. 'Of fun?'

Again, a genuine smile danced across his lips. 'Not at all. You will have to educate me in that regard.' Touché, she thought, pleased to see him in such good humour. 'But I would like you on board, Phoebe. I am suddenly only too aware, as my own father was, that I need to make provisions for the future of the company, and you at least carry the family name. Besides, I detect a kindred spirit – a games lover and an enquiring mind.'

'I'm not sure your directors would welcome a female, in *any* capacity, but I am happy to learn about what you do, and help in any way I can. And with that in mind, shall we play a game?' she suggested. 'Teach me something new.'

'Hmm . . .' He rubbed at his whiskers. 'Then I shall take this opportunity to introduce you to poker – which truly separates the boys from the men. I want to launch a Bellingham poker set in a smart leather box, and persuade the British to embrace the game. I will be interested to see how you handle it.'

They adjourned to the drawing room and any lingering awkwardness from the night before fell away as they became absorbed in their pursuit, even though Phoebe quickly realised the bluffing element would be her downfall. They chatted easily, as cards were laid and counters scooped up – invariably by Sidney, who remained patronising regarding her play, if increasingly more affable. And the only time her heart raced was when he studied her face in his efforts to establish what cards she might be holding.

She was pleased her announcement hadn't soured relations between them. They would always be wary of each other, but she was no longer desperate to see him homeless and humiliated. Everyone made mistakes in life, and they should be allowed to atone for them. His acceptance of her was exactly that – his way of making amends for his behaviour towards Leonard.

'My game, I believe,' he finally said, gathering her remaining counters and adding them to his pile. 'Honestly, Phoebe,' he half-joked, 'your poker is no better than your chess.'

Phoebe shrugged. She enjoyed these diversions immensely but suspected she didn't have the necessary ruthlessness to be a winner. After all, hadn't she come to the Hall to play a game of sorts and lost that too?

Chapter 35

Mrs Murray finally had a promising reply from her advert in the Suffolk Chronicle for a replacement kitchen maid as autumn marched on. The new girl, Enid, settled in well, and was willing if somewhat clumsy, but this was offset by Mr Bellingham's surprise decision to engage a local builder to fit a new staircase down to the kitchens and address some of the more frustrating issues the staff had been wrestling with – like the infuriating backwards cupboard doors and ridiculous tap. It caused chaos in the household and Phoebe's help was needed more than ever. Below stairs, Murray was heard to grumble at the thirty years it had taken him to confront his father's heartless alterations. Above stairs, she was doubtless suitably grateful to him for his thoughtfulness.

Unfortunately, the structural changes to the kitchens also led to the discovery of the listening pipes that Sidney had ordered to be disassembled, and the housekeeper was furious.

'Am I to understand that all these years you have been eaves-dropping on our conversations below stairs, sir?'

Phoebe witnessed the confrontation as Murray, once angered, was not prepared to hold back, and had come marching into the library. The older woman's bottom lip quivered, suggesting an emotional side to her that Phoebe hadn't witnessed before.

'My father used them, not me. I have no interest in your chit-chat, nor would it be gentlemanly to listen in to the conversation of others. To be honest, I've given them little thought over the years, but I understand Burton was aware of their existence.'

'Och, no wonder that sleekit man always seemed one step ahead of the comings and goings.' She tutted. 'Never liked him much and was glad when he left. But I'm still surprised at you, sir. They should have been removed twenty years ago.'

'Yes, well, better late than never, eh?'

The housekeeper scowled. 'And there's nothing else you've kept from me?'

'No, you know the truth of the puzzle,' and they both looked towards Phoebe, who was nestled in a window seat. She was pretending to be engrossed in a book, but inwardly felt her stomach lurch.

Did she really need to go through the charade of solving it now? It was not going to prove straightforward and she wondered what tricks would be played and turns it would take.

She kept her expression neutral and her eyes down as she wrestled with her thoughts – not wanting to disappoint Sidney by abandoning the puzzle, but equally not wanting any further part in the twisted games of Clement Bellingham.

Now that she no longer had an official job, the weeks dragged for Phoebe. Sidney went away for a while, abroad on business, so she didn't have his company for the evenings, and often took to sitting with the servants. Sometimes, during the day, she found herself in the folly, perhaps with a book, but more often than not purely with her muddled thoughts for company, and the puzzle was largely forgotten. In the Hall, she helped where she could, as everyone knuckled down to prepare for winter. The outdoor staff were busy splitting and stacking logs, raking up leaves, repairing fencing, collecting seeds, and generally putting the gardens to sleep. In the house, chimneys were swept, thicker blankets and quilts were taken from cupboards and aired, and menus were adapted to suit the limited seasonal produce that was available.

Phoebe wasn't used to having so much free time and wondered at the gentlewomen who had no fires to lay, no floor to sweep, and no clothes to mend. She couldn't imagine herself embroidering fancy work purely for show, and it was too late in life for her to learn an instrument. Instead, she decided to use her time productively and began to read more widely, often curled up in one of the high-backed leather library chairs, with a shawl about her shoulders to fend off the autumn chill. She tried to keep out of Ada's way, conscious of how it would seem to the housemaid to stumble across the young Miss Bellingham doing nothing when there was so much work to be done. Sometimes, she sat in the nursery, looking through the Bellingham board games of the past, or wandered into Sidney's study and perused the games and ideas strewn across his desk. She'd already offered several suggestions for his picture puzzles and was pleased that he wanted to include her in the company. It was an outlet of sorts for her restless mind.

When Sidney finally returned at the start of December, and it grew dark before the day had really begun, they settled back into their previous routine of spending their evenings together. She enjoyed playing board games with him, mainly because it was one of the few times Sidney smiled. How could you fail to, when the basic premise behind *Grab It* was to snatch the counters between you and your opponent when you landed on a 'grab it' square? The physical contact when their hands met left her uneasy and strangely thrilled at the same time. She also found these frivolous games more enjoyable than some of their more serious pursuits, such as poker, when they could spend the whole evening barely speaking as his mind worked out the possible permutations and combinations of the cards, and he returned to the stony-faced, unreadable man she had first met.

Douglas occupied an alarming proportion of her thoughts, and more disturbingly, her faintly inappropriate dreams. She'd never obsessed about a man like this before – about what might be beneath his clothing or how it might feel to be touched by him in a manner designed to excite and stimulate.

She thought back to the warmer weather when she'd first arrived at the Hall and had occasionally glimpsed Douglas working in the gardens shirtless. How she'd been fascinated by the curves and grooves of the muscles across his broad, tanned chest, the smear of dark blond hairs across his collarbone and the trail that led from his navel to below his waistline. There was something about being privy to those areas of his body that were normally hidden from view that had made every nerve ending send frantic signals coursing around her trembling body.

It was increasingly frustrating to her that their relationship hadn't developed since the day they'd held hands walking back from Halesham. The only further indication of his feelings had been the nearly kiss in the corridor before the dinner party, and perhaps she'd mistaken his intentions. Sometimes he would light up a Woodbine from the packet he kept in his breast pocket and stare at her across the kitchen or the gardens in silent contemplation, and her heartrate would accelerate accordingly. But most of the time he appeared distant and withdrawn, and she longed for him to look her way. Perhaps he was conscious that she was his employer's niece, suspecting Mr Bellingham wouldn't allow such an attachment. And he would be right – Sidney was unnecessarily wary of his under gardener – but she would be twenty-one soon and old enough to make her own decisions.

Phoebe decided it was time to find out how Douglas really felt about her.

She ventured outside and was delighted to find him by the vegetable plot, repeatedly thrusting a spade into the soil as he dug the nearly barren patch over, his heavy breaths condensing in the air before him. Brassicas and parsnips were all that remained down the far end. Those broad shoulders of his stretched at the fabric of his shirt, and a wet streak between his shoulder blades hinted at his exertions.

'Hello,' he said, grinning and wiping his brow with the back of his hand. 'What brings you out here?'

'I'm collecting eggs,' and she lifted up her basket. 'Although the girls aren't laying so many with the colder, shorter days.' They'd been moved to the barns now that winter was fast approaching.

'But you're the mistress of the house – part of the Bellingham family,' he said. 'You should be clicking your fingers for staff to fetch the eggs as you recline across the antique sofa sipping sherry. You're too elevated to mix with the likes of us.'

Ah, so she was right. He'd backed off because of outdated and noble values regarding their positions.

'I'm still the simple country girl from Cambridgeshire, brought up in a series of tiny cottages, daughter of the village schoolmaster, making do with altered hand-me-downs and emptying chamber pots.'

Douglas cocked his head to one side as if to concede she had a point.

'Despite his belated but most welcome decision to accept me here, my uncle hasn't stopped me from helping out, particularly in the kitchens. I have precious little else to do with my time and he knows how much I love to bake. As long as I'm discreet, and am not to be found on my hands and knees scrubbing the floors when he has guests, he won't object. Because I certainly don't consider myself superior to anyone who works at the Hall.'

'Good to hear.' Douglas grinned again and her insides wobbled. 'And I'm pleased he's beginning to show you the respect you deserve. Well done for persevering. He recognises what we all knew from the beginning – that you are a kind and gentle soul. You're his only family, Phoebe, and he will come to love you, as we all do.'

His words made her head giddy. Did *he* love her? Perhaps not as a fellow member of staff but as something potentially so much more? Maybe she hadn't imagined that moment before the dinner party after all.

He propped the spade up against the wooden barrow and stepped in front of her as she tilted her head up to meet his eyes, hoping he couldn't hear her thudding heart.

'Look, I know I've kept my distance recently but I didn't want to rush you, or make assumptions about your feelings, and then my mum said something about your grandmother . . .' He paused, clearly wondering whether he should impart this information to her. 'There was some scandal when she disappeared. Seems someone else went missing from Halesham at around the same time. A young man called Christopher who was a bit of a scoundrel, by all accounts. Mum remembers him as having a reputation with the ladies, especially when the daughter of the Bell found herself in the family way and pointed the finger at him. It's possible he bolted to avoid taking responsibility, but he worked here and was fired shortly before Sylvia Bellingham disappeared. The staff talked, as staff invariably do, and noticed he spent an awful lot of time in the gardens with the mistress before her husband went crazy and threw him out. But then perhaps it was just a coincidence.'

'He worked at the Hall? In what capacity?'

There was a pause. 'He was a garden hand.'

Sidney's over-protectiveness finally made sense, although it was the first she'd heard of any illicit romantic entanglement involving Sylvia Bellingham, and she felt somewhat uneasy. Had the poor woman flipped out of the frying pan and into the raging fire by running off with another unwholesome man?

'Ah, and you think my uncle is worried that history is about to repeat itself?'

He shrugged. 'I certainly think it's on his mind when he sees me speaking to you, and it's been on my mind too, since I found out. I don't want to make things difficult for anyone, but I do know how I feel and would very much like to know if you feel the same. Before the dinner party . . .'

'Yes?' she whispered, encouraging him to continue.

'In the corridor . . . and the looks you give me sometimes, across a room, or at the table . . . there's something dancing in the air between us whenever we're close and I know I'm not imagining it . . .'

Phoebe thought she might burst, right there in front of him, as he stretched out the thing he was trying to say, like unravelling a ball of wool in search of the end. He put his hand up to her face and tucked a loose strand of her dark hair behind her ear, letting his fingers rest on her cheek when it was done.

'I want to ask you something. Don't feel you have to say yes, but how would you like to make this thing between us more formal? Be my sweetheart? Step out with me?'

Phoebe swallowed hard. 'I would like it very much indeed.' She felt a bubble of warmth in the pit of her stomach which swelled and grew, spreading through her body and creeping to every part of her.

'Even if your uncle disapproves?' He raised one eyebrow.

'Oh, most especially then.' She smiled. 'He's disapproved of me since the start, wanting me gone and out of his life, and then shoving me in the kitchens as some kind of twisted revenge for past wrongs he suffered. Despite his denials, he still thinks of me as naive, foolish and gullible, but this tiny country worm is turning. I am determined to be a stronger, better person, if only to make him proud of me.' The truth of her own words took her by surprise. Sidney's opinion of her mattered. It mattered more than she could ever have imagined.

She looked up at Douglas and smiled again, and he lowered his head and brought his free hand up to cup her face, leaning in for a hesitant kiss. Everything that was her was pulled to him. If there was some way she could have melted into his body at that moment and become a part of his being, she would gladly have done so.

His lips were slow, gentle and undemanding. He seemed as unsure of how to proceed and how much of himself to give as she was. Douglas was no Lothario. Sidney had another agenda when he'd warned her off his handsome gardener. Was it connected to his mother? Yet there was a part of her convinced something else was going on. She wasn't sure what it was yet, but knew he would do everything in his power to prevent her from being with Douglas, and this worried her.

With wobbly legs but a singing heart, she reluctantly parted from her newly acquired beau and went to the barns in search of eggs, still worrying about how Sidney would take the news of her attachment. Her thoughts clarified as she walked. He would forbid this relationship, but if she were to solve the clues and claim back the inheritance, she would be a woman of independent means and able to offer Douglas financial support with his business endeavours. There was no longer a desire for revenge, but instead a desire to prove herself to Sidney and to achieve something by her own merits. She had no intention of ousting him, but having all that power would make his objections moot. If she owned the Hall and she held the purse strings, then his outdated opinion would no longer matter.

She needed to focus on the next clue.

I, Andrea, am reformed to help you gather letters.

Idling through a well-worn book on Greek mythology from the library, and reading about how Ariadne helped Theseus find his way out of the Minotaur's maze with a ball of string, Phoebe's daydreaming, eternally flitting, brain finally made the connection with Halesham Hall. It was suddenly obvious that *I, Andrea* was an anagram of Ariadne.

She thought back to when Sidney had sent her into the maze not long after she'd first arrived, and remembered the decorative lead plant label at the foot of the hedge by the entrance. She was certain she would find more letters scattered throughout its twists and turns.

'Do you have a sketch pad or some paper I may borrow?' she asked him at breakfast the next morning.

'In the study. I use it when I design the boards. Help yourself.' He toyed with his eggs. 'I wasn't aware you sketched.'

'I need to solve the maze. It's the next clue.' He looked up. 'Ariadne,' she explained.

'Ah. Yes. Clever.' One of his eyebrows rose to the occasion.

'Come on, then,' she said, sliding back her chair and walking towards the corridor. 'You know you're curious. And let's be honest, you desperately want to witness either my success or failure. Perhaps one of those scenarios might make you smile.' She stopped and turned. 'Although, had I not witnessed rare glimpses of these almost mythical occurrences myself recently, I'd be inclined to think tales of Sidney Bellingham demonstrating good humour were fanciful fabrications, told to the village children in an attempt to make them believe you are human, after all.' And not waiting for a response, she continued on her journey as Sidney allowed the remaining eyebrow to join its counterpart in surprise.

'So, what is it that you think you know?' he asked a few minutes later as they stood together at the gap in the imposing yew hedge, Phoebe with a shawl about her shoulders and Sidney in a thick coat.

'That if I follow the correct route out of the maze – Ariadne helped her lover find his way *out* with the string – I shall find a series of letters that will spell the next clue. So I must find my way to the centre, and then back to the entrance. Hence the sketch pad.'

'I hope you're not expecting me to help.'

'I would be most disappointed if you did. To get any real sense of satisfaction from a task, one must complete it independently of others – even if it is only the polishing of shoes.' She gave him her widest smile and skipped into the maze.

Half an hour later, watched over by an infuriatingly silent Sidney, Phoebe stared at the two words she had written, and wondered what on earth *ascending bones* could mean.

Chapter 36

1899

Jane's words about the board game raced around my head. *Find the Culprit* was developed by Father on the back of Conan Doyle's success, and the Everett Winchester detective, whom the game revolved around, was a thinly disguised Sherlock Holmes. It had sold well when I was younger and been reissued several times. I hadn't played it often, as you needed at least four players, although I had a vague recollection of an early version being in the nursery cupboard. Jane must have seen it on the afternoon we went up there together.

The premise was simple enough: a crime was committed at a large country house and you travelled around the board – a ground-floor plan of the fictional Brampton Manor – finding the solution to a series of logic problems and humorous riddles, in order to gather information and solve the case. For example, a valuable necklace was stolen, by the housekeeper, because she was in debt. Or the gardener was murdered, by the lady of the house, because he was blackmailing her. But you had to follow a complicated path through the rooms in a specific order, so that you could collect the Crime, Perpetrator and Motive cards. *Winchester's three destinations.* I couldn't remember which rooms held these key cards, and which rooms you merely collected a 'Help or Hinder' card from, but I did remember Father saying he'd based the board on a simplified version of Halesham Hall. In the game, though, there was a secret passageway, and I had no idea if such a thing really existed.

Suddenly aware that time was of the essence, I crept from the folly, carefully picking my way through fallen branches and negotiating patches of wet soil where the sun had failed to bestow her charms. Only when I was far enough away not to be heard did I rejoin the path and race to the Hall. Mrs Murray was standing at the foot of the main staircase, overseeing her staff.

'Out of my way,' I shouted as I pushed past her and up the stairs, not even stopping to remove my muddy boots. One of the under housemaids was at the far end of the hallway, the string mop still in her hands and a resigned look across her face as all her hard work was undone by the thoughtless young master of the house. Feeling guilty, I abandoned my boots at the top of the stairs so as not to tread further mud over the carpets.

I raced along the corridor and flung the nursery door open so violently that it crashed into the wall. There was a stack of games piled in the ceiling-height cupboard and my eyes scanned the boxes until I found the one I needed. Tucking it under my arm, I hastened to my room, closing the door behind me as I looked across at the image of the woman who had haunted my childhood dreams – her omniscient eyes seeing into my soul, reminding me how I'd been equally beguiled by the hypnotic Jane.

My eyes locked with hers, and at that moment my heart turned to stone. I would solve this puzzle – I was so close – and then where would Leonard and his precious love be? Homeless and penniless, if I had anything to do with it. As Father so often said,

'Cross me once and you are lost to me. There are no second chances.' Despite my protestations otherwise, *surely* Leonard had known what Jane meant to me and he'd taken her nonetheless.

And for that they would both pay dearly.

Lying across my bed, I set out the board. I could see that the first two crime cards were in the dining room and the games room. The final clue – the identity of the perpetrator – was in the secret passage, as in the narrative of the game, this was where the suspect was hiding.

There was a knock at my door and I flung my quilt over the game – fortuitous, as Leonard entered almost immediately, without waiting for my reply.

'Sidney.'

I rolled over and gave him an indifferent glance. 'Feeling better?' I enquired, challenging him to perpetuate his lie.

'What? Oh, yes, much.' He shuffled his feet and couldn't meet my eye. 'Wondered if you'd taken any of the games out the nursery? Had a fancy to look through some of our older editions and see if there was anything worth revising.'

Lies, lies, lies.

'Really? Never known you to take such a keen interest in the business before,' I said. 'How dedicated of you, particularly as you are under the weather today.'

'Yes, well, show the old man willing and all that.'

'No,' I said. 'In answer to your question, I've not touched them. Ask Murray. Perhaps she's given some away to the church bazaar.' I rolled back to face the window. 'They are so rarely played with now that we are older.'

'Right. Only Jane recently mentioned a couple that I'd forgotten about . . . so I thought . . .'

'Ask Jane then. Next time you . . . see her.'

It had been on the tip of my tongue to say 'Next time you

bed her', but I was learning to be less hot-headed. Besides, Leonard hadn't even afforded her the dignity of a bed. So I held my tongue. One of Father's many lessons in gameplay. Don't let your opponent know you're rattled.

'Right.' He nodded slowly to himself. 'Perhaps I'll have a word with Murray.' And he slunk off back down the corridor.

Not entirely sure what I was looking for, I headed to the dining room when the coast was clear. The clue said 'Turn the tables', so I took this literally and began my search beneath the large mahogany dining table. I crawled around, running my hand along the joints and looking closely for places a clue could be concealed. Eventually I found a card, identical in style to the ones from *Find the Culprit*, wedged between the underside of the tabletop and the supporting apron. One simple word was printed on the reverse: *Under.* I was sorely tempted not to replace it, knowing Leonard was on my tail, but I knew better than to break the rules of my father's game.

Next, I dashed to the games room and flew under the large billiard table. After much scrabbling around, I found a second card in a similar location, wedged under one of the muntins between the rails. This time the word *the* was printed on the reverse. My heart accelerated. Now I had to trust there was indeed a secret passage at Halesham Hall. It was, after all, entirely possible Father had ordered one to be constructed during the building works. The night my new childhood bedroom was presented to me came to mind. I had seen him disappear down the west corridor, only to appear moments later in the study. A passageway made sense and I wondered how many times he'd used it to evade people, or simply to nip to the library for a research book. Now I only had to hope I could locate it.

The library had a multitude of shelves, although it was a

somewhat clichéd location in which to conceal a secret door, having been much overused in mystery novels. But the book-lined walls rather lent themselves to such a thing.

Twice, as I methodically searched the room, someone entered. First Murray and then the ever-snooping Burton. Twice, I pretended to be looking for a volume of Greek poetry. I tipped back spines, rapped on panels and let my hand trace down the uprights, looking for catches or gaps. It was only when I felt a slight draught from one section that I stumbled across the door. A narrow section of shelving pushed inwards to reveal a low, dark tunnel. I grabbed the lamp from the small side table and proceeded inside, closing the door behind me.

After a few feet, I met with a set of stairs taking me below floor level and into the deep underbelly of the house. There was a musty smell and when I placed my hand on the stone wall to steady myself, it felt cold.

The dancing light from my lamp bounced off the curve of the bricks that lined the passageway and I kept walking, still not sure where I might locate the final card. Surely there would be no table down here?

After about fifty yards, I spied three amateur artworks hanging on the stone wall, totally out of place. I raised the lamp to inspect them and there was a landscape, a portrait and a bowl of fruit on a table. I lifted the still life from the wall and turned it over to find the final card, with the last word, *sun*, printed on the reverse. I now had the entirety of the clue: *Under the sun*.

An unpleasant draught circled about me and, as I continued along the passage, I heard the faint moan that I had sometimes imagined when I was near the staircase that led nowhere. As the noise became louder, light flooded in the passageway and I noticed a narrow slit up high, concealed by an almost invisible zinc mesh. Looking more closely, I recognised the white wainscotting. That eerie chill felt by us all as we stood at the bottom of those incomprehensible stairs was suddenly clear to me, as was the moaning. A small set of wide pipes, cut so that the draught from outside would play over them, was mounted on the wall. More of Father's games – a deliberate manipulation of the atmosphere to unnerve those with weak nerves or fanciful imaginations.

Moments later, I stepped out into the east wing study, the simple door hidden by busy wallpaper and hanging pictures, extinguished the lamp and headed nonchalantly for one of the exterior doors. Only when I was clear of the Hall did I race towards the woods, absolutely certain of where I was headed.

I knelt before the long stone bench in the folly, tugging the top slab towards me with all my strength. There, in the corner, bathed in light from the stained-glass window, was a small brown cardboard box, obviously reused from a parcel, as it had an address written in copperplate across the front. I opened the lid and inside, wrapped in an offcut of linen, was a large iron key. A small, yellowed paper label was tied to it with string, and in my father's distinctive handwriting were the words *Turn the key and look inside . . .*

The irony of the hours I'd spent lying across the bench, inches from the key, was not lost on me, and I knew, without a shadow of doubt, that I'd reached the end of my quest. Finally, I could open the locked room at the top of the stairs that led nowhere, and see what lay beyond.

Chapter 37

'I have it!' I shouted, flinging open the door to the drawing room, where Murray had indicated I would find Leonard, and holding the key aloft. 'I've solved the puzzle and have the key to the room at the top of the stairs.'

I could easily have climbed the staircase unobserved, and opened the locked door to claim my victory silently, but there was a part of me that needed to see Leonard's face as I did.

'The board game,' he said, swivelling in the desk chair at the inlaid oak bureau and turning to face me. 'You had it all along.'

I didn't respond, or even ask which game he was referring to. I didn't need to. High on the heady cocktail of arrogance and glory, I strode across the room and thrust the key so violently under his nose that he had to lean back.

'How does it feel to have been outwitted by your little brother? To lose everything to someone ten years younger, with more intelligence and drive than you?'

Leonard's eyebrows rose as he closed the fall of the desk and stood up from the chair. 'Well played, little brother. I'm impressed.' He put his hand out to shake mine, but I let it hang there.

I shook my head in disbelief. 'Don't pretend that you don't care. That you can take this on the chin and carry on. Show me a good loser and I'll show you a loser.' My father's words echoed around the room.

'I mean it, Sidney, I'm pleased for you. Frankly, I'm sick of the old bastard's games and I just want out. Meeting Jane was the best thing that's ever happened to me. I thought I wanted all this . . .' and he swept his hand across the room, 'but the truth is, I felt nothing but relief when you came in just now. The stupid game is over and I feel unshackled.'

I gave a laugh that I hoped conveyed my disbelief. 'But she won't want you now when she realises she backed the wrong horse. Oh, she'll pretend for a while that it doesn't matter and it's you she loves, but will she still want to tie herself to you when I have the Hall, the company and the wealth?'

'You're wrong, Sidney. And it's why I love her. She asks for nothing and wants nothing.'

'Father will never allow it.'

'Then we will willingly leave the Hall, for without her *I* am nothing.'

'Fine sentimental words, but you can't fool me. Take her. I don't care. She is not what she seems – she has secrets.'

'Yes, I know.'

I assumed that, like me, he also suspected her of hiding things, but it made no difference to him. He apparently loved her regardless.

'She's agreed to be my wife and we will be married as soon as possible. I shall easily find a teaching post in a small village somewhere and we will start again.'

'Teaching?' I scoffed, ignoring the devastating blow that Jane had accepted his proposal. It cut deeply but was not a wound I could allow myself to focus on in that moment. 'In some backwater, in a draughty hut, to waste your time on unruly labourers' offspring who aspire to nothing more than to emulate the pathetic lives of their parents? What a waste of your time and your talents, Leonard. You disappoint me.'

Having stayed calm thus far, it seemed my brother was finally beginning to tire of my taunting. He reached forward and grabbed my collar, thrusting his face closer to mine. 'You know nothing, Sidney. Nothing.'

Burton entered the room and I wondered how long he had been listening to us from the corridor. Leonard released me and we stepped apart. There was anger building in both of us. Perhaps it had been bubbling away unobserved for years, but it was about to erupt with a fierceness neither of us had anticipated.

'Your father wants to see you both,' he said. 'I don't think it will be many days now. The physician has been sent for but he is deteriorating rapidly.'

Time really was of the essence. It was important that Father knew I'd succeeded, even if he did not have long left to live with this knowledge.

'I found it, sir,' I said, waving the key at my father as we entered his bedchamber. I did not allow my pride at succeeding to be overshadowed by the fact that it was Jane who had solved the last clue. Would I have considered the board game had I not overheard her suggest it? Possibly. However, Leonard, with his lack of interest in the family business, most certainly would not have done.

Father stared at me for a long time before speaking. He was propped up by a mountain of pillows and looked alarmingly small all of a sudden.

'Then it is all yours. You must open the door and discover what lies behind. My money was always on you, Sidney.' He coughed a phlegmy cough, unable to properly clear his throat, and then smiled.

For the first time since my elation at discovering the key, I felt uneasy. I didn't like his smile – the cruel one he'd employed so many times in the past, particularly when he knew something I didn't.

'Go then,' he commanded. 'Unlock the door, and return to tell me what you find.'

I nodded and left the room, with Leonard following behind. He might profess not to care, but he was naturally curious. Those pointless stairs and the solid locked door had haunted our dreams for years.

I felt the chill around my ankles as I mounted the first step, and even though I now knew the atmosphere was manufactured, I couldn't help but feel the ethereal presence of my mother. She was always somehow on this staircase, hovering beside me, faint whispers of her lavender perfume in the air. Here and at the folly – the two places she watched over me.

My brother and I climbed the staircase in silence until I stood on the top landing with the key in my hand, my fingers quivering as I went for the keyhole. My mind returned to the night my mother had disappeared. There had been so much blood on his hands and I replayed the words he'd spoken to himself after an anxious Murray had left him alone in the hallway. 'She'll not grace the Hall again. Ever.' So many times over the years an unwelcome and stomach-churning thought had flitted through my brain. He'd been so certain her departure was permanent . . . Could he be responsible for that permanence? I shivered. I'd always been so excited about what might lie behind this door, sealed for years and promising glorious things, but now I was fearful.

'Come on then.' Leonard was irritable and impatient. 'Put us both out of our misery.'

The key slid into the keyhole and, with some difficulty, I

managed to turn it anticlockwise, always expecting a further trick – for it to turn the wrong way, or for the door not to open at all. But the bolt gave a satisfying clunk. I turned the cut-glass knob to swing it open – rather surprisingly, towards us both rather than into the room – and, as we both stared open-mouthed at the sight before us, I realised I'd been right to be suspicious.

Chapter 38

1920

Phoebe had a sweetheart and it made her feel like a woman for the first time in her life. She'd come to the Hall with her tiny cottage ways and lack of life experience, but she now looked forward to what the future might bring, hoping her parents would have approved of her choice. Douglas was a hard worker, a cheerful and engaging companion, and treated her respectfully. They visited Daisy again and spent another pleasant afternoon in Halesham with his family, but both agreed not to advertise their attachment any wider yet, as Phoebe wanted to be one step ahead of Sidney when he found out. If Murray suspected anything was going on between them, she said nothing.

Still needing to prove her worth to Sidney, if only for him to respect her as an adult and accept her decisions in life, the *Ascending bones* clue played relentlessly on Phoebe's mind, but to no avail. She'd looked through the library, studied the murals, and had even considered a kitchen connection – Mrs Murray's stockpot undergoing a quick inspection. But it was whilst looking through the games in the nursery that she found a very expensive-looking and highly ornate set of dominoes, all of which had tiny bones in place of the standard dots and a pirate-like skull on the back. It was a bone connection, but was it the right one?

Down in the kitchens, still her much-preferred place to be for meals and where she often retreated to chat to Mrs Murray when Sidney was absent, she explained that she was trying to solve a series of puzzles set by her grandfather. She wondered if the word bones meant anything to them, or if there was some place about the Hall where bones might have a particular significance?

'Oh, that damn puzzle. It was an evil thing for the old Mr Bellingham to do. No wonder the brothers fell out. Poor Master Leonard spent a lifetime preparing to step into his father's shoes and wee Sidney spent his childhood knowing he was to all intents and purposes redundant. I honestly don't know who I felt the most sorry for.'

Phoebe had come to a similar conclusion. The relationship between Sidney and Leonard had always been complicated, but she understood now that both had been at fault, both had been devious and both had a right to feel angry with the other.

'One of the old gardeners used to play dominoes down in the sheds, puffing away on his pipe and mumbling in such a broad dialect that I couldn't understand him, but I remember he always called them "bones",' Murray said, after a considered pause. 'Young Mr Bellingham learned the game from him when he was very wee, but then the poor soul was always short of playmates.' She rolled out the pastry for a meat pie as she kept half an eye on the new girl.

'There are dominoes running up one of the staircases,' Ada offered, joining in the conversation. She was mending linen again in the far corner, the kitchen being by far the warmest room in the house. 'I should know, I've dusted them often enough. Tiny things burnt into the wood. They go up, well, they come down too, but could that be it?'

Thanking them both, but rejecting any further offers of help, Phoebe went to the staircase, determined to solve the next part alone. Their suggestions had, however, been most welcome, as she'd never heard of dominoes referred to as bones before. Mrs Murray had always been on her side and keen for her to remain at the Hall, but Ada appeared to be heading that way too – the grunts weren't as frequent and the snide comments had stopped.

It took Phoebe a while but she eventually realised that the dominoes, running up the stairs in a random order, could be lined up to match the static dominoes on the top and bottom newel posts by turning the balusters. She was rewarded with another clue, burnt into the oak underneath the handrail, and went straight to the library to investigate. She pulled out Volume II of the enormous leather-bound encyclopaedias, balanced it across her knees and curled her legs beneath her.

'Murray thought you might be in here.' Sidney entered, still wearing his coat and clearly not long returned from visiting the print works. 'She informs me you've been playing about on the east-wing staircase in my absence? I'd rather hoped you would share your puzzle-solving with me.' His face resembled the spoilt child told he could not play with the big boys.

'I'm afraid I can't wait around until you happen to be free,' she teased, feeling so much more at ease with him in recent days. Their honesty had broken down some of the barriers between them, and she was pleased she'd come clean about Leonard. 'When inspiration strikes, I have to act.'

'And the next clue?' he asked, smoothing his moustache down. 'Clearly inspiration has also struck with regard to this and that's why I find you in my library?'

Her finger was tracing down the entries. 'I'm looking for a chap called Chappe, for it surely must be a name,' she explained.

Murray entered. 'Och, there you are, sir, and still in your coat. Sanderson has taken you a tray through to the drawing room. We thought you would like a cup of tea and some cake. You must be chilled to the bone.'

'Bring the tray here,' he said. 'I wish to sit with my niece.' Phoebe looked up from her research, unimpressed by his manners. He noticed her reproachful expression. 'If you would be so kind,' he added, unbuttoning the coat and tossing it over the back of a chair.

Murray nodded, swept the coat up and retreated.

'Semaphore,' Phoebe said with immense satisfaction, having returned to her investigations. 'I've heard of it before, and am certain Father taught the boys this at Scouts. I remember them standing on boxes and waving flags about.'

'Your father was a Scout leader?'

'After the war,' she clarified. 'The Scouting movement lost a good many of its leaders for king and country, and some of the boys in his class encouraged him to take on the role.'

'A noble man indeed. I think perhaps I would have liked the Leonard you talk of, had I ever got to know him properly.'

'The age gap?' she surmised.

'Yes, but my stubbornness also. There are several things in my past I am beginning to regret . . .'

She thought he was about to open up further about her mother, but Sanderson appeared with the tray, shattering the moment, and Phoebe closed the heavy book with a thump. A flutter of dust danced in a beam of winter sun streaming in through the windows.

'This obviously refers to the frieze leading to the study.' She replaced the encyclopaedia, selected the volume that would contain semaphore, and walked towards the door.

'Where are you going?' he asked, mid-pour.

'To solve the next clue.'

'But my tea?' He looked at the tray. 'I want my tea.'

'I'm not stopping you.'

She collected a sheet of paper and a pencil from the desk and skipped off to the corridor.

Twenty minutes later she was scratching her head regarding the Winchester reference as Sidney sat, leaning against the wall, a tea tray by his feet and more of the fruit cake in his stomach than was probably good for him.

Christmas was nearly upon them and frosty windowpanes and frozen puddles signalled the undisputed arrival of winter. The household, meanwhile, busied themselves with preparations for the more cheery aspects of the season. Boughs of holly and ivy adorned the stairs and mantels, Douglas cut down a Norway spruce for the girls to decorate, and Ada and Phoebe spent a pleasant morning sorting through a box of Christmas ornaments Mrs Murray had ordered fetched from the attics.

'I can't believe you're stepping out with Douglas,' Ada said, avoiding her eye and unpacking some delicate paper snowflakes. 'You really aren't his sort.'

The news that they were together was now known amongst the staff, but Phoebe immediately felt on her guard.

'Am I not?'

'No, you're too nice.' The comment surprised Phoebe and she waited for elucidation. 'He's a chancer, that one. Make no mistake.' It was an odd choice of word for Douglas. Admittedly, he could be a bit cheeky sometimes, and often teased Mrs Murray or the younger girls, but away from the banter of the staff, Douglas was quiet and unsure of himself, taking things at her pace, even when she wished he'd move a bit faster.

Was Ada warning her off so that she could bag the

handsome gardener for herself? After all, he was a very attractive and affable man. It was the only explanation, and Phoebe couldn't help but wonder what the housemaid had said to him in the corridor the night of the dinner party. Ada's motives might be different, but she was as unhappy about the thought of Phoebe and Douglas together as Sidney was, which only inclined Phoebe to dig her heels in deeper. The doubters were wrong. There was something special about Douglas, and when they kissed – those snatched moments around the yard or in a deserted corridor when no one was watching – she felt such an intense draw to him, she wanted to press her body so close to his that they became one. She was thankful that he had a steady head and knew to pull away before she got lost on a wave of almost uncontrollable longing. He took everything so slowly – always checking she was comfortable with his overtures. In fact, he was moving at such an unhurried pace that her inner woman was torn between her gratitude that he was so thoughtful and her frustration that he never pushed things even a little bit. Wasn't she desirable enough? It was times like this that she wished her mother was around to guide her.

'I'll consider myself warned, then,' was all Phoebe could reply, and an uneasiness hung in the air between the two girls.

Ada snorted, picked up a small box of red silk bows to hang from the tree, and changed the topic of conversation.

'This is the first Christmas since I've worked here that we've really embraced the festivities. Mr Bellingham seems cheerier somehow. Did you know he'd organised the delivery of small gifts to the elderly and housebound of Halesham? And offered to fund a Christmas party for the school?'

Sidney was a safer topic of conversation and it pleased Phoebe that he appeared to be mellowing.

'Although Mrs Murray said before the war he used to really

live it up,' Ada continued, 'with fancy friends from London and boisterous dinner parties, where the guests stayed for several days. But then the war was no time to celebrate and he wasn't home for seventeen or eighteen – serving abroad. It never felt right to be singing, dancing and playing board games when men like him and my oldest brother were huddled in a trench somewhere, fighting for their lives.'

Sometimes things pop into your head from nowhere, particularly when you've been wrestling with a knotty problem for a while. Somehow her subconscious brain had continued to rifle through her memories and acquired knowledge, looking for some link to the puzzle. Ada's mention of board games enabled her to dredge up a Bellingham game she'd looked at in the nursery a while ago, remembering how much the vicar's wife had loved the delicious mystery of it all. A game about culprits with a detective who was called Winchester . . .

And, as the rain clouds gathered in the heavy Suffolk skies and hungry birds pulled the last of the berries from the trees, she spent her afternoon racing around the Hall, looking under tables and searching for a secret passage. Eventually, she laid three cards before her on the small writing desk in the library that spelled out *Under the sun*.

Chapter 39

Phoebe knew immediately what the clue meant – *in silvis* – the stained-glass window in the woods. She grabbed a coat and a small lamp, and headed across the lawns. It was barely four o'clock and the shortest day was almost upon them.

'Where are you going at this hour?' Sidney was striding back across the grass and returning to the house, Satan running freely at his feet.

'On the trail of your grandfather's puzzle,' she said. 'I'm heading to the folly.'

'In the dark? Aren't you afraid of the evil spirits?'

'The faeries are my friends, remember?' she teased.

A sceptical eyebrow drifted towards his hairline. 'I've actually just come from there. The tranquillity of the place settles my restless mind, but I should very much like to witness your progress. May I come with you?' he asked.

'To laugh at me when I fail?'

He didn't answer.

'I can't really stop you, can I?' she pointed out. 'It's your land.'

'Sort of,' he said and put out an imperious hand to take the lamp from her. Again, proof that he knew he was only guardian of it all until the final clue was solved.

They headed off together, back across the lawns, down the path and then deeper into the mass of dense trees. Satan scampered madly about in the shadows and darted between the tree trunks, thrilled to find that his walk had been extended. He picked up small branches and fallen pine cones and periodically dropped them at his master's feet, rewarded by pats on the head and words of affection.

'My father built this in memory of my mother,' Sidney said, as they reached the little tumbledown building. 'Another stupid metaphor for love and how it decays. Like the Aphrodite in the maze – unreachable.'

It was sad to Phoebe that something so broken represented love, which she always considered as powerful and healing. What a strange and damaged man Clement Bellingham must have been. She thought back to the door knocker and realised her first impression had been right. There had been a woman at Halesham Hall, trapped and unhappy, desperate to escape.

Sidney kicked at a broken branch, the damp surface already beginning to freeze and glinting ice crystals reflecting back the light from the lamp.

'My father said she ran away.' Phoebe wondered if he might open up to her in this dark space where he didn't have to meet her eye.

'Yes. I was six.'

'Where did she go?'

He shrugged. 'No one knows. Quite deliberate on her part, I think. He was terribly cruel to her, and I suspect she worried that his cruelty would be directed at anyone involved in her escape. And yet I am certain he never loved anything or anyone as much as he loved his wife. Look at how he lavished her with gifts, even turning the west tower into a sewing room to indulge her favourite pastime.'

'You mean she was kept locked up *in a tower*?' Phoebe asked incredulously.

Sidney looked thoughtful for a moment. 'I admit to not having considered it from that point of view, but I suppose she was restricted, being encouraged only there or in the gardens, as she also had a fondness for flowers.' He sighed. 'The truth is, his adoration of her was so intense, it destroyed them both. Love is not a healthy emotion – it's too powerful.'

'It can be, but I've been lucky enough to be brought up in a household brimming with love and it had the most positive impact on me. I've spent a lifetime observing the devotion of my parents and have, at times, even felt jealous. Father always said it was the only reason he got through the horrors of war.'

She stepped into the folly, turning away from him and allowing her hand to trace the bumps of the stone and ridges in between. It was important he didn't feel scrutinised when she asked her next question.

'Was there never anyone else, after my mother?'

She heard his footsteps halt and turned back to see a confused Satan, circling his master and looking up at him with expectant eyes.

'Not anyone that mattered.'

He chose not to comment further as he walked towards the stone bench, and she pulled her heavy wool coat tighter around her shoulders. Her breath condensed in little clouds before her, and Sidney looked almost ghostly as the light cast his eye sockets in shadow and illuminated the recesses of his face.

She followed him to the window, but no shafts of golden light fell at her feet like they had back in the summer. This was where the clue was leading her – the glorious stained-glass sun in memory of a lost love. A swirling wisp of dark emotions hung in the air and a wave of unhappiness encircled her, ushered by the breeze that scampered through the trees and into every dark corner.

Kneeling in front of the stone bench, she ran her fingers under the solid top, suspecting there would be a cavity beneath it – like a tomb. She shivered. With no offer of help whatsoever, Sidney watched as she tugged at the slab, glad of her mittens to protect her hands from the rough surface, and managed to pull it back far enough to reach inside, wary of what she might stumble across. Surely even he couldn't be so unkind as to allow her to delve her hand unwittingly into the long-buried bones of his mother.

He stepped forward to give her more light.

'Aha!' She scrabbled around in the dirt and pulled out a box – seemingly reused from a parcel sent long ago, with an Italian address across the front in a dark blue-black ink.

Sidney watched silently as she unwrapped the linen to reveal an old iron key, and her heart thumped so violently she was sure he could hear it beating in the still air. She'd done it. She'd solved the puzzle that he'd been unable to complete. She could claim the Bellingham treasures.

'I'm impressed, Phoebe,' he finally said. 'And now you get to open the door.'

Chapter 40

1899

Leonard and I stared at the brick wall directly behind the door. The staircase led nowhere. There was absolutely nothing at the top of the stairs.

'I don't understand,' I said, putting my hands out to assess how solid the wall was.

Leonard was shaking his head. 'The bastard. He's really done it this time. If he wasn't dying, I'd a mind to kill him myself. There never was a room.'

'No, this can't be it. The deeds . . . The treasures . . .' I was panicking, scrabbling at the coarse bricks with my fingers. 'I can order Burton to bring up a sledgehammer,' I said. 'Perhaps Father bricked the entrance up?'

Leonard was frowning, his eyes closed as his hand traced out squares in the air. 'There's no point. Think about it. All the twists and turns in the staircase and no windows to orientate yourself. God knows why neither of us worked it out before, but this is an exterior wall, Sidney. Smash through that and my guess is you'll come out, thirty foot in the air, above the rose beds. The staircase leads nowhere. It never did.'

'No!' I yelled and kicked at the wall, only succeeding in

scuffing the toe of my brown leather brogues and sending an unpleasant jolt up my leg. Everything I'd been striving for had been snatched away from me at the last, and in both instances it was family who had betrayed me – the people who should have had my best interests at heart.

'I'm sorry,' he said, feigning sympathy. 'I know you wanted this.' He put his hand on my shoulder but I shrugged it away.

'You're loving this, aren't you?' Tears were stinging behind my eyes, but I refused to let them fall.

I'd lost the girl *and* the inheritance, and my anger was bubbling so furiously it had to spill out somewhere. Unfortunately, it was about to explode over my father.

'You utter bastard. There is no room,' I shouted, returning to my father's bedchamber and standing at the foot of his bed as his shrewd eyes sized me up.

I couldn't swear to it, but I thought he was smiling. It was the discreet, almost undetectable satisfaction of the victor in a game at the moment they realise you are defeated.

'You, sir, are an evil old man who deserves to die.' Once I'd uttered the words that had been spinning in my head and looking for an escape, I couldn't stop more tumbling from my mouth. I was crossing a line but no longer caring. My father couldn't rise from his bed to strike me as he had done in the past when I'd displeased him.

'So, you've reached the end of your quest, then?' he said. 'Solved the house?'

'Yes, and all I found was a damn brick wall, so I'm done now. You've had your fun at our expense. Years of it. Well, you can lie in a cold grave and rot and perhaps then it will be our turn to laugh.'

'You disappoint me, Sidney, and I don't believe you even know why. But, nonetheless, someone must head up the company, and you at least found the key.' He paused to catch his breath. 'Bellingham Games shall pass to you, for I must see that settled before I die, but you will both be granted an income from your employment and may remain in the house for your lifetimes, or until you locate the deeds. Every eventuality has been covered in my will.'

I was too angry to properly assess his words, and too proud to question him further. All I could do was direct further vitriol at him.

'But you lied to us. You said everything was behind the door.' I grabbed the collar of his nightshirt, pulling his smug, dying face closer to mine. He had a sweet, sickly smell about him, the smell of a man not long for this world, overlaid with the sweat and urine that all invalids carry with them.

'Sidney,' came a warning from Leonard, who had followed in behind me, but my fury was unstoppable now, like bubbling red-hot lava spewing from a volcano. '*You said*,' I repeated, as spittle shot from my mouth, '*it was all behind the door.*'

Even facing death, my father was victorious. He gave a cruel smile and this time there was no ambiguity – it spread from one side of his walnut-skinned face to the other. 'That was always your problem, boys. You only heard what you wanted to hear.'

'And your problem has always been that you are a bitter, evil old man who only sees what he wants to see. Leonard is shortly to marry one of our maids – Jane – a servant girl who comes from God knows where, hiding God knows what, and who has been at the Hall barely five minutes. Not just screw her, but actually marry her. How will that sit with your desire for respectability and family honour? A servant swanning around the Hall, lording it over the staff.' If Father was disappointed in me for missing something I couldn't understand, he would damn well be given cause to be disappointed in Leonard as well.

'Is this true?' It was rare for my father to be surprised by anything, always having the unnerving ability to second-guess most situations, but he looked faintly alarmed at my announcement. He tried to shuffle further up the bed but didn't have the strength. 'Marriage?'

'I love her, sir.' Leonard looked daggers at me. It was his news to deliver, and he had doubtless contrived a more palatable way to present his plans to our father, or was waiting until he was not around to object. In my blind fury, I was dragging my brother down with me.

'Damned that you do,' he spluttered. 'I forbid any such union. Sidney is right. How do you think it would reflect on the company? On our family name that I have devoted my life to advancing?'

'I've already asked her and she has accepted. I *will* do this, sir, with or without your blessing.' It seemed we were both so much braver now our father was no longer a physical threat.

'You will not.' There was a prolonged spell of coughing and when he was able to speak again his voice was barely a whisper. 'If you're worried you've put a little bastard in her, she can be paid off. Don't feel obligated. That's their cunning. Give her some money to shut her up or get it dealt with. I know a woman in town.'

I don't think either myself or my brother wanted to question why he should know about the services of such a person, but Father's suggestion that Jane was expecting did at least explain their sudden rush to the altar. I knew they'd lain together, and now Leonard was doing the honourable thing. Perhaps it wasn't love, after all – perhaps it was duty.

'But I love her,' Leonard reiterated, as though this fact was so powerful that it eclipsed all the obstacles.

Father scoffed. 'Love? You've barely known this girl five

minutes. You know nothing of that emotion.' He spat the words out. 'I could write a book about how it consumes and decays. The maggots of your desire feed off the festering flesh of your obsession, until there is nothing but bones left behind. It's an illusion – albeit a pretty convincing one to begin with. I loved your mother. That was my downfall. I put her on a pedestal and worshipped her. I courted her for two years and was not deterred by her constant rejections. Three times – *three times* – I proposed. But all the while she was playing me . . .'

He paused to get his breath, desperate to say his piece, even though it was killing him, as my brother and I exchanged a glance. I wanted to know where this was leading, but was also scared of the truths that might spill out.

'The two weeks we spent in Italy for our honeymoon were truly the happiest of my life, but you cannot know what it is to love someone so much that you hardly dare touch them. Perfection in my eyes . . . I could not bring myself to consummate the marriage for weeks, even though she did not understand my reluctance to come to her bed. Because once I had, she would no longer be an innocent. No longer be perfect . . .'

Another anxious glance passed between Leonard and me. His love had been disturbing beyond words, unhealthy. I'd always known he doted on her, forever bringing gifts and concerned that they weren't to her liking, but I'd been a small child and not seen beyond those material offerings.

'And having ensnared me, she began to turn me into something I couldn't control. Her flirting with other men, the way all eyes were on her wherever she went, how everyone wanted to be with her, talk to her, touch her. So I stopped her from going out. I could not share her with these lecherous others. The lady's maid had to go – they were conspiring together. Your mother had to be curtailed for her own good. She had to be *disciplined* for her own good . . .'

There was a gasp from Leonard. 'My God, man – you beat her.' It wasn't a question but rather a sudden realisation on his part. 'The bruises. She always insisted she was clumsy. That she'd fallen or met with some accident.' His head was shaking and he staggered backwards to collapse in a bedroom chair against the wall. 'How could you?'

I looked between the two of them. I knew nothing of this, too young to have picked up on the signs, but her fear the night she fled was now clear to me.

Father's eyes closed and remained like that for a while as the truth of his cruelty swirled around the room, settling on dusty surfaces, waiting to be disturbed and flutter into the air again. The silence stretched between us for some moments. I wondered if he'd passed away – if that was it, and we would receive no further explanation.

'You know nothing, son. They drive you to it. And as the rider has to whip his horse, I had to curb her disobedience.' His eyes hadn't opened but he was still with us, still keen to justify his beastly actions.

'No wonder she ran away.' Leonard's head was now in his hands as he leaned forward over his knees. Perhaps he felt guilty for failing to see any of this earlier, for failing to stop it. But Father wasn't finished.

'You'll understand soon enough. Especially if you take up with some kitchen whore. They profess to feel the same and then abandon you when they become a mother. Close their legs and kiss only the child.'

The truths were tumbling out like coal from a bucket – black and dirty. My father's twisted logic knew no bounds. He was a jealous bully and a violent tyrant. Could this explain the large age gap between Leonard and me? Was that why my mother had called me her happy accident? It had seemed such an odd phrase to me at the time, and I'd not understood what she meant. With only a child to lavish her love on and be loved in return, he'd sought to control even that, preventing any further procreation. But I had somehow been conceived, and she had loved me, even if it was only actively demonstrated when he'd not been around to witness it.

He opened his eyes then, and stared at Leonard with a look that threatened the violence his physical body could not deliver.

'So don't you dare insult me or our precious family name by taking up with an ill-educated tart of a kitchen girl.'

'I *will* be with her, Father.'

'Then you are no longer a son of mine. You will be disinherited. I swear it. The company shall go to Sidney permanently – even if he has failed me at the last.'

Although keen to defend myself, I didn't want to interrupt this interchange. I liked where it was leading and was content to let the two men battle this out without further input from me. To distract Father now, when I was on the verge of being handed the Bellingham crown, would be foolhardy, even though I could barely contain my glee at this unexpected turn of events.

'Do your worst,' my brother said. Despite everything, I admired his courage and sacrifice in that moment, as he would not be swayed by the threats of the old man. I remained the sycophant, eager to please and ingratiate myself with my father. Eager, if I'm honest, to become the heir, to inherit the house, the wealth and the respect.

'So be it,' my father muttered, and asked me to ring the bell. Burton appeared at the door almost instantly, but he was a man given to lurking at doorways, and doubtless had heard every word.

'Burton, instruct Mrs Murray to fire the kitchen maid and arrange for Dartington to come here promptly.'

Chapter 41

1920

Phoebe stared at the brick wall behind the door in utter disbelief. She'd solved the puzzle and there was nothing – no deeds or treasures, and no opportunity to claim back an inheritance taken away from the rightful heir on the whim of a twisted old man. It didn't make sense.

Sidney stood beside her on the top landing of the staircase that led nowhere, and she realised how unnervingly accurate the Bellingham boys had been with their naming of this quiet corner of the east wing.

'I don't understand. Where is the next clue? This absolutely can't be the end.'

'That's exactly how I felt. But it's the final and cruellest embodiment of my father's malice. A stupid quest to the end of the rainbow where there never was a pot of gold.'

'Hold on a moment,' she said, absorbing his words and taking a step away from him. 'You got to this point too? You *knew* that there was nothing behind this door and yet you let me go through all this?'

He shrugged as the truth of her own words echoed around her head. The old Mr Bellingham's promise had been a lie. Her stomach concertinaed. She had so badly wanted to prove her worth to Sidney, and even though her motives for solving the puzzle had changed, she felt hollow. It had all been for nothing, because, like the maze, it was unsolvable. But what hurt her most at that moment was the betrayal by a man she'd come to trust. She thought Sidney Bellingham had changed, that he was different to his father, but he wasn't. He was still playing cruel games.

'But . . . but my father said you hadn't solved the puzzle. He said the birthright was still there for the taking. He was told so by your father on his deathbed.'

Reverting to form, Sidney let out a mocking snort. 'Oh, I see your motives more clearly now. And you thought you'd claim it? Whip the Hall away from me and waltz off into the sunset with my mother's pearls?'

Was it her imagination? Or did he look somewhat forlorn at the possibility he'd been played too? Well, what's good for the goose . . ., she mused.

'Not for myself. To prove it could be done.' This was almost true. She'd never wanted the wealth, only to crush him into the dirt. And then when she'd believed him to be a decent human being after all, her motivation had changed. She'd seen an opportunity to validate her relationship with Douglas, and had been keen to prove herself worthy to Sidney. Worthy of what, she hadn't decided.

'Leonard always had a more charitable side to him, but he was wrong. The puzzle ends here. It was our father's last game with his sons. His ultimate revenge. Life had dealt him so many disappointments and he made sure we understood that this was the way of the world. I've thought a lot about it over the years and am convinced he simply got rid of Mother's possessions – scattered them to the four winds. As for the deeds, I searched for them for a while but have long suspected they were lodged with Dartington, to be handed over at some point in the future – perhaps even to a grandchild, after his own sons let him down so badly. Ha! The chances of that are now non-existent. Leonard's child is not blood and I will never procreate . . . No one would have me.'

He smiled, pleased at his own joke, but perhaps he was right. The possibility it was all a charade was certainly borne out by Clement Bellingham's past behaviour. Phoebe felt her heart sink.

'The continuation of the company was his main concern, and I suspect he always intended to hand it to me. I was the more fitting successor and he knew that. If he said anything to my brother about the puzzle not being completed, it was merely to keep us playing, to have a last laugh from beyond the grave. But with Leonard gone, there was no point in investigating any of this further – I had everything I needed, and was never a fan of Solitaire.'

He looked at Phoebe's desperate face, noticed her building emotion and disbelieving eyes, and shook his head. 'It's not worth getting upset about – the puzzle was another empty box. He did it to me all the time.'

Mrs Murray had told her about the non-existent birthday gift Sidney was presented with on his seventh birthday. It explained his behaviour towards her, letting her try to solve the unsolvable, but you had to be better than the bullies in life, not emulate them, or it became an endless circle of destruction.

Confronted with his total lack of feeling, she wondered if she'd been wrong to reconcile herself to him. Had their friendship also been a game?

'I'm tired of being manipulated by you,' she said, wanting to cry but not prepared to give him the satisfaction. No wonder he'd had the whispers of a smile dancing around the edges of his mouth all the way back through the woods. He'd anticipated her failure. How foolish to mistake it for a sign that he was beginning to thaw, that he was happy to be around her and proud of her success in solving the clues.

'Don't blame me – blame my father,' he said. 'I felt the same crushing disappointment that you feel now. He spent years telling us everything he treasured was at the top of these stairs – that a mecca containing everything of value to this family awaited us.'

'So letting me experience the misery you endured makes you feel better?' she asked. 'Does it give you satisfaction to hurt me in this way? Were you testing me?'

She glared at him and he was forced to drop his eyes to the floor.

'I wanted you to understand,' he said, shrugging his shoulders, suddenly looking slightly vulnerable and childlike. 'And to do that, you had to feel the things I felt. *This was my life.* A constant and unrelenting stream of games and tricks. You get to the point where you feel nothing – where you anticipate that everything is an unkind joke and every hope you hold will end in disappointment.'

But his explanation didn't wash. 'All your excitement at my endeavours has really been you secretly laughing at me. You knew there was no room. You have been mocking me and enjoying every step of the journey, all the while allowing me to believe you valued my friendship.'

Sidney, whose face had gone from cool indifference to concern, stepped forward and put out his arm, but she shrugged his touch away.

'But I do. You've got this wrong, Phoebe. My excitement at watching you work through the puzzles has not been in anticipation of your failure. My God,' he whispered. 'Do you really believe I'm so very like my father?'

'What else am I to think?'

Satan, sitting at their feet, looked up at the pair of them. Sensing Phoebe's distress, and perhaps aware that his master was responsible for it, he shuffled closer to her feet and licked at her curled fingers, which hung limply by her side. They both noticed his actions.

'It was a test, but not in the way you think. You've proved how bright you are by solving this. You may not be a Bellingham by blood, but you have the same sharpness of mind and determination to succeed. You fit in here. I didn't think you would, but I was wrong.'

He sounded almost desperate as Phoebe backed away from him and he took cautious steps towards her. He was gabbling and his usual reserve had evaporated.

'Things have changed since you arrived. *I've changed since you arrived*. This has always been a family business and I want it to stay that way.' He paused. 'I want you legally recognised as my heir.'

He tried once more to make physical contact, to reassure, and put his arm out to her elbow, but she snatched it away. She was done with this house and this man.

'Why would I want this horrible house? The unhappiness seeps from every wall and swirls around in the particles of dust that float through every room. Sylvia Bellingham spent twenty years trapped here, desperate to escape, and I only hope that wherever she went she found peace.'

She would not allow herself to become another victim of the Hall, like his mother.

'I'll be twenty-one soon and independent. I know what my parents left isn't much but I look at you and am more certain than ever that money brings with it no guarantee of happiness. If you had been brought up like me, and witnessed the unselfish, undemanding love my parents had for each other, you would understand. But you weren't, and for that I pity you, Sidney. I pity you more than you will ever know.'

His eyes narrowed yet again, and his temper finally surfaced. 'You know nothing of what I've been through. I have loved, twice, and both times completely and with every fibre of my being – different types of love, but love, nonetheless. You talk of your parents' love as though you understand it, but how can you? You've never experienced it.'

'And you, equally, know nothing about me,' she said, certain that her feelings for Douglas were heading this way. She was pulled to that young man in exactly the manner he described – so much so, she barely trusted herself around him, and understood completely why so many young couples raced to the altar.

Their faces were closer now, but the anger and frustration they were both feeling was muddying the atmosphere. They stared at each other, both passionate about the points they were making, and then something swept over Phoebe that she couldn't define, but that made her heart race and her mouth dry.

Sidney's eyes dropped for the smallest fraction of a second to her lips, and something rolled in her chest, leaving her breathless. He was playing with her again, some lesson she was too naive to appreciate, but this one was cruel, unkind and possibly inappropriate. It was the final unexpectedly heavy straw. He would never change. She'd thought she was getting somewhere with him, but it always came back to his stupid games.

'Why on earth would I want you to name me as your heir? I don't want to be a part of this cycle of bitterness and destruction. This is not my home and I must think about leaving. Besides, despite your attempts to interfere, I'm with Douglas now. He asked me to be his sweetheart and he doesn't play silly games with my emotions. Instead, he makes me feel valued and treats me like a woman – not a child.' It wasn't how she had intended to deliver the news, but her hackles were up, and it was important he understood that she and Douglas intended to make their own way, forge their own path, without handouts from him.

A vein pulsed in Sidney's forehead and his nostrils flared. 'You little fool. Then you are beyond my help.' If looks could kill, Phoebe would be six feet under.

She started to walk back down the stairs to the main body of the house. As she turned at the half-landing, she heard a low growl, followed by a heavy thud, where she could only assume he had either punched or kicked the wall. She glanced back, to see him slide down the door and, tearing at his hair, rest his head in his hands.

Perhaps if she hadn't had Douglas, Phoebe would have packed her bags that very night, not caring where she went, just to escape the suffocating atmosphere. But the thought of her young man, his shy smiles and their stolen kisses, meant a small and happy part of her wanted to stay at Halesham Hall, at least until she knew where their relationship was heading. Besides, she intended to enjoy the Christmas festivities, having played such a large role in their preparation, and the staff were her friends – even Ada.

She found Douglas later that afternoon, lifting parsnips the size of a small child's arm from the soil. He saw her walking across to the vegetable gardens and put down his fork, the biggest grin spreading across his face.

'Here comes my girl,' he said, announcing his ownership of her to anyone who would listen, and raised his arms to catch her as she ran to him. It was a lovely feeling – to be cherished so.

'Oh, Douglas,' she said, relieved to find comfort in his embrace. Woodsmoke hung in the air from an earlier bonfire and the wonderful outdoorsy smell of him lifted her spirits as her head rested on his chest and his lips toyed with her hair.

'What's the matter? You look glum.'

She looked up into his darling face. 'It's my uncle.'

'Isn't it always?'

'More games, more cruelty. I've had enough. I had such great plans to steal back my father's inheritance when I first arrived . . .'

Douglas pulled back and frowned at her.

'It's a long story connected to Clement – my grandfather – devising a stupid puzzle to decide which son should inherit. I thought it was possible to reverse it, but it turns out I was wrong, and now Sidney has resolved to accept me as his niece after all, and wants to leave me everything in his will regardless.'

'But that's wonderful – you've got what you came here for. I'm both surprised and impressed, Phoebe. I never had you pegged as the devious sort. With that sort of cunning, you'll make an excellent head of the Bellingham household.' He grinned. 'We could take on the world.'

Phoebe shook her head. 'You don't understand. I thought it was what I wanted but it isn't. I reach my majority after Christmas and although the sum I inherit will be small, I will finally be independent. Perhaps it's time for me to think about applying for a position somewhere.'

'Don't be so hasty, little one.' Douglas's face crumpled into a worried frown. 'Why shouldn't the inheritance fall to you? You have Bellingham blood running through your veins, for good or ill. Don't let pride make you push it away. He has no one else, Phoebe. What will he do if you leave and refuse to be part of his life? Bequeath his worldly goods to some charity? Consumptive females? Foreign sailors? Or a ragged school?'

There was something holding her back from admitting the truth of her parentage to Douglas. Perhaps she didn't want him judging her mother or thinking less of her. Sidney was the only person who knew and, for the time being, she wanted it to stay that way.

'I honestly don't care. Keep to the arrangements he had before I arrived, I suppose, whatever they were. Money doesn't make you happy – he's proof enough of that.'

'Tell that to the old boy who sleeps under the railway bridge in town. Mr Bellingham might be a miserable git who has no one who truly cares about him, but at least when he cries himself to sleep, he does it in a warm, comfortable bed, with his stomach full and a roof over his head. It is foolish to take umbrage over such a trivial matter, when you have a cosy room here of your own. Your plan is working – you've started to worm your way in . . .'

She didn't like Douglas's use of the word worm, as if she was a creature who didn't belong, something inching into the dead flesh of a corpse. An uncomfortable feeling bubbled inside. Did Douglas really not know her, after all?

In fact, she began to wonder if she really knew him.

Chapter 42

'Good evening,' Phoebe announced, stepping into the drawing room later. A much more melancholy sound came from the phonograph – it was not a time for jazz music, it appeared. 'May I join you?'

Sidney scrambled to his feet, a half-empty decanter of whisky by his side, and directed her to the opposite chair. Satan was flopped across the deerskin rug in front of a roaring fire, two large paws resting either side of his large head, his silky ears spread flat to the floor. The room looked cheery where Mrs Murray and Ada had hung holly boughs from the picture frames. She'd helped to make the berries from dried peas and red sealing wax, as the hungry blackbirds had stripped the bushes bare that winter, and the spicy scent of his whisky added to the seasonal atmosphere. But Phoebe didn't feel full of festive cheer. She felt empty and confused.

He began to pace in front of the fire, and Satan lifted his head and followed his master's inexplicable zigzagging with his doleful eyes. There was a moment when Sidney's gaze met Phoebe's as they both tried to assess the lie of the land. Harsh words had been spoken by them both, but surely he recognised that they needed to resolve things calmly, one way or another.

'You may be an innocent in so many regards, but I must acknowledge your surprising cunning.'

She frowned.

'You came to the Hall to overthrow me, did you not? Pretending you wanted nothing but family, and all the time carrying the weight of the injustice you perceived your father had suffered.'

'Yes,' she replied.

'And you have failed.'

'So it would seem.'

'So now what? Arsenic in my plum pudding?'

'Don't be ridiculous. I didn't want you dead. I wanted you to pay for what I thought you'd done to my father. But I was wrong about so much of the past and I no longer feel the anger towards you that I once did. However, it was mean of you to let me pursue the puzzles knowing I would fail, and if I were a man, I would probably have punched you on the staircase.'

'Good God. What has happened to you? These are not the words of the naive girl who arrived at the Hall that stormy afternoon all those weeks ago.'

'She is older and wiser,' Phoebe replied. 'Someone has taken it upon himself to teach her a few harsh life lessons. Well done, Sidney. I think I'm now ready to face the world and all its unkindness.'

'That's not what I intended.' His voice was low as he hung his head over the cut-glass tumbler as if to take a sip but then placed it down on the side table and sank back into the armchair. 'But I've lived that life, too. I've had all the joy knocked out of me over the years, on occasion quite literally.'

Her patience was wearing thin. 'It's easy to keep blaming your father – to say he was the architect of the Hall and all its foibles – but I don't see him walking these dark corridors any longer. Whilst I can see that you are trying, you could have changed things much sooner – made it easier for staff, and made the Hall a brighter, happier place to be, but you chose not to. I believe you enjoy the games as much as he did.'

'But I have addressed the issues in the kitchen. The dining room has been refurbished. I've done those things for you, Phoebe.'

She shook her head and stared at her hands. 'You're worse than me. I may be naive and far too willing to give my heart, but I'd rather be like that, with the smallest hope of finding someone, two parts of a whole like my parents, than like you, so cynical you'll never find anyone to share your life with – apart from Satan, and he would love you even if you were his namesake.'

She looked up at him, trying to engage eye contact and stress her point.

'You have a choice, Sidney. You can sit in this house and let it consume you or you can set about altering all those things that make it such an unpleasant place to live. You have staff who respect you and will follow your lead. Try looking for the good in people, instead of only seeing the bad. Find a wife. Fill this house with laughter and light, maybe even children, instead of silence and shadows. All of these things are in your power. Being loved is within your power.'

His eyes met hers, but only briefly. He was clearly uncomfortable because he knew she had a point.

'And you think you've found these things in Douglas?'

'My heart is my own affair but, yes, I believe he has real feelings for me.'

He shook his head. 'You're too trusting, Phoebe. You still need someone to protect you from yourself.'

'As much as it pains me to say it, the only person I need

protecting from is you. If I stay here much longer, your cynicism will eat away at my soul. You're wrong about Douglas. But then how can I expect you to see the good in people when you can't even see it in yourself?'

Somewhere deep inside, she knew Sidney was battling his demons. Look at how he'd pulled her from the unsolvable maze. How he was starting to address issues in the house. Even his misguided attempt to warn her about Douglas was proof of sorts that he cared.

'I'm sorry I let you go through the charade of unlocking the door. It was thoughtless of me. I'm not a good man, Phoebe, and I warned you this house has ghosts. Stay and help me become a better person.'

For the first time since she'd known him, he looked almost contrite. She took little satisfaction from the fact that, in a few short months, this man had gone from ordering her off the property to trying to manipulate her emotionally by implying that his salvation rested entirely in her hands.

'You don't need me to oversee your deliverance. The power lies inside yourself. I watch you with Satan when you think no one is around, and there is a deep love between you and Mrs Murray that goes beyond employer and housekeeper – if only you would both acknowledge it. Because I can't stay here for ever, and we both know that. I have to pick myself up from my parents' death and carry on with my life. Find somewhere I do belong and start again.'

But even as she said these words, she doubted herself. She wanted to leave but she didn't – all tied up in the same beat of her confused heart. Halesham Hall and the people within it had come to mean so much more to her than she dared to admit.

Chapter 43

Later that evening, Phoebe went down to the kitchens and hung around until everyone but Douglas and Mrs Murray had retired. She wanted some time alone with Douglas, if only to help her focus her thoughts.

The older woman lingered with them, finding things to do as if she'd elected herself Phoebe's unofficial chaperone. Phoebe sat at the long refectory table, repeatedly stirring her now tepid cocoa, willing the older woman to leave so that she could sink into his arms and for everything to be all right. She looked across at him, perched on the edge of a low chair in front of the range, polishing a pair of brown leather boots so vigorously she felt sure he would wear a hole in them. The smell of turpentine reminded her of her father's Sunday night shoe-cleaning ritual – the waves of grief less ferocious now, even though she knew the tide would never stop coming in completely. Mrs Murray was sitting opposite, darning a grey woollen sock – a job she would normally have done in her own sitting room.

'I notice the master is crabbit tonight,' Murray said. 'He hinted you might be leaving us soon. I'll be sorry to see you go, lass.'

Douglas looked up and frowned.

'Nothing is settled, but this isn't my home. He won't let me work in the kitchens any longer so I need to find employment, make a life for myself. I'll keep in touch and come back to visit, but I hope you will take care of him when I leave.'

'Aye, I'll look after him. I've been doing so since he was six years old. I'd do anything for that laddie.'

Phoebe reached across the table and clutched the older woman's hand. 'Then remind him. He needs to know that he is loved.'

'Och, I don't know about that.' Mrs Murray focused intently on the needle and the darning wool. 'It's not my place, and he doesn't cope well with emotions – although I'm hardly one to talk. I guess he never had anyone to show him, to tell him that sometimes it's fine to be honest about how you feel, and that there are positive things you can do in negative situations. Instead he bottles things up. Whenever he's angry he lashes out at innocent people, usually staff, and when he is truly wounded, he tries to cover up his pain by pretending he doesn't care. And yet he wears the pain of that caring across his face as clear as day.' Her eyes misted over and she shook her head gently from side to side. 'Even at six years old, I remember him telling me he hadn't really loved his mother all that much. That her going was a blessing. Somehow, in his head, that made things better. And Leonard told me that he only found out the truth of Sidney's real feelings for your mother on the day of the funeral. He'd been so insistent that he didn't care for her. It's a form of self-defence, see? It's how he protects his broken heart.'

Mrs Murray glanced at the wall clock. 'Bed for you now, miss,' she said, eyeing Douglas, who'd stood up and was pouring himself some more beer from the large jug. He'd had a few over dinner, perhaps drowning his sorrows because she was talking of leaving.

Phoebe reluctantly pushed her chair back. Mrs Murray wasn't going to let them be alone together, so she took her mug to the scullery and rinsed it out, standing it upside down on the wooden draining rack. When she returned to the kitchen, the room was empty. The housekeeper had doubtless ordered Douglas to bed too, preserving Phoebe's virtue being her last task of the day. Phoebe picked up the small oil lamp and carried it carefully up the servant stairs to the main body of the house, towards the central staircase, but as she walked along the dim corridor, the door to the drawing room swung inwards.

'In here,' a voice whispered.

Phoebe held the light aloft to see Douglas's face winking at her in the shadows. She slipped inside and placed the lamp on a side table.

'There was no way old Murray was going to leave us, and I wanted to be alone with my best girl. Come here,' he said, reaching out for her, sliding his broad hands around her slim waist and crushing her body to his as he kissed her. He tasted of beer and the Woodbines he so loved, but his lips were warm and she revelled in the embrace.

'I can't believe you've let him drive you out,' he said as the spine-tingling kiss finally ended.

She shrugged. 'I'm weary of it all – the games, his changeable moods. I'm glad he and I have a better relationship and I realise I was mistaken about the past, but there are things you don't know. I shouldn't be here and certainly don't deserve to be named in his will or be involved in the company.'

'Then you're cutting off your nose to spite your face.' Douglas shook his head. 'Do you have any idea how fortunate you are to be in this position? Most of us are born into poverty and stand little chance of clawing our way out of it, but you have this fantastic possibility knocking at your door. He's in a great position to help me, help *us*, with the future. This has gone far enough. Instead of either alienating him or playing the part of some self-righteous little madam, why don't you apologise and gratefully accept the things he's offering? There's a good girl.'

Phoebe was glad of the dim light, because it hid her perplexed expression as she tried to work out what Douglas was saying.

'When he realises we're serious about each other, and if you keep playing your part, it's highly likely a few handouts will come your way. He's got more than enough money. Let him support us to follow our dreams. A few hundred would set up that import business I talked about and then I can escape this pathetic excuse of a life – at another man's beck and call – and start again in the city.'

'*Your* dreams,' Phoebe corrected, her stomach beginning an uneasy churn. He'd really thought this all through to an alarming degree, but with the rash assumption that she wanted the same things as him. 'I'm a country girl. Cities suffocate and intimidate me.'

He leaned further into her and pulled her closer. 'Come now. There's no need to be anxious. I'll look after you.'

It's interesting how the same words can be said in different ways and have multiple meanings. Intonation and accompanying facial gestures can make subtle and sometimes uncomfortable differences. Those words should have made her feel safe and loved, but when Douglas said them, they sounded controlling. There was no acknowledgement that she wasn't happy about moving to a city, as if that wasn't up for debate – just the bold statement that he would look after her when they did.

'It's all very noble but high morals don't pay the bills.' He was nuzzling into her hair again, his breathing getting heavier and his grip getting tighter. 'Do the wide eyes, pander to his vanities, talk about the importance of family – the sort of thing you do so well.'

She pulled back, looking into his pale blue-grey eyes in the flickering light. They weren't as open as she remembered. There was a darkness about them she hadn't noticed before. Had she been played?

'Is it me you want or my uncle's money?' she asked, desperately hoping she was wrong about all this.

Douglas shrugged. 'Both. But there's nothing wrong with that. If the prettiest hen lays the biggest eggs, you take them both and run.'

'And if I refuse? Resolutely insist I'm not to be included in his will?'

Phoebe rarely felt emboldened, but at that moment she did. Standing up to domineering men was becoming a habit. She pulled her shoulders back and refused to break his gaze. She was still young, but she had values and principles that she held dear, and would defend them to the grave.

For the first time, Douglas looked less sure of himself. 'But that's not going to happen.' His eyes were fierce now, and his voice threatening.

Phoebe began to panic. How could she have thought herself in love with someone she barely knew? All those hours fantasising about a man who she suddenly realised wasn't what she'd thought he was at all. She'd completely failed until that moment to spot the burning resentment that he'd carried since childhood. He'd seen a way to elevate himself into higher social circles and shake off the shackles of his lowly birth. Was she just a means to an end? She could see the answer in his eyes.

How could she have been so naive?

'You were so close, Phoebe. You'd done so well. For him to talk about making you his heir was such a coup. Somehow you broke through his reserve and suspicion. But I won't have that possibility waved at me, only for you to go all righteous and it get snatched away. Understand?' he growled.

It was frightening. She'd never seen him like this before – angry and focused. Where had the lovely, open Douglas gone? The shy man who'd presented her with a freshly picked apple and who took a whole afternoon to summon up the courage to hold her hand? An uncomfortable knot formed in her stomach. Had it all been an act?

She took a step away from him, her back now up against the wall. 'Do you even like me?' she asked. 'Or have you been playing games too?'

'Me play games? Ha,' he scoffed. 'Running around like some virtuous maiden, throwing me longing looks across the gardens and flirting across the table. You were like a bloody dog, following me about and hoping to be petted. My God. Do you have any idea how hard it's been for me to play the long game? To take this slowly? There have been times when your kisses have told me all I need to know. I could have had you a hundred times – you know I could. I felt the passion in your quaking body and tight grip. The fire was burning in both of us and it would have been so easy to make love to you. You would have yielded in a heartbeat, but I walked away.'

She knew he was right. Despite all her mother's warnings about the machinations of men, and her moral upbringing and sense of self-worth, in the heat of those moments, she would have surrendered to him totally.

'I've been a fool,' she acknowledged, with a painful swallow. 'This is wrong. You don't have feelings for me – not really. I don't want to be your girl any more, Douglas. I'm sick of being manipulated by others. It's games with all of you.'

'That's as maybe, but the funny thing is,' he said, taking everything she said with alarming calmness and leaning towards her like a hunting cat, 'despite everything, I know you still want me.'

His face was inches from hers now and he put one hand on

the wall behind her, preventing her from moving towards the door. She tipped her head backwards to get away from his hot, beery breath, but his face came closer. And there was some truth in his statement. Under his penetrating stare, the weird fizzes and chills coursed madly around her body. She'd grown up in so many ways since arriving in Halesham and this awakening of her sexuality was the most powerful. Douglas had opened a door to a flood of carnal feelings and all-consuming emotions. She longed to be touched, ached to be kissed, but no longer by him. This was all wrong.

'We could have had it all,' he mused, shaking his head. 'A future at the Hall and a thriving company waiting in the wings until Bastard Bellingham passed it over to his trusted nephew-in-law. And now you've made me show my hand and ruined everything. Perhaps I should have held back on the beer tonight. Still . . .' He winked and her stomach rolled again. 'No reason why we can't have a bit of fun before we part ways. How about an early Christmas present – for me and for you?' His head was uncomfortably close to hers as he whispered these unwelcome words into her ear.

'That was when I was foolish enough to think I loved you.'

'Oh, but you will,' he said, as his mouth came for hers and her head had nowhere to go. 'After this, you'll want me more than ever. Let me give you a taste of what a future with me might hold, and then perhaps you'll rethink your silly behaviour.'

His kisses were violent and forceful, his lips bruising hers and not allowing her to catch her breath. The arm blocking her escape route slid behind her back and yanked her slender frame to his once more, pressing hard on the small of her back. Their two bodies locked.

'No,' she shouted, finally twisting her face away. 'I will not let this happen.' Her mother had been taken advantage of like this, and was then left to deal with the consequences alone. Perhaps she would have spent her whole life being a victim had Leonard not come along. But that would not be Phoebe's future. She simply would not become another version of her mother.

'I'm pretty sure no one is going to hear you. Besides,' his lip curled, 'I don't think you really mean it.'

'Don't you?' She cocked her head to one side.

Finding an inner strength, both mentally and physically, she lifted her leg sharply and made sure Douglas knew that no meant no. He groaned and crumpled before her, collapsing at her feet, just as the drawing room door burst open and light from the corridor illuminated them in the gloom.

Sidney stood silhouetted in the doorway, his wide eyes searching for the source of the shouts that had surely drawn him to her. He focused on the writhing Douglas and assessed the situation.

'I heard voices, but it rather looks as if you have everything under control, Phoebe, and have finally recognised this man for the scoundrel that he is. Better late than never.'

He gave her an approving nod and then strode over to Douglas, who had slid back up the wall but was still hunched forward, clearly in a lot of pain.

'You're fired, Douglas. I want you out of my house and out of my sight,' he said. 'Your employment here is terminated with immediate effect and, if I have anything to do with it, you won't find work in Suffolk again, never mind Halesham.'

'You bastard, Bellingham,' he hissed.

'I may not be a particularly nice man, but I would never force myself upon a woman – particularly an innocent.'

Douglas fixed Sidney with an intense stare. 'How dare you judge me and my actions when everyone knows about your past. All those women . . .'

Sidney shrugged. 'Always reciprocal and not as many as people think. A few grains of truth and an overactive rumour mill. And not one of those women was in love with me the way this poor, misguided woman is with you. You don't deserve her. She is a kind, loving and gentle soul, an honest individual who sees the best in everyone – even me.' He paused and narrowed his eyes, flicking a glance at Phoebe and then dropping his gaze to the floor, as he said the words again, but more quietly this time. 'Even me.'

'You utter hypocrite, Bellingham. This poor girl is related to you by blood. She turned up on your doorstep looking for some compassion and a family, and you turned her away in a damn thunderstorm, of all things. And then, *then*, you had the gall to treat her like a servant. All she wants is love – at least I was prepared to give it to her, whatever my motives were. You, on the other hand, treated her like dirt from the start.'

The truth of his words made Sidney flinch, but it also inflamed his anger, and he lunged for the collar of his accuser as Douglas sidestepped. The two men were similar in height but Douglas was younger and broader. She had no doubt that if this turned ugly, Sidney would come off worse, and her heart tugged in his direction.

Tired of watching things play out as though she was no longer in the room, she stepped forward. 'Stop this, both of you.' Her best bet was to place herself between them. Surely neither would risk hurting her? Manoeuvring herself into the gap, but facing Sidney, because she believed he was the one who would listen to her, she looked up into his scowling face. His eyes flicked briefly to hers and there was something behind them that made it impossible for her to tear her gaze away.

'Just let him go. He's not worth it,' she begged, but Douglas had started hobbling across the room the instant she'd used herself as a barrier, and had already moved to the door that led to the garden. He might have been the stronger of the two, but Sidney was more of a man than he would ever be. Her heart flipped then, because she knew the master of Halesham Hall would have taken on his servant to defend her honour, doubtless as aware as she was that the odds were not in his favour. But then men, she was learning, had an innate desire to assert their physical strength in any potentially volatile situation, and almost always had to have the final word.

The door slammed and Douglas disappeared into the night, leaving Phoebe and Sidney, eyes locked. A curious atmosphere circled the room, slowly settling to the floor like the dust motes about them.

'Are you all right?' he asked, and she nodded, stepping forward and letting Sidney put his arms around her. She wasn't sure how long they stood together in the dark room, a white spear of moonlight slicing through the heavy curtains to her right and the glow from the oil lamps, a softer orange hue to her left. Perhaps it was only a minute or two, but it felt so much longer, and it felt good. It made her realise how much she needed someone in her life to comfort her in times of crisis, to heal her wounds and lean on, so that whatever the future held, she wasn't facing it alone. Was that why she had so foolishly latched on to Douglas? Because he had cunningly slid into her life to fill that gap?

Finally, Sidney broke the silence. His warm breath travelled across her cheek as he spoke.

'I was wrong about you. Seems to me, Phoebe Bellingham, that you are a much stronger and more capable woman than I believed.'

Chapter 44

1899

Father finally passed away on the thirteenth of September, five days after he threatened to disinherit Leonard should he go ahead with the marriage. The clocks were stopped, the mirrors were draped in black crepe and the few photographs we had were laid face down. Burton sat with the body until the burial, suitably lubricated so as not to mind the unpleasantness of the task.

The funeral, held on the fifteenth, was attended by Leonard and me, some of the senior household staff, and a handful of dusty, dry old men who worked for Bellingham Games in various capacities, probably thinking they'd better show willing in case their jobs were on the line. None of his business acquaintances came, I noticed. No one from the city. Not one of the self-important men he'd lavished his hospitality on over the years. Not even the gentleman from Cross Ridge, father of Leonard's preferred bride. The truth was Clement Bellingham wasn't liked. Everyone paid him lip service during his life, but he had garnered no respect on a personal level, formed no true friendships. Perhaps some of his longer-standing acquaintances even knew of his treatment of our mother – a revelation I was still coming to terms with.

Dartington read out the hastily updated version of the will to us that afternoon, the one he'd been summoned to alter on Father's deathbed. He sat behind Father's desk (which irked me beyond reason) and peered over the edge of his wire-rimmed spectacles. I was seated next to my brother but would not meet his eye, deliberately tilting my body from his.

'Essentially, the company will pass to you permanently, Sidney, when you are of age, and in its entirety, for finding the key,' he said, summing up the two pages of legal jargon for us, and tapping a bundle of papers together on the desk to neaten them up. 'It was important to your father that the future of Bellingham Games was secured, and I know he has faith in you to nurture and grow his legacy.' He turned to my brother. 'And you, young man, have some serious decisions to make. You *will* be disinherited should you go ahead and marry that girl. He made it perfectly clear that you are to make a more suitable marriage, possibly that Cross Ridge woman, and then you can continue to draw a not insubstantial income for the remainder of your life, and play a more junior role in the company, under Sidney's direction.'

I'd underestimated the old man's strength of feeling regarding the family reputation, but would not allow myself to feel guilty for exposing Leonard's intentions. I waited for my brother's outrage, but it did not come.

'I will not give her up. We marry tomorrow.'

'Then you are disinherited. Sidney becomes custodian of Halesham Hall until such time as the stipulations within the will are met.'

'What? I don't understand. Why don't I inherit the house?' I asked. Not content with the company, I wanted it all. Hell, after what Leonard had taken from me – I deserved it all.

'And I fail to see your confusion. Whoever solves the puzzle is entitled to the Hall and the family wealth. As he used the word "whoever" to me on his deathbed, I can only assume this was deliberately vague, to allow future generations, or even Leonard himself, to claim victory. I think he harboured hopes that your brother would come to his senses regarding his marriage plans. Alas, he has not. I also understood from Clement that he had made this arrangement perfectly clear to both of you on numerous occasions, but as neither of you have produced the deeds, I can only assume that you failed in this endeavour.'

'But I did solve it.' My voice was becoming agitated and I thumped my fist on the desk, leaning aggressively towards him. 'I opened the damn door and there was nothing there.'

'More tricks,' Leonard said dispassionately. 'More gifts of empty boxes and windows that look out on nothing.'

Dartington, unmoved by my temper, reached down for his case and calmly replaced his papers. 'Nothing was ever straightforward with your father – you and your brother should know that more than anyone. Now, if you'll excuse me, I believe Murray mentioned sandwiches, and I do have a rather long journey home . . .'

Leonard and I rejoined the pathetic cluster of mourners assembled in the morning room, but they made no attempt to scrabble for kind words or fond memories of the deceased, unlike at other funerals I'd attended. Instead, we found other, safer topics of conversation – the weather, the harvest and a dusting of politics.

I stood as far away from my brother as I could, quietly fuming over his determination not to give Jane up. Mrs Murray told me that Leonard had lodged her in Halesham since her dismissal, clearly biding his time until our father passed away. It would not take long for the Chinese whispers to spread around the county. There was nothing the townsfolk liked more than a scandal – and the more moneyed you were, the juicier the scandal became.

Practical matters distracted me from my simmering anger.

'You'll stay on, of course?' I said to Murray as she offered me a plate of dainty sandwiches.

I was only too aware of the huge burden of responsibility about to befall me. As detailed in the will, Father had arranged for people to oversee the business whilst I finished my education, but with Leonard shortly to be disinherited, I was now head of the house, under Dartington's guardianship. I had little idea of the minutiae that role entailed. Nor, to be honest, did I care. If I could secure old Murray, the staff would continue much as before and I needn't be bothered with the details.

'If that's your wish, Master Sidney.'

'I think Mother would have wanted you to. Besides, what do I know of running the Hall?'

'You do know that I only remained because she made me promise?' The older lady gave me a direct and earnest stare. I frowned. 'Promise that I would do my best to protect you both from him. Be a watchful eye. That duty has been discharged, I believe.'

As I absorbed her words, my respect for this no-nonsense but ultimately kind woman grew even more. Perhaps, in some ways, she'd slipped into the role of the mother I'd lost – her servile position blinding me to the extent of her love and care. She'd always been on my side, concealing her true loyalties from Father, and playing a complicated game in order to protect his sons and the staff from the worst of his schemes and his temper.

'And you never once heard from her?'

She shook her head. 'Not once these nine years, sir. We agreed it was too risky for me to know her plans, or to attempt any communication, especially as Burton oversees all post that comes to the house. I trusted she would find a way . . . if she could.'

Unspoken thoughts hung heavy in the air between us. Had she also seen his hands that night? I wondered.

I looked across at Leonard and noted his contented smile and calm resignation – serving to fuel the slow-burning fire I'd been nursing these past couple of weeks.

Burton was pouring a tray of whiskies for the older gentlemen. I walked over to him and took a tumbler from the tray, aware it might raise eyebrows, but not caring.

'Have one yourself,' I said magnanimously, caring not that my position was custodial and under the guardianship of Dartington. It was mine unless someone said otherwise, and I would embrace the role with relish.

He gave a supercilious smile. 'Thank you, sir.'

I felt sorry for him, as he was unaware that his services were shortly to be dispensed with. His drinking had started to affect his work and I had no time for a man whose ultimate loyalty would always lie with my father. Let him have a few final drinks, I thought, and this time with the master's blessing.

I knocked back the honey-coloured liquid in one, trying not to splutter and draw attention to my unfamiliarity with alcohol. It stung, burning a passage down the back of my throat. The taste would take some getting used to, but the almost instantaneous, heady after-effects were most welcome. They dulled the pain of losing the girl I loved and the disappointments of the staircase.

I made small talk with Father's employees, who all but bowed and scraped at my feet, clearly annoyed that the new head of Bellingham Games was a mere boy. Three more large whiskies found their way into my stomach as I listened to their nauseating flattery. The intoxication was liberating. Aside from some illicit rum smuggled into the dorms and the alcohol I was occasionally permitted with formal meals, I hadn't experienced the delight of this rite of passage. Now, more than ever before, I wanted to prove I was the adult. I had the body, brains and now the power that went beyond my years, overriding the increasingly irrelevant year of my birth.

'That's enough, old boy,' Leonard said, as I staggered towards an equally unsteady Burton for a fifth.

'Dammit, I'll drink whisky if I feel like it. You're not the boss of me.' I glared at him. 'If I'm old enough to oversee all this . . .' and I swung my arm clumsily across the room, the drink spilling from my glass, its smoky aroma more potent for being released so recklessly into the atmosphere, 'then I rather think I'm old enough to do as I damn well please. Fill me up, Burton.'

The butler looked uncertainly between me and my brother but obeyed. He knew which side his bread was buttered and that I was now in a position to see him dismissed in a heartbeat. I waited for him to replenish the glass before a wave of uncontrollable malice swept over me.

'And please know that your services at the Hall will no longer be required as of tomorrow. If you go quietly, any reference will not mention your propensity to help yourself to the contents of the wine cellar.'

The damn fool stared at me then, like a landed fish gasping for air, and Leonard reached for my arm.

'Sidney, you're behaving like an idiot. What's this all about?' he asked.

'What's this all about?' I parodied, poking him roughly in

the chest with my free hand. 'I'll tell you what it's all about. It's the betrayal of one brother by another. It's about stealing.'

With every sentence, I jabbed him harder, forcing him to take several steps back. And each time I advanced a pace of my own.

'Stealing? You have *everything*, Sidney – you saw to that.'

'But you have the only thing I want,' I said. I swung a fist at his head, but, less intoxicated than me, Leonard easily dodged the punch.

Realising there was potential for the situation to spiral out of control, Murray began herding people from the room and asked the footman to fetch the stable lads, whose group presence and strong arms might restrain the feuding Bellingham brothers. Burton was in no fit state to intervene, sprawled across the chairs. Besides, he knew now that his time at Halesham was at an end. Why should he get involved?

'Stop this,' commanded Murray, wringing her hands but wisely standing back from the two rutting stags who both had something to prove. This moment had been a long time coming.

'I love her,' I growled. 'You took her from me.'

'You told me she was a friend,' he said, perplexed, trying to hold me at bay as I gripped his shirt. 'I didn't know you had real feelings for her.'

'Well, guess what?' I growled, throwing him to the floor. 'I lied.'

'Oh God, Sidney. I'm sorry.'

'Sorry? Bit late for that, dear boy,' I said with gritted teeth. 'You came back early and spoiled everything. I just needed a bit more time, and then suddenly there you were, playing the dashing knight and sweeping her off her feet. You are a total bastard, waltzing back in and stealing the girl I love.'

'She's not a possession,' Leonard pointed out. 'And as much

as you believe that you love her, you're still so young. I promise that you will get over this and realise there is someone better out there for you.'

My anger intensified. He'd kicked at my Achilles heel and I was done with being patronised for my lack of years. I launched myself at him, my teeth gritted. An animal growl came from deep within as the pair of us tumbled to the ground, overturning a small tripod table and a potted fern. The ceramic pot split and soil tumbled out over the carpets. Murray gasped as I threw a punch that had so much force behind it that had Leonard not been able to block it, I dare not think of the damage I would have done, because in that moment I wanted him dead.

Although I was by far the strongest, my agitated state of mind and inebriation affected my reactions and my coordination. All those lessons I'd learned from Father deserted me. I wasn't thinking clearly – I was about to overplay my hand and give him a stronger desire to win.

'Take her then,' I shouted. 'Oh, I forget – you already have, up against a dirty stone wall in the woods, like she was a common prostitute. Debasing her for your own ends. You disgust me. I would have treated her better.'

It was a low blow. How ashamed would she be to know their most intimate display of affection had been witnessed, and that I had been watching? Spying. But by giving herself to my brother, she had lost all my respect. I didn't know which of them I hated the most.

'Don't you dare talk about her like that.' And suddenly the intensity of Leonard's anger matched mine, and the fury and hate in his eyes scared me.

He rolled over and got to his feet, as did I, but this time his hands were curled into fists and ready to throw punches of his own. There were a few haphazard interchanges before he caught me with a left hook and I was thrown violently against the sideboard. There was a crash of glasses as a tray slid from the table and the crystal tumblers shattered around our feet. Murray gasped and gave someone instructions to fetch a brush. Daisy appeared and started to cry, standing with the brush in her hand but not moving. I felt for the edge of the table to steady myself and returned the punch, catching him across the mouth, splitting his lip. Daisy screamed as scarlet blood oozed from the cut and seeped between the gaps of his teeth, giving him the look of Satan himself.

Leonard took advantage of my momentary hesitation, rugby-tackled me to the ground and pinned both my arms to the floor with his knees. I was defeated and braced myself for the final, powerful punch.

But Leonard didn't move.

'Go on,' I urged him, just wanting this whole thing done with. 'Hit me. You know you want to.' Still he did nothing, but looked at me with a wave of pity. Anything but that. 'HIT ME!' I shouted. 'I would if I were in your shoes.'

'But I'm not you, Sidney,' he said, and rolled to the side, allowing me to scramble to my feet, pulling my waistcoat back in place and tugging at my cuffs as though I could dust all this unfortunate unpleasantness away.

Two of the stable hands arrived at the door, pausing to assess the situation. Daisy was now sobbing as though a murder really had taken place, but our physical fight was over.

'I want you gone and I want you gone this instant,' I said. Leonard looked across at me in surprise.

'What? You can't do that.'

'I can and I will. Did you think everything would change when Father died? That I'd overrule his decision to disinherit

Chapter 45

1920

The run-up to Christmas was proving particularly tough for Phoebe. There were so many traditions and happy memories tied up with the season: from receiving her first stocking, to felling the tree with her father; from evenings making paper chains, to hours spent playing games with her mother. It was a time of family and belonging, but she had no blood relatives and belonged to no one.

On Christmas Eve, and with so much time on her hands, Phoebe baked an array of festive treats and the atmosphere seemed more relaxed than it had ever been. Sidney seemed to accept that she would soon be leaving but, for now, they would enjoy the season together, at least until the New Year.

Although perhaps not aware of the extent of Douglas's machinations, none of the staff seemed unduly surprised he'd been fired, particularly as it wasn't the first time. Phoebe realised she'd misjudged Ada, who finally confided that her cousin had been briefly involved with him the previous year and he'd treated her badly. The housemaid's reluctance to share his past misdemeanours was driven by her fear that Phoebe would mistake her interference for jealousy – which indeed she had. Even

Murray admitted she'd given the cheeky under gardener one too many chances as a result of her past fondness for Daisy.

Phoebe realised it was time to come clean about her parentage and her mother's true situation when she'd arrived at Halesham Hall all those years ago. These people were her friends and deserved the truth. It wasn't fair to let them think Sidney was completely to blame, and it was important to her that they understood why she must make her home elsewhere.

'Well, I never did.' Murray sank into the pine kitchen chair. 'She hid it extremely well because, I can assure you, she wasn't the first of my girls to find herself in that unfortunate position. The wee lass must have been lucky with her sickness, and what with the old Mr Bellingham so ill by that point, perhaps no one had time to pay proper attention to the laundry. Missing monthlies was always the first sign.'

'You would have realised soon enough,' Phoebe admitted. 'My birthday is early February.'

The housekeeper nodded. 'She was lucky. Leonard was a good man – one of the best. You must miss them both so much.'

'He was, and will always be, my father,' she said. 'Regardless of biology. And I'm sad that he never got to hear me tell him that.'

Just before supper, an impromptu game of snapdragon was played in the servants' hall. Sanderson had extinguished all the lamps and set the plums on fire. Much hilarity ensued as they tried to retrieve them from the bowl with scalding lips and shrieks of laughter. Ada noticed the master first and gave an embarrassed cough to alert the others. With no one answering his bell, he'd crept down to the kitchens to investigate. How long he'd been watching from the shadows, no one knew, but the game came to an abrupt end when he was discovered. As all eyes turned to him, Phoebe noticed he no longer looked so angry with the world, but instead sad, like a little boy on the edge of the school yard, watching all the other children play and desperately wanting to join in.

Later, feeling sorry for him, she presented Sidney with a knitted stocking to hang up. He looked incredulous at first.

'I'm not five, Phoebe.'

'No, but you didn't have much of a childhood. Indulge me.'

They hung the stocking on the mantel shelf in the drawing room in anticipation of an overnight visit from Father Christmas, who would fill it with sweets and treats.

'Was this something you did with your parents?' he asked, as they stood back to admire their handiwork.

She nodded, unable to speak without emotion.

'I'm sorry.' His voice was gentle. 'I should have thought to do these things for *you*. To make this season more bearable.'

'I am much happier giving than receiving,' she said. 'Besides, I don't want you to feel you must step into Leonard's shoes.'

He looked momentarily horrified at the thought. 'No, never that. I do not wish to replace your father. Our relationship is . . . entirely different.'

Yes, she thought, even if she hadn't quite sorted out what exactly their relationship was. Men were complicated beasts, and Sidney Bellingham more than most.

Watching his face, so full of childlike wonder as he opened small parcels of fudge, coconut ice and marzipan fruits on Christmas morning, Phoebe's heart flipped.

'You know me so well,' he said, grinning like the Cheshire Cat. 'I have always had a sweet tooth and your fudge really is excellent.'

After breakfast, he drove Sanderson and Murray to church in his motor car, insisting the long walk would be difficult for both of them. With his chauffeur now dismissed in disgrace, he didn't seem to mind what tutting this reversal of master and staff roles might give rise to in the village, and Phoebe knew him well enough to know that he cared not a jot for the judgement of others.

She chose to walk to church with the remainder of the household, enjoying being part of a gaggle of excited girls, skipping and chattering their way down the wide lanes to Halesham. To her relief, Douglas wasn't at the service, but Daisy threw her a disgusted look across the pews and she wondered how creative her son had been with the truth of his dismissal. Sidney noticed the cool glances from his former housemaid and threw a protective arm around Phoebe, guiding her gently to the front pew, where the Bellingham family had long since established their place in the village hierarchy.

After an uplifting service, where frosted breath filled the church as the congregation sang with gusto, everyone returned to the Hall. Phoebe and Sidney sat together in the refurbished dining room, enjoying their sumptuous meal of goose with braised ox heart and pheasant pudding. It was a muted affair in this formal setting and she missed eating downstairs, surrounded by people and their chatter. When she'd been working in the kitchens, the heat from the range, the glorious food smells floating around and the babbling company of the staff had made below stairs the place where she was most content. However, the conversation between herself and Sidney was friendly and relaxed. After too much food, and possibly in Phoebe's case too much rich wine, the staff were dismissed for the remainder of the day. The pair of them then retired and embarked on a very long game of *Empire* – Sidney keen to show off the flagship game of the company.

As darkness fell, Phoebe nipped to the kitchens to prepare

some cold salt beef and pickles, and they sat together in front of a crackling fire, reading in companionable silence.

'I wanted to warn you that there are some unpleasant rumours circulating the village,' Sidney said, shattering her reverie as the phonograph played softly in the background. 'Mrs Murray brought them to my attention and it doesn't take a genius to work out where they originated.'

'Oh?' She put down her book.

He sighed. 'Why is having you in my life so complicated but so simple at the same time?' It was rhetorical, so she remained silent. 'There are suggestions that our relationship is . . .' He struggled for the words. 'Not appropriate.'

Phoebe looked blank for a moment and then realised what he was trying to say.

'Oh. Douglas.' She cast her eyes down to her hands. 'I should have listened to your warnings about him sooner.'

'Perhaps if I had been more pleasant to you upon your arrival, you might.' There was a pause. 'Did you love him?' he asked, reaching for a piece of coconut ice.

'I thought I did. I'm not sure. Perhaps I don't really know what love is.'

'Did you think of him every waking minute, pick up objects he had touched and hold them close, knowing his hands had been on them moments before? Did you smell his clothes, bring his abandoned articles to your face to inhale any vestige of him, and to remind yourself of his scent? Did you contrive to be near him at any given opportunity, and linger longer than you should when you met? And did you earnestly believe that he was your destiny, that you belonged together, whatever obstacles presented themselves?'

So many of those applied to her feelings for Douglas that she nodded.

'Then you have my sympathy, for I have been there, but in my case it was just obsession – particularly given my age at the time. I suspect real love is a more gradual layering of feelings and understanding. I don't believe you can truly love someone if you don't know them, and I never took the time to know your mother properly. Had I done so, I would have realised that she was right in every way for Leonard. Not me.'

Phoebe felt awkward, and not only by Sidney's frankness. She hadn't known Douglas at all, and had been thoroughly taken in by his act. It was humbling and humiliating, but she wouldn't allow herself a lifetime of bitterness because of it.

'Damn my brother for being so honourable and good. I was beastly to him,' he admitted. He held her gaze and she saw him take a slow swallow as he prepared to speak further. 'The truth is, as I'm sure you have worked out, that I was furious with Leonard for stealing Jane away from me. Murray, or perhaps even Daisy, must have told you about my unforgivable behaviour back then. An irrational anger that I couldn't control and allowed to bubble and fester into a hatred of my brother, instead of taking time to consider that she had never been mine in the first place. A foolish boy of nearly sixteen obsessed with a pretty girl and thinking I had some right to her.' He shook his head slowly from side to side. 'I drove a wedge between my father and Leonard, said nothing when my brother was disowned, and after Father's death and my imminent elevation to head of the household, I banished him and your mother. I'm so sorry.'

She looked at the repentant man before her and her heart lurched.

'I forgive you,' she said, and reached forward to lay her hand upon his – an intimate gesture in an intimate moment.

She felt like the older, wiser person as the ticks of the clock counted out the next few seconds. So many times she'd witnessed flashes of the adolescent behaviour he talked of as though it was in the past, but he clearly couldn't shake it off completely. Living in his privileged world, and denied of any real love, perhaps he'd never quite grown up. However, you forgave those you cared for – much as she held no ill will towards her parents. And she did care for Sidney, she knew that now.

His eyes rose to meet hers.

'Then can we not leave the past behind us? Start again? Because I'm asking you nicely, *begging you*, not to leave.'

She was used to a gamut of reactions from him – anger, frustration, impatience. But this was different. His calm honesty was welcome, but perhaps too late. She was painfully aware that this drifting state of affairs couldn't continue indefinitely. It would be unfair to abuse their relationship and expect him to finance her food and shelter for much longer. In her mind, she was waiting for the legal independence that came with her twenty-first birthday, when she would no longer have to rely on small sums forwarded by the family solicitor. She would finally be in control of her own financial affairs – however meagre they might be.

'I don't belong here . . . Sidney.' Speaking his Christian name aloud for the first time was a frightening thing – strong and separate. It made him just a man, and for reasons she couldn't explain, that was a stomach-clenching concept.

He narrowed his eyes in that all-too-familiar, and somehow suddenly endearing, way of his. 'Then I challenge you to a game.'

'I don't understand.'

'It's quite simple. If you win then you are free to leave Halesham Hall. If I win then you stay.' He raised both eyebrows, daring her to accept.

'Don't be ridiculous. I cannot decide my future on a game.'

'Things of far more importance are settled on such. The throw of a die, the spin of a wheel . . . the building of a Navy and one man's desire to capture the lands of another.'

'No. I will not be manipulated again by a man.'

He shook his head. 'You aren't ready to face the world alone, Phoebe. It's a dangerous and cruel place. You'll be swallowed up and spat out by it, and I don't want that.'

'You still see me as naive and vulnerable, don't you?' she said.

'After witnessing you handle Douglas, I do not doubt that you have the resolve, but one young woman against a cruel and male-dominated world will never win – however courageous she may be. I want you to stay, and this is the only way I can persuade someone as stubborn as you to remain here.'

'Ah, but only because you're convinced you'll win.'

'Then it is not me who is underestimating you – it is you doubting yourself.'

Damn the man for twisting everything. She swallowed hard.

'Perhaps the real question is this,' he said, looking down at her and tipping himself almost imperceptibly closer. 'Do you *really* want to leave?'

Chapter 46

Never a particularly wilful child, there was nonetheless a determined side to Phoebe that she had only discovered since arriving in Halesham. Sidney was correct to label her as stubborn, but perhaps it was only because life had hitherto not presented her with such an infuriating adversary. There was something about being confronted by him that made her dig deep. She'd stuck her chin up in the air and met his eyes with a fierce determination the previous evening and replied, 'Then we shall settle this once and for all tomorrow, over a game of poker.'

'Can we not settle it over a Bellingham game? *Empire*, perhaps?'

'No, you set the challenge so I get to choose what we play. After all, you said it was the game that truly demonstrated who was the man and who was the child. Perhaps it will answer that question for both of us.' And she'd swept from the room.

Flinging herself across the bed, she'd regretted allowing herself to be goaded so easily, but they'd played poker on a few occasions and her choice of game had been deliberate. There was no way she could beat him at chess, and she was certain he would have an advantage in any of the Bellingham games she might have suggested – after all, he'd invented most of them. But in poker, your hand was decided the moment the pack was cut. This increased the odds in her favour, even though the real skill was in bluffing your opponent and holding your nerve. Sidney had often delighted in pointing out her tells and belittling her amateur game, and she would turn this smugness against him. She realised that in order to move forward with her life, she needed to play him, in both senses of the word, and win.

As sleep wrapped heavy arms about her, sensual dreams like those she'd had in the midst of her infatuation with Douglas came to her again, but now it was a faceless figure who caressed her body and whose soft breath travelled across the curves of her skin, not the strong arms of the gardener holding her tight or creating knots in her stomach with his piercing pale eyes.

The following day she spent half-packing, even though victory was far from certain. Should Sidney win, and that was indeed the most likely outcome, a deal was a deal and she would honour it. Truth be told, she still didn't belong anywhere, and the Hall was as good a place as any for her to stay whilst she decided on her long-term future. At least it was big enough for them to co-exist relatively independently. But then the poker wasn't simply about staying or leaving – it was about so much more.

She kept to her room for most of the day and then spent a restless hour fiddling about, dressing for dinner, wrestling with her muddled thoughts. When the gong was sounded, she entered the much less nauseating dining room, to be informed the master wasn't hungry and would wait for her in the drawing room. Her own appetite was equally absent but she politely ate her meal and then wandered down to face him.

As she stepped through the door, she noticed his eyes linger on her for longer than usual. Not to be intimidated, she returned the scrutiny.

Satan padded over to greet her as she walked towards the green baize card table. She nodded a thank you as Sidney slid out her chair. What was it about the atmosphere in Halesham Hall? Sometimes it held the whispers of ghosts, and the bitterness and cruelty of the past was only too obvious in the fabric of the house, but that night something far more intoxicating and dangerous was swirling around – for her, at least.

'Can I pour you a drink?' he asked, and she noticed for the first time that there were no staff present. Sanderson had been with her while she dined but not followed her to the drawing room. It was usual for him to be standing silently in the corner of the room, as motionless and indifferent as a potted fern, and staring ahead like a statue, ready to jump at the smallest command and then return to his station – dismissed from the minds of the company but hearing and seeing everything.

'No Sanderson tonight?' she enquired.

'Just us.'

Even though she hadn't answered his question regarding the drink, he walked to the sideboard and poured two large brandies, placing one in front of her as he sat down opposite. She wouldn't touch it – she needed to remain focused.

An uncomfortable silence permeated the room. This was no time for small talk – they both had too much riding on the outcome.

A brand-new pack of cards sat in the middle of the table and three equal piles of assorted ceramic red, white and black chips were piled up before both of them. She reached out to pick one up, hard, smooth and cold in her hand, and turned it over and over in her fingers. It was a beautiful thing in its own right – the centre inlaid with a filigree number five, encircled by a web of leaves and scrolls. Bellingham Games' finest, and an example of Sidney's successful targeting of the moneyed classes.

He gave a brief recount of the rules and then slid the cards from their cardboard packet, shuffling them and placing the pack in front of her. They cut to deal – Sidney won with a ten, and she hoped he couldn't hear her increased heartbeat. Her palms were clammy, and she wiped them down her thighs under the table where he couldn't see. Her throat felt dry and it was difficult to swallow, but she would not reach for the brandy. It was important to prove to him that she wasn't the innocent girl who'd landed on his doorstep all those months ago. He had to see her as an equal – especially should she be forced to remain.

She gambled cautiously to begin with, only committing when she had a good hand, and the first half an hour the silent play saw no clear winner. He didn't make comments about her tells this time. He was not here to mock, he was here to win. She studied his face, his hands, his manner. Was there some give-away in his own reactions?

It was a game for the self-confident and fearless, she reflected – neither of which described her. And he'd readily agreed when she'd suggested it because he knew that her inability to bluff and her inherent honesty would put her at a disadvantage. But even the most skilful player in the world would struggle if not blessed with good cards, and in the first few hands she was lucky – a full-house, a straight and two high pairs saw her sweep his chips to her pile. What cards Sidney held on the occasions she bowed out, she didn't know – his face remained impassive. But gradually her luck began to wane and she noticed her pile diminishing, and his growing.

His body language changed subtly as he became increasingly confident of victory. He stood to pour another brandy and loosened the stiff collar of his shirt. Satan wandered over and he bent down to rub his silky ears, no longer reluctant to whisper kind words to his loyal companion in front of others. He sat back in his chair, stretching out his legs, and the hint of a smile occasionally danced at the edge of his mouth.

But she'd had a plan from the beginning: be the readable little creature he'd come to expect, let him wallow in his smug observations. And then, when the stakes were higher, show him she was no gullible fool after all. She was sick of everyone assuming she needed looking after, directing and overseeing her life. Douglas may have played her like a well-worn fiddle, and Sidney, sitting across from her, remained convinced he was in control. Well, no more. Phoebe Bellingham would take on the world alone. She may have stumbled and fallen, but she was stronger now and understood the game of life so much better.

Betting boldly, she forced him to pay more attention to her as she began to claw back some of her losses. He sat up straighter, a frown toying with the edge of his eyes. Totally out of character, she pushed a large pile of chips into the centre.

'You're bluffing,' he said. She made no reply and for the first time in the game she picked up the brandy glass in front of her and downed the whole drink. It burned a scalding path down her throat but a satisfying one.

Sidney shuffled slightly in his chair and rubbed his hand across his moustache. He continued to play in his unemotional way, but she'd spotted the almost imperceptible telltale signs. He was unnerved.

The pot grew slowly, and she could sense him unsure of himself for the first time. She noticed his hand waver a fraction over his chips before he decided to see her. Had he folded, it would all have come to her, but he needed to satisfy his curiosity as much as she wanted him to see her hand.

Placing his cards slowly on the table, with only a modest pair of threes, he clearly expected to lose – but as she laid her own cards on the soft green fabric before her, he realised she had absolutely nothing.

'Interesting,' he said, scooping his winnings towards him without his eyes leaving her face. She stared straight ahead and kept her expression neutral. 'Is the little fox cub trying to out-fox its master?' Again, she chose not to reply.

The atmosphere shifted, the tension in the room all but dripping down the wallpapers. Sidney rang for Sanderson to adjust the fire and open a window. He complained of feeling hot, and although he was careful not to show it, she knew he was also bothered.

She glanced down at the five cards in her hand, spreading the last two apart to reveal the pair of queens – the jolly-faced Queen of Hearts in her enormous red-puffed sleeves, with hearts in the white slashes, holding a posy of scarlet flowers, and the gaunt Queen of Spades, practically in mourning dress, with a sweeping of black hair across pale skin, a black fan in her hands. She looks like me, Phoebe thought. If only I wielded that sort of power.

She swapped just two cards when her turn came, glanced at them only once and laid them face down on the table before her. Her expression gave nothing away.

This is it, she thought. This is my moment.

The sound of the clock dominated the room, each tick reverberating in the air, counting down to whether she would stay or leave Halesham Hall. Sidney lit a cigarette, not bothering to ask if she minded, and drew on the end as if by inhaling the smoke he was drawing on some inner power. They studied each other, both raising their bet, and both with a grim look of determination across their face. With neither prepared to concede, finally Sidney pushed his remaining chips to the centre. As she'd dealt, Sidney was the first to lay.

'I have a straight,' he said, placing the four and five of diamonds, the six of clubs, the seven of spades and the eight of clubs. He watched her face for some sign of disappointment or possibly glee – he could not be certain of her hand. Still she gave nothing away and the clock continued to tick in the background.

'Come on, Phoebe, don't keep a fellow in suspense. What's it to be? Are you free to leave me and all my evil schemes, or can I keep you locked up in my tower for eternity?'

She narrowed her eyes and collected her cards from the table, fanning them out in her hand with a measured calm.

'I have two pairs,' she said, and she knew, without daring to look up at him, that a flash of victory would pass across his face. However much he tried to rein it in, there was still something of the child about him.

'Then I win and you must stay.' He sounded smug. Two pairs were not a match for his straight.

'A pair of Queens . . .' – and she carefully laid those most regal of women before her as Sidney reached out to scoop up his winnings, 'and another pair of Queens.' The coquettish Queen of Diamonds and rather appropriately smug Queen of Clubs joined their sisters on the table.

Sidney froze. His lips parted slightly as though he was about to say something, but his words tangled in his throat.

'So, actually, I won,' she said triumphantly, stating the obvious, but she felt a perverse pleasure in rubbing his nose in her unexpected victory.

'I underestimated you.' He stroked his chin with his left hand and glared at the cards as though he could intimidate them into changing the result and snatch back victory.

She stood up and reached her hand across the table, although he did not take it. 'Thank you for your hospitality these past few weeks. Christmas was wonderful and not as desolate as it might have been without my parents. It has been kind of you to allow me to stay for as long as you have. I hope you understand my reasons, and we must stay in touch. I've been corresponding with the vicar's wife back in Chettisford and shall be staying with them for a while. She was a good friend to my mother. There are still a few arrangements to sort but I'll be gone by the end of tomorrow – if that won't inconvenience you too much.'

'You can't go.' He looked almost desperate as he squashed his half-smoked cigarette into the glass ashtray. Curls of smoke twisted upwards and then dissipated into the emotion-laden air.

'Surely, as a gentleman you will honour our agreement? You know in your heart that I don't belong here – a cuckoo in the nest. I appreciate you've tried to improve things, but honestly,' – she sighed, 'I find you too much like hard work. You are an infuriating and mercurial man to be with. You judge everyone and everything, yet give nothing of yourself away. And whilst I can appreciate that you are a product of an unfortunate upbringing, you don't show those you love how much you care about them – playing games all the time.'

'Me play games? That's rich coming from the girl who led me to believe she was my niece until her conscience got the better of her.'

'That's the point, Sidney. I have a conscience. And I can admit when I'm wrong. I came to the Hall determined to seek revenge for my father, but the truth was more complicated and I realised he wasn't the only injured party back then. Besides, he wouldn't have suited this life. He was never cut out to run the company and my parents were happy with their choices. Whereas I don't think you know how to be happy. You don't embrace your emotions or give anything of yourself away.'

'I can assure you I am a man of feelings. I may not skip

around kissing children and smiling at rainbows, but passions burn deeply within me.'

'So deeply they hardly ever surface,' she pointed out, trying to dislodge the ridiculous image of Sidney skipping. 'And yet I know you're right, because I see how you are with Satan.' Hearing his name, the dog looked up from his semi-slumber and his tail began an enthusiastic swish. 'You pretend he's such a burden, a stupid inconvenience, but we both know you would do anything for that animal. And how about Mrs Murray – a woman who has stood by you for nearly forty years. Can you even admit how special she is to you? Are you afraid of what people will think? Or has your father done so much damage that you don't know how to undo it?'

'When I love, I love completely,' he said. 'Without compromise and with total honesty. Murray has my love, Satan has my love, and you . . .' He paused, either considering what exactly she meant to him, or too afraid to admit what his feelings really were.

There was a moment when they were both acutely aware that his next words could potentially change everything between them. She took a hesitant step closer to him – part challenge and part hope. 'Yes?'

But the sentence was never finished because, with his eyes still locked on hers, he stepped to the side of the card table and lurched towards her, pressing his lips ferociously on her mouth as he gripped her shoulders. Drawn in by his warmth and the power of his kiss, her head was pushed backwards, and her insides stirred up like a hive of frenzied bees. The shock of it all made her freeze at first, but then she acknowledged that this was the reason she'd been unable to leave the Hall: Phoebe had fallen for Sidney, even though there were so many reasons why this was a bad idea.

There was the tiniest fraction of a second when she contemplated responding with her own lips before he pulled away, almost as abruptly, and waited a beat, looking to her for a reaction. Too shocked to say anything, she felt his eyes upon her, before he stormed from the room, leaving her grasping at the edge of the table for support, unsure of what had just happened and what she should do next.

His striding footsteps echoed up the corridor, and an eerie silence descended, until a small tower of ceramic counters, balanced precariously near her hand, toppled over, several crashing on to the highly polished floorboards below and skidding around her feet.

Chapter 47

1899

Leonard and Jane's wedding was to be a quiet affair that wet September afternoon. How he had organised everything so quickly, I didn't know, but Murray told me in confidence that they were leaving for Cambridgeshire immediately afterwards – far away to make a fresh start – and that I must part with my brother on good terms. I told her Leonard could go to hell as far as I was concerned, and gathered, sometime later, she'd received a similar response from him. We were both too stubbornly Bellingham to put our differences aside.

I wrestled with a lot of things that morning, certain that I never wanted anything to do with my brother ever again. It was an unthinkable act of betrayal, made worse because I'd been wrong about both their motives, even though I could barely admit it to myself. Neither of them cared for the fortune. The beautiful simplicity of love was enough.

I gathered the box of keepsakes from my wardrobe and took it down to a neglected end of the gardens, where the firewood was chopped and bonfires were occasionally lit to dispose of the weeds and hedge clippings. Determined to burn these foolish mementoes, I placed the box on a small faggot where white ash already dusted the ground, and took a box of matches from my pocket. But instead of throwing the lit match on the sticks, I found myself hypnotised by the crackling flame, and watched it burn all the way down to the tips of my fingers, hastily shaking it out before I caused myself injury. I struck another, this time hovering it over the box, ready to drop it and let the fire consume those painful memories. Again it burned down to my fingers. So I lit a third. But it was hopeless. It was impossible for me to destroy these things. I loved and I hated her all at once, and couldn't reconcile the two emotions. It was for the best that they were leaving for Cambridgeshire, and I would make no endeavours to locate them in the future, for I knew I would be pulled to her again and again if she was nearby. I would forever be her Hylas.

I returned the box to its hiding place and, looking at my pocket watch, I realised the service would be underway. The promised rain began to fall from the leaden skies as I headed to the parish church, pulling my wax jacket tighter around my body. Unseen by anyone, and hidden in the trunks of a cluster of trees outside the churchyard, I watched as Mr and Mrs Leonard Bellingham, with their pathetic handful of possessions tied to the back of a farm cart, left Halesham down a bumpy lane, never to return.

For months, I'd had a recurring dream where I stepped from the trees, walked up to my brother, shook his hand and wished him well. It would have been so simple. I knew more than most that you have no control over who you fall in love with and that, equally, you can't make someone love you. But on that rainy, grey day, I was as much a victim of my youth as I'd ever been.

Instead, I returned to the Hall and dismissed half the staff. Leonard's room was cleared and I ordered a bonfire set. I organised a meeting with the man Father had nominated to oversee the business until I reached my majority, briefed Murray on how things should run during my absence, and finalised my plans to return to school. By nightfall, weary of the emptiness, I climbed the staircase that led nowhere and let my head rest on the door that had promised so much but delivered very little.

Occasionally, I wondered if there was more to the puzzle, but I couldn't see how. The door key was the end of the road, and there were no further clues to chase. I had everything I needed, and Leonard had made it perfectly clear he didn't intend to challenge that. Perhaps I shouldn't have been so surprised that my father had played with us both in such a cruel manner. After all, his repeated warnings to me as a boy had been clear – 'Put your trust in no one – not even me.'

As always, I imagined I could smell lavender on that top landing, and thoughts of my mother filled my head. Memories and dreams intermingled, and for the first time since my father had left me curled up in a cold, dark hallway, outside my new childhood bedroom, I cried – both for my mother and for the loss of the woman I was still in love with. Abandoned by both, I promised myself no one would ever get close enough to break me like this again.

Over the following years, my anger festered and grew. I flunked at school, but didn't care. My financial future was secure enough and I embraced the invincibility of youth and the arrogance of the wealthy. I was my father's son and utilised the skills he'd taught me. At twenty-one I took over the company in an official capacity. By the time I was twenty-five, I was directing every aspect of Bellingham Games as it went from strength to strength. Work was the only thing that made me truly happy.

Father was right. I had a natural aptitude for games and developed many of them myself, working from the study, leaving others in charge of the business premises and warehouses.

With success and wealth began a repeating pattern of self-destructive behaviour that endured throughout my twenties, an excess of 'wine and women, mirth and laughter' – perhaps not as many women as the gossips suggested, but enough. And then, in 1914, the whole world tipped on its axis. The country went to war, and two years later, when unmarried, single men no longer had any option but to enlist, I left the company in the safe hands of a manager, and the Hall in the safe hands of Murray, and travelled to foreign shores, hardly expecting to return. And yet, despite the deeds I did and the sights I witnessed, I did.

My mother came to me once, twenty-eight years after she'd disappeared. She sat beside me on a rough bench of planking, wearing a pale yellow summer dress. The bench was spattered with mud and the brains of a young corporal who had been standing not ten feet from me only moments before. An artillery shell had thrown me against the wall and my head had hit the side of the trench. There had been a tremendous noise before the violence of its landing, and clumps of dirt rained down for several moments afterwards in the eerie almost-silence that followed.

'You'll get through this,' she said, reaching for my trembling hands and taking them in hers. I remember the softness of her skin because there was nothing soft in my world any more. No soft voices, no soft material, no soft flesh next to mine in the night.

'There is a time coming,' she said, holding my gaze, 'when you will be loved unconditionally, despite the shadows. Don't let it slip through your fingers. I know that you feel alone in this world, but you will find yourself cherished and adored. Embrace it. Don't push it away.'

She stood up and stepped over what was left of the corporal, and walked down the trench and into the dark. I stared after her until the pale yellow of her dress disappeared.

In the January of 1920, staying with a chap from my old regiment, I reluctantly took part in a pheasant shoot. I'd only been out of the army for a few months, it having taken until the previous summer to be demobilised. I was finding my feet again in the Bellingham company, which had thrived during the conflict. (All small boys wanted games that emulated the military endeavours of their fathers and uncles, and *Battlefield* and *Waterloo* had sold beyond my expectations.) The shoot was an attempt to return to our pre-war lives, but the efforts of these disillusioned survivors were futile. Hunts, dances, dinner parties, Saturday-to-Mondays – yet many of us did not have the heart when all we could think about were the men we'd left behind. Such wounds as the country had suffered were not so quickly or easily healed. The old way of life was slipping away and our politics shifted in an alarming direction.

The horn blew to signal the end of the first drive and I unloaded my gun and put it back in my slip.

'Good shooting, Bellingham,' my friend said. 'You're on form today, old boy.'

I knew I'd shot well – seven birds down – but I was becoming increasingly uneasy about holding a gun again, and about the company I was keeping. A pleasure-seeking lifestyle had suited me in my twenties but sat uneasily with me now.

We were distracted by a black and white cocker spaniel dashing in front of the guns, rolling around on its back, barking at nothing and generally having a whale of a time – oblivious to the formal nature and strict etiquette of a shoot.

'For God's sake, man, get that bloody dog on a lead,' my friend shouted.

He strode over to the gamekeeper, who was wrestling with the hound as it rolled around at his feet, paws in the air, preferring to be petted than collect the fallen birds.

'Shoot it, Mason,' I heard him say. 'Take him to the woods and do it quickly. I can't be embarrassed like this. The dog is no use to me – he has the very devil in him.'

'Right you are, sir,' his man said, grabbing the hound by the collar and turning away.

There was a moment as the enormous brown eyes of the pathetic beast looked up at his temporary custodian, and his tail wagged happily as he trotted behind, oblivious to his fate. A flash of the little boy I had once been, the hopeful, loved, trusting child before my mother had left and my father had embarked on years of harsh life lessons, hit me with an unexpected rush. That dog wanted to be cared for and so did I.

I looked at the guns standing about me – entitled fellows in their tweeds and shooting jackets – and wondered what I was doing there. Didn't these people realise that everything had changed? We couldn't go back to the high living of the belle époque. They were clinging to a lifestyle that was slipping away. People no longer wanted to work in service, at the beck and call of the fabulously wealthy, and were finding better pay and conditions elsewhere. Besides, the war had seen so many heirs to these large estates killed, and I'd seen enough senseless killing to last a lifetime. Although at least the birds would make it to the table.

'Stop,' I shouted. 'I'll take it. Give the dog to me.'

'Come on, Bellingham. He's next to useless. I know you don't have a gun dog of your own, but this is madness.'

'If you don't want it, give the damn dog to me.'

Used to my black moods and not wanting to make a scene, particularly as the Earl of Kettling was among the guns, he conceded. 'Very well. Take the damn beast, if you must.'

The gamekeeper handed him over and the animal looked between the two of us, wondering which of us to bestow his overflowing affections on. Who would give him the much sought-after tummy rub? The gruff gamekeeper or the sour-faced man he did not recognise?

I reached out to pat his soft head – 'It's all right, boy. You're coming with me,' and he tipped his head to one side, questioning my decision.

'Good luck, sir, that bloody dog is untrainable.'

'Perhaps I don't want to train him. Perhaps I just want the company of a dumb animal.'

And despite the unforgivable breach of etiquette, the damage done to a long-standing friendship and the bemused whispers that I knew would circulate in my social circle for weeks afterwards, I picked up my gun and headed for the house. Thirty minutes later, I drove out of the tall iron gates, with the dog beside me in my Model T, and my head set to the future. For the first time since I could remember, I was unconditionally loved, even if I wasn't sure how to return that emotion.

'It's fine, old boy,' I said, taking my eyes off the road for a moment to look at the creature that had transferred his affections wholly and absolutely to me without questioning where we were going or what sort of man I was. 'We're going to be just fine.'

This, I decided, was the prophecy of my mother.

But I was wrong.

Chapter 48

1920

The kiss stayed with Phoebe for hours, keeping sleep at bay and leaving her head in a total mess. Her first reaction, as she stood alone in her room the following morning, was to question what game he was playing now. Embarrassment had crept up from her toes after Sidney had left the room, leaving a flush of heat in its wake. She knew that had he not broken away, the kiss would have become deeper – it would have meant something – to her at least. But he was playing games again and she felt as much of a fool as she had when Douglas had revealed his hand. Yes, Sidney was furious at losing, but his sudden desire to kiss her made no sense. It came from nowhere and was further proof, as if she needed any, that remaining here would not be good for her. She craved a simple and uncomplicated life, where people said what they meant and there was no edge to their words and no emotions unnecessarily manipulated.

Passions had been running high and the sticky air from the roaring fire had fuelled them both to speak freely. She'd goaded him into proving he had feelings and the thought that those feelings might be directed at her had been unexpected. And yet, there were tiny glowing embers lingering in her body from that bright and evanescent burst of flame. This damaged and confusing man was such a bundle of contradictions. Reading him was harder than understanding a book containing only blank pages, but was it possible he did feel something for her? Was it possible that the kiss had been real?

Ada entered, pulled back the curtains and deposited a large jug of hot water on the washstand.

'You'll be pleased to know I'm leaving today,' she told the maid. 'One less thing to do – wait on me.'

'I get paid the same, regardless of how many people are staying at the house. But we will miss your baking.' That was perhaps the closest Ada would get to admitting there was a fledgling friendship between them. 'Can I help with your packing?'

'No, I shall manage. Honestly. I don't have much. No fancy ball gowns or endless hat boxes, like many who have stayed at the Hall over the years.'

'Where will you go?' The maid poured some of the hot water into the basin and placed a clean towel on the foot of the bed. Phoebe was glad there was no animosity between them now.

'Back to Chettisford. One of my mother's dearest friends will take me in. After a while, I shall look for work, perhaps in a kitchen or maybe one of those tea houses that are so popular – I'm certain Mrs Murray will give me a good reference. But I'll come back to visit.'

'Good,' said Ada, and the girls exchanged a smile.

Phoebe washed, dressed and took herself down to the dining room for breakfast. By lingering in the bedroom, she'd hoped Sidney would be out on business or tucked away in his study working, but no, he was at the head of the table, an open copy of *The Times* in his hands, staring out of the window, and a plate of cold food untouched in front of him.

She lifted up one of the domed lids, not caring what she ate but knowing she must eat something, helped herself to some porridge, and then poured a strong coffee. She could feel his eyes on her back as she moved, but when she turned to take her seat, he'd returned his gaze to the window.

'Apologies for my silly joke last night. It was the brandy and the shock of defeat.' And that was the matter dealt with swiftly and without emotion as he moved on to other matters. 'If you want Sanderson to run you to the station later, I have no objection. Perhaps you would like to visit at Easter? I know Murray would be pleased to see you.'

He lifted up his newspaper and concealed his face with the large pages. Phoebe's mouth dropped open and she stared at the banal headline across from her, unable to see the vexing man behind. He was an unsolvable puzzle in his own right. One minute he was begging her to stay, the next he was all but seeing her off the property. And yet the only thing that had changed was that kiss.

She took a mouthful of the porridge but it tasted of nothing. There was a rustle of paper and she looked up as Sidney took a sip of his coffee, dabbed at his mouth with the clean white napkin and rose from his seat. He nodded as he passed, leaving his food untouched and any words of goodbye unsaid.

After forcing herself to eat breakfast, Phoebe took herself off to the folly. She felt a strange affiliation with that tiny, run-down building. It was abandoned and unloved, lost in a beautiful tangle of trees in the shadow-haunted woods, and seemingly unwanted by anyone. She felt lost herself, stumbling around in her life with no clear direction.

It had tried to snow in the night, a half-hearted attempt that left the ground dusted with an icing-sugar coating of white crystals, but the sky threatened a more substantial offloading later. Slate-coloured marshmallows hovered in the dark sky above.

Although the decision to leave the Hall had been hers, there was still something holding her back. Why else had she not packed her trunk and left at first light? A confusion of feelings flitted through her muddled head. Halesham Hall was where her mother had fallen in love, and where the man who had brought Phoebe up as his own had spent his formative years. In their own ways, Leonard and Sidney had both shaped her – Leonard seeing her through childhood and giving her a happy and stable home life, and Sidney quite the opposite, making her face the harsh realities of life and forcing her to grow up. How was it possible these two brothers had turned out so differently? And then she wondered if it was simply that Leonard had been able to escape. The invasive tendrils of creeping ivy had wrapped themselves round Sidney's ankles and bound him to the Hall, refusing to let him go. Nervously, she cast a glance at the frozen woodland floor, subconsciously searching for that most smothering of plants, but any ivy clinging to her now was only in her head.

She curled up on the icy-cold stone bench under the stained-glass window, the chill of it biting through her clothes, and closed her eyes. The exhaustion of her inadequate night's sleep draped heavy arms about her shoulders and before she knew it, she was lost in bewildering dreams . . . Standing at the imposing front door of the Hall, she reached out for the knocker, gripped the brass hand and held it tight. The door dissolved before her eyes and she was clutching the fingers of a pale, frightened woman. In her gut, she knew the shadowy figure was Sylvia, even though she had no idea what the woman looked like. Had she been murdered by her husband all those years ago? Was she trying to communicate? Phoebe tried to articulate these questions, but no words came from her mouth. Did this faceless woman want the truth to be unearthed? Would they ever even know what had happened to Clement Bellingham's poor wife? She could be buried anywhere on the estate – even in this folly. Show me, Phoebe willed the figure. Show me what you want me to do.

Woken by a noise, she saw Sidney standing in silhouette by the non-existent wall, Satan by his feet, tail wagging, with large, white, rapidly melting flakes glistening on his black and white coat.

'So this is where you've been hiding. Murray said you'd disappeared. I believe Sanderson is anxious to know when you would like to be taken to the station. The snow is falling more heavily now.'

She sat up and rubbed at her eyes. How long had he been standing there, watching her?

'Sorry. I come here to think sometimes.'

Sidney frowned. 'Yes, me too.'

Was that why he was there now? she wondered. He needed to think?

'I must have dozed off. I didn't sleep well last night.'

She got to her feet and rubbed her stiff arms, noticing how dark the skies were and how silent the world was when it was blanketed in white. There was an icy stillness to the air inside the folly which mirrored the icy stillness of his glare.

'I'll head back and see if Sanderson is free. It won't take me long to finish packing.'

'Quite frankly, I expected you to be gone by now. I'm weary of your comings and goings, your idle threats and your dallying about.' He adjusted his leather gloves and flung the loose end of his scarf over his shoulder. 'Anyway, I came to replace the key, if you would kindly step aside from the bench. It's been sat on my desk for days and I should return it for some other gullible soul to find. *Turn the key and look inside.*' His tone was bitter. 'We blindly followed this last instruction but were both played by a cruel and unfeeling man. Perhaps another stranger will wriggle out of the woodwork pretending to be related to me, and I can set them on the merry task of solving Father's pointless riddle. It's always good for a laugh, to watch the face of someone as they open the door and find nothing but bricks behind.'

She looked at Sidney in complete astonishment, her insides lurching forward. How could he have gone from that kiss, with all its underlying power, to delivering such unkind words? She knew he was the only person to have solved the riddle besides herself and the thought that he was still amused by her futile exploits was upsetting.

He took the small cardboard box from the deep, square pocket of his Norfolk jacket and walked towards her. She stepped to the side and watched him heave the heavy stone seat and replace the key, noting the Venice address across the front once again and wondering if it had any connection to Sylvia and Clement's honeymoon. Had she loved him at the start? she wondered, and hoped the marriage had offered the young bride at least some happy memories.

'And now, if you wouldn't mind, I came here to spend some time alone. It would be most convenient if you were gone by the time I return.'

'Of course.' She turned to leave, walking past him as he moved out of her way, but paused before venturing outside. Was it really going to end like this? 'Goodbye, Sidney.'

He didn't answer but spun on his heels to face the stained-glass window, his arms behind his back in a stiff, formal manner that almost made her laugh out loud. She stepped from the relative shelter of the tumbledown folly and into the gloomy woods, melting snowflakes running down her face, hiding her tears, and crunched her way back to Halesham Hall one last time.

Phoebe turned things over in her mind as she gathered her undergarments from the tall chest of drawers. She recalled her foolishness with Douglas as she collected her brushes from the dressing table and laid them gently in between her folded clothes. How ridiculous she had been to believe herself in love after so short a time. To love someone you had to know them – for all their strengths and all their faults. She analysed Sidney's behaviour, how he had warmed to her in the last few weeks, and how she had foolishly believed she was starting to get through to him. And then Mrs Murray's words came to mind – how he dealt with disappointment badly and kicked out, denying his true feelings. Pretending that he hadn't loved his mother and his initial denial that he'd ever had feelings for Jane. It was the reaction of a child when they weren't allowed something – I don't care, I never wanted it in the first place. Was that what he was doing? Protecting himself because she'd been slow to respond to the kiss? Because she hadn't thrown her arms about him and acknowledged her feelings?

She closed the lid of the trunk and stroked the address label, written in her mother's neat hand. It was the one her parents had taken on honeymoon to Skegness. Two days, all they could afford, in a small hotel by the sea. A happy memory for them.

Something in her brain clicked – a satisfying clunk as a gear spun and another cog dropped into place to become part of the machine, allowing it to function smoothly, work faster. Of course, what would be one of the most special memories for any couple? The first days they spent together as a married couple. The honeymoon.

And then she suddenly knew two things with almost certainty.

And the fierceness of that knowing, and all the repercussions that came from it, hit her with a force that was almost physical.

She opened up the trunk and began to put all her belongings back in their rightful places: undergarments back in the drawers, brushes on the dressing table and books on the nightstand.

Phoebe Bellingham was going nowhere – because she'd worked everything out. She knew why Sidney was being so relentlessly unpleasant to her. And she knew the answer to the unsolved riddle of the stairs that led nowhere.

Chapter 49

'Why are you still here?' Sidney said as he stepped into the main entrance hall, a flutter of snow and a biting wind following him in. He handed Sanderson his wet coat and gloves, glaring at Phoebe, who was perched on the bottom step of the main staircase.

'Pray tell me what exactly I must do to get rid of you? Throw you over my shoulder and carry you down the driveway? You're the one who was so insistent you were leaving that you played cards with me to let you go, and yet here you still are.'

'The key is not the key,' she said, rising to her feet and wringing her hands together.

'What nonsense are you spouting now? Sanderson, take Satan through and towel him down. And tell Murray I wish for tea. I'm chilled to the bone.'

The manservant nodded and took Satan's lead.

'The locked door is nothing to do with the room,' Phoebe explained. 'Because I believe there *is* a room at the top of those stairs, but we were looking in the wrong place. The key was the box, with its Rio del Palazzo address. Murray mentioned to me once that your parents honeymooned in Venice?'

Momentarily forgetting his glum mood, Sidney couldn't help but engage with her words.

'And the painting on the opposite wall is of the Bridge of Sighs.' He was finally on the same page as her. 'My God, the old man tried to tell me. He used to say, "Everything I value is at the top of those stairs." Words chosen very carefully, because now I think about it, he never once said behind the locked door.'

'I've spoken to Mrs Murray, who thinks the box might have contained a gift from your father. He commissioned a watch for her as a wedding present but there was some delay and it was posted out after they had left for Italy.'

'Perhaps the only time they were truly happy,' Sidney reflected. 'Before they returned to England and my father's jealousy and controlling ways began to destroy the marriage. Sanderson,' he called, and the poor man returned to the hallway. 'Fetch me some tools from the sheds.'

'And the key from the folly,' Phoebe said. 'I've got a strange feeling we'll need that too.'

They stood at the top of the staircase in the east-wing corridor, traces of lavender still lingering in the air. Sidney was biting at his bottom lip and running his hands over the panels, so focused on the task in hand he'd forgotten to be angry with Phoebe. He tapped intermittently at the wall with his knuckles as Phoebe examined the key to the door.

'It could be hollow. It's difficult to say,' and he reached down for the hammer.

'*Turn the key and look inside*,' Phoebe mumbled, reading the label attached to the old key that Sidney had gone back for, claiming he was cold and wet anyway, and that Sanderson had far more pressing demands on his time. They had both previously believed it signalled the end of the quest but she realised now that it was, in fact, the final clue. The words were instructing them to look inside the key itself – not the locked room. She twisted the top and bottom of the shaft in opposite directions and two of the collars separated, revealing a key within the key – a small hexagonal bar – which she held out to him as he turned to her.

'The sconce is a handle,' she said. 'Is there a hexagonal recess somewhere?'

Sidney pulled out the wax candle stump and peered inside. 'Yes, in here.'

Phoebe stood on her toes to place the newly revealed bar into place. There was a click as she turned it and using all her strength, she pushed on the cleverly disguised door. There was a crack as the paint between the panel and the stiles split and it swung inwards to reveal a room. A much stronger scent of lavender drifted out on the stale air.

The space was small and black, and the light from behind them was poor, but as their eyes adjusted to the dark, windowless space, they could see it was filled with a multitude of objects.

'All my mother's things,' Sidney whispered, with childlike wonder. 'Her clothes, her ornaments, her paintings, her books . . . We thought he'd sold everything, or perhaps even burned her possessions.'

'How odd. What was he playing at?' Phoebe stepped over the threshold and ran her hand across a pile of gowns laid over a low table.

'Who knows? I've given up trying to rationalise my father's behaviour. I think he was ill, in here,' and he tapped at his forehead. 'He was a clever man but some of the things he did were beyond the actions of a rational man. Leonard was damn well right, however – I gave up too early. The puzzle was never completed.'

'It's like a shrine.' Phoebe stared in wonder at Sylvia's personal effects, piled high around her. 'Except you visit a shrine. You worship at it. This room has surely been sealed for years.'

'I guess he wanted all traces of her gone, but perhaps he couldn't bear to destroy them.' He scrunched up his face in pain and shook his head slowly from side to side. 'This unnerves me far more than I care to admit, Phoebe. His obsessive behaviour . . . I . . . I kept a box of your mother's things all those years ago, when . . .' He couldn't finish the sentence. 'Was this where I was heading?' His questioning eyes looked at hers.

'It's hardly the same thing,' she reassured him, knowing even she had held on to one of Douglas's handkerchiefs. Clement Bellingham's obsession had been on a ridiculous scale. 'Forget what I've said in the past when I've been angry or frustrated. You aren't like him, Sidney. He was dangerous and violent, for all his genius. You are a much better man.'

Her words seemed to soothe him and he returned his focus to the room. 'To think everything was the other side of the wall all along. It beggars belief.'

'Perhaps he kept these things for Leonard and you, expecting them to be found at some point, when the time was right? Your mother had a legacy too, don't forget. Maybe not a house or a company, but possessions that deserved to be passed down, and I don't think he wanted that legacy lost, even if he couldn't cope with it around.'

'Perhaps,' he said, absent-mindedly caressing a cream-coloured satin gown with Brussels lace trim and an enormous bustle. It hung over a dressmaker's mannequin. Sylvia's wedding dress, Phoebe surmised. 'But Leonard and I didn't find them – you did.'

'There are an awful lot of purple things.'

'She loved lavender, but Murray told me in later years that my father took it too far – part of his obsessive need to please her. I realise now that this was rooted in the guilt he felt over his violence. It was as though he could do what he wanted to her, as long as he bought a gift to make everything all right again afterwards. A clumsy way of showing his love, without really listening to what she wanted, which was kindness and trust. Murray said she began to despise the colour. She continued to wear the scent, though, and when I smell it, I always think of her.'

Sidney looked a little lost for a moment, staring ahead and not focusing on anything in particular. He was building up to something, she was sure of it. There was a stillness about the room – the deep breath of time before the exhale of something significant.

He parted his lips to speak but then something caught his eye.

'My rabbit!' he exclaimed. 'Mother made it for me when I was little.' He picked up a slightly misshapen handmade animal, its species only properly determined by the long ears and puffball tail, and briefly clutched it to his chest. Perhaps embarrassed by such a childish show of emotion, he pulled it away, and then examined it, his face crumpling into a frown. 'But he never had a patch on his stomach like that.' He peered at the square of fabric, edged by neat blanket stitches. 'I recognise the material. She was cutting up this dress the day before she disappeared.' He tilted it towards her so she could see.

'Was he threadbare? Perhaps she was repairing him for you?'

He shook his head. 'No, I loved that rabbit and was always very gentle with him. Father used to tease me. "Six and still clinging to that like a baby." I would tell him Mother had made it, that it was special, and he would scoff and call me pathetic. I was distraught when he went missing.'

My God, she thought, to be consistently subjected to such negativity and mocking was heartbreaking. Her childhood had been cushioned by kind words and encouragement every single day.

'There really was no limit to your father's malice,' she said.

'Fancy taking a treasured toy away from a small child.' Her heart flipped as she watched him place the soft mohair to his cheek and let it rest there for a moment, before burying his nose in the toy and drawing in a breath.

'I can still smell traces of her,' he said. 'Yardley's Old English Lavender.' He sighed and then held the rabbit out at arm's length. 'Patches hide secrets,' he murmured.

Phoebe had absolutely no idea what he was talking about, but watched with interest as he tugged at the stitches and pulled off the patch to reveal a small, folded piece of paper. He angled it towards the scant light from the doorway. '*Remind Leonard that patches hide secrets*. That makes no sense.'

'Perhaps it does,' Phoebe said, thinking on her feet. 'You were six when she left?' He nodded. 'She wanted to leave a message behind but you would have been too young. My guess is she left a note for Leonard, who might be better placed to deal with it, or keep it from your father, and this was her backup.'

'So Leonard had something she also patched?' He was beside her now, opening boxes and lifting up stacked items. 'She made him a monkey when he was a baby, but I'm guessing Father confiscated that too – not realising she'd left her sons a message hidden in those precious hand-sewn toys.'

'Is this it?' Phoebe held up a brown velvet creature with tiny, rounded ears and a pale pink face. Sidney took it from her and pulled at an identical patch. Another small piece of paper fell to the floor, and was there for a heartbeat before he retrieved it – his face changing from confusion to shock as he read the words.

'Oh my God. She emigrated,' he said, turning the paper to Phoebe to reveal a contact postal address for Montreal, Canada. 'At least, this implies she planned to. But the question is, did she ever make it?' He put the paper down and took her hands in his, desperate for her attention. 'I saw him return the night she left, Phoebe. His hands were covered in blood . . .'

Phoebe looked up at this desperate man, a wisp of hope emanating from him, and his touch travelling through her like the warm glow from a large brandy. She gently squeezed his fingers.

'Then you must investigate,' she said. 'And find out once and for all.'

The afternoon flew by. Sidney ordered for his mother's possessions to be removed from the room and Mrs Murray became quite emotional as she oversaw this monumental task. Phoebe left them to it, as the two people still alive who had loved Sylvia Bellingham best. Each object they uncovered would have memories and meanings for them, but they held nothing for her. She still had things to confront him about but she would wait until the household was calmer and he came to her.

Sidney was not present at dinner, and she sat alone, moving pieces of smoked fish around her plate as Sanderson looked on. Afterwards, she took herself to the library, picked up a volume of poetry and sat on the window seat, in the low light of a crisp winter evening. Spring would be here all too soon. Bulbs would burst from the ground and heartening smears of colour would appear once again on the landscape. The darkness and shadows would come to an end.

'Ah, there you are.' Sidney entered the library and walked over to light one of the rope-twist oil lamps standing on the centre table. Phoebe's book lay untouched on her lap. She'd been looking out across the gardens, lost in thoughts and uncertainty and hadn't noticed how gloomy the room had become because the snow was reflecting the scant light, making it seem brighter than it was.

'The room has been cleared,' he said, as the lamp gave a soft glow to the library. 'Many of my mother's personal possessions have been returned to her empty bedroom temporarily. Perhaps you would like to assess the wardrobe at some point? The styles are dated but the fabric is good quality. And you must look through the jewellery – some of it is very valuable.'

'Sylvia's possessions have nothing to do with me. I don't think I should be making decisions about them, even though I appreciate the thought.'

Sidney tapped his hand to his forehead and gave a tiny snort.

'Sorry, I've gone about this all wrong. I've been so knocked sideways by the shock of everything, that I forgot you don't know what's going on. All this is yours, you see,' he said, his arm sweeping the room. 'You came to Halesham Hall determined to reclaim Leonard's birthright and you've succeeded. It is I who shall have to move out, for everything here now belongs to you.'

Chapter 50

'Father was quite specific in his will,' Sidney said, as Phoebe finally realised that she'd inadvertently accomplished the very thing she'd come to the Hall to do all those weeks ago – evict him. 'I'm not sure he envisaged anyone other than Leonard or me solving the final clue, but regardless, it's yours, Phoebe, all of it. I've been on the telephone this very afternoon to my solicitor to confirm the details. I've merely been a caretaker all these years.'

'Nonsense. I don't want it. Besides, we opened the room together.'

'Then you must sell it, but the instructions are clear – whoever finds the deeds inherits Halesham Hall and everything in it, and the deeds were in the concealed room you alone discovered.'

Her mind was spinning and her heart was thumping. She didn't want this sinister old property, not even on her father's behalf any more. Fortune had never been her driving ambition in life, just a momentary obsession that she'd clung to in her grief. The more she analysed her behaviour, the more she suspected that she'd come to destroy Sidney as a way to avoid confronting her parents' deaths and the news that Leonard had not been her father. It was far easier to go on the attack than deal with difficult truths. Something Sidney also understood.

She engaged his eye and swung her legs to the floor. This inheritance nonsense was overshadowing something far more important to her, and the very thought of it was making her feel physically sick.

'There is only one thing I want here and if I can have that, I will gladly give you the Hall – legally and above board. You may even give me a shilling for it, if it makes you happier to think money has exchanged hands.'

'One thing?' Sidney was clearly confused, and stroked at his moustache. 'Something of my mother's? One of the paintings, perhaps?'

'You really don't know me very well, do you?' she said, disappointed that he should assume the most valuable item was the thing she coveted.

'No, quite right, you would want something of sentimental value. Something with special memories, perhaps. Something relating to your father. The monkey?' His face scrunched into a frown as he contemplated various possibilities.

'Honestly, Sidney, considering that you believe yourself to be so good at games, I'm surprised your brilliant mind hasn't picked up on the clues by now. But I have every faith that you will get there in the end. Please let me know when you do.'

She swept up her book and walked towards the door, but as she passed, he reached out and grasped her wrist. She spun to face him and their eyes locked. Heat pulsed up her body, from her toes to her cheeks, which were now aflame.

Her words hung between them for a while as she studied his confused face. Perhaps she'd got everything wrong, misread the signs, and would instantly regret taking a chance on this man. But there had been subtle changes in his behaviour since she'd told him they weren't related: his frequent inability to hold her gaze, the nervous fiddling with his cuffs, the way he looked at her sometimes when he thought she didn't know, and that powerful kiss – rooted in passion but vehemently dismissed as a joke. Did he think he was being noble, believing he was saving her in some way from himself?

Added to which, she'd been unbelievably slow to acknowledge her own feelings – the waters muddied by his involvement with her mother and her misguided feelings for Douglas. But the night that the under gardener had fled in disgrace and Sidney had held her in his arms, everything had felt right. She loved the man standing before her – his vulnerability, his stubbornness, his everything.

His eyes fell to her lips as her eyes fell to his. He swallowed hard and released his grip.

'But . . . but you didn't react and I panicked. I thought I'd got everything wrong.'

'You didn't give me a chance.'

She bravely closed the gap between them and stood less than six inches from his tightly buttoned waistcoat and ostentatious silk cravat, gazing up at him with her wide eyes, attempting for the first time in her life to manipulate someone with a look. How hard could it be? Some women made a career out of it.

'Phoebe.' His voice was softer now. He was less sure of himself. 'I'm old enough to be your father.'

'Barely,' she replied. 'Sixteen years is nothing. Most of your wealthy friends have played fast and loose with the ladies for years and then picked up a young bride half their age, who happens to have plenty of money and a family name that suits their purposes. Besides, you don't act like a thirty-seven-year-old man – most of the time you behave like a spoilt adolescent. And don't look at me like that – Mrs Murray thinks the same.'

He shook his head. 'I'm no good for you. I'm cynical and bitter, shuttered and miserable. You should be with someone who brings out the best in you, who is bright and gay, and sees the good in others, like yourself. I'm too damaged.'

'And yet I still love you.'

He dropped his eyes to the floor and shook his head, but she was having none of it. She stood on her tiptoes to collide her mouth with his. It was clumsy, but it did the trick. After a moment when he remained motionless, not reacting to her overtures, even he couldn't fight his real feelings any more, and she felt his tense body relax, his hand reach around her back and pull her close, and his lips finally respond to her own.

She'd known all along that there was love inside him, desperate to surface. And as the kiss intensified, their laboured breaths and desperate, searching fingers spoke of the ache in both their bodies to prove this love in the most intimate manner. Eventually he summoned enough strength to pull himself away.

'Of course I love you – how could I not?' he finally said, resting his forehead against hers. 'I can't keep lying to myself, or to you. You bring sunshine everywhere you go and your dogged perseverance is an admirable quality in one so young. From the moment you first stood up to me in the study, when I threatened to set Satan on you, I was intrigued. And when you admitted the truth about Leonard, I started to look at you differently – as a woman and, to my astonishment, an equal. Thoughts of you have haunted my dreams, Phoebe, and consumed my days. You win. You played the much better game and you deserve your victory.'

'Of course I do,' she agreed, putting up her hand to stroke the side of his face. 'Because this time I wanted it so very, *very* badly.'

Chapter 51

'Is there something going on I should know about?' Mrs Murray asked the following morning, as Phoebe sat down to breakfast.

'What makes you say that?' she asked, wondering what the canny housekeeper was referring to.

They had been careful, Sidney leaving her long before the rising sun allowed her fingers to creep over the horizon, splashing the world with colour and waving her palms over the snow-covered fields, bringing light, warmth and joy to that small part of Suffolk where joy had been an unwelcome visitor for far too long. Ada was no fool and would know which beds had been slept in. Having been part of that downstairs world herself, Phoebe was only too aware that staff invariably knew more secrets than those whose secrets they kept.

She had led him through the house and up the dark stairs after that kiss, holding the oil lamp to light the way. And he shook his head when she stood on the threshold to her room, tugging him towards her. He insisted for the first time that he would not be selfish – that he would wait. Instead, they had compromised and Sidney stayed with her but simply held her in his arms and even in that period of deepest slumber, had refused to let her go.

Mrs Murray gave Phoebe a look that brooked no nonsense.

'Because I've known that man for thirty-seven years and this morning I saw something in his eyes I don't believe I've seen since he was a wee laddie. Simple contentment. And after losing the Hall, I'd rather braced myself for one of his foul moods.'

Phoebe smiled, saying nothing, but it was enough for the housekeeper to give a delighted sigh.

Sidney breezed into the dining room, looking particularly resplendent in his single-pleated trousers and jacket, and kissed Mrs Murray on the head as he walked to the row of covered dishes along the back wall, lifting the first lid and allowing wafts of a smoky kedgeree to escape into the room.

'Sir!' The housekeeper was flustered and threw an embarrassed look at Sanderson, who stood quietly at the end of the sideboard, staring ahead impassively. 'I hardly think that's appropriate.'

'Why not?' He scooped several spoonfuls of the yellow rice on to his plate and swung into the chair next to Phoebe, instead of his usual seat at the far end. 'You've been like a mother all these years. Looking out for me and silently guiding me in the right direction, keeping everything ticking over while I gadded about like a damn fool, making a mess of my life.'

'Well, it rather looks as though you have someone else to do that for you now,' and she looked over to Phoebe. 'Although I have a feeling the poor wee lass has bitten off more than she can reasonably be expected to chew.'

'Ha. This one will give as good as she gets. Don't you be worrying about her. I rather think it is me you should be feeling sorry for. Look.' He stuck out his leg.' She's even got me polishing my own shoes.'

After breakfast, he took Phoebe upstairs and they went through his mother's possessions together. She was most struck by the handful of photographs – including a radiant Sylvia and a besotted Clement. You could see the adoration in his eyes. How sad, thought Phoebe, that his love turned to something far more sinister over the years.

'Have you written to the address?' she asked Sidney.

'I have people on it,' was all he replied.

Had Sylvia made it to Canada or not? Her silence after all these years was ominous.

'And now, I have something to show you,' he said, reaching for Phoebe's hand and tugging her back out into the corridor and down the main staircase.

They grabbed their coats and his strong hand gripped hers as he led her outside, across the courtyard and over to the maze. Stubborn patches of snow still remained where the surprisingly strong late December sun had failed to seek them out.

'All done, sir,' said the heavily whiskered, elderly gardener, nodding at his master as he pushed a barrow of yew clippings out the entrance and towards the distant plume of bonfire smoke. Even Phoebe knew it was not the best time of year to be pruning. What had Sidney been up to?

'Shall I lead the way?' he asked.

'Not at all. I'm confident I can remember. You wish me to try to get to the centre?'

He nodded and let her step past him into the puzzle of green.

As she rounded the last corner, there was a gap in the hedge that had not been there before. A gateway had been cut into the yew, allowing her to enter a small square where Aphrodite stood, alone, rather lichen-speckled and melancholy.

'You led me here, my darling,' he said, following her in. 'I was closed off to love, trapped in a maze of my own making, but the barriers have gone. I'm no longer wandering around aimlessly, facing dead-end after dead-end.'

Phoebe walked over to the statue and ran her hand along the

undulations of cold stone. Sidney moved beside her and let his lips fall to the top of her head.

There were bare patches of soil where the bushes had been allowed to creep further and further towards the solitary figure over the years, unchecked and untrimmed, surrounding her and trapping her even more. But now the goddess of love stood in her clearing, and looked down with serene eyes at the lovers before her.

And if you were the sentimental sort, you might even say she was smiling down at them.

Chapter 52

1921

'Sir, there's a telegram for you.'

Sanderson handed Sidney a small envelope as Phoebe sat at his feet, her shoulders resting against his knees, caressing Satan's silky ears and enjoying the warmth of the crackling fire.

February was proving even more brutal than January but, twenty-one at last, with an engagement ring on her finger and a spring date set for the wedding, her glowing heart more than compensated for the plummeting temperatures outside.

She felt him tense without having to look up at his face. Telegrams had been things to be dreaded for so long, imparting, as they did throughout the war, news of the most distressing kind, and even now, delivering information deemed to be urgent, they were always viewed with suspicion.

Gazing down at the dog, she heard the paper rustle and stared intently at the darting orange shapes in the fireplace whilst he read and digested whatever information lay within.

'Oh my God, Phoebe,' he finally said, leaning forward with wide and unbelieving eyes. 'He's found her. She's alive. My mother is alive.'

Chapter 53

It was a cold and wet spring day when Sylvia Bellingham stood in front of the imposing gothic front door of Halesham Hall. She noticed the flakes of lilac paint on the neglected woodwork, remembering how, when Clement painted it to please her all those years ago, the neighbours had thought it odd. But then he'd never been a man to conform – part of his genius and part of his lunacy.

Escaping Halesham Hall had been the hardest thing she'd ever done, but she'd honestly believed Clement was close to killing her. Not on purpose, of course. He loved her above all else, but he hated himself, and it was easier to take that hatred out on another – someone who loved you, and would always forgive you – than face up to it.

The recently dismissed garden hand, a young man by the name of Christopher, had met her down by the waterfront under the cover of darkness. They had forged a friendship during her hours in the gardens, tending her roses, and he too was looking to escape – his mistakes, however, were of his own making. Careless with his romantic entanglements, but a kind and thoughtful man, he'd persuaded her to come with him and start again in the New World. They had planned to travel as man and wife to avoid suspicion, and had agreed to part when they reached Montreal.

'He can't hurt you now. I'll make sure you come to no harm.' He had put his strong arms about her and they had stood at the stern as the boat pulled away, watching her husband pummelling his bare fists into a tree in his anger as his vitriolic abuse drifted through the night air and over the water towards them. She had been blind to her husband's true character when she'd married him, flattered by his devotion, but she felt nothing for him as the boat pulled away.

'What if he comes after us?' she had whispered.

'He won't. Bullies pick on those who are weak and alone. You are no longer either. Besides, he will imagine we are crossing the Channel to France. He will not come looking for us in Canada.'

She had fervently hoped Christopher was right. Had she taken the boys, her husband would not have let her go. Without them, he might. The Bellingham name was everything to him and his sons were a vital part of that legacy.

They had sailed down to London and then caught a train up to Liverpool, the choice of circuitous route deliberate, but on that transatlantic journey, Sylvia had unexpectedly fallen in love. This love was not blind. Her eyes were wide open as the charade she executed with Christopher became increasingly real. When she clung to his arm as they walked about the decks, and looked into his eyes as they were watched by their travelling companions, the looks she got back made her heart lurch. When she cried for the boys she had abandoned, he held her tight and offered calm words of reassurance. And one night, when he had believed her elsewhere and stumbled into their cabin, he had seen the bruises that she had talked of, and stood before her in shock. She had let him trace the marks with his gentle fingers and kiss the tears that fell from her eyes.

'Marry me?'

She shook her head. 'I'm already married.'

'Would you if you could?'

'Yes,' she had whispered, because she knew that Christopher loved her and would never raise a hand against her. She knew that with him she would be safe.

'Then we will find a way . . .' And they had.

Sylvia rapped on the brass knocker – a slender hand reaching out from an engraved surround, its limp fingers curled around a solid ball. *That was me*, she thought sadly, *trapped and so desperate to escape.*

A housemaid opened the door and not ten foot behind her stood Sidney. She knew him immediately – his features so like Clement's and his colouring always darker than Leonard's.

His eyes met hers. For a moment she saw the love her son had for her in his returning gaze, but it was quickly replaced by a cold expression. She would have to earn his love again, not that she blamed him for being guarded – she had done something unforgivable. Now she would have to justify her actions, to tell him that she had daughters whom she had always been there for, whom she had kissed and comforted, cherished and protected. Would he even understand why she'd been forced to abandon her sons? Why she had not been in touch?

She'd tried to explain all this to the private investigator who had knocked on her door back in February. How she had wrongly assumed her husband was still alive and still had the power to hurt her. That her sons had never tried to trace her so she believed her return would be unwelcome. That her second marriage had been a lie because she was not free to marry another. That her three beautiful daughters were illegitimate. How could she have risked returning to England and exposing this?

It still hurt that she had lost Christopher to cancer five years ago. He had always loved her, even though he had eventually strayed again, as she had always known he would. She smiled to herself. Murray had always had the measure of him, telling her in the days before her planned escape that it was rather like asking the fox to guard the hens. Dear Murray. She'd had such a good friend in the wily and formidable housekeeper, and wondered what had happened to her over the intervening years. Was she even still alive?

'Come in, Mother,' Sidney said. 'I believe we have lots to discuss . . .' His words snapped her out of her thoughts as a young woman appeared by his side, someone Sylvia didn't recognise. This pretty gay thing clutched at her son's arm and gazed up at him adoringly.

'Be kind,' she heard the young woman whisper.

Sylvia tentatively stepped into the hallway as the maid took her coat, and was relieved to discover that the shadows had gone. She took a deep breath. Reconciliation with her son would not be easy. Dark secrets would invariably tumble out, perhaps on both sides. But as she followed the pair of them along the corridor, her heart lifted, because she knew that whatever damage she had done by leaving him, Sidney had found love. As she had warned him so many years ago, life was a complicated blend of love lost, love found and love that endures. And she was absolutely certain that, much like her own love for her son, the young woman by his side would always be a love that endured.

Acknowledgements

As always, it takes a whole team to produce a book and so my grateful thanks must go to Headline Accent for their continuing and fantastic support. In particular, I wish to acknowledge the genius of my editor, Kate Byrne, and her assistant, Sophie Keefe, but I am also indebted to the copy editor, proofreader, cover designer (isn't the *Halesham Hall* cover a real beauty?) and all involved in the marketing and promotion of my books. Thank you also to my dear agent, Hannah Schofield, who guides me through it all.

For research help, Hannah Dale, from the archive department of Cheltenham College, who helped me to understand more about private schools at the turn of the twentieth century. So much didn't make it into this book but will undoubtedly prove useful going forward.

Thanks to the amazing (and divinely Scottish) Rae Cowie for beta reading a very early draft of this novel to ensure Mrs Murray sounded authentic. The storyline has changed considerably since then, and her insights were very much appreciated. Plus, I now know what a wee scunner is! I look forward to supporting her first novel in the way she has supported me. (So hurry up and finish it, Rae . . .)

As ever, thank you to the Romantic Novelists' Association, without whom I would not be published, and who continue to support and cherish romantic fiction, despite the obstacles the genre faces in a rather judgemental world. Also HUGE thanks to the Society of Authors, who have propped me up in some pretty dire times recently. These splendid organisations exist so that authors don't have to face everything alone, and for that I am truly grateful.

There is a small group of local authors without whom I would be rocking gently backwards and forwards, dribbling onto my lap: Heidi Swain, Clare Marchant, Rosie Hendry, Claire Wade, Kate Hardy and, last but absolutely not least, Ian Wilfred. (How many times have we choked on our cups of tea at his astute observations?) But there are so many authors out there who are equally precious to me, and I worry by naming some I will offend others, but Kate Smith, Mary-Jane Reilly, Lisa Firth, Suzie Hull, Victoria Connelly, Henriette Gyland, Anita Chapman – on this occasion, and for various reasons, you have been named. Thank you all.

The Heidi Swain and Friends Facebook Book Club (do join if you haven't already) has been such an amazing support over the past year, so a big shout out to the tireless Sue Baker and Fiona Jenkins, who really know how to share the love. And extra thanks to Fiona, who has made me see the world in a completely different way since I have known her. Love you, honey.

To Rachel Gilbey – Blog Tour Queen and simply lovely person.

To family and friends, to independent bookshops, to Eye Library in Suffolk (happy retirement and big hugs to Julie Shepherd) and to each and every one of my marvellous readers . . . I love you all.

Jenni x
Twitter @JenniKeer
Instagram @jennikeer
Facebook /JenniKeerAuthor
TikTok @jennikeer